Patricia Grey was born in Highgate, went to school in Barnet and college in London, and now lives in South Hertfordshire. She became a secretary and worked in all manner of companies from plastic moulding and Japanese banking through to film production and BBC Radio, eventually ending up as contracts manager for a computer company. The background for both BALACLAVA ROW and JUNCTION CUT, her first novel, was supplied by her parents, who grew up in Kentish Town.

Also by Patricia Grey

Junction Cut
Goodhope Station

Balaclava Row

Patricia Grey

HEADLINE

First published in 1994
by HEADLINE BOOK PUBLISHING

First published in paperback in 1995
by HEADLINE BOOK PUBLISHING

10 9 8 7 6 5 4 3 2

ISBN 0 7472 4658 0

Printed and bound in Great Britain by
Caledonian International Book Manufacturing Ltd, Glasgow

HEADLINE BOOK PUBLISHING
A division of Hodder Headline PLC
338 Euston Road
London NW1 3BH

For John

Prologue

Thursday 17 October 1940
'Bad raid last night,' Ethel Murray said.

It was a stupid remark. She knew that. They were all bad raids. Had been for the past six weeks, ever since the Luftwaffe had started the Blitz on London. But Ethel had never heard of companionable silences; any break in the conversation she saw as a chasm which she had to fill. So Ethel pitched in words, sentences, and whole monologues with enthusiasm, unconcerned by the lack of response from her passenger.

Occasionally she stole a sideways glance at him as he swayed and rocked with the bumpy motion of the lorry. He was too old to be of interest to her; in Ethel's experience once they were past twenty-five they started to get staid and set in their ways, like her dad. This one wasn't as old as Mr Murray Senior, but she guessed he must be at least in his late thirties; the dark cropped hair that framed his thin face had flicks of grey on the ends as if it had come too close to the paintbrush, and there was a cobweb of fine lines deeply etched in the skin beneath the graphite-coloured eyes. But it was his skin that fascinated her most; it was the particular shade of dirty beige that her mum's old lace curtains had turned when they'd been left to soak in cold tea.

He was certainly no chatterbox. Didn't say a word.

Just stared blankly through the windscreen although there wasn't much to see; the streets were still dark and the grey morning was struggling to rise in the east.

Ethel made another stab at conversation. 'It's dead difficult driving after the bombs; what with all the pot-holes, and the bricks and glass and things in the road.' To emphasise her point, she spun the wheel to take the next corner. The churns in the back clanked together warningly.

'Don't oversteer, girl,' he said. 'You'll have us over.'

Ethel sniffed. 'I know how to drive, thank you. I deliver all over London.' She didn't bother to admit that she'd only been doing so for four weeks, since the last of her brothers had been called up.

Seated in the cab high above the pavement, behind the green and red board that announced 'Murray & Son – Carriers', Ethel stared down pityingly at the scurrying pedestrians and headed towards Camden Road.

'I'll have to put my foot down a bit. The milk train was late. They stopped it out past Stevenage on account of the raid on London. I'm supposed to pick these up at five o'clock. From King's Cross.'

Well he knew that, she scolded herself mentally. That's where she'd met him. Struggling to heave a heavy churn up on to the lorry tailgate, and willing herself not to ask a couple of grinning porters for help, she'd been grateful when another pair of hands had seized the other handle and lifted it effortlessly into the lorry's back.

It wasn't until the last one was in position that it had belatedly occurred to her that he'd be expecting a tip. Whilst he banged the tailboard up and fastened the chains, she thrust her hands into the deep pockets of her dungarees. Her fingers found nothing but dust in the heavy seams.

'I'm sorry,' she'd began to say. 'I don't have . . .'

She'd found herself talking to empty air. Relieved to be rid of the embarrassment, she'd trotted to the cab, climbed on to the running board, opened the driver's door – and found him sitting in the passenger seat.

'I'll need a lift,' he'd said.

'I'm going up to Kentish Town,' Ethel offered.

'I know.' He waved the delivery docket she'd left lying on the dashboard.

That was the last thing he'd said until his comment on her driving abilities two minutes ago. Well, she'd show him!

She did. Her performance culminated in an impressive demonstration on how to reverse down a 'closed' street at forty miles an hour.

'For heaven's sake, girl,' her passenger said when they eventually came to a neck-wrenching halt. 'Watch where you're going in future or you'll have this milk turned into butter before it's delivered. Go on up there a bit now and we can cut down Sandalls Road.'

Ethel opened her mouth to ask how he knew where she wanted to go, and then remembered the delivery manifest. It wasn't, she decided, very nice; reading other people's delivery papers *and* yelling at them. With a toss of her brown curls, she decided not to speak to him any more.

It wasn't a resolve she could keep for very long.

3

Blithely crashing and grinding her way into third gear, she told her passenger that she thought she might join up.

'I quite fancy driving one of them big army trucks,' she confided. 'Or a tank. I'd really like to have a go in a tank. You think they'd let me join the Army?'

This wasn't a random question on Ethel's part. Despite her empty-headed chattering, there was a strong streak of shrewdness in her make-up. She'd been puzzling for some time over his background, and had privately christened him 'The Silent Soldier'.

At first, the cropped hair had led her to wonder whether he'd just been discharged from prison. But when he'd stabbed his right leg forward for a non-existent brake as she'd hurtled towards a policeman who'd been reckless enough to step out in front of the lorry, she'd glimpsed the khaki trousers beneath the long, shabby raincoat. And as the light increased outside she was able to make out a paler band of skin at the top of his forehead. It ended abruptly in a straight line, as if he were used to wearing a hat which sat over his eyebrows. Regular Army or reservist probably since he was too old to have been conscripted yet.

She repeated her question: 'Do you think they'd let me join the ATS?'

Without turning his head, he replied, 'I should think so, love.'

'And would I get to drive a tank? Do they let women do that?'

'No.'

'That's not fair! I bet I could drive one as well as any man. I reckon I'd sort them out, don't you?'

'I reckon you'd scare them to death.'

'Really? You think I'd frighten the Wehrmacht?'

'Them too.'

She was still puzzling over this remark when, with minimal damage to the gears, she rocked and lurched her way across Leighton Road and rolled into the yard of a small dairy tucked away behind Willingham Terrace. A morose, ferret-faced man who'd been sitting on the back doorstep rose to meet her.

'Morning, Mr Monk.'

'It's nearly afternoon. Two flaming hours I've been sitting here. And she wouldn't even let me slip back to me digs and get meself a slice of toast and a scrape of dripping.'

'Sorry. But the train was held up. They wouldn't let it come through until the "all clear". Isn't that right, mister?'

She stood on tiptoe and peered into her cab. It was empty.

'Where's he gone?'

'Where's who gone?' Felonious Monk asked.

'Me passenger. Didn't you see him?'

'Didn't see nobody 'cept you.'

Bewildered, Ethel stared round the yard. It was empty apart from herself, Felonious and the dairy's bad-tempered skewbald which was kicking noisily at its stable door.

She ran over to the open gates and looked both ways down the deserted street. There was no sign of a thin figure in a flapping raincoat.

The Silent Soldier had disappeared.

Chapter 1

'We're two short.'

Ivy Thomas glared at Felonious, her gleaming eyes sweeping over his thin figure as if she suspected him of concealing a pair of large metal churns about his person.

'It's all she left.' Fel extended the signed delivery note.

Ivy scowled but didn't pursue the subject. 'Get them shifted then, you lazy lump. It still needs to be bottled up and we've lost two hours already. I don't know why I bothered to give you a job. I must be going soft in the head.'

Muttering under his breath Fel manhandled the churns into the dairy, climbed on to a chair, and tipped the first one into the hopper. Ivy thrust a bottle under the optic, pushed upwards, and released the creamy liquid.

'Don't stand there on one leg looking like Eros,' she ordered. 'Start putting the tops on.'

Clambering down, Fel took up one of the caps and clamped it into position. For the next hour they worked feverishly, with Ivy filling and Fel capping, with occasional breaks to tip another churn into the dispensing hopper.

'I'll do the last few,' Ivy said eventually. 'You go hitch up Kitchener.'

'Can't you do it?' Felonious pleaded.

'No I can't. The cart's a man's job. And don't go upsetting that horse. He's more use to me than you are.'

Miserably, Felonious trailed out to the stables where Kitchener waited with an anticipatory gleam in his bloodshot eye. Fel was well aware that the horse enjoyed these early morning sessions. It was a battle of wits to see how many kicks and bites he could land before he was finally immobilized between the shafts. Today, Felonious managed to get off with two partially crushed toes and a nibbled ear.

'Get this round quick,' Ivy instructed, heaving crates into the back. 'Before they all start switching to the Co-op. And remember it's regulars only. There's not enough for casuals so don't go selling any off the back of the cart.' She accompanied this instruction with a sharp slap on Kitchener's rump. The horse trotted forward briskly scorning Fel's frantic shouts to 'whoa up'.

Kitchener ambled around Torriano Cottages and along the Avenue, stopping automatically at their customers' houses. Each time Felonious refilled his carrying crate, he was aware of the horse staring into space with an expression of nonchalant unconcern. The first week in this job had taught him that if he forgot and strayed too near the front of the cart, Kitchener's iron-shod rear hoof would lash out with the speed of a striking snake and make painful contact with Fel's ankle-bone.

'Beat you,' crowed Fel as he completed the last delivery in Torriano Avenue. 'Now let's go down the Gardens.'

Kitchener swished his tail, flicked his ears, and

continued to contemplate the passing clouds.

'Go on, you stupid four-footed glue-pot, you know where to go.'

Stooping, Felonious picked up a stone, hurled it at the broad brown and white rump, and yelled, 'Go on, giddup.'

Kitchener got up. He galloped along the Gardens and into Balaclava Row at full speed, stopped abruptly with all four feet planted wide, and would have succeeded in dislodging the entire day's milk supply if the cart's sides hadn't been so high.

Panting and gasping, Fel caught him up. Lugging a full crate from the cart, he staggered up to the door of the Home Harbour Cafe and elbowed it open. A fish slice sailed past his ear. Fel ducked and threaded his way through the tables to the counter at the far end.

'Morning, Miss Maria, Miss Josepha. Here's yer milk. Where'd you want it?'

'Cow!'

'Josepha, *please*, not in front of the customers.'

A salt cellar flew over the counter and was fielded by a plumpish dark-haired women before it could plunge into the tea urn.

'I'll just leave it here on the counter then, shall I?'

Banging it down by a display case Fel raised his cap to the two olive-skinned young women, and backed out past the few diners who were continuing to munch steadily, ignoring the hail of insults that flew around their heads.

The jeweller's shop was closed. Fel rattled the handle of the locked door. It wasn't like James Donald to be late up. Moving round to the windows he tried to squint through to the shop premises. There was no sign of any movement behind the black velvet curtains that backed the bow-fronted windows. For a moment, Fel's gaze lingered longingly on the display trays; all the good stuff would be locked in the safe in the back room of course, but even so just the sight of the little glittering groups of cheap costume jewellery brought a reminiscent tingle to the end of his fingers. He found himself calculating how much he could get for the carriage clock at the back of the display.

Pushing away such treacherous back-sliding he put the bottle on the step and moved quickly down the line of shops. There was no point trying the next one; it had been closed ever since he took over this round. Pity really, he mused, the Wellers had served the best fish and chips in Kentish Town.

At the grocery store the young woman behind the counter greeted him with a wan smile. 'Morning, Mr Monk. What a relief to meet someone who wants to give me something, instead of the other way round.'

She took the two pint bottles and slipped them under the polished wooden counter. 'There, now I really have got something under the counter.'

'Been giving you a hard time have they, Missus Goodwin?'

Rose nodded. 'Everybody's convinced I've got several pounds of butter stored under here. Not to mention bushels of tea, barrels of sugar and any amount of bacon and eggs.'

'Whereas, fact of the matter is, 'e's got 'em stored away in the back, eh?' Felonious whispered.

'I heard that!' The voice that roared from the store room was followed by a large rotund figure in grocer's beige. 'I heard that,' Albert White repeated. 'Implying I'm playing favourites. Keeping back the choicest bits for me regulars.'

'Felonious was only joking,' Rose said, laying a hand on her employer's beefy arm with its generous thatching of white hairs.

'That's right,' Fel agreed. 'Just me little joke. No offence intended.'

He stepped jauntily out of the shop, making a mental note that there was something of interest in the back of White's shop.

In the cobbler's he was greeted with a lecture on the laziness of folks who overslept just because there had been a bit of an air raid and raised his eyebrows in sympathy at the women who accepted the milk bottles. How Lexie put up with the miserable old bugger day in and day out was beyond Fel. It made you glad to be an orphan.

It was a relief to reach the last shop in the parade.

Helen Fortune smiled at him with genuine warmth and paused in her massaging of shampoo into a client's wet hair to invite him to put the milk in the back and make himself a cup of coffee if he liked.

'I'm afraid I can't offer you tea, we're out again. Matt's so heavy handed with the caddy spoon. But there's a bottle of Camp in the cupboard. And you too, Mrs Green?'

Beneath her mound of perfumed lather, Mrs Green murmured that coffee would be just the ticket.

Shuffling through to the back room, Fel lifted the kettle on to the gas ring and poured half an inch of the thick brown liquid into the bottom of three cups. There was no sugar, but a partially used tin of condensed milk was standing on the side. Fel added a dollop to each cup to sweeten it, sipped experimentally, and grimaced. He'd never get used to the stuff. You just couldn't beat tea. A lot of people felt the same judging from the talk you heard in the street. There was probably a fair bit to be made by anyone who could lay his hands on a few packets of Horniman's. An image of the locks on the back door of the grocer's shop swam into his mind.

Before you could say 'clink', he'd gulped down a mouthful of the hot liquid, scalded his tongue, and rushed through into the shop, slopping puddles liberally into the saucers.

'Here yer are,' he gasped. 'Just like yer muvver never made.'

Trussed up in towels like a Turkish pasha, Mrs Green sipped noisily. Behind her back, Helen yawned loudly, excused herself, and drank several inches of the sweet liquid gratefully.

'Bombs keep you awake too, love?' Mrs Green asked sympathetically.

'Not really. I was on duty at the ARP post last night. It was my turn for the bicycle.'

'What d'you do with that then?' Fel asked, blowing across the pool of coffee he'd tipped into his saucer.

'Jump on it whenever it looks like we've had a hit in our area, pedal like mad until you find it, then pedal like mad back to the post so they can log it.'

'Did you find many last night?'

'No. Just a couple of incendiaries,' Helen admitted. 'Most of the bad ones fell south of here. I hear Mornington Crescent tube was flooded.'

'I 'ope they didn't hit the Black Cat factory,' Mrs Green

remarked. 'I couldn't do without me fags. Got to have something for yer nerves these days, haven't you?'

Helen yawned long and loud again. 'Oh excuse me,' she said. 'I'd better get on with winding you up before I fall asleep in the basin.'

Fel looked through the glass door and saw Kitchener regarding him with beady eyes. Sometimes he had the ridiculous impression that the horse was spying on him and reporting back to Ivy Thomas. 'I'd best be getting on too.'

As he was leaving, he saw a mangy black and white dog circling the pint outside the jeweller's shop. The animal sniffed and nudged the top with his black velvet nose.

'Get off!' Fel hurried across and seized the bottle. For a moment he thought the dog was about to make a fight of it. But it slunk away, and squatted down at the end of the road.

Fel looked at the bottle and then back at the mongrel. If it nicked the bottle, or broke it, Donald might complain to Ivy Thomas. And Ivy might decide to dispense with his services. With a sigh of the put-upon, Fel trudged round the back of the parade, made his way along the narrow path, and unlatched the door to Donald's yard.

The small, brick-enclosed area was empty apart from the rubbish bin and a man's bicycle which had been carefully covered by an oiled tarpaulin. Unlike other shops in the parade, the back windows on the ground floor were heavily barred with thick iron rods. From habit, Fel ran an experimental finger around the base of the bars, checking if the fixing was secure. It was.

He rapped sharply on the wooden door. With the smooth movement of well-oiled hinges, it swung slowly inwards.

'Hello? Anybody in?'

Hovering on the balls of his feet, ready to run if anybody challenged him, Fel edged a little further into the silent room.

He looked around curiously. James Donald used the back room as a workshop for his jewellery business. Creeping cautiously round, Fel examined the benches with their neat rows of tiny tools used for working and repairing the precious metals and semi-precious stones. He slid open a few of the drawers in the chests that lined the back of the bench and poked a curious finger amongst the unset stones, clips and fastenings. A small smelter was sitting on one of the benches. Fel peered inside hopefully; but the machine was cold and empty. He tried the door into the shop but found it was securely locked and bolted. Disappointed, he turned away and saw something that he'd missed on his initial tour of the workroom. A tingle of anticipation slid up and down his spine. In two strides he was across the room and running his hand lovingly over the thick, cold metal of James Donald's safe.

'Beautiful job. Lovely bit of workmanship.' His fingers caressed the brass handle and explored the metal dial. He wasn't a safe man, never had been. But he knew several good petermen. 'Fifty-fifty, that's fair,' he told himself. 'I found it.' His ferrety face creased. 'Or maybe sixty-forty would be better.'

The sight of the milk bottle in his own hand brought him back to reality with a jolt. He was a respectable

14

working bloke now. Here on legitimate business.

With a last lingering look at the safe, he crossed to a door in the side of the room and peered up the steep wooden steps that led to the flat above the shop.

'Hello? You up there, Mr Donald? I've got yer milk. Shall I bring it up?'

There was no answer again, but since he'd got this far, Fel decided he might as well go on.

The wooden stairs were uncarpeted but clean. Fel made his way up to the carpeted landing.

'Milk!' he tried again. Getting no response, he opened the nearest door. It was the bathroom. Backing out again, he tried the door opposite and found himself in the Donalds' sitting room. The blackout curtains were still drawn and it took him a few moments to adjust to the darkness. Blinking and trying not to trip over the furniture, he groped his way to the window and twitched back the heavy curtains sufficient to show him the room was unoccupied.

But there was evidence that James hadn't gone far. The jacket and waistcoat of the black suit that he always wore in the shop were lying across the back of the sofa. On the occasional table, in front of the new GEC radio, were his watch, tie-clip and cuff-links. Fel's hand was already on the way towards them, drawn like a pigeon to scraps, when the floorboards outside creaked loudly.

Jumping back guiltily he hurried outside, calling reassurance. 'Only the milk. Overslept, did you?'

The hall was empty. Puzzled, Fel checked the kitchen and found it equally deserted. If James was here, there was only one place he could be. Whistling loudly to show his innocent intentions, Fel mounted the stairs to the second landing.

The door on the left led to a pink-papered bedroom. Patchwork counterpanes in various rose hues covered the twin beds. Along the wall-shelf several forlorn dolls hung limply against a collection of children's books. On a small wooden table the front of a doll's house was partially pulled open to reveal the Lilliputian furniture inside. Above the beds, two handmade pictures, decorated with cut-out illustrations of fairies, declared these to be: 'Mavis's Bed' and 'Evelyn's Bed'. The whole room had a dusty, cold, unused feel.

Felonious remembered Helen French telling him that Mrs Donald and the girls had gone to live with her folks in the country somewhere as soon as war had been declared. Hoping he wasn't about to interrupt Mr Donald in a reunion with his better half, Fel rapped loudly at the last door and opened it a fraction of an inch. 'Mr Donald, you there?'

Thirty seconds later he was haring down the wooden stairs and bursting out into the back alley as if an entire troop of German paratroopers had just crashed through Donald's roof. He barely noticed the excited mongrel which had followed him into the flat and now circled him with hysterical yaps.

Out of Balaclava Row, up the Gardens and back into Torriano Avenue he fled. Once there he turned right, heading instinctively for the shelter of his digs, remembered belatedly that he was now a respectable citizen, turned left and saw two coppers coming towards him. Their uniforms, from the tops of their tin helmets to the tips of their wellingtons, were covered in a fine film of red powdered dust. It wasn't until he was six inches from them, that Fel realised their hands and faces were also plastered with layers of the same brick debris.

He opened his mouth to speak and discovered he was still clutching the milk bottle thrust out before him like a relay runner's baton.

'Thanks, mate,' the younger constable said. Pushing off the top, he tilted his head back and tipped half a pint of Ivy's milk down his parched throat. Wiping the back of his hand across his mouth and leaving a pink gash amongst the terracotta mask, he passed the bottle to his companion.

'Eer, you ain't supposed . . .' Fel started to protest.

'That your horse?' the first copper asked.

Turning round Fel found that Kitchener was following him at a slow ambling pace. As he watched, the horse stretched his neck into someone's front garden, flipped the top off a metal bin, and rooted out a lump of stale bread.

'Oi, get that 'orse out of me bin.' The instruction was followed by a boot which flew out of the top window.

'You heard, mate,' the older policeman said. 'Shift it.' He handed back the empty bottle. 'Thanks for the drink.'

Fel hurried over to scoop up Kitchener's trailing reins, avoided the lethal teeth, and hauled the horse back into the middle of the road. The two coppers had reached the far end of the road. Fel had already opened his mouth to shout after them when a sudden horrifying picture flashed into his mind: he saw himself touching James Donald's safe. His hands caressing the door, the handle, the lock.

'Dabs all over the place,' he moaned to Kitchener. 'What am I going to do?'

The horse trod heavily on Fel's toe and barged him out of the way as he made for the next street on their route. Fel limped after him. They stopped. A pint was delivered to the waiting hands of a complaining housewife. They moved on again. Felonious worked automatically, his mind racing as he tried to decide what to do. Go back and wipe off his fingerprints? He'd been all over the flaming flat; it would take days to clean the place proper.

'And what if I missed one?' he said to the impatient horse. He was bright enough to realise that it would look even more suspicious if the police found just one print. Anyway he couldn't imagine himself working in that darkened bedroom. Cleaning and polishing while that thing was on the bed. A great shudder went through Fel's body. He couldn't do it.

He finished the round and stabled Kitchener again in record time. Collecting his money, he bought chips and sausages from the fish and chip shop opposite the Palace cinema, absent-mindedly fed half to the dog which was still slinking behind him, and spent the rest of the afternoon in the Mother Shipton, nursing a pint until the barman slung him out.

When they re-opened, he was the first back through the door; retreating again to his favourite corner. The dog crept under the table. Occasionally it cocked an ear or an eye in Felonious's direction as he muttered and moaned to himself under his breath.

There was no getting round it. Whichever way he looked at it he was in dead lumber. He didn't doubt the police were going to try and pin the blame on him.

They were like that; never giving an old lag a second chance. And there was no point in making a bolt for it; in these days of ration books and identity cards they'd pick him up in no time. He looked desperately round the filling pub, searching for a way out of his problems.

'Room for a little one? Oi, lover boy, I'm talking to you.'

With a start, Fel realised he was being addressed. He found himself being thrust to the corner of his seat by a determined set of hips encased in a tweed skirt. He was drowned in an overwhelming scent of rose perfume as the owner of the well-upholstered rump settled herself more comfortably and continued to shout at her friend over the noisy sing-song.

'Just 'aving a bit of a kiss and cuddle, weren't we? And this frosty cow complains. So this woman police sergeant comes over and give us an earful. Tells us we can't do it in a public shelter.' A double gin disappeared down her throat in one swallow before she continued. 'Jealous if you ask me. Great tall streak of a thing she were. Don't suppose she's ever had it. I mean, gentlemen like a bit of meat on the bones, don't they?' She finished on a shriek of indignation. 'Oi, watch where yer putting yer hands.'

Felonious continued to keep his fingers firmly dug into the substantial roll of flesh around her upper arm. 'This shelter you was in, where is it?'

The woman shuffled her bottom round on the seat and gave him her full attention.

'Where's this shelter, miss?' Fel repeated.

'Up around Carker's Lane. But there's no need to go all that way. I've got a room round the corner; it's nice and cosy. And no nosy coppers. Eer, where you goin'?'

Felonious was already pushing his way through the smoke-filled bar towards the door.

Oblivious to indignant shouts to mind the blackout, Felonious flung himself into the street. Miss Sarah, he thought, relief flooding through him, that was who he needed.

The drone of heavy bombers, like a flight of gigantic bees, grew louder as he puffed up Kentish Town Road until the sky above was filled with the thunder of engines. Ahead of him the night was suddenly alight with a Jacob's ladder of searchlights. The boom of the anti-aircraft guns on the Heath added to the din as they tried to hit the planes caught like flies in amber in the brilliant shafts of light.

Felonious hurried on, expecting to hear the angry whistle of descending bombs any second. But the planes had already discharged their loads and were swinging eastwards again.

'Bloody typical,' Fel muttered. A stick of bombs on Balaclava Row would have solved all his problems. Even as he thought it, he pushed the idea quickly away. He didn't wish the folks in the shops any harm. He was just strongly attached to his own skin and wanted to stay that way for as long as possible.

His arrival at the public shelter was greeted with a hissed instruction from the shelter marshal that he 'couldn't bring that cur in here. Read the notice. It says no animals.'

'It ain't mine. Show 'im the notice if you don't want him to come in.'

Barging past the man, Felonious hurried into the

shelter and tripped and crashed his way over the huddled figures trying to sleep on the slatted benches and concrete floor.

The only light came from the far corner. Squinting into the dimness Fel saw a small lamp set up against a tea urn. Three women were grouped around the make-shift wooden table. Two wore the uniform of the WVS, the other was in the dark blue of the Metropolitan police.

Sergeant Sarah McNeill heard Felonious approach long before she saw him. To a chorus of yells, squeals and curses, he trod over the slumbering shelterers and practically flung himself into her arms.

'I never done it,' he announced.

'Done what?'

Fel grasped her shoulders, stuck his mouth close to her ear and whispered: 'Murder, Miss Sarah. Someone's done Mr Donald in.'

Chapter 2

Sarah did not receive his news with quite the amount of gravity that Felonious thought it deserved. In fact, she was downright sceptical.

He found her quite willing to believe he'd found a body; but she was inclined to think it was more likely that James Donald had died as the result of blast damage. She'd learnt from experience over the past few weeks that an exploding bomb could produce strange effects. Only last week she'd had to deal with a case where a child had slept on in a blast-damaged house, blissfully unaware that the rest of the occupants lay dead in the next room.

She suggested to Fel that perhaps his 'murder victim' was one of these freaks of circumstance. Fel indignantly informed her that James Donald weren't no freak.

'He had ones and twos of everything he was supposed to have far as I could see. 'E's been done in. You come and see, Miss Sarah. And tell 'em I never done it.'

With a sigh, Sarah had eventually agreed on a compromise; he'd stay in the shelter until she came off duty the following morning and then they'd both walk round to Donald's shop.

Now he scuttled along beside her in the dark, chilly morning, his ferrety face bobbing at her shoulder height. Despite his agitation, Sarah maintained an even pace.

23

She was a tall woman, too tall in her own estimation, although she was careful never to appear embarrassed by her height. Her long hair, brown at the roots but tending to blonde on the tips was tucked up under the helmet that framed a long serious face. As usual she was regarding the world with a slightly quizzical expression in her cool blue eyes. She wasn't pretty in a conventional sense; but she had the sort of looks that stuck in the mind after everyday glamour had faded.

Now she said, 'When did you find this body, Fel?'

'On me round yesterday.'

'Collecting the rent?'

'Rent?' Fel stared blankly for a moment, then shook his head. 'Nah. I don't do that no more. I'm on the milk now.'

'Milk?' Sarah's brow wrinkled in a frown. 'What time was this?'

'Dunno. About nine-thirty, ten. Something like that.'

'Ten! Ten o'clock in the *morning*! Why on earth didn't you come into the station and report this yesterday?'

She sounded sharper than she'd intended, her indignation fuelled mainly by the realisation that, had he done so, she could be on her way home to bed now rather than putting in some unpaid overtime.

Fel extended a sulky bottom lip. 'Knew you'd ask that. It's always the same with you coppers. Trying to make out everything I do is suspicious. It's not easy going straight you know,' he said indignantly. 'Nobody wants to give an old lag a chance. They think I can't be trusted.'

'That's because you keep stealing things, Fel.'

'Yer, well . . . everybody's got their little weaknesses, ain't they? Watch out!'

They both sprang away from the kerb as a delivery lorry, churns rattling noisily in the back, screeched round the corner on two wheels.

'She'll be expecting me in to bottle that up,' Fel said, increasing his pace. 'We'd better get on quick so's you can do somefing about this stiff.'

Wrapped in his coat last night, trying to sleep on the hard concrete floor of the shelter, Fel had half-heartedly tried to convince himself that yesterday had all been a nightmare. One look at the quiet, untouched workroom told him it hadn't been.

'Up here,' he said, leading Sarah towards the stairs.

On the first landing, he stopped and pointed. 'He's up there. Right-hand door.'

'After you.'

Felonious glared but was forced to proceed her up the stairs. 'In here.' Thrusting the door open, he stepped back as a warm, sickly smell hit their nostrils.

Covering her mouth, Sarah made her way across to the drawn curtains and twitched them apart.

James Donald lay relaxed on his back with covers drawn to his chin, his arms resting outside on the neatly turned down pale-green bedspread. It was only as she stepped nearer to the bed that she saw the man's eyes were open, the sightless pale grey irises staring with an expression close to disbelief at the cobweb cracks in the white-washed ceiling.

'See, Miss Sarah. Done in.' Fel called from the landing.

Sarah hesitated. There was nothing to suggest that

Donald hadn't died of natural causes. Yet there was something wrong with the scene. What was it?

'Why d'you think he was murdered, Fel?'

Felonious couldn't give her a coherent reason. He just knew. 'I seen people who been called Upstairs. And I seen them that 'ad a 'elping hand up the treads. And you take my word for it, miss. Someone stuck a boot up this one's backside and 'elped 'im along a bit.'

It was a perfectly normal bedroom: matching pale-green curtains and bedspread; a flock wallpaper in a darker shade of viridian; solid walnut furniture chosen for durability rather than style; a square rug either side of the bed and – Sarah stooped quickly – a flower-decorated chamber pot beneath. So, what was worrying her?

Pursing her lips, she stood, hands thrust in her pockets, foot tapping, considering the scene. Then suddenly it came to her: the arms.

Sliding her hand under the cold flesh, she grasped the edge of the bedclothes, easing them away from the body. It confirmed what the arms had already told her; James Donald wasn't wearing a pyjama jacket. Peeling the clothes to his waist, she discovered that he wasn't wearing any trousers either.

Fel edged closer. 'Cor, he's starkers!'

It was very odd: respectable lower middle-class men in Kentish Town went to bed in solid flannelette pyjamas. The absence of a pair of these articles on the Monday morning washing line would have caused instant gossip amongst the neighbours. So where were Donald's?

She bent closer to the man's chest, overcoming her revulsion enough to touch the patch of wiry pale-brown hairs that flowed in an inverted 'V' shape from his solar plexus. At the base of the hairs, staining the chalky skin, was a vivid purple bruise.

'Reckon that's what done for him?'

Sarah jumped. She hadn't noticed Fel creeping closer until he hissed in her ear. 'I've no idea,' she said briskly, drawing the clothes back again. 'But you keep your mouth shut about what you've seen.'

Followed by Fel, who seemed to believe the closer he stuck to her, the less chance there was of him being charged with murder, she clattered back to the first floor and quickly checked the kitchen and sitting room.

'What you looking for?'

'A telephone. Did he have one?'

'Dunno. In the shop maybe. But the door's locked.' Realising he had made a tactical mistake, admitting he'd been trying to get into a jeweller's shop, Fel quickly offered the information that there was a phone in the hairdresser's.

None of the shops were open yet, but a vigorous knocking on the back door of Helen Fortune's resulted in the window of the flat being thrust open.

'Yes? Who's there?'

Tilting back her head, Sarah replied, 'Police, sir. Could I use your phone please?'

'Yes. Of course.' The window closed and a few seconds later the back door was opened.

'Has there been an incident? I could fetch my sister if you like, she's had first aid training.'

'That won't be necessary, thank you, sir. If I could just use the phone?'

By the time Sarah had finished quietly talking to Agar Street Station, Matthew had roused his sister and they were both hovering in the back storeroom, trying to appear helpful but not over-inquisitive. Helen offered tea.

'Slip along to Rose and ask her if she can let us have a quarter, Matt. I'm sure Albert won't mind if it's an official incident.'

Matthew returned within minutes. He was a good-looking young man in his mid-twenties. Not as dark-haired as his sister, but they both shared the same hazel eyes and clear cream skin. He flicked a packet of tea to his sister and informed her that he'd drank the last of the milk. 'Lucky you're early this morning, Fel,' he remarked. 'The dairy won't mind letting us have a couple of extra pints, will it? Seeing we're catering for an incident.'

'Mr Monk isn't here to deliver the milk,' Sarah said. 'He's assisting the police with their enquiries.'

She saw by the way Fel sagged like a punctured balloon that it was an unfortunate turn of phrase. It meant only one thing to Felonious. He was nicked.

'Why didn't he report this immediately? We've already lost twenty-four hours.'

'He was scared, sir. He thought we'd charge him with murder. Will we?'

Chief Detective Inspector Jack Stamford didn't reply immediately. With an unconscious gesture he thrust a hand through his dark auburn hair. He was in his early forties now, but there was no sign of any grey amongst the copper thatch above the square face. Likewise the tall figure beneath the well-worn suit still suggested muscles rather than the approach of any middle-aged softness.

Moving along the bed, his shrewd brown eyes took in the long, naked figure. Leaning close to the corpse's chest, he examined the bruise in the centre of the rib cage. As he was about to straighten up his attention was caught by a fine white thread dancing gently in the victim's nostril cavity as it was caught in the draught from Stamford's exhaled breath.

'Do you have any tweezers?'

'Not on me, no.'

'Try the dressing table. But be careful about finger-prints.'

Sarah nodded. Using her handkerchief, she gingerly drew the top drawer out and found a small felt case decorated with cross-stitches in wool along each of its seams. One side held a shaving brush and comb, the other had pockets for a pair of nail clippers, a pair of scissors and a set of tweezers. A linen name tab, pasted on to the lining, proclaimed in wavering red embroidery: 'Happy Birthday, Daddy, love E and M.'

Wordlessly, she passed the tweezers to Stamford and watched while he fished the thread from Donald's nostrils, placed it in an envelope and scrawled information on the outside before sealing it securely.

'Suffocated?' Sarah asked.

'Maybe. But we'll have to wait for the post mortem to know for sure. Perhaps it was some kind of seizure and the bruise has no connection with the death. How tall would you say he was?'

Sarah ran a speculative eye over the corpse. 'Five ten?' she suggested.

'Weight?'

'Heavyish. Thirteen stone?'

'I agree. Big enough to put up quite a fight anyway if someone was trying to asphyxiate him.' Stamford turned one of Donald's arms, running a finger lightly over the livid weal around the wrist. 'Or trying to tie him up. Was the back door open when you arrived?'

Sarah nodded. 'And Fel said it was yesterday when he came in.'

Jack straightened, wincing at the dull ache which shifted position and lodged itself firmly into the small of his back. 'Bomb hit a couple of nights ago,' he said, catching Sarah's eye. 'Trapped a couple and their baby in the coal cellar. I was helping to shift bricks until the heavy rescue team arrived.'

With the arrival of the Blitz the demarcation line between CID and uniform had blurred; if help was wanted both plainclothes and uniformed donned tin hats and wellingtons and mucked in wherever needed.

Jack massaged the tender spot. 'The spirit's willing, but the lumbar region is weak,' he admitted with a rueful grin. He ran one more glance around the room. 'There's not much more we can do here. Let's leave it to the doctor and the forensic team, and we'll go and have words with Mr Monk.'

Felonious was perched on a wooden stool in the hairdresser's back room; his hands pressed together and clasped between his knees, his shoulders hunched and his bottom lip thrust out mulishly as he shot resentful glances at the plainclothes policeman who was guarding him. 'I never done it,' he said as soon as Jack and Sarah entered the room.

'I don't suppose you did,' Jack agreed.

'Don't you?' Fel looked at Jack in surprise, torn between relief and indignation. 'Why not?'

Jack tapped the side of his nose. 'We detectives have ways of knowing these things.'

'Yeah. You mean you've found a clue already.' Fel was impressed.

'So why don't you tell me all about yesterday morning?'

Before Fel could oblige, the door to the flat stairs opened slightly.

Helen had changed into the plain claret dress she usually wore to work in the salon. She'd also found time to apply a light dusting of powder and a lick of the dark red lipstick that best suited her black and white colouring. Seeing the flicker of admiration in the chief detective's eyes as he looked up, she was glad she'd made the effort.

'I'm sorry to interrupt,' she apologised. 'But I've made some tea upstairs, if you'd like a cup. And my brother was wondering if it would be all right if he goes to work?'

'Of course. I'm sorry we're holding you up like this. We won't be here much longer. In the meantime, we'd love tea. Why don't you go upstairs and collect it, Constable, whilst I have a word with Felonious.'

DC 'Ding Dong' Bell didn't need any further urging. With an expression of deepest gloom on his long face, he drooped after Helen in a way that suggested the weight of the world was on his shoulders.

'Doesn't he ever smile?' Jack asked.

'Only at the children's Christmas party. He does a wonderful conjuring act.'

Jack tried to picture this bizarre scene, gave up, and settled down to listen while Felonious trotted out his story again.

It had acquired certain refinements since the previous day. Fel had only tried the doors to the shop and the safe in order to spare the police the trouble of discovering whether Donald had been robbed. Once he'd found the body he had, of course, looked in all the other rooms, just to check that the murderer wasn't still hiding in the flat.

'I expect I left me dabs all over the place,' he explained earnestly. 'But I was just trying to do me bit and save you the trouble.'

'Most thoughtful,' Jack said. 'And did you take anything from the flat? Just until we wanted it, of course.'

'No!' The indignation in Felonious's voice sounded genuine. The door opened at that moment to readmit Ding Dong and a tray of tea. Both officers turned at the sound and consequently failed to see the slight frown of worry that crossed Felonious's narrow face. He opened his mouth to say something, thought better of it, and accepted his tea instead.

He'd just finished noisily slurping it up, when Matthew Fortune clattered down the stairs. The pyjamas and dressing gown had been exchanged for a dark grey, pin-striped suit, the dark hair was now hidden under a soft felt hat, and in his left hand he was clutching a briefcase and umbrella. He waved both at the trio: 'The intrepid civil servant goes to do battle against the Hun. Matthew Fortune, Inspector,' he added, extending a hand to Jack.

Stamford shook it and glanced down involuntarily as his senses told him something was wrong. The thin white hand that was sliding out of his fingers was only two thirds of the size of its fellow.

'Polio, Inspector.' He pushed the hand into the pocket of his jacket. 'It doesn't bother me, but I find it embarrasses other people. So if you'll excuse me, Sergeant, I won't raise my hat, I'll just wish you good morning and be off to fight the good fight at the Ministry of Misinformation.' With a nod and smile he strode briskly out into the backyard.

Jack raised silent eyebrows: a bitter young man, he suspected, trying to hide it behind an act of light-hearted carelessness.

'Can I go too,' Felonious asked hopefully, 'since you ain't nicking me?'

Jack considered. 'I suppose so,' he conceded. ''But don't talk to anyone about what you've seen here. Can we still find you in Leighton Road if we need you?'

Fel agreed they could in a tone that suggested he very much hoped they'd never want to, and sped thankfully away to face the wrath of Ivy Thomas and Kitchener.

Helen Fortune slipped quietly into the room and collected the cups. 'I was wondering,' she said awkwardly. 'I mean, I thought at first James had had an accident. But it's not that, is it?'

'There are certain aspects of Mr Donald's death that we need to investigate. Is there a Mrs Donald?'

'Oh yes.' Helen set her tray down again. 'Gwen took the girls to the country last September. They're staying with her family. I have the address upstairs, if you'd like it?'

'That would be helpful. Shall we come up with you?' Jack precluded her refusal by picking up the tray before she could retrieve it. Ding Dong was despatched back to Donald's shop to await the divisional surgeon and forensic team whilst Stamford and Sarah made their way up to the Fortunes' flat.

Its layout was identical to the Donalds', but it had a lighter, airier feeling, mainly due to the Fortunes' preference for pastel shades rather than the rather heavy, flocked wallpapers favoured by Mrs Donald. Like the jeweller's shop, it puzzled Stamford slightly: this was an out-of-the-way location with a slightly rundown feel, yet the fittings in both the shops and the living quarters, whilst admittedly old-fashioned, were of the kind of quality that he would have expected to find in Bond Street or Burlington Arcade, not Kentish Town.

Helen led them into the living room, excused herself for a moment, and returned with a small black book stuffed with loose scraps of paper. She extracted one. 'Here you are. I asked James for it last Christmas so I could send them a card.'

It looked like a sheet torn from a child's exercise book. Jack twisted it to read the address properly. 'Aldbury?' he said on an interrogatory note.

'It's somewhere in the west of Hertfordshire apparently. Near enough for James to get there and back in a day anyway.'

'Did Mrs Donald ever visit him here instead?' Jack asked.

'Not often. A few times.' Helen's hazel eyes grew larger and the pupils dilated. 'I've just realised . . .' She looked between the two officers. 'Someone is going to have to tell her, aren't they? If you'd like me to . . . I mean, we aren't particularly close, but if I could help . . .'

'That's very kind,' Jack said. 'Is Mrs Donald the sort of woman who's likely to become hy—' He nearly said hysterical but changed it to, 'likely to become deeply distressed?'

'No,' Helen admitted. 'Gwen is quite . . .' She hesitated, searching for the right word and eventually finished, 'Gwen is quite sturdy, emotionally speaking.'

'Were they a close couple?'

'I suppose so. It seemed like most marriages. Not wrapped up in each other, just, sort of, comfortable.'

'And the children? What about them?'

Helen's face lit up. 'Oh they're both devoted to the girls. Couldn't do enough for them.'

'How old are the daughters?'

Wrinkling her brow, Helen made a moue with her mouth. Holding up her fingers she counted silently. She had her brother's long, slim hands, but without their disfigurement.

'Evelyn must be nine now, I think. And Mavis is a year younger. Poor little things.' She sat, chewing at her bottom lip, removing the lipstick in small globules.

Jack examined her covertly for a moment, whilst appearing to tuck the address sheet into his wallet. She was a lot older than her brother; nearer his own age of forty-one. Her figure was what he supposed might be described as curvaceous, filling out the plain dress very pleasingly in the hip and bust areas. But it was her hair that he found fascinating. It was a deep black shade shot through with blue lights; but instead of wearing it in the pleats and twists that were fashionable now, she'd cut it in a plain simple chin-length bob and straight fringe. It could have looked mannish if it hadn't been relieved by her lively eyes and full mouth. He asked if she knew whether James Donald had any enemies.

'Good heavens, no. He wasn't interesting enough to have any enemies,' she blurted out. 'Oh dear, that sounds dreadful, doesn't it?' she moaned, as Jack smiled broadly. 'But you must know what I mean.'

'Yes, I know. Tell me about the other people in this row. What about the cafe?'

'That's the Brownes. At least,' Helen said. 'Maria is a Browne. Josepha's a Scionne or something like that. They're half-sisters, same father, different mothers.'

'Italian?'

'Maltese. They came here with their father about five years ago. But he got fed up and went back to sea. He was, in fact he probably still is, a ship's cook.'

'What about the other side of the jeweller's? The fish and chip shop.'

'The Wellers. But the shop's been closed since August. They went down to Cornwall when Alice's mother had a bad fall and they haven't been back since. Lexie, in the cobbler's, will have their address if you need it.'

Jack nodded at Sarah's notebook, obviously meaning her to take notes. She flipped a page and they continued.

The grocer's they discovered was run by Albert White. But he lived with his widowed sister, not above the shop.

'The Goodwins rent the flat,' Helen explained. 'At least, Rose does. Peter was killed at Dunkirk.'

'And the people next door?' Jack indicated the dividing wall.

'Frank and Lexie Emmett.'

'Which of the neighbours would you say was closest to the Donalds?'

'None of them,' Helen replied promptly. Seeing the detective's expression she struggled to explain further. 'They weren't that sort of people. I mean they passed the time of day with you but they weren't the sort of people you got close to.' She shrugged an apology. 'I'm sorry, there was nothing special about them. They were just ordinary.'

Sarah felt a trickle of ice slip down her spine. Looking across at Stamford she knew he'd experienced the same sensation. Helen Fortune's words brought back an uneasy echo of the last murder case they'd worked on: the death of the 'just ordinary' schoolgirl, Valerie Yeovil. A young lady who'd turned out to be anything but ordinary in the end.

They both saw Helen's surreptitious glance at her watch. Jack stood up. 'We won't keep you any longer. But another officer will be back to take a formal statement later.'

'Yes, of course. Although I don't think I can tell you anything that will help.' She accompanied them to the back door and asked them to tell Gwen Donald that she'd be pleased to give any help that was needed. 'They've no phone at the cottage. But there's one in the post office, I remember James called it last week. She could ring me from there.'

'I'll let her know,' Jack promised.

They stepped out into the lightening morning. In the way of English autumns, the weather had changed again. The cold winds of the last couple of days had given way to a milder spell which was drawing a slight mist from the dank field behind the shops.

Jack looked around; once again he was struck by the odd location of this parade of shops. The short row of houses known as the Gardens ran down to the edge of the rough field; Balaclava was stuck on to the end of this street like a boot on a leg, except that there was a gap at the 'ankle' leaving an access between the last house in the Gardens and the start of the Row. The front road was a cul-de-sac, coming to an abrupt stop at the edge of the grass. The trodden footpath at the back went nowhere except back round to the front of the shops. On the other three sides of the field were unbroken lines of backyards, except for one place to the left where he could make out a gap between two houses in Leighton Road.

'Do you think the murderer used the back entrance, sir?'

'Well if he didn't come in that way, he certainly went out that way,' Jack said. 'The bolt's still across the front door.'

Making his way down to the cafe end, he was aware of a flutter of activity behind each backyard gate. He walked carefully past a young girl leaning against the gatepost of the cafe's yard, pointedly ignoring the fact she was dressed in a pink slip and knickers and little else.

'Josepha! Get back in here. You want the police to think we're running a whore house?'

The girl looked lazily over her shoulder, flicking untidy brown hair from her face and revealing a fierce bruise under one eye. 'What's the matter, Maria? You scared they'll ask for their money back when they see you?'

Sarah, who'd been treading carefully behind Stamford on the narrow track, trying not to obliterate any footprints, was forced to jump back quickly as a metal colander flew out of the open gate and bounced across the field before coming to rest against a hillock of nettles. Taking a deep breath, she spoke quietly but firmly to the girl. With a shrug and a whisk of her pink-clad rump, the girl padded back inside and banged the gate loudly shut.

Rounding the corner of Balaclava Row, they found the mortuary van had already drawn up outside the Donalds' shop. The untidy brunette had skipped through the cafe and was now lounging in the front entrance. She'd been joined by another olive-skinned young woman, a few years older than herself. Presumably the 'Maria' she'd been cheeking. This woman, however, had already dressed in a crisp white blouse and black skirt and had pinned her hair into a matronly bun behind her round face.

The two women betrayed no embarrassment in their open curiosity, unlike the proprietors, assistants and customers from the other shops in the Row, who huddled in groups on the pavement, trying to give the impression they were engaged in casual chit-chat rather than watching the proceedings at the Donalds' with avid interest.

Snatches of conversation drifted across to the two police officers.

'It's gas, definitely gas, that's what I heard. Seeped up from the sewers and done him in in his bed.'

'What the police here for then? The way I heard it he strung himself up from the banisters when they broke in and found him with a radio in the attic sending messages to the Germans.'

'Good God,' Stamford muttered. 'Where do these stories *start*?'

He half smiled at Sarah, expecting her to share his amusement, and was met instead with an enormous yawn.

Hastily apologising, the sergeant covered her mouth and blinked tears of sleep from her eyes. 'Night duty,' she explained. 'Public shelter.'

Stamford was instantly contrite. 'Look,' he said, 'there's not much we can do today. I'll get the others started taking statements from the neighbours and see what can be done about contacting Mrs Donald. You get some sleep and I'll see you tomorrow. All right?'

Sarah bit her lip. 'Yes . . .' she paused, wondering how to phrase her next question. 'Look,' she said eventually, 'you seem to be assuming I'm going to be working on this investigation. I mean, last time, it was just a temporary transfer, and now I'm back in uniform.'

Stamford was momentarily thrown. He *had* been blithely taking it for granted that she'd be assisting him with this case as she had done in the Yeovil case five months previously.

He looked into Sarah's long-jawed, serious face. 'If I can arrange it, would you like to assist me again?'

Sarah's face lit up, transforming it from interesting to attractive. 'Yes, sir. I'd like that very much.'

'Good. Let's get back to the station then.'

'Oi, wai' a minute.' Josepha pointedly ignored Sarah and spoke directly to Stamford. She'd pulled a grubby, crumpled pink frock on, but had made no attempt to add shoes or tidy the strands of long brown hair. She smelt of cheap, over-perfumed soap and iodine. 'Is it true what they say? James is a goner?'

'Mr Donald is dead, yes. Was he a friend of yours?'

Josepha paused for a moment, her potentially pretty face spoilt by the enpurpling bruise and the sulky mouth. Then she spun on her heel and sauntered casually back to the cafe. 'He liked me,' she called over her shoulder. 'Lots of men like me.'

'I bet their wives don't,' Sarah said softly. 'I wonder if it was one of them gave her the black eye.'

They left the street, aware of the eyes burning into the backs of their necks. It was always a temptation to turn around suddenly and catch the gawpers out; but years of beat training enabled them both to walk slowly and unconcernedly to the corner and turn it.

The excited shopkeepers and their customers followed every step with avid interest.

As a consequence no one noticed the flutter of movement above from the unseen watcher who'd been following the police activity with a keen interest ever since Felonious had first dragged Sarah through the back gate of Donald's yard.

As the police passed out of sight, the watcher risked stepping forward and squinting down through a gap in the curtains at the collection of watching bystanders. The stronger light caused him to screw up his eyes and deepened the spider's web of fine white lines that radiated into taut skin the colour of tea-dyed lace curtains.

Chapter 3

'Funny job for a woman,' Lexie Emmett said.

The two stood side by side on the pavement, watching the police officers moving away, talking quietly together. Lexie's red head was four inches taller than Rose's fair one and there was an eleven-year difference in their ages, but apart from that there was a superficial likeness about the two women. They both had an air of dowdiness that was reflected in their simple hairstyles, lack of make-up and plain dresses, black in Rose's case and a faded blue in Lexie's.

'I thought about joining up,' Lexie announced after a moment of silence.

'What? The police?'

'No. Not them. I don't like the uniform. I quite fancy the Wrens. But I don't suppose they'd let me in. I'm not posh enough. The ATS is more my level. Bet they'd let you in the Wrens though, Rose,' Lexie said enviously. 'You talk ever so nice. Just like a lady. I suppose they learn you that at the teacher training?'

'Not really. If you live amongst people for a while, you start speaking like them. I don't think I sound particularly posh.'

It came out more sharply than she'd intended. She didn't want to be thought posh or different from the other girls in Kentish Town. She wanted to turn the clock back ten years and be common little Rose

43

Tammie from St James's Gardens again. 'Sorry,' she apologised, seeing the flicker of surprise in Lexie's eyes. 'I didn't mean to snap. It's all this business next door. It's a bit of a shock. What do you think is really happening in there?'

'No idea. Helen would know, the police were in her shop for ages talking to her. Helen,' she said reflectively, returning to her theme, 'volunteers for everything. She's *involved*. Not like us. We never do anything. Never even go out or nothing. Should we go in and ask about Donald, d'you fink?'

Rose's reply was interrupted by a sudden roar from the cobbler's shop.

'Lexie. What yer doin' out there? There's customers waiting to be served.'

Lexie scurried in and Rose realised that the crowd outside her own shop had now drifted inside and were standing impatiently by the high wooden counter.

'Yes, Mrs Parmentier, what can I get for you?' she said, quickly lifting up the flap and slipping into the serving area.

'Quarter of boiled ham please, love.'

Rose looked at the blandly smiling face framed by a crisp halo of curls coaxed into troughs and waves by the heavy application of marcel wave lotion and kirby grips.

'You're not registered with us, are you, Mrs Parmentier?'

'Not presently, love, but I want to change. See I've brought me ration books.'

Rose's heart sank. A change of grocer usually meant one thing; a row over the allocation of rationed goods with the previous one. Flicking through the proffered books she saw her instincts were right.

'I'm afraid you've no coupons for ham left for this week, Mrs Parmentier,' she said, extending the open books so that they could be clearly seen by the rest of the customers. 'Could I get you something else instead?'

'I don't want nothing else, thank you.' Mrs Parmentier drew herself up, looking Rose straight in the eye. 'I didn't get my full share from that crook up the market. Keeps his thumb on the scales,' she said to the growing queue behind her.

There was murmur amongst the shoppers, part agreement, part impatience.

'I'm afraid you'll have to take that up with the local Food Office. I can't sell you any ham unless you've got the coupons. What about a tin of salmon? We've had a delivery of that.'

'I'll have one of those,' called a voice from the door.

'Me too,' agreed the woman behind Mrs Parmentier.

The whole shop laid claim to a tin. Including Mrs Parmentier. Rose breathed a sigh of relief.

'And,' Mrs Parmentier added. 'I'll take me ham too. You can give me a bit of me next week's ration. No need for anyone to know and no harm done.'

'No I can't do that.' Seeing the stubborn set of Mrs Parmentier's thick lips, Rose braced herself for an argument. She was saved by Albert suddenly surging through from the back with half a dozen tins clutched in his massive hands.

'It's all right, Rose, I'll carry on here. You get on with filling out those counterfoils out the back.'

With his back to the shop, Albert accompanied this instruction with a broad wink. Rose understood.

They'd had a delivery and he wanted her to check it.

'Certainly, Mr White.' She passed over the disputed ration books. 'Mrs Parmentier wants to register with us. And all these ladies want a tin of the salmon.'

'Only six left, ladies,' Albert boomed, laying the evidence out along the counter. 'First come, first served.'

Rose found the remaining tins concealed under the tea-towel by the scullery sink at the back of the shop. Stacked beside it were a pile of biscuit tins. Removing an order sheet from the clip-board by the door she started counting, comparing it with the delivery manifest the driver had left and her own order form. She'd just finished when Albert returned.

'All hunky-dory, love?'

'They've only sent half of what we asked for.'

Albert tutted and shook his head. 'I don't know. Where's all the food gone, eh? There was plenty a few months ago. Hardly any shortages at all. We can't have eaten it all in that time, can we?'

Rose sat back on her heels. 'I don't think it's shortages exactly with a lot of things. It's the distribution. You know what it's like in here. Soon as we get something in, everyone buys one, and then we're out of stock again. It would be easier if everything was on ration.'

Taking a key from his pocket, Albert unlocked an enormous cupboard that stood against one wall and added the salmon tins to the considerable stock of tinned goods, sugar, tea and dried fruits that were already piled inside. This was his special store. It was opened for privileged customers: friends, family and those who couldn't walk far such as the elderly and mums with small children. 'Won't do the others no harm to use up a bit of shoe leather,' he'd explained when Rose had remarked she didn't know if that was quite legal.

'I wish that cellar weren't so damp,' he grumbled now. 'Be much easier to keep this lot down there. Pass a tin of them biscuits, love. And take some for yourself.'

'I don't need any, thank you. I haven't finished the last lot yet.'

Albert paused in his packing. 'Take some salmon then. You got to eat something. Keep your strength up. You're looking peakier than Elsie.'

'How is Mrs Finch?' Rose said, glad of the chance to change the subject.

'Same as ever, love. That bomb that hit Camden Road tube night before last blew in Elsie's windows; she's still picking glass out of everything.'

'Oh, Albert, I'm sorry. She must be in a terrible state.'

Prior to the war, Elsie Finch had served in her brother's shop. But the previous September she'd taken off her white apron, announced she was going home, and hadn't been seen outside her house since. Not even the peaceful lull of the 'Phoney War' prior to Dunkirk could tempt her out. For the past thirteen months, Elsie had been living in terror of being caught up in an air raid, and now it seemed her worse fears had been realised.

'You should have said something,' Rose said. 'I can manage here if you want to go home and stay with her.'

'No need,' Albert assured her. 'Now it's happened, she's found out it ain't half as bad as she thought it would be.'

'That must be a relief.' An unwelcome thought occurred to Rose. 'Does that mean she'll be coming back to the shop?'

'Lord no, love. You don't want to worry about that. Our Elsie has nerves the way other people have mice. Soon as you get rid of 'em in one place, they break out somewhere else.' He shook his head sadly. 'It's the planes now. Convinced that one's going to get shot down and fall on her head she is.'

The ring of the shop bell summoned him and he went back to the front leaving Rose to finish her stocktaking. The clang and jangle of the brass bell announced the coming and going of several more customers. Rose finished writing, put several empty biscuit tins carefully to one side for return to the manufacturers, and knew she ought to go back in and help serve. But the familiar lassitude was stealing over her again. Folding her hands in her lap she stared blankly at the calendar on the opposite wall. It was dated 1938 but no one had bothered to take it down. The picture was of rolling hills clad in purple heather.

Peter's voice whispered in the still storeroom. 'One of the chaps at work knows someone with a cottage up near Fort William. We could go up there this summer if I can get leave. We'd have time on our own, just you and me. That's what we need, isn't it, Rose?'

He'd touched the back of her neck, disturbing the wisps of fair hair that curled into the nape. She felt them stir now but it was only Albert returning.

'Someone to see you, Rose.'

'Who is it?'

'Your mum.'

Reluctantly Rose ducked through the dividing

curtain. 'Hello, Mum. How are you?'

'Well enough.'

'And Dad?'

'He's well too, as you'd know if you came round to see us.'

'Sorry, Mum. I've been busy.'

'Doing what? Counting tins of peas? It's not as if you've got homework to mark or anything.'

Marge Tammie was a faded and coarser version of her daughter. But Marge still believed in 'making an effort', and as long as her supplies of lipstick and powder held out she wouldn't be seen dead outside without a lick of both.

'Don't start again, Mum,' Rose pleaded.

'I'm not starting anything. I'm entitled to have my say. It cost us a lot, me and your dad, keeping you on at the Central. And then sending you to the teacher training college. We made sacrifices for you. And for what? So you could be a grocer's assistant? There's girls left school at fourteen doing better than that.' Marge warmed to her theme. 'I suppose while you had a man to look after there was some excuse. But Peter's gone. There's plenty of women in your position, my girl, and making a better job of it. It's time you pulled yourself together.'

'Yes, Mum. Can I get you anything?'

'Have you got any salmon?'

'Only paste.'

Marge sniffed. 'Well I suppose that will have to do then. Give me two jars. What about a bit of butter?'

Rose sighed with exasperation. 'Mum, you know you're not registered here.'

'What's that got to do with it? It's a fine thing when

49

you can't oblige your own mother. We may as well get something out of you wasting all that education behind a grocer's counter.'

'Mum! I can't . . .'

A hiss from the curtain attracted her attention. A large hand was extended clutching a half pound of butter. 'Here, love, give this to your mum.'

'You're a gentleman, Albert,' Marge said, tucking the package quickly into her wicker basket. 'Me Victoria sponge just don't taste right made with that vitaminised margarine. What about some tinned pineapple?'

An upraised thumb appeared, followed a moment later by two tins of pineapple chunks.

'Aren't you going to ask me what I want this lot for?' Marge demanded.

'No.'

Marge refused to take the hint. 'I've invited Mr and Mrs Goodwin round for their teas on Sunday. You come too and we'll have a good old family natter.'

'I'll see. I may be busy.'

'Don't you give me no more of that "busy" nonsense, madam. If we'd have known you was going to go all hoity-toity on us, we'd have sent you to Haverstock Hill.'

'Mum, I'm not . . .' Rose's voice failed. She cast a desperate glance at the back curtain, hoping Albert would come to the rescue again. But this time relief arrived from another direction. The bell rang sharply and a morose-looking man whom she recognised as one of the policemen who'd been called to Donald's shop came in.

Marge departed hastily, pushing the butter and

pineapple to the bottom of her basket as Ding Dong politely held the door for her.

He'd come to take their statements regarding their movements on the night before last. Neither had anything of interest to tell him. Albert had gone straight home to his sister's house as soon as he'd locked up the shop and Rose had spent the night in the flat, scorning the public shelters as usual, despite the air raid. They'd neither heard nor seen anything out of the ordinary.

'What's happened to James, then?' Albert demanded. 'Robbery was it? They're saying he disturbed a burglar. 'Ad a heart attack?'

'Is that what they're saying,' Ding Dong remarked, closing his book. 'Well people will say all sorts, won't they? Thanks for your help, the chief inspector will be in touch if he wants to ask anything else.' Raising his hat to Rose, he moved away, opened the door and then paused. 'By the way, you ain't got any more of them tins of pineapple have you? The lady wife is very partial to chunks with a drop of condensed milk.'

Once the constable had departed, the inside pockets of his raincoat bulging with booty, Rose apologised to Albert for her mother. 'You shouldn't have given her the butter. It's not fair. I won't draw my ration next month.'

'Rubbish, love. I told you, you got to eat. You don't eat enough to keep a sparrow alive now. And you don't want to fret about what your mum says. Parents don't know the rights and wrongs of everything, do they?'

'Thanks, Albert.' Rose's lips briefly brushed the old man's cheek. She wondered how much of the truth Albert knew.

'Go make us a cup of tea whilst we're quiet, eh?' Albert suggested.

Rose did so, pouring Albert's into a huge chipped white mug and her own into a willow-pattern tea cup which she carried into the backyard. From here she could hear the rustle and subdued mutter of the police officers in Donald's backyard. If she had stood on a crate she could have seen what was going on, but she was too embarrassed to try. Lexie had no such scruples. Her red curls suddenly popped up over the grocer's back wall.

'They think it could be murder,' she hissed at Rose. 'That copper, the one who looks like a moth-eaten sea-lion, just come to take our statements.'

'Ours too. We couldn't tell him anything though.'

'Me neither. I wouldn't know if the invasion was on, stuck down in that flaming cellar night after night. Honestly, Rose, I'm beginning to feel like a bat. One of these days I'll just hang upside down from the water pipe and save meself the bother of making up the beds.'

Rose smiled weakly. 'Can't you just stay up in the flat?'

'Tried that. But 'e ain't been down there five minutes before 'e starts.' Imitating her father's peevish voice she whined, 'Lexie, Lexie, I got this terrible pain in me chest. It's all the worry of you being up there I reckon. Best come down an' keep yer old dad company.' She sighed heavily and laid her arms along the top of the wall. 'God, I'd give anyfing for a bit of excitement in me life. I wish they still 'ad them gas mask drills and first aid classes.'

Startled, despite her own problems, Rose said,

'Why? I didn't think they were particularly exciting.'

With a mischievous wink, Lexie admitted she'd never gone to them. 'A couple of hours an evening away from 'im and no questions asked. It was too good to waste on learning 'ow to stick bandages on.'

'Didn't he go to the classes?'

'Nah. You know Dad. Reckons it's the hospitals' business to look after casualties, not 'is. Same with the fighting, unfortunately. I thought I might get rid of 'im on this Home Guard thing, but he won't 'ear of it.' Mimicking her father's voice again, she chanted, 'Fighting's the Government's business. That's what I pay me taxes for. I ain't paying the shoeshiner then using the polishing rag meself.' Blowing out a heavy sigh of desperation, Lexie wailed, 'I could really fancy a night out at the pictures and a fish and chip supper after.'

'Good idea,' Rose said abstractedly, her mind drifting once more around the mess of her own life.

'Honest? Great! How about tonight?'

Startled that her casual remark had been interpreted as an acceptance, Rose raised her blue eyes to the other woman's sparkling grey ones. 'We can't. What if there's a raid?'

'If we went to the Gaisford or the Palace we could always nip down the tube if it got bad.'

'I thought you weren't supposed to use the underground for sheltering.'

'Can't stop yer, can they? If yer've bought a penny ha'penny ticket they got to let you in. Or we could stay in the cinema if you like. One of the customers was telling me they ran the programme all over again last week 'cos the raid was still going on after they'd played "God Save the King". Go on, Rose, say you'll come,' she urged, the idea of escaping the cellar bringing a flush of colour to her pale cheeks. 'Just for a couple of hours. We could see the big picture and the news.'

'What's showing?'

'Who knows? Who cares?' Lexie said, sensing Rose was weakening.

'All right. Knock for me when you're ready to go.'

'Soon as I've washed the tea things,' Lexie promised, leaping down from the crate and hurrying back inside.

'Where you been?' Frank Emmett said sharply, his eyes examining his daughter suspiciously whilst his hands moved automatically over the upturned shoe on his last.

'Just talking to Rose in the backyard.'

'You haven't got time to chatter, there's work to be done in here. Those black boots are finished, put a coat of polish on them.'

Obediently, Lexie picked up a rag and smeared a thin coat of blacking over the worn boots. Whilst she worked, she cast considering looks in her father's direction, wondering whether it would be best to tell him now or leave it until later. He wasn't in a good mood; he'd already ruined several pieces of leather attempting to cut out a sole. His blade slipped again and he bit back a curse as it clattered to the floor.

'I'll get it.' She passed it across. His fingers fumbled and the knife fell again.

'That was your fault, I didn't have a proper grip,' Frank snapped.

'Sorry.' Obviously now was not a good time to break

the news. She'd wait until he sweetened up.

She should have known better. An hour later, he'd used up a good portion of their month's leather allocation and was moaning that the grinder was a bloody fraud who'd taken his money and not bothered to do more than show the blade to the whetstone.

Realising that things weren't going to improve, Lexie decided she might as well get the moment over. 'Dad.'

'Hmmm,' Frank mumbled through a mouthful of nails.

'Rose and me . . .' The tinkle of the counter bell interrupted.

Muttering under her breath, Lexie went out into the main shop.

The postman thrust the afternoon post into her hands.

'What's that?' Frank demanded as she returned to the back.

'A crate of kippers,' Lexie murmured with irritation.

'What?'

'Nothing. It's the post.'

Frank removed it from her hands and peered closely at it. 'Copy of the *Fish Fryers Review* for Fred Weller,' he announced. 'And a letter for you.'

The postmark and handwriting were scrutinised thoroughly before he passed it back to her and informed her it was from Alice Weller. 'Well, what does she say?' he said a few moments later.

Swallowing to release the constriction that had gripped her throat as she scanned the single sheet of paper, Lexie said baldly, 'They're not coming back. Alice's mum can't manage on her own no more and

the rest of the family can't take her. Fred's found a
bloke in Penzance with a fish round that wants to go
halves. They want me to keep an eye on the shop until
they can come up and sort it out.'

Alice had added two postscripts:

P.S. You know there will always be a bed down
here for you, don't you, love?

P.P.S. Can you send me tweed coat please. Take
the postage from the cash in me sewing box.

'Daft if you ask me,' Frank grumbled, spitting out
nails and hammering them into the upturned
leather sole with precision. 'They'll soon be sorry
they've given up a good little fish and chip business
like that.'

Lexie blinked away tears and folded the letter into
her pocket. Since her own mother had died in the
1919 influenza epidemic she'd regarded Alice Weller
as a kind of favoured aunt. She had a sudden
miserable sense of being completely alone.

'Rose and me are going to the pictures tonight,' she
announced to the back of her father's head.

'Oh yes. That will be nice for you,' Frank responded.

Lexie wasn't fooled by this mild response. She knew
what was coming. And it did.

By closing time she'd been called into the shop four
times by her father so some customer could relate in
detail their relatives' experiences in bombed-out
buildings.

'Comes of not taking shelter properly, that does,'
her father would say, shaking his head sadly at the

end of these sagas. 'Be right as rain they would if only they'd stopped inside.'

'I'm going,' she said, shuffling shoes into pairs along the shelves. 'To the pictures. With Rose. Soon as I've fixed your tea.'

'Please yourself.'

Frank stomped upstairs and buried himself behind the paper whilst she cooked sausages and mashed potatoes.

When it was served he took a couple of mouthfuls, dropped his cutlery with a clatter and pushed the plate noisily away. 'I don't feel hungry.'

Despite her determination not to look, Lexie couldn't miss the fist massaging the centre of his chest and the grimace of pain. 'What's the matter?'

'Nothing. Don't worry about it. Go out and enjoy yourself.' Levering his chair back noisily, Frank sat watching her eat. The silence was punctuated by small groans and deep sighs.

Lexie munched grimly on throughout the rest of the 'I'm-about-to-expire-any-second' performance. By the end of the meal, the familiar sensation of bile had risen in her stomach and she knew she couldn't go through with it.

'I'm sorry,' she apologised to Rose. 'I *know* he ain't really ill. But then I keep thinking, what if he really is this time?'

'Don't worry. I was only going because you wanted to,' Rose said. 'We'll go another day.'

'Some hopes,' Lexie thought, hurrying back through the darkened yard to her own shop.

'I've made the cocoa,' Frank greeted her, waving the thermos. 'And I put them sausages back in the larder. You can heat 'em up again tomorrow. I may feel more like them then.'

Lexie nodded, up-ending a meat cover over the plate of sausages that were now cooling in a pool of congealing grease. She noticed, but didn't comment on, the empty plate that had contained a quarter of cheddar before she left for Rose's flat.

'Come on quick,' Frank urged. 'Let's go down to the cellar before the sirens sound. Better safe than sorry, eh?'

'You go down. I think I'll just pop round to Alice's and get that coat she wants.'

'Hurry up then. You don't want to be up here when the bombs start.'

'Five minutes,' Lexie promised, taking a bunch of keys and a torch from the kitchen drawer.

She didn't need the light to find her way out of her own yard and into the Wellers'. It was a route she'd trodden at least once a day since she was sixteen. Inside the back room that still stank of fish, although it hadn't seen a fin or fillet for over three months, she switched the torch on and made her way upstairs by the shaded light.

The Wellers had departed leaving their curtains open and the blackout down and it hardly seemed worth putting it up in order to rummage in the wardrobe. Balancing the torch on their chest of drawers, so that the thin beam gave her a little light, Lexie burrowed into the clothes that smelt so strongly of Alice, a potent mixture of cod and lavender water, and found the thick, serviceable coat that Alice wore every winter.

Holding it folded over both arms, she made her way

back downstairs. Halfway down she remembered the postage money.

It was scarcely worth going back. She could always use her own money and pay herself back later. On the other hand, it was an excuse to stay out of that damp prison of a cellar for a moment longer.

The sewing box was in the second bedroom. Not having any family the Wellers had always used the room as a cross between a lumber store and a sewing room. Entering quietly, on soft shoes, Lexie stifled a scream of fright as a dark figure loomed out of the empty room towards her.

A second later she giggled in relief as she realised it was just the tailor's dummy with a half-finished dress pinned in place.

'You're getting as big a bag of nerves as Dad,' she scolded herself, taking the top tray out of the sewing box and scrabbling up a handful of loose change from the bottom compartment. A coin dropped from her fingers and rolled away across the uncarpeted boards.

'Damn.' Crouching so that the torch beam wouldn't be seen from the window she played the feeble circle of light over the sewing table, assorted stacks of magazines and books, a couple of dilapidated deck-chairs, broken seed boxes, several pairs of shoes and a pair of boots.

A glitter of light between the boots betrayed the errant shilling's location. As she watched, it tilted slowly and fell flat to the floor.

Paralysed, and with a scream frozen halfway up her throat, Lexie crouched behind the torch beam and stared in horror as the boots moved and started to walk towards her.

Chapter 4

Jack had spent a frustrating Friday trying to resolve his worst difficulty on the Donald case.

He'd already spoken to their irascible pathologist who had agreed that, to save time, the post mortem could be done on Sunday to confirm that they were dealing with an unnatural death. In the meantime (and on the assumption that they were involved in a murder investigation) the two detective constables had been set to take statements from the neighbours, although Stamford didn't hold out much hope that they'd get a great deal of help from that source. The combination of the blackout and bombing raids had all but eliminated the detective's best friend: the incurably nosy neighbour.

The favoured theory seemed to be that Donald had been surprised by a burglar. Which was very neat and convenient, but seemed to overlook the fact that nothing appeared to be missing.

'Maybe whoever done it, shut the safe up again,' Ding Dong had suggested. 'Could be empty as a greengrocer's onion box in there for all we know.'

It was a valid point. There was also the possibility that some of the stock *was* missing. They needed a complete cross-check between the invoices and stocklists. And they needed the combination to that safe.

'We need to get in touch with Mrs Donald,' he'd

said to Sarah as they made their way back to Agar Street Station. 'If she's up to it, she's probably the best person to do the stock-check.'

'Will you go down there, to this Aldbury place?' Sarah had asked.

'Hmm, I think so. We can bring her back with us.'

'*We?*'

They'd reached Kentish Town Road. Glancing right and left before crossing they were aware of the differences that a few months had brought to the area. Last time they'd both been involved in a murder case, this street had had an air of normality that was scarcely disturbed by the sandbagged station entrances and posters urging enrolment in Civil Defence. Now, despite the cheery 'good days' from the passing shoppers, the atmosphere had subtly changed. Partly it was due to the boarded-up shopfronts with their handwritten posters defiantly declaring them 'Open for Business as Usual'. The street had received a direct hit three weeks previously and whilst the council's repair parties had relaid the road and pavement surfaces in record time, the glaziers were fighting a losing battle to keep up with the constant demands for their services.

'People look tired, don't they?' Sarah had remarked, putting her finger on the other marked difference between the months before Dunkirk and the months after.

'I don't suppose anyone's been getting much sleep,' Stamford had agreed as they'd hurried across the road and up into the station entrance.

'No, sir.' Perhaps it was an association of ideas, but she'd found herself unable to stifle an enormous yawn.

'What time are you due to go off duty?' Jack had asked.

'I should have gone off at six o'clock this morning. I've been on night duty in the shelter all week. I'm due on again tonight.'

'Go off now then,' Jack had instructed. 'And, unless you hear to the contrary, assume you'll be skipping the shelter tonight and coming with me to Aldbury tomorrow. I'll fix it up while you're getting your head down.'

And that's where his problems had begun.

When he telephoned Chief Superintendent Roland Dunn to ask if he could arrange her temporary transfer to CID again, as he had done when they'd worked on the Yeovil case a few months previously, he met a blank refusal.

Apparently Dunn was being put under pressure by a female CID inspector at the Yard to appoint more women officers to CID and he didn't want to provide her with any ammunition for her case.

'Anyway,' he barked irritably. 'Four months ago the regular detective sergeant from Agar Street was on sick leave. I understand he is now back at his desk. Or have I been misinformed?'

'No. He's here.' Through the glass partition that separated his office from the general office, Stamford contemplated the subject of their conversation.

Detective Sergeant Alfred Agnew had arrived back from eleven months' sick leave in August. He'd brought with him a medical report that had made Jack's hair stand on end. Over the past twenty-five years DS Agnew had suffered from everything from dandruff to athlete's foot with all imaginable afflictions in between. At the bottom of the report the MO had added a pencil note: 'If this man was a horse – I'd shoot him.'

'I have a weakness in me blood,' Alfred had sadly informed Stamford. 'It seeps into me pores and causes me to be afflicted.'

It appeared to have seeped into his clothes as well, since the fibres on the tweed jacket and brown trousers that he always wore were rotting away in patches that suggested they'd caught one of Alfred's nastier skin diseases. To make matters worse, someone had once informed him that tobacco smoke was a barrier against germs. Looking through the glass square of his office, Jack found it difficult to locate the sergeant amongst a swirling smokescreen that would have brought a tug of envy to the heart of any destroyer captain on the Atlantic convoys.

'I can't work with him,' Jack said in despair. 'I'd spend most of my time trying to *find* him.'

'I beg your pardon?'

'Nothing, sir. What I mean is, the sergeant is plainly not a well man. He should be retired on medical grounds.'

'Yes, well, I believe there is a move afoot to do just that. But in the meantime, he is the official CID sergeant. You can't expect us to assign a woman when there's a man available to do the job.'

'You did say I could have a free hand when you asked me to get Agar Street CID sorted out,' Jack reminded him.

His original transfer had been on a purely temporary basis for one particular case, but Dunn had asked him to stay for a while and, in the older man's words, 'Lick some discipline into that office.'

It was a request that suited Jack very well since he lived a few streets from the station and had been spared the difficulties of travelling to Scotland Yard after the efforts of the Luftwaffe to disrupt the transport system.

Eventually, Dunn grudgingly agreed that if Sarah's inspector could spare her, he'd 'turn a blind eye for a few days. Shouldn't take you any longer than that to clear the matter up, should it?'

'No, sir. Thank you, sir. I'll just stick a poster up asking the murderer to give himself up,' Stamford added under his breath as he replaced the receiver.

Thankfully, the inspector of female police was quite amenable to his appropriation of Sergeant McNeill for a few days.

'No problem,' she said. 'The women constables can handle most situations and the WVS ladies are taking on a lot of the welfare work. I have first call on the sergeant though if anything out of the ordinary happens.'

By the end of the day the detective constables were able to give him verbal summaries of the neighbours' statements. As he'd suspected, nobody had seen anything, heard anything or knew anything.

'He was a steady sort of chap by all accounts,' Ding Dong said, flipping his notebook shut. 'Sort of bloke you'd never notice normally.'

'I bet he wishes he'd stayed that way,' Stamford remarked. 'You're on the rota for Saturday aren't you, so see if you can get those statements typed up, will you?' He checked his watch and found it was nearly six o'clock. 'You'd better get off home before the sirens sound.'

Before Jack himself left, he had a quick word with Detective Sergeant Agnew. He'd half expected the man to be offended at Sarah's involvement in the case but, to his relief, Alfred accepted the news with pleasure.

'I'm no good on the legwork any more, sir. It's me arches. They collapsed one morning 'bout six years ago. One minute I was walking along straight as any guardsman, next thing I'm shuffling like a blooming penguin. Much better to let the young lady do the legwork. You let me know if there's any deskwork you want done.' He stuffed a large portion of what appeared to be shredded sock into his pipe bowl and sucked vigorously. 'Providing it's not small print. Small print brings on me headaches.'

Escaping from Alfred's fumigation zone, Jack seized his hat and coat and made his way home. He reached the Square to find his neighbour, Eileen O'Day, standing at his front gate peering into the sky, her eyes screwed against the fading light.

Eileen was his closest friend in the Square. She'd taken a neighbourly interest when he first bought the house; befriended his Dutch wife, Neelie, when he'd brought her home to live in Kentish Town; appointed herself his cleaner and cook when Neelie had walked out; and firmly taken over the care of his daughter, Annaliese, when she'd been rescued from the path of the advancing German Army without her mother.

Now she said, 'Did you hear any sirens, Jack?'

'No.'

'Me neither. It's nearly half six. What's happened to them? I hate all this waiting. You don't know whether you're coming or going.' She brought her gaze back to earth. 'Sammy's slipped off somewhere, the little devil. I told him to stay in after his tea, but he got out when me back was turned. Just wait until I get my hands on him. I'll slipper his backside 'til he can't sit down for a week.'

Jack understood. It was the idea of her youngest being caught outside in the open when a raid started that was bothering her, rather than the punctuality of the Luftwaffe.

'Has he taken Annaliese with him?' he said sharply.

'No, love. She's in the kitchen. Maury's watching her. Do you want to come across? I put a plate of macaroni cheese on top of the saucepan in case you hadn't eaten.'

Jack clicked his tongue impatiently against the roof of his mouth.

'I know,' she said before he could speak. 'I shouldn't waste me rations on you. Only cheese and macaroni aren't on ration. And if you don't want it, it'll do for Pat. He's coming off duty at six tomorrow.' She'd been preceding him down the hall passage of her own house whilst she spoke, now she reached the kitchen and called cheerfully into the warm fug. 'Here's your dad home, Annie. Come and give him a kiss.'

Flicking a couple of barley-sugar twist plaits from her shoulders, the little girl climbed down from a wooden chair on which she'd been kneeling, came across the room, and lifted her face obediently. Jack scooped her up, planted a kiss on the tender skin and gave her a fierce hug.

'So what's this then?' Jack said carrying her across to the scrubbed kitchen table.

'We're doing a jig-saw, aren't we, Annie?' Eileen

said answering for her. 'And Annie's telling me the names of all the things in the picture. We're learning ever such a lot of new words, aren't we, lovie?'

Annaliese nodded. Twisting around in her father's arms, she wriggled to be set down. As soon as he put her back on her feet, she slid round the rim of the table and took Eileen's hand.

'Early days yet,' Eileen said quietly, seeing the expression on Jack's face.

He gave her a half-smile. But neither of them really believed that time had anything to do with it. It was four months since Annaliese had been scooped out of the path of the advancing German forces in Belgium and hustled on to a boat by a group of fleeing refugees. But instead of becoming closer to her father, she seemed to distance herself more and more from him, clinging instead to Eileen.

'She'll be missing her mum,' Eileen murmured under her breath. 'No news?'

'No,' Jack said in the same low tones. 'Nothing. The Red Cross are still dealing with military prisoners. They haven't the facilities available to trace missing civilians.' And still less, he thought to himself, to trace the grave of the nameless young woman to whom Annaliese had been found clinging after their refugee column had been strafed by the Luftwaffe.

'Do you want this macaroni cheese then?'

'No thanks.' He added quickly, 'I ate in the canteen.'

'I'll eat it,' Maury offered, suddenly emerging from behind the newspaper that he'd been scanning intently ever since Jack entered.

'No you won't,' his mother informed him. 'Pat can have it when he gets in.'

'For breakfast?'

'It's good food. No reason to waste it.' Using an old towel, Eileen rescued the covered plate from the top of the boiling saucepan, wiped off the drips and set it on the table. 'Take it across to your place will you, Jack? Pat said he'd drop in first for a bath. That's all right, isn't it?'

'Of course. I've told you. Any time.'

'Can I come over too, Mr Stamford?' Maury asked.

'No you can't,' Eileen snapped. 'You can get the tin bath in and heat up water on the stove, same as the rest of us. Or go down the public baths. Pat's got a dirty job. You haven't. In fact, I've been meaning to ask you what you *do* do now? I hear you ain't been on the linen stall up the market for three weeks. So what have you been doing with yourself?'

'Bit of buying, bit of selling, you know,' Maury said vaguely, waving the paper, open at the personal ads, at her. 'Fink I'll just go get yesterday's paper. I left it down the Anderson.'

He slid out of the kitchen. The wary look he cast in Stamford's direction before he went wasn't lost on his mother.

'He's turning into a spiv, Jack,' she said, shaking her head. 'I don't know what to do with him.'

'Don't worry. Once he's conscripted the Army will soon sort him out.'

'Be too late by then. Pat says he'll either be a millionaire or inside by the time the call-up catches up with him.'

Jack gave her shoulder a reassuring squeeze. 'Do you want me to go and see if I can find Sammy?'

'No, love, you sit down and play with Annie for a

bit. He'll be back when the sirens start.'

She was right. As Jack left at ten o'clock he encountered a nonchalant Sammy strolling up the front path to the accompaniment of the wailing air raid siren and the distant roar of guns somewhere to the south. It was so well timed, Jack suspected he'd been loitering outside waiting for the alert to distract his mother.

'It won't work,' he whispered to the boy. 'She's been waiting to deal with you for the past three hours.'

'I fort she would be,' Sammy hissed back. 'But she can't give me much of a whack in the Anderson. There ain't no room to get a decent swing.'

Jack couldn't argue with that: he'd never bothered to have one installed in his own garden, and one night of trying to squeeze his six foot frame into one of the homemade wooden bunks in the O'Days' shelter had left him vowing to risk the bombs rather than try that exercise again. Nowadays his own air raid precautions consisted of setting up his bed under the solid kitchen table and hoping for the best.

Tonight it worked well enough for him to sleep soundly until the sound of running water woke him at six-thirty. Rolling out of his blankets he made his way up to the first floor landing and found Pat O'Day stripping off his fireman's uniform in the bathroom.

'Sorry, Mr Stamford,' he apologised. 'Didn't mean to wake you. All right to use the bath, is it?'

'I've told you time and again. You're welcome to it any time. So's your mother, if only you could persuade her to use it.'

He'd had the bathroom, with its indoor lavatory and fitted bath, installed when he bought the house with a small legacy left him by a great-uncle.

'Mum don't like taking liberties. Nor baths in single gentlemen's houses. Got her reputation to think of after all.'

'That's ridiculous . . . No one could think . . .' Jack started to splutter, then realised Pat was pulling his leg. Slinging a towel at the young man's head, he went into his bedroom and started laying out the clothes he'd need for the trip to Aldbury.

'Busy night?' he shouted through to Pat.

'Not too bad,' Pat replied, shaking water from his face with noisy gurgling. 'We got called out to an incident down by the Veterinary College about eleven. Clump of incendiaries. Luckily they didn't get much of a hold. We managed to get the lot out by twelve. After that we was just on standby. How about you? What's going on down Balaclava Row?'

Jack told him. As he talked, he reflected that, even a few months ago, he'd have fobbed Pat off with a non-committal answer. Whenever he'd thought about Eileen's eldest, he'd still tended to see the gawky fifteen year old in a flat cap and too-long trousers draped over his boots, who'd stood in the Square watching him move his few possessions into the house eleven years ago. But Pat had grown up imperceptibly under his nose, without him really noticing until the Blitz had started.

'Finished,' Pat said emerging from the bathroom with one towel wrapped round his waist and the other rubbing at wet hair.

Jack jerked a thumb at his wardrobe. 'Help yourself to clean clothes if you want any. I'll grab a shave. By the way, there's a plate of macaroni cheese in the kitchen. You're supposed to have it for breakfast.'

Pat gave a despairing grimace but by the time Jack had shaved, dressed and come downstairs, he was stirring the mixture over a low gas. He'd also set out two plates. 'Wouldn't let me suffer alone, would you, Mr Stamford?'

'I would, if I didn't think you'd report me to your mother. And by the way, don't you think you're old enough to drop the "Mr Stamford" and call me "Jack".'

Pat continued to stir the bubbling mass, but the back of his neck flushed a pale pink. 'Righto, Mr Stam . . . er, Jack.'

He doled out two portions of the solidified mass on to the plates and they washed it down with mugs of tea.

'Don't the Goodwins live over one of the shops in Balaclava Row?' Pat asked as they disposed of the last forkful.

'A Mrs Goodwin lives there,' Jack agreed. 'She works in the grocer's shop. I gather she's a widow. Husband killed at Dunkirk. Why, do you know her?'

'I knew both of them. Rose and Peter. They were in my class at Riley Street.' Pat drained the last of his tea. 'They were the clever ones. Passed the exam for Haverstock Central. Brightest two in the class. Well,' he amended, 'second and third brightest anyhow. Girl called Molly Winslow was the cleverest. But her parents wouldn't let her go to the grammar. Reckoned it was a waste of time educating girls. She got a job in the wallpaper factory after she left school.'

'But Rose's parents wanted her to take her Higher Cert?'

'That's right. Dead proud of her they were. Sent her to teacher's training college as well.'

'So what's she doing behind a grocer's counter?'

Pat shrugged. 'Dunno. You could ask Mum. She knows Rose's mum. It's funny,' he said, collecting up the dirty dishes, 'she told Mum that Rose got real stuck up after she married Peter. Never used to come near them for weeks at a time. I don't see it meself. It don't sound like the old Rose. She seem standoffish to you?'

'I didn't speak to her.' Jack recalled to mind the pale-faced young woman he'd seen hovering outside the grocer's shop. 'She seemed . . .' He tried to find the right word. Not sad exactly, but distant from the life that was going on around her. 'Detached,' he finally said. He glanced at his watch. 'I've got to go. I have to pick up my car and my sergeant and head for Aldbury.'

'Is it the chain-smoking compost heap? Or the one Mum calls "that nice Miss McNeill".'

'It's *Sergeant* McNeill, yes. Tell your mother I don't know what time I'll be back. But I don't suppose she'll mind keeping Annaliese, will she? And Annaliese certainly won't mind.'

He knew from the expression on Pat's face that he'd sounded more bitter than he'd intended. He had a sudden impulse to confide the real source of his worries to Pat, but the young man turned away and the moment was gone.

Stepping out into the lightening autumn morning, he set out for Agar Street and once again pushed away the niggling persistent policeman's instinct that was increasingly whispering to him that this child who'd been found clutching Annaliese's passport was not, in fact, his daughter.

Chapter 5

Rose's Saturday started miserably and ended in blind terror.

She'd woken at six o'clock with a pounding head-ache which wasn't entirely due to the fact the sirens and guns had kept her awake until the early hours. Peter had been there, in the flat again, last night, walking through the dark bedroom and bending over her bed, only to disappear when she jerked out of her dream state and sat up with a dry mouth and pounding heart.

In her half waking, half sleeping state, she'd heard the all clear sound and half an hour later had crawled out of bed. Boiling the kettle, she used half for washing and made herself a cup of tea with the rest. Dressing and flicking a comb through her simple hairstyle only occupied a further fifteen minutes. By the time she was ready to face the world, it was six forty-five and the shop didn't open until nine.

Taking the shop account book from her kitchen drawer, she sat down and started checking and totalling the columns of figures under each customer. By eight o'clock she'd finished and busied herself tidying the stockroom until eight-thirty when Albert arrived.

'You look proper peaky again,' he greeted her. 'What have you been doing with yourself. Did you eat a proper breakfast? I told you to cut yourself a rasher of that bacon, didn't I?'

Rose ignored the second question and answered the first. 'I've been checking the books. Have you any idea how much money people owe us on account?'

It was Albert's turn to wriggle out of answering an uncomfortable question. 'They've already started queuing out there. Wonder what's making us so popular this morning?'

He found out when he turned the sign to 'Open' as the clock was striking nine, and was immediately besieged with requests for tinned salmon and pineapple.

'Comes of doing a good turn,' he muttered to Rose when the last of the stock of these items hoarded in the back room had disappeared into eager shopping bags and the shop was empty again. 'How was I to know none of the other grocers had had a delivery this week?'

'Never mind, Albert,' Rose laughed, standing on tiptoe to kiss his cheek. 'You'll get your reward in heaven.'

'I'm going to have mine now. Big mug of cocoa and a slice of our Elsie's Tottenham cake. Call me if you get busy.'

He'd barely let the curtain fall, when the brass bell announced the arrival of another customer. Rose looked up and smiled at the tall young man who'd come in. 'Yes, sir. What can I get you?'

'Hello, Rose. Don't suppose you remember me?'

Rose stared. There was something vaguely familiar about the open face with its thatch of light brown hair and merry brown eyes. A recollection clicked at the back of her mind. A memory involving ink wells and her own long fair plaits.

'It's Pat, isn't it? Patrick O'Day. Well fancy that, I haven't seen you for years. Silly, isn't it, when we only live a few streets away from each other. You're still living in the Square, aren't you?'

'That's right.'

She waited for Pat to buy something but instead he continued to stare at her. Eventually Rose said, 'You're not on duty then?' Which, she realised instantly, was a pretty inane question since she'd surely have noticed if he'd parked a London fire brigade engine outside the shop.

'No,' he agreed. 'It's me twenty-four off.'

'I'm sorry?'

'We work forty-eight hours on, twenty-four off,' he explained. 'I'm off until six tomorrow morning.'

'Oh yes. I see.' Another silence stretched between them. 'Can I get you something?' Rose asked, indicating the shelves of goods behind her.

'What? Er, no. That is, I mean.' Pat took a deep and audible breath and said quickly. 'Look, I came to say I was really sorry to hear about Peter. I've been wanting to say it, only not having talked to yer for so long, I thought it would look a bit funny just walkin' round and coming straight out with it like.' His voice trailed off uncertainly as he watched the emotions flitting across her face. One of them looked suspiciously like the beginning of tears. 'I haven't upset you, have I? I didn't mean to, honest.'

Rose swallowed the lump gathering in her throat. 'No,' she said. 'Of course you haven't. It was kind of you to come.'

'Oh, good.' Pat exhaled, visibly relieved. 'Tell you the truth I was wondering all along Leighton if this

77

was a good idea, or if I was just gonna stick me foot in it and upset you.'

'I'm not upset.' She smiled brightly to prove the point. 'After all it was four months ago.'

'Dunkirk, wasn't it?'

'Yes. No.' Rose bit her lip. 'I mean he was wounded at Dunkirk, but he died a couple of weeks later, in hospital here. They'd had to amputate his leg.'

'That must have been rough.'

Rougher than you'll ever know, Rose thought bitterly. 'You must be getting it pretty rough yourself,' she said. 'I've seen some of the engines going back to the fire station.'

'Yer, well, you know.' Pat shrugged, embarrassed. 'It's not all work, we have a laugh sometimes too.' He took another breath, his voice becoming firmer. 'As a matter of fact we're fixing up a dance. Some of the auxiliaries have got up a band and we're going to have a bucket for contributions to buy a Spitfire. It won't go on late. I mean not after eleven o'clock. I was wondering whether maybe, you'd . . .'

What he was wondering was interrupted by the tinkle of the bell.

'Why didn't you wait for me?' Sammy demanded. 'Didn't Mum tell you I had something really good to tell you?'

'You were out. How'd you know where to find me?' Pat gave his youngest brother a look that would have shrivelled a sensitive soul.

Since Sammy had a blithe conviction that his company was welcome everywhere, he remained noticeably unshrivelled. 'Me and Piggy followed you, didn't we, Piggy?' he demanded of the boy who'd slid in after him.

Piggy nodded behind his owl-like glasses.

'We was pretending you was a German spy and we was tracking you down. Good, weren't we? Bet you didn't see us at all, did you?'

'No. Now go follow someone else.' Pat tried to push him out of the door, but Sammy wriggled free.

'But I got somefing to tell yer. It's good. About school.'

'Go on then, tell me. But make it quick.'

Sammy drew himself up and puffed up his chest to make his announcement. 'Posh Perkins has left. He's been called up. *And.*' He took an even deeper breath to get the full effect from his next statement.

'And Miss Gilbert's dead,' Piggy said.

'*I* was gonna say that. He's my brother. I should have told,' Sammy shouted indignantly.

Before Pat could tell him off, Rose said, 'Miss Gilbert dead? I can't believe it! She's been at Riley Street for ever. She taught my mum.'

Elbowing Piggy out of the way, Sammy grabbed the centre of attention again. 'Yesterday morning it was, miss. One minute she was teaching the first years and next fing she just gives this terrible scream, clutches her throat, and drops down dead.' Just in case his audience should be unable to picture this scene, Sammy flung his arms out, spun round like a top, clutched his throat with a strangled gasp and dropped to the tiled floor.

'Get up out of the way,' Pat ordered, dragging him to his feet, as the next customers tried to open the door and found it blocked by Sammy's prone figure.

'Is he all right?' one of the women asked.

Rose explained.

'Miss Gilbert dead. Well I'll be blowed. She can't be. She's been at Riley Street since Adam was a lad. D'you hear that, Ada? Miss Gilbert died.'

It was all the encouragement Sammy needed to repeat his performance. This time, however, it ended with Pat catching him as he fell and lifting him bodily out of the shop with a hissed instruction to push off.

He turned back to find the customers and Rose looking at him expectantly. 'Serve the ladies first,' he said quickly.

The ladies wanted bacon, butter and lard. With the slicer set to its thinnest gauge to make the ration go further, Rose drove it across the home-cured joint. She was uncomfortably aware of Pat hovering in the background.

After the correct money and coupons had been exchanged, the two women departed, still chattering over Miss Gilbert's sudden demise.

Pat cleared his throat.

'Now, what did you want to buy?' Rose said hastily.

'I er . . .'

The blessed bell rang out again. Four small boys poured into the shop followed by a plump, dark-haired young woman issuing instructions. 'Don't touch. Put that down, Danny. Joe, get your hand out of that biscuit box.'

'Well blimey. It's Molly, ain't it? Molly Winslow? Ain't that funny, I was just talking to someone about you this morning. Ain't it amazing? I don't see neither of you for years then we all end up in the same shop together.'

It was perfectly obvious that the dark young woman had no idea what he was talking about. Rose prompted her.

'You remember Pat O'Day, don't you, Molly?'

Her face cleared. 'Pat! Course I do. My, ain't you grown since Riley Street.'

'So have you, Molly.'

'Outwards maybe. But that's what comes of having four kids. I'm Molly Barlow now. I married Cyril. Used to sit at the back of the class.'

Somewhat smugly she went on to inform them that Cyril was too valuable to be conscripted into the forces. As a fully trained fitter he was doing 'war work' somewhere 'up north'. 'We'll be joining him soon. He's renting a place for us. We can afford it easy now. Guess how much he earned last week?'

Pat shook his head wordlessly.

'Twenty quid.'

A low whistle escaped Pat's lips.

Molly looked pleased. 'Yes,' she said, addressing Pat but flicking a sly sideways look at Rose. 'I reckon my dad did me a favour not letting me go to the Central.'

'Did you want to buy something, Molly?' Rose said deliberately keeping her voice non-committal.

'I really come down here to pick up the kids' shoes from the mender's, only he ain't done them yet. They were saying in there that you 'ad some pineapple.'

'We're sold out.'

'All of it?'

'Yes.'

'Been a real wasted journey then, ain't it? Come on, kids, let's get up the market.'

She led her brood out and Pat drew a deep breath. 'Look, Rose, I was just wondering, Oh . . . bug—' He bit back the rest of the sentence and moved to let the next customer take his place.

'Hello, Lexie. What can I get you?'

Lexie dumped a brown paper parcel, secured with string on the counter. 'It's all right, serve the gentleman first. Albert not around?'

'He is now, me dear.' Albert pushed his way through the back curtain, stretching his arms above his head and yawning vigorously. 'I nodded off. You should have called me, Rose love.' He blinked and registered Pat's presence. 'Yes, sir? What can I serve you with?'

Pat pointed at the shelf behind the grocer. 'Box of that, please.'

The item was pushed across the counter. 'Anything else, sir?'

'Er, no. No thanks.'

'That's just fourpence then.'

Defeated, Pat retreated.

'Now, Lexie, what can we do for you, love?'

'I come to settle what we owe.' Lexie took a large purse from the depths of her capacious inner pockets.

Rose ran a finger down the relevant page and announced the total came to eleven shillings eleven halfpence.

'For a bloke that goes off his food at the drop of a hat, Dad don't 'alf pack it away,' Lexie grumbled, handing over a ten shilling note and a handful of change.

'Our Elsie gets like that. A good fright puts a real edge on her appetite.'

'Oh me dad ain't frightened. Only lives down in

that cellar every night for my sake according to him. How is Mrs Finch? Still not going out?'

"Fraid not. Doctor's given her some new nerve tonic along with 'er sleeping drops, but it don't seem to make no difference.'

'I was thinking I'd go see her.'

Albert beamed. 'That would be kind. She'd enjoy that. You going down there now?'

'No, I can't leave Dad on his own for long on Saturday. It's one of our busiest times. I'm just going along to the post office to send Alice her winter coat. It looks like her and Fred are stopping in Cornwall.'

Rose called her back as she opened the door. 'Lexie, I was thinking, about the pictures. Would you like to go tonight?'

'The pictures?' For a moment Lexie looked flummoxed. 'Er, no I'm a bit busy. That is . . .' A frown creased into a V between her eyebrows and then her face cleared. She smiled broadly. 'Yer, good idea. The pictures would be just the ticket. I'll come round for you after tea.'

'I could come for you if you like? Your father might make less of a fuss if I'm there.'

'No. Don't do that,' Lexie said firmly. 'Best to let me handle him. Wait for me to come to you, all right?'

'If you think that's best,' Rose said equably. 'See you after tea, then.'

'Yeah. See ya.' Lexie departed with a broad grin on her face that was nearly equalled by that on Albert's.

'That's right, love,' he said, patting Rose jovially on the shoulder. 'Get out and enjoy yerself. Finish up early if you like. Give you time to titivate yourself up a bit. And don't worry about cleaning up. I'll do the slicer, and the floor don't matter for once.'

'No thanks, Albert. There's plenty of time.' She turned away to clean the meat slicer. He was so pleased for her, she hadn't the heart to tell him the real reason she was going out. If Pat came back she wanted to be able to say truthfully that she was busy tonight.

'Bit of a surprise about the Wellers, isn't it?' she remarked casually.

The silence that followed warned her something was wrong. Looking around she found Albert fussing with the shelves, moving tins this way and that, then putting them back where they'd been in the first place. She knew him so well now that she hardly needed him to mutter that Fred Weller was the same age as him and that he expected it was all getting a bit much for him, what with all these new forms and things they made you fill in these days. Rose understood. Albert was in his mid-sixties; over the past few months she'd watched life become more tiring and confusing for him as rationing, food regulations and air raids all took their toll.

'You're giving up the shop!' She hadn't meant it to sound like an accusation, but when Albert turned back to face her, he hung his head like a kid that had been caught out scrumping.

'Our Elsie's taken it into her head that she wants to move to the country. Derbyshire. Finch took her up Derbyshire for their 'oneymoon. No raids up there, see?' He eased a finger round his clean collar. 'There's only 'er and me left,' he pleaded. 'Her and Finch not 'aving been blessed and me never 'aving taken the long march to the altar.'

Rose laid a hand on his arm. 'You don't have to make excuses to me, Albert. Of course you must go if you think that's best for Elsie.'

Relief flooded over Albert's face, flowing into the worried creases and restoring his normal good-natured smooth complexion. 'It won't be yet,' he assured her. 'And I expect whoever takes over will want to keep you on. They'd be daft not to. I'll tell 'em so.'

'Ta, Albert,' Rose said, reverting to her childhood language briefly.

For the rest of the day she kept up a deliberately cheerful pose, determined that Albert shouldn't feel guilty about his decision to move. By the time she'd returned to the flat, cooked her tea, washed up and changed into a plain black skirt and mauve blouse, she was surprised to find that she'd succeeded in deceiving herself as well and she was almost looking forward to her evening out.

Switching off the lights, she swished back the heavy blanket that served as blackout, and peered up at the sky. In the distance the underbelly of a barrage balloon, like a great silver fish bloated by disease, danced and dipped as its cable tightened. A movement below caught her eye. Lexie scurried down to her own back gate, tying a scarf round her hair and pulling her coat closer.

Rose readjusted the curtain, twitching it to cover any potential chinks. The balloon was continuing to jerk and dance in a very peculiar fashion beyond the opposite rooftops. She paused for a moment, trying to decide whether it was winched up or down. After a few feet of going down, it seemed to stop, spring upwards quickly, then be drawn back towards the winch again. She guessed the cable had jammed and the unseen crew were making an attempt to free it. A final vicious jerk seemed to do the trick. The balloon rose suddenly, soaring into the grey clouds. It wasn't until she saw the dangling severed end of the cable that Rose realised it had broken free. Instinctively, she ducked as the cable whipped and snapped like an enraged serpent. But the wind was blowing from the west and, with a final parting swipe that demolished a chimney stack, the balloon ascended into the clouds and disappeared eastwards to cause havoc over Hackney Marshes.

Tucking the curtain into place, Rose shrugged herself into her own coat and hurried downstairs to let Lexie in. But when she reached the yard there was no sign of the older woman.

'Lexie,' she called softly, stepping into the open, and pulling the door close. 'Lexie?' she said, raising her voice very slightly.

It was stupid, she realised, whispering. There was no reason to, but somehow the blackness seemed to have that effect on people. 'Keeping your voice down so's not to wake the ghosts up,' was how Peter had once described it. The thought of him conjured up the vision of him. A sudden, violent chill shot down her backbone. Whisking round, she rushed back inside, banged the door shut, and fled back upstairs to the dark flat.

It was half an hour before a soft rapping on the back door called her downstairs again.

'All ready?' Lexie asked.

Rose locked the back door. 'Did you forget something?'

'What?'

'I saw you a while ago, coming out of your yard. Did you go back for something?'

Lexie clicked her tongue in silent annoyance. It was obvious Rose hadn't seen her slipping into the Wellers', but she'd have to be far more careful about her visits in future. Since the heart-stopping fright she'd received on her visit to collect Alice's coat, she'd already been back several times, fetching supplies and information to the fugitive holed up there. The last thing he needed was her drawing attention to him.

Smiling brightly at Rose, she agreed: 'Yes. That's right. Forgot me torch. Which cinema d'you want to go to?'

'Whichever we can get in, I suppose. It is Saturday night. Do people still go as much now as they did before?'

'Dunno. I 'ad enough trouble going before the war. Let's go find out.' Linking arms with Rose, Lexie drew her along the road at a bouncing pace.

Rose looked sideways at the other woman. In the deepening dusk she couldn't see the expression on Lexie's face, but she caught the occasional glimpse of sparkling eyes and felt the springy tension in the thin body. 'You're in a good mood,' she said. 'Something happened?'

'Happened? No, what ever happens to me? I'm just glad to be out, that's all. Tell you what, if we can't get in the cinema, let's go to the pub.'

'What? On our own. Without a man?'

'Why not? There's a war on, you know,' Lexie laughed. 'Let's live dangerously.'

As it turned out, they didn't need to experience

any greater danger than the one and three's in the Palace.

'Two seats in there, miss.' The usherette's dancing beam probed along rows of knees until it settled on the two vacant spaces. Obediently, Lexie and Rose pushed past, murmuring apologies and trying not to trip over toes.

'Phew,' Lexie said. 'Just in time for the news. Hold me seat a sec while I get comfy. Rose, what's the matter?'

Rose shrank against the seat back, huddling down into the warm blackness. 'Shhh,' she begged.

'What's the matter?' Lexie repeated in a sibilant whisper that drew more requests to 'shhh' from surrounding seats.

'It's the Goodwins. They're there. Three rows down.'

'What, your in-laws?'

'Please, Lexie, keep quiet. I don't want them to see me.'

'All right. Toffee?' She unscrewed a tattered bag and extracted a sticky lump.

'No. Thank you.'

To the accompaniment of Lexie's chewing and the relentlessly cheerful tone of the commentator, she sat through newsreels depicting smiling young men in uniform, none of whom it seemed were dejected by the recent setbacks and all of whom were eager to get back into the fray.

With each flickering frame of fresh, untouched faces, she found her eyes being drawn to the back of the man sitting ramrod straight three rows ahead. In the unlit auditorium, the colour of the tightly clipped hair was indistinguishable, but the thin line of the narrow head with its slightly protruding ears was unmistakable. Without any effort she could conjure up Jonas Goodwin's face, with its pinched lips, long nose and high cheekbones.

She shut her eyes to block it out, and instead it was looming over her again. His arms were on either side of her, pinning her to the hospital wall. The overwhelming stench of disinfectant and death was filling her nostrils as he pushed his face close to her and hissed, 'May God forgive you for what you did, girl. Because I won't. You hear me? I won't!'

A wave of nausea surged into her throat at the memory. The blaring music of the main picture caught her by surprise. 'I want to go,' she murmured to Lexie.

'Don't be daft,' she whispered back. 'This is a good picture. Everyone says so. I've been 'oping they'd show it again.'

Rose twisted uncomfortably. To push her way out now might attract the very attention she was trying to avoid. Sliding deeper into her seat, she took deep breaths and tried to concentrate as the swirling mists of eighteenth-century Cornwall closed around Jamaica Inn. It proved to be impossible. When the National Anthem finally rang round the auditorium, she grabbed Lexie's hand, dragged her bodily past the customers standing to attention and burst out into Kentish Town Road before the Goodwins had left their seats.

'What the 'ell's the matter with you?' Lexie protested, forcing Rose's fingers off her wrist.

'I want to get home. There might be a raid.'

'No there won't. It's too late. They're not coming tonight.'

The assurance had hardly left Lexie's lips when the screaming wail of the siren on the police station roof shrieked into the night.

'Oh blimey,' Lexie gasped. 'What do you want to do? Go back in?'

Rose looked behind her. The Goodwins were just pushing their way into the foyer.

'No. I can't hear any planes. Can you?'

'Don't think so.' Lexie cocked her head.

'Let's go home then.'

'Right ho. Run then.'

Linking hands, the two women rushed across the road and dived down the opposite street. Gasping in mouthfuls of air, they ran along the unlit pavements, dodging and stumbling around the columns of street lights, post boxes and water hydrants. Scurrying pedestrians fleeing in the opposite direction loomed out of the black void, the glowing orange tips of their cigarettes giving Rose and Lexie sufficient warning of their presence to let go of each other's hand and weave around them. An ARP warden bawled across from the opposite pavement, shouting to them to get under cover.

'What does he think we're doing? Training for the next Olympics,' Lexie puffed.

'Come *on*,' Rose said, tugging her along.

The batteries in the park barked defiantly and were joined a moment later by those on Hampstead Heath. Above the repetitive crash of the guns, they could hear the remoter 'pak' of exploding shells. Flashes of light illuminated the row of houses in brief bursts showing them that everyone else had taken the warden's advice and found cover. They were the only people left in the street.

Lexie stopped abruptly, jerking Rose to a halt. 'What's the matter. Are you hurt?'

'No. Me flaming suspender's gone.' She started to hop on one foot.

'What are you *doing*?' Rose moaned.

'Taking me stocking off. These are me only decent pair.'

'For heaven's sake, Lexie.' Rose hovered, uncertain whether to abandon her or stay.

'Got it.' Lexie shuffled her shoe on. 'Gawd,' she squealed as a hail of shrapnel hit the road, spitting and fizzing in sparks of light as the lumps disintegrated further on impact.

'Run,' Rose instructed.

She was younger than Lexie, but Lexie had the longer legs. They reached the back of Balaclava Row in a dead heat.

'Go into ours,' Lexie shouted.

'Will your dad . . . ?' Rose started to call back. She stopped as another sound drowned out her words. An enormous screaming row, as if someone was tearing a gigantic sheet, filled the sky directly above their heads.

For a moment, both women stood still, trying to make sense of the racket. Then Lexie screamed. 'Oh God, Rose. It's a bomb. Get *down*.'

Flinging herself forward, she knocked Rose face down in the mud and weeds.

Chapter 6

Aldbury proved to be a pleasant village a few miles east of Tring, huddled beneath a sweep of tree-covered hills clad in a profusion of colours that ranged from honey and gold, through apricot, amber and scarlet to cinnamon and caramel. But even here the signs of war were unavoidable; from the military camp on the hills to the searchlight batteries on the common and the mud fort plastered around an ancient elm tree in the middle of the village.

'What on earth is it?' Sarah said, staring bemusedly at this bizarre structure.

'I think it's intended to hold the crossroads against the invaders,' Stamford replied. 'The holes must be loopholes for rifles.'

Their examination of the village's civil defence preparations was being regarded with suspicion by two old men seated on a wooden bench outside the public house. Eventually one rose, made his way slowly towards the open driver's window and demanded to know their business.

'We're looking for Mrs Donald,' Jack said, extending a scrap of paper with the address.

'From Lundin, are you?' the man said, chewing slowly.

'Yes. Do you know Mrs Donald?'

'Maybe.'

He plainly thought they were up to no good. The

car was unmarked and Sarah had changed into a plain black coat, twisted her long brown hair up into a sweep on top of her head and topped the lot off with a narrow brimmed felt hat, pin-tucked and decorated with two ribbons at the back. Tilted over one eye it did tend to make her look rather more like a foreign agent than a Metropolitan police officer.

Reluctantly, Jack fumbled for his warrant card. He'd been hoping to avoid showing it, since it would inevitably make Gwen Donald the centre of gossip and speculation. It was the hitchhiker that saved the day; for the first time since they'd picked her up on the Berkhampstead road, she spoke.

'I think,' she announced, 'I'm going to be sick.'

Stooping to peer at the girl huddled on the back seat, a handkerchief pressed to her mouth, the old man assimilated the breeches, smock, gaiters and boots. His face suddenly broke into an understanding smile. 'Oh, you be fetching the new land girl!'

He waved at the nearest row of cottages. 'Gwen's place be the second one. But she'll be up the farm this time of day.' He became animated, issuing streams of conflicting instructions, drawing diagrams in the dust with his stick. Eventually Jack resorted to letting in the clutch and sliding gently away from him.

'It sounds like we're both heading for the same place,' he said over his shoulder to the girl.

'Oooooh . . .'

Jack pushed the accelerator to the floor and prayed it wasn't far. For once, it seemed someone was listening to his prayers. Despite the complicated directions, the farm turned out to be no more than a mile outside the village.

The yard was deserted as they turned into it, but at the sound of their engine a man emerged from the barn, wiping his hands on greasy trousers. As he came nearer, striding across the straw-strewn cobbles, they saw that his height had deceived them. Despite being nearly six feet tall, the face under the cap was that of a boy.

'Help you?' he asked. The hitchhiker crawled out of the back seat and promptly threw up. The boy grinned. 'You the new land girl?'

A low moan greeted his question.

'We're looking for Mrs Donald. They said in the village she'd be here.'

'Aunt Gwen's in the dairy.' The boy pointed to a stone building attached to the farmhouse. With another chuckle in the direction of the doubled-over girl, he strolled back into the barn. They heard the murmur of voices followed by a burst of laughter. The land girl straightened up, hauled up the corduroy breeches which came up to her armpits, and shouted: ''Ope all ya doors are low ones, Lofty.' Diving back into the car, she struggled to extract a large suitcase tied with string. Jack reached over her head.

'Allow me.'

'Ta, mister. Yer a gent.'

With Jack carrying the case, they made their way across the yard towards the dairy. A pungent smell of burning straw and roasting flesh stung their eyes and caught in the back of their throats.

'Phew,' Sarah remarked. 'I thought they'd repealed the law about burning witches.'

She'd meant it as a joke, but on cue the boy appeared again carrying a metal bucket in which a dark red liquid slopped and sloshed against the sides. They caught the unmistakable, slightly sweet, tang of blood. He raised his free arm and pointed again at the dairy. 'Through there, mister. Aunt Gwen will sort her out.'

Jack nodded.

'Aunt Gwen' proved to be a stoutish, short woman of fiftyish who greeted their appearance in the cool, stone room with a brusque, 'I hope you're going to be more use than the last one they sent us. What's your name?'

'Aggie Kemp, ma'am.'

'You don't need to call me ma'am. I'm Mrs Donald. You'll be lodging with me. Have you done this sort of work before?'

'No, ma . . . Missus.'

'What was your last work?'

'Seamstress, missus. In Whitechapel.'

'You'll find it very different out here.'

'I bleedin' 'ope so.'

'And we'll have less of the language please, miss. I don't want my girls picking up filth.' Gwen fluttered a plump hand at one of the stone shelves that ran along two walls of the dairy. 'You can leave her case under there, sir. I'll take care of her now.' She offered Jack her hand, obviously intending it as a goodbye.

'Mrs James Donald?'

'That's right, sir.' The smile on her plump pink face turned to bewilderment as Jack produced his warrant card.

'Police?' she said. 'I thought you was from the Woman's Land Army.'

'So I gathered. Can we talk privately, Mrs Donald?'

There was no point in beating around the bush any more. 'It's about your husband. I'm afraid we have some bad news.'

She took the news of her husband's death with the stoicism that Helen Fortune had predicted. It was only when the possible manner of it was explained to her, that she swayed and would have fallen if Sarah hadn't caught her and lowered her on to the one seat in the dairy, a low wooden stool.

'Murdered?' She looked between the two officers, staring up at them from her low perch. 'It's a mistake. Who'd want to murder Donald?'

Jack had never had much faith in the robbery theory but he used it now as the simplest explanation to offer the bewildered woman. 'We need to open the safe. And to check the contents of the shop. To see what, if anything, is missing. Are you familiar with your husband's business, Mrs Donald?'

'Oh yes, sir. I did all the books before me and the girls come out here.' She moved her head from side to side, rather like a cow trying to dislodge a troublesome fly. Her eyes looked at something many miles away.

Jack said, 'We'd like you to come back with us today, Mrs Donald.'

Gwen placed both hands on her knees and levered herself to her feet. 'I'll have to wait for the girls to come back. Ruby, my sister, has taken them into Tring in the car for a bit of a treat. I'll have to wait,' she repeated belligerently, as if she expected an argument.

'Of course,' Jack agreed. 'As long as you like.'

Gwen gathered herself together. 'Best be getting on with my work then. Can't leave everything for Ruby.'

Picking up a wooden churn she tipped the contents on to the top of a shallow wooden trough mounted on legs to lift it to waist height. 'Now where's that girl got to?'

Sarah looked through the window. 'I think she's gone across to the barn. Shall I get her?'

'No. Don't do that, miss. You stop here with me. You can give me a hand to wash the butter, if you don't mind?'

'No, I don't mind. But I've never done anything like . . .' Sarah gestured vaguely at the mysteries of the dairy. She was a London girl, born and bred. Milk and cream came from the Co-op and butter and cheese came from Sainsbury's as far as she was concerned.

'Nothing to it, miss. Just pick up that bucket of water and pour it over the butter as I roll.'

Gingerly, Sarah did as she was instructed. Gwen Donald leant on something resembling a fluted rolling pin and drove it along the two wooden battens on each side of the trough, forcing the yellow butter into a flat slab. 'More water, miss,' Gwen panted, her face growing red with the force that she was exerting on the roller.

Refilling the bucket from the tap, Sarah poured again.

'It's a dairy farm, is it?' Jack asked.

'What?' Gwen looked up, as if she was trying to recollect who he was. 'No. Not now. They used to have a lovely dairy herd when I was a girl. But it's all gone now. They've ploughed up the pastures for arable. Ruby just keeps a couple of cows for herself. Dairy's hardly used now. Another bucket, miss.'

'You're from here then, Mrs Donald?'

'Born and bred, sir.' The butter was driven before Gwen's anger, its fat, waxy surface taking the full brunt of her grief. 'Not here. The farm's only been in the family a few years since Archie started renting the place.'

'Where did you meet your husband? Here or in London?'

'London, sir.' The cold tide crashed over the slab again. 'I was in service. Cook. That's enough, miss.' The butter was scraped from the trough and flung into a bowl. A handful of salt crystals was mashed in with vicious energy. Whilst she worked, Gwen talked in short, breathy bursts. 'Parlour maid. Was getting married on Saturday. No time off. Ring needed adjusting. Thursday my half day. Asked me to pick it up.'

The butter thudded on to the trough again. Sarah moved towards the tap.

'No. No water this time, you'll wash the salt out. Has to have salt,' Gwen panted. 'To keep.'

Jack prompted her again. 'So you and Mr Donald started courting after you collected the parlour maid's ring.'

'Courting?' Gwen's neck muscles bulged as she squeezed the golden mound flat again. 'No, sir, we never did much courting. See Donald's parents had just died and he wanted to know how to make pastry, never having had the need before. So I went round on me next half day and showed him. And the next week he took me up to tea in Fortnum's and asked me to marry him. And I said yes.'

Knocking on the tap, Gwen held her hands under the cold water, dried them roughly on a bleached sack hanging by the sink and drove her fingers into the butter slab. Pulling an earthenware crock towards her, she flung the handful into the bottom with a grunting exhalation of air. 'We were both too old for any of that courting nonsense. Donald was thirty-seven and I was turned forty,' she said between grunts and lobs. 'And I'd a fancy for my own place and children before it was too late. So I took Donald. And I did my duty by him, ask anyone.'

The last of the butter hurdled into the crock neck. Seizing a wooden mushroom with both hands, Gwen brought it down on the fat with a vicious 'thud'.

'When did you last see your husband?' Jack asked.

'La . . .'

Before Gwen could finish her reply the door behind Jack burst open. The expression on Sarah's face told him something was wrong. He spun round and found himself facing a squat, muscular man in shirt sleeves, grubby trousers and rubber boots. In his right hand he was clasping a large, viciously bladed knife.

'What's going on, Gwen?' he demanded. 'The new girl says these two are police.' The man advanced on Jack.

Surreptitiously, Sarah reached behind her and located the rim of one of the heavy shallow bowls lined up along the stone shelf.

Gwen paused in her pounding. Her face was shiny and suffused a deep rose shade by her exertions. 'It's Donald, Archie. He's been taken.'

'Taken?' Puzzlement changed to enlightenment on the man's thick-browed face. 'Oh, I see. You mean he's . . .' He passed his hand across his throat and seemed disconcerted to find the knife in it. Muttering an apology, he transferred it to his left hand and thrust the right at Jack.

'My brother-in-law,' Gwen made the introduction. 'The lady and gentleman have come to take me back to London, Archie. The stock's to be checked.'

'Got the shop did they? Much damage was there?'

Once again Jack had to explain that James Donald's death wasn't the result of enemy action. Archie's reaction was so predictable, it was becoming positively monotonous.

'Murdered? Who'd want to murder James?'

'The police think it was burglars.'

Archie hovered. His thick fingers clasped the knife, blade upwards, like a spear. He was caught on the dilemma that faced most people when confronted with the news of death; he couldn't think what to say. 'Ruby will be home soon,' he offered finally.

'Yes. I'll wait for Ruby,' Gwen agreed. 'You get back to your work, Archie.' Lifting the wooden mushroom over her head, Gwen brought it down on the compacted butter with all her strength. The earthenware crock cracked with a loud retort under the force of the pressure, split into two sections and deposited the butter on the floor with a resounding 'thwack'. Gwen stared at the mess. She looked around at the watchers. 'I've spilt the butter,' she said in a dazed tone. Her voice rose in a wail. 'I've spilt the butter.' Two large fat tears welled in her eyes and started to slide down her red cheeks. Crouching on the floor, she tried to scoop up the slippery mess.

'It don't matter, Gwen. Leave it.' Archie came across the room, his heavy boots clattering on the stone floor, his demeanour competent. Farmyard disasters he could handle. Taking up the bowl Sarah had been intending to use as a weapon, he flicked the mass into it. 'I'll feed it to pigs. No need to take on.'

Sarah crouched by the distressed woman and put one arm round her shoulder. 'Perhaps we could go across to the house, Mrs Donald? I'll make you a cup of tea.'

Sarah had got the weeping woman to her feet. With one arm round her waist, she led her to the door. Jack's attempt to help was met with a flinch and stiffening of muscle under the plump arm. Allowing his hand to drop, he mouthed to Sarah over Gwen's head: 'You take her in. Try to get her talking.'

Sarah's cool blue eyes flickered their understanding.

In order to give her time to gain Gwen's confidence, Jack thrust his hands in his pockets and took a stroll round the farmyard.

The first shed he looked in was no more than three walls and a roof. A few items of lethal-looking farm machinery were drawn up against the back wall. A small brown hen, perched on a set of wicked spikes, fluttered indignant feathers at him.

Taking the hint, he took himself off and located the pig sty by the excited grunts and squeals. Several fat porkers were leaning over the low stone wall watching something with intent interest. Jack turned to follow their line of sight and saw Archie, his gangling son and a large bearded man staggering out of the rear door of the barn with the carcass of one of the porcine spectators' late relatives, its skin scraped and singed of its bristles.

At the sight of Jack, the three men stopped and

stared. Raising his hat, he called across, 'Warm work?'

'Yes, sir,' agreed Archie readily. 'Very warm.' With a jerk on the limb he was cradling he urged the other two on towards a tenter frame standing a few feet from the door and consisting of two upright stakes and a crossbeam. His son had the other front leg and the third man was supporting a wooden yoke to which the pig's back legs had been lashed. When they reached the frame, he heaved the yoke on to two pegs and waited whilst the others tied it into place.

Fascinated, Jack stepped closer as the land girl, her pasty face now returned to a healthier shade, backed out of the barn dragging a galvanised metal bath. 'Where'd ya want this, mister?' Squinting under her armpit, she spotted Jack and grinned. 'I fink I'm getting the 'ang of this farming lark.'

'Put it there,' Archie ordered, slapping a boot next to the frame. 'And stand by to lend a hand with the horribles.'

It was clear that this order meant as little to the girl as it did to Stamford. They were both enlightened two minutes later, when the bearded one tied his apron round the pig's corpse and slashed confidently with his knife. 'The horribles' spilled into his taut apron and were manoeuvred into the bath with a sickening squelch.

Jack wondered if the girl was feeling as sick as he was, but apparently it was only combustion engines, not guts, that had that effect on her. With sparkling eyes, and much hitching of the slipping breeches, she helped to carry the bath to the kitchen.

Jack followed, mainly from a mischievous desire to see Sarah's reaction when she was confronted with the spectacle. He was pleased to discover it was the same as his.

'Fine pair we are,' Jack said ruefully, as they stood outside the door sipping their tea. 'Fat lot of use in an air raid.'

Sarah's chin jerked up immediately, her eyes flashing at this implied criticism of her toughness. 'I've been in air raids,' she said. '*And* seen victims blown to pieces.' Then she stopped and blushed. 'I sound like a kid boasting I've got the biggest bit of shrapnel, don't I? Didn't mean to, sir.'

'I know. It's hard, isn't it? Trying to sound compassionate and not get too involved at the same time. Have you found out anything more from Mrs Donald?'

'Two bits of information.' Sarah took out her notebook and flipped it open with a professional one-handed movement. 'The last time she saw her husband was on the ninth. It was his birthday and she went up to take him presents from herself and the girls. She stayed overnight and came back on the Thursday morning.'

'And what about the last time they spoke?'

'Same time, I suppose.'

'I don't think so. Helen Fortune said James called the post office in Aldbury. I assume he spoke to his wife.'

A flicker of disgust at her own incompetence passed over Sarah's face. 'Damn, I forgot the flaming phone call.' A flush stained her high cheekbones as she realised she'd allow the common accents of her background to slip out.

Stamford took pity on her. 'It's probably not important. What was the second thing?'

Sarah drew him further from the farmhouse door. 'I wasn't sure whether it was important or not. You see, I asked Mrs Donald whether the shop was a good business, and she said the regular sales were just steady, but they made quite a good living from the "specials".'

'Making copies of bits and pieces,' Gwen Donald had explained. 'Donald was good at that. He could make you a bracelet in gilt and coloured glass that you'd swear was gold and precious stones.'

Intrigued, Sarah had asked, 'Who did he do this work for?'

'Anyone who asked. There was never anything criminal about it,' Gwen had said sharply. 'It was ladies mostly, run up a few more bills than they should and didn't want their husbands or the neighbours finding out. So they'd sell a bit of their jewellery and Donald would make them a copy so nobody would be none the wiser. Sometimes it was the husbands, of course. I didn't really hold with that, but business is business, isn't it, miss? And it wasn't for us to tell them how to carry on.'

'Why? How were they carrying on?'

'Giving their girlfriends a little present from their wife's jewellery box, that's what. And then getting Donald to make a copy so's it wouldn't be missed. I don't think carryings on like that are anything to laugh about,' she'd bridled, as Sarah had attempted to swallow a smile.

'Yes,' Stamford agreed. 'A definite possible under the "motives" heading. Where did he find these customers?'

'Word of mouth. You know how it works, sir. He

does a job for one customer, and next time a friend's a bit short, they mention this obliging jeweller they know. According to Mrs Donald, they knew they could trust him to be discreet.'

'And, this time, somebody made doubly sure he'd never open his mouth?' Stamford murmured, nodding his approval at his sergeant's reasoning. 'Could well be. We'll know more after we've got Mrs Donald up to London.'

They had a long wait. It was a couple more hours before Ruby finally returned from Tring in a wheezing Austin Seven into which she'd crammed two nieces, two daughters, several large sacks of animal feed, and all the household shopping that the farm couldn't provide.

After more explanations and lamentations, Gwen had to be driven back to her cottage to collect her case. And once that had been done, they were delayed one final time by the arrival of Ruby. 'Just a little something from my husband,' she'd explained, pushing her offerings at Stamford. 'Don't take offence.'

Despite all his protests, he'd not been allowed to refuse. The eggs, safely cradled on Sarah's lap in the back, were perfectly acceptable. And he could live with the two rabbit corpses staring sightlessly up at him from the passenger seat. But the final gift he could definitely have managed without, rationing or no rationing. Applying the brakes as he drew up outside the Donalds' jewellery shop, he breathed a silent prayer of relief that was the last time he'd have to listen to a tidal wave of 'the horribles' slurping against the lid of the white enamel dish wedged on the car floor beside the gear stick.

Gwen had her own set of keys to the shop. She walked through the front with scarcely a glance and dropped to her knees before the safe. Despite Jack's assurances that there was no need to, she insisted on checking the contents immediately, and pronounced them intact.

'How can you be sure? If you haven't been involved on a regular basis with the business for over a year?'

Rising stiffly to her feet, Gwen insisted that she was pretty sure. 'I had a look in here when I come up for Donald's birthday. And it don't look to me like there's anything added nor taken away since then. I'll check the books proper, like you say, sir, but I don't reckon they took anything from here.'

It was the same with the flat. After a cursory search, she insisted that nothing was missing. 'Where was he?' she asked suddenly.

It was Sarah who answered. 'In the bedroom, Mrs Donald.'

They'd returned to the kitchen. Gwen pulled open a drawer and sorted amongst the cutlery. 'There'll be arrangements to make,' she said, her back to the officers.

'I'm afraid you won't be able to bury him quite yet. There will have to be an inquest. In the meantime, is there someone you could stay with tonight?'

'Stay with?' Gwen looked at him as if he were mad. 'Why should I want to stay with anyone? I'll stop here. If that's all right?'

It was, the forensic teams had long since completed their business, but Jack had assumed she might be nervous. Gwen dismissed the idea, vigorously flicking curtains into place and setting a match to the gas.

'I'll be quite all right, thank you, sir. I'll make a start on the books soon as I've had my tea.'

'What if there's a raid?'

'There's a cellar, sir. Under the shop. Donald used it sometimes. I'll be perfectly all right, thank you.'

It was a dismissal. She wanted him to go so that she could be alone. He sensed it but was reluctant to fall in with her plans. Throughout the hours at the farm and during the drive to London he'd had that constant spine-tingling sensation that told him there was something he'd missed – or something that he hadn't yet been told.

Apparently Sarah had received the same message. She'd moved into the hall, shielding herself from Gwen's vision by keeping the partially open kitchen door between them. With an expressive lift of her eyebrows, she signalled Stamford to come out.

'I'm sure she wants to tell me something, sir,' she murmured. 'I kept getting the impression she was about to speak in the car, and then she'd suddenly have second thoughts. I think it's because you were there. It would probably be best if you went now and left me with her.'

'Certainly, Sergeant,' Jack said. He replaced his hat. 'And what time would you like me to report back in the morning?'

'Oh I don't think that will be necessary, sir. I'm sure I can get her to confide in me this evening.'

His sergeant's expression was as straight-faced and calm as his own. Stamford cracked first. 'All right,' he said, grinning reluctantly. 'Let me know as soon as you get anything out of her.'

He delivered the car to the station and the rabbits

and dish of pig's innards to Eileen. To his surprise, she greeted the offering with delight. 'That's grand, Jack. I'll not need to touch the meat ration for days.'

'Do you know what to do with them?' Jack said doubtfully, peering at the unappetising mass.

'Course I do. We always had a pig when I was girl. None of this waste like they have now. What didn't go down our throats went into the pig and got served up on the plates again next year.' She stood the dish carefully in the larder. 'Are they short of food on this farm?'

'Not that I could see, why?'

'It's much too early to kill the pig. There's a good six weeks fattening time left. We never sent ours to the pig man until the end of November.' She turned in surprise as Jack threw back his head and burst out laughing. 'Whatever's so funny?'

'Nothing.' He shook his head in despair at his own naivety. 'I'll tell you one day.'

Still chuckling, he made his way back to his own house to change out of his suit which now stunk of farmyard and singed pig. He couldn't help admiring Archie's nerve. No wonder the man had been so put out at finding a couple of detectives lodged in his dairy. When Sarah turned up he'd have to tell her they were now a pair of corrupt coppers; they'd accepted a bribe in return for keeping quiet about the illegal slaughter of an extra pig over and above the farm's yearly ration. There was no point in trying to recoup the situation; he had no doubt that if the local coppers called at Archie's now, all traces of the surreptitious butchery would be cleared up and the meat safely stored elsewhere. It would be his word against the three of them. He just hoped that whatever Sarah got out of Gwen Donald made their deviation from the straight and narrow worthwhile.

She didn't disappoint him.

Chapter 7

'He had a what?' Jack repeated incredulously.

'A mistress, sir,' Sarah said, keeping her voice low since she was standing on Stamford's doorstep.

He seemed to realise that it wasn't an ideal location to discuss a possible murder case. Taking her elbow, he drew her into the hall, snapping on the light. A beam of yellow illumination fell on the front garden and spilled across the street. Jack quickly flipped the switch to 'off' again. 'Oh damn, I haven't got the blackout up anywhere. I've been across at Eileen's all evening. Wait here while I get the curtains across in the dining room.'

'Is your daughter asleep?' Sarah called in a sibilant whisper.

'No idea,' he called back in normal tones. 'She's across the road. With the raids coming practically every night, Eileen thought it best to put the children to bed in the Anderson rather than mess about getting them down there when the sirens sound.'

'Haven't you got one here?'

'No. My precautions consist of huddling under the kitchen table. I'm afraid you'll have to join me if an alarm goes.' He reappeared in the hall as he issued the invitation and at the same moment the air outside was filled with the steadily rising wail of the siren.

Sarah paused, her tall slim figure framed against the still open front door. She wasn't entirely sure whether Stamford's remark had been intended as a joke. Or whether she wanted it to be. She knew she liked him, and appreciated that he was one of the few policemen who was prepared to take a woman officer seriously. But she'd suppressed any stronger attraction because Stamford was not only a senior officer but, with his wife missing somewhere on the Continent, there was no way of knowing whether he was a married man or a widower.

Eileen solved her dilemma by hurrying across the street, the creaking of an unoiled gate hinge announcing her presence. In the partial starlight they could both see the paler fringe of her nightdress beneath the man's overcoat she'd thrown on to come out.

'I thought it was you. Come over to our house. We can squeeze you down the Anderson with us.'

'Thanks, but it doesn't sound too bad. I can't hear any planes, can you?'

Sarah stepped back out into the front garden and both women stood craning their heads back at the star-filled sky.

'I don't know, I can hear a sort of rumble, can't you?'

'It's a train,' Sarah asserted.

'Are you certain?'

'Absolutely,' Sarah said in a firm voice that finished on a gasp of alarm as the anti-aircraft guns opened up.

'Go on,' Jack urged, pulling his front door closed behind him. 'You'd better do as Eileen suggests and take cover in the Anderson. We can talk later. If you can still stand.'

'Are you sure there's room, Eileen?' Sarah asked, following her down the hall into the kitchen and puzzling over Stamford's cryptic comment.

'Course there is. We've got four bunks fixed up down there. And there's only me and the kids tonight. Maury's out somewhere and Pat sleeps in the house, or over at Jack's. Ask him what he's doing tonight, will you?'

Since Pat was currently adjusting the wick on a lamp that was sitting on the kitchen table, this seemed an odd request.

'I'll stay here, Mum. In case you need anything.'

'Tell him he can use one of those eggs Jack brought back for his breakfast. What are you two doing out of bed?' This last demand was directed at Sammy who'd just wandered in the back door, leading Annaliese by the hand.

'I came to see when you were coming out. With our jam sandwiches and cocoa. And Annie come 'cos she don't like being out there by herself. On account of the ghosts.' Raising his hands over his head, he swooped on Annie with a mock howl. She squealed with fright, but her brown eyes, peeping out from beneath the knitted pixie hood, were dancing with laughter.

Eileen drew a sharp breath as a louder 'crump' outside was followed by a threatening rattle from the kitchen window and a furious barrage of shells from the guns. 'Get outside to that shelter *now*,' she said in a tone Sarah had last heard coming from a police drill instructor at Peel House.

Even Sammy seemed to realise that his mother meant business. Seizing hold of Annie again, he scampered back down the garden, the bottom of a cut-down pair of his brother's pyjamas flapping beneath an oversized jumper and drooping over his wellington boots.

'I can loan you a nightdress if you like?' Eileen offered. 'And you can have a wash up in my room if you want.'

'I'll sleep in my clothes,' Sara said. She always did if she was in a shelter. Somehow the idea of being dragged from her own flat in her knickers was acceptable, but the thought of having the rescue service uncovering her unconscious body, clad only in her nightdress, from the wreckage of a public shelter made her go cold.

'You'll need blankets,' Eileen said, putting down the plate of sandwiches and thermos flasks she'd just picked up. 'Oh God, that one sounded close!'

'You go out to the children. Pat can show me where the blankets are.'

Gratefully, Eileen retrieved her food again, added a hot water bottle and a torch, threw an instruction over her shoulder to tell Pat it was the blankets from Brendan's bed that she wanted, and hurried out.

Pat placed a box of matches next to the lamp, stood up and grinned at Sarah. 'I bet you only stayed so you could find out what I've done, didn't you?'

'Right first time.'

Reaching over her shoulder, Pat picked up a box and handed it to her. 'Know what that is?'

'Rinso?' suggested Sarah, reading off the label.

'Rinso,' agreed Pat. 'I bought it this morning.'

Sarah mulled this fact over whilst Pat sprang up the stairs and returned a few moments later with an

armful of blankets. 'And?' she asked passing back the
soap powder and scooping up the bundle of covers.

'Mum uses Persil and yellow soap. And she buys it
herself.'

Enlightenment dawned on Sarah. 'She thought you
were criticising her laundry.'

'Yep, I'm condemned to do all me own scrubbing,
mangling, starching and ironing from now on.'

'Why did you buy it then?'

Unable to admit that he'd been trying to fix a date
with Rose, Pat said vaguely, 'It was a sort of mistake.
I was thinking of something else.'

Sarah laughed. 'Well it looks like you're going to
get housemaid's hands. Unless you can talk some
gullible female with a yen for blue bags into marrying
you.'

She'd said it light-heartedly, partly to take her mind
off the air raid that was getting nearer by the second.
The deep brick red flush that flooded across Pat's
cheeks caught her by surprise. She would have liked
to ask who the girl was – but she didn't know him
well enough to probe that deeply. Wishing him good
night, she felt her way cautiously down the dark
garden to the Anderson, trying to avoid pitching head-
first into the vegetable patch.

'Mind the step down,' Eileen said, playing a weak
torch beam across the floor. 'Soon as you're in we can
wedge the door across and I'll light the lamp, let us
see what we're doing. Just squeeze in between the
beds there.' Sarah obediently followed the small circlet
of light which darted backwards across the wooden
duckboards. 'Sammy, push the door.'

There was a scrambling at Sarah's ear level,

followed by the rumbling scrape of metal and the rattle of a curtain. The soft golden glow of an oil lamp filled the shelter and Sarah saw what was behind Stamford's parting shot.

The Anderson was six feet six inches long, four feet six inches wide and six feet tall at its highest point. Into it Eileen had crammed four bunks and a shelf to hold food, thermos, torches etc. In addition, she'd left sufficient room at the door end to allow a hammock to be slung widthways across the shelter, and had further cut down the height by putting duckboards across the floor. For a woman of five foot three and for children under ten it was tolerable. For anyone of above normal height, it was an exercise in contortionism.

Eileen was seated at the head end of one of the lower bunks, tucking the hot water bottle down beside Annaliese. 'You take this top one, love. Sammy, get down off there and get in the lower bed.'

Grumbling that he wanted to sleep in the top one, Sammy levered himself into the gap, kicking off his boots as he did so.

'You'd better put your shoes on the shelf,' Eileen informed Sarah as she climbed with difficulty into the space between the top bunk and the curved roof. 'They won't get wet up there if we flood tonight.'

'Does that happen often?'

'About once a week, that's what I had to put the boards down for.'

'Pat says it's because the River Fleet runs under here, Mum.'

'Daft if you ask me,' Eileen grumbled, handing out the jam sandwiches and clambering into the other top bunk. 'What they want to build a house on top of a river for?'

'It's not just us,' Sammy mumbled through a mouthful of bread and margarine. 'It's all over Kentish Town.'

'Then there are a lot of daft builders around.'

For a few minutes they munched in silence. Other scents mingled with the smell of the jam: damp earth, a burning lamp wick, Lifebuoy soap, stale nicotine from the blankets and fresh cocoa from the thermos. It was pungent but not unpleasant, and definitely an improvement on the stink she'd had to put up with in the public shelters, Sarah reflected, twisting uncomfortably as she tried to accommodate her long legs within the bunk.

Stretching out brought them into painful contact with the end wall. Wriggling on to her back, she bent them and found her knees jammed against the roof. She finally settled for lying on her front, huddled into a ball, with one arm and most of her legs hanging over the bunk. 'Are you sure I'm not taking anyone's place?' she asked hopefully. 'What if Maury comes back?'

'Oh don't worry about that. He can sleep in the hammock.'

'That's 'cos Maury's a midget,' Sammy remarked.

Annaliese giggled, suggesting Sammy had been increasing her vocabulary again.

'Don't call your brother names,' Eileen said. 'He's a bit touchy about it,' she hissed across at Sarah. 'I keep telling him it's what's in the package that matters, not the size of it. Though,' she continued with a despairing sigh, 'some days I think it might be less worrying not to know what's under the brown paper. Are you ready for the light out?'

'Shouldn't we leave it on? In case one of the children wants to go to the lavatory in the night?'

'Sammy's got eyes like a cat, and Annie wakes me.'

'Oh. That's all right then,' Sarah said in a small voice. The sinking wick seemed to suck the light back into the lamp. Cramped and uncomfortable she lay in the dark, listening to Sammy's noisy breathing and the crash and rattle of the explosions which thankfully seemed to be fading to the south as the German bombers aimed at St Pancras and King's Cross Stations.

With four people crammed inside, the Anderson started to heat up. Sarah could feel clammy sweat sticking her skin to her blouse. She moved cautiously and felt the curved surface of the metal roof a few inches above her head. A spasm of panic gripped her throat, constricting her saliva. Desperately, she swallowed, but the darkness seemed to be closing in, touching and crawling over her skin. Ever since she was a little girl she'd been terrified of enclosed spaces. The advent of the bombing raids had left her with a constant horror of being buried alive. The trouble was, she couldn't tell anyone. Instead she'd been forced to move amongst the shelterers and her own WPCs a picture of calm authority. In a way that had helped; she'd almost managed to fool herself some nights, so convincing had her performance become. But there was no one to act for here.

A louder explosion thundered outside. She was certain she could feel the shockwaves vibrating in the metal walls of the shelter despite the heavy covering of earth that had been flung up over it. Turning on her face, she buried herself in the pillow. Her arm dropped over the side and swung limply in the darkness. A small hand crept out of the lower bunk and fastened itself around the middle finger. Instinctively Sarah drew the little girl's hand into her own and rubbed a comforting thumb over the soft skin. At least she wasn't the only chicken in the shelter tonight.

'Everything looks better in the morning,' Sarah's first sergeant had been fond of informing her. In her experience, this wasn't true. The morning just brought daylight, which meant that instead of creeping up on you, troubles could locate you more easily and sock you straight in the mouth.

In her case it gathered itself up and landed a knockout punch on the front steps of Agar Street Station. She and Stamford had paused on their way to Gwen Donald's to see if there were any urgent messages. There was a car driven by a WVS volunteer parked at the kerb and as they went in a WPC hurried down the steps and leapt in.

'Morning, Sarge,' she called back.

'Good morning, Jeannie,' Sarah said raising a hand in friendly greeting.

'If you want breakfast you'd better hurry, the canteen's just stopping serving.'

'Thanks,' Stamford said. 'But we've eaten ours at home.'

He was facing the car. Sarah was looking towards the station. She had plenty of opportunity to see the two PCs descending the steps grin and nudge each other as they heard Stamford's remark and absorbed the crumpled appearance of her clothes.

Why on earth couldn't he have said they'd eaten theirs in Eileen's kitchen – together with three of Eileen's children and his own daughter. Saying something herself now would just look like she was producing an alibi.

By the time they'd checked the office she was painfully aware of the whispers and giggles preceding her around the station.

Stamford seemed oblivious to them. No doubt he was wondering why she was scarcely speaking to him as they made their way back to Balaclava Row. Well, let the tactless idiot wonder, she thought rebelliously. It would have been bad enough living with the rumours if there had been any foundation to them. But to put her in that position without any justification was just what you'd expect from a flaming man; and she didn't care if he was a chief inspector!

'Many men are thoughtless in my experience,' Gwen Donald stated. 'They can't be bothered with the *detail*. But not Donald.' She tapped the pile of invoices and receipts spread around her on the kitchen table. 'Everything's recorded and entered up in the ledgers, just like I'd expect. It will take me a couple of days to check everything, but I really can't believe that anything is missing.'

She was wearing a freshly pressed blouse and skirt, her hair was tidily tucked up by hair grips, drifts of thicker powder, in the heavier lines around her nostrils and under her chin, showed that a powder puff had been pressed on to her weather-roughened skin. The breakfast dishes had already been washed and returned to the cupboard. The kitchen was swept, and windows had a vinegary scent that suggested they were newly washed.

'What about the "specials",' Stamford asked. 'Are they all accounted for?'

'As far as I can see. There weren't many recently. People don't seem so shy of admitting they're a bit short since the war started.' She swung a lined ledger book so they could see the entries. 'This was the last one. It was collected last week.'

Stamford read the cramped, precise writing in Indian ink. 'There are no names or addresses.'

'That's right. They were given a number.' Gwen's square-tipped finger pointed to four digits in the left hand corner of the ruled-off box. 'And when they came back, they just quoted that number. Most customers preferred it that way, not having to give a name.'

'It strikes me as a dangerous system. If you can't identify the customer, how did you know you weren't assisting in a crime? An insurance fraud, say?'

Gwen drew herself in, pursing tight lips. 'Like I said, sir. What people did in their private lives was no concern of ours. But we never did nothing wrong.'

What you mean, Sarah thought, recognising the type, is that whilst you didn't know for certain it was illegal, you were happy enough to take the cash and keep quiet. 'Tell the inspector about your husband's affair, Mrs Donald.'

Gwen coloured and shot a look that plainly said 'traitor' at Sarah. 'I don't think that's necessary, is it, miss? I don't think it's quite nice, talking about such things in front of a gentleman.'

'Oh Mr Stamford isn't a gentleman. He's a police

officer.' Sarah accompanied this assurance with a bland smile in her superior's direction. 'And you obviously think it had something to do with his death, Mrs Donald. Why else did you ask whether it was a woman who found him?'

'Well it weren't, were it? So there's no more to be said on that subject.'

'Assuming your husband was murdered, you'd want his killer to be caught, wouldn't you?' Stamford asked. 'I think you owe it to him to tell us the truth.'

Gwen swept the papers into one pile. 'Well, no one can say I didn't give Donald everything that was owed to him as his wife. Ask anyone. I kept this place spotless. And he never had any cause to complain the way I took care of the girls. And as for the other business.' Her eyes fluttered unconsciously to the ceiling. 'Well I never denied him. I kept all me vows.'

'But your husband didn't keep his end of the bargain?' Sarah was beginning to form the impression that that was what this marriage had been; a bargain struck between two people for the production of children.

'He strayed,' Gwen admitted.

'Did he admit it?'

'I didn't ask. Not at first. I wanted time to think. I never expected that sort of carrying on from Donald, see. It flummoxed me a bit.'

'So what did you do?'

Rather than reply directly, Gwen opened her handbag, extracted a scrap of paper, and passed it to him. It was an advertisement cut from a newspaper.

'French's Private Investigation Agency,' he read. 'Investigations undertaken with the utmost discretion.'

'I waited a few months. I thought maybe it would pass like. But I could tell it hadn't. He was still happy. So I wrote to Mr Fox, told him I wanted Donald investigated.'

'Who's Mr Fox?' Stamford asked.

'He's the gentlemen who wrote back to me. Mr Laurence Fox. Ever such a nice polite letter. He explained to me all about their charges and said he'd have to watch the flat for at least a week, so I should send enough money for five nights. Or I could have a special rate for seven days.'

'And I suppose you took that?' Stamford said. Sarah knew from his tone that he suspected the absent Mr Fox of being a confidence trickster.

'That's right.'

'Did you ever hear from him again?'

'Of course I did. I've stood behind that shop counter for eleven years, you think I haven't learnt how to spot a fraud? He sent me a letter. I had to pretend it was from a girl I'd been in service with, our Ruby's that nosy sometimes.'

'So what did the fair-dealing Mr Fox have to say for himself?'

'He said I was right. He was certain Donald was carrying on. And he could get into the flat and get a third party's connobation . . .'

'Corroboration,' Sarah suggested.

'That's right, miss. That's what he wrote. And pictures too if I wanted them for the divorce. But they'd cost extra.'

'How unexpected,' Stamford murmured under his breath. 'Did you take up his offer?'

'No. I couldn't see no point. I didn't want a divorce.

I just wanted to know I was right, so's I could tackle Donald and tell him to act his age or I'd keep the girls with me down at Aldbury for good.'

'And did you?'

'Yes.' An expression of smug satisfaction passed across Gwen Donald's troubled face. 'When I come up for his birthday, I told him straight I'd give him two days to think about it and then I wanted his answer.'

'Was that why he phoned you? At the post office in Aldbury?'

'How did you . . . Oh, I suppose Helen said.'

'What was his answer?'

Gwen looked triumphant. 'He'd seen sense. I knew he would. Said he'd tell her it was over.'

'Tell who?'

Before Gwen could reply, they were startled by a loud thumping on the front door of the shop. It had an official ring to it, and Stamford half expected Gwen to summon him downstairs. Instead, she returned to the kitchen carrying a metal bucket that she must have taken from the workroom. Standing it under the sink tap, she spun it full 'on'. 'Turning the water off,' she explained over her shoulder. 'The bomb last night did something to the water pipes.'

'What bomb?' Sarah asked. They'd come in the front way and the street had appeared unscathed.

'Came down out the back. Two houses are gone across the way. Direct hit. You can see from the sitting-room window if you want.'

They didn't especially, but she'd already left the tap running and was walking down the passage. 'I left the curtains drawn, no point opening them when I don't sit in here.'

She flicked them open with an efficient twist of her wrist. 'See.'

They did indeed. The row of tall terraced houses across the field resembled a set of lower dentures whose two middle teeth had been punched out. Even with the window closed they could smell the familiar cordite and pulverised bricks. Rescue workers were picking over the pile of stones, timbers and crushed furniture like maggots on a half-chewed apple. A smaller device had dropped on the scrub, stripping away the nettles and couch grass and gouging out a crater from the thick yellow and grey London clay.

'Was anyone hurt?'

'I've no idea about the houses. I believe Lexie was outside. And one of the others too. I heard a bit of fuss going on but I didn't bother to go out. I don't think it was bad. I didn't hear no ambulance.' She seemed oddly indifferent. 'Anyhow, she's all right now. Look.'

Squinting sideways they could make out a red head bouncing down the backyard of the cobbler's shop and stopping at a brick outhouse.

'Washing,' Gwen sniffed. 'You never used to find no respectable women doing their laundry on a Sunday. When I was a girl we didn't even cook on the Sabbath. Still it will just get covered in muck from the bomb site. Serves her right. If you've seen what you want, shall we go back to the kitchen? Oh blast it, the bucket!'

Her alarm was well founded. The sound of water gushing and pattering on to the linoleum carried into the passage.

'I'll get it,' Sarah called, lifting the bucket from off the plug-hole.

'Be careful, miss, the handle is . . .'

Gwen's warning came too late. Sarah dropped the bucket back into the sink with a gasp of pain, sending an even larger tidal wave of water over the floor and into her shoes.

'Are you cut?' Gwen asked pushing past Stamford.

Sarah extended her hand. Blood was just beginning to well from a straight cut that extended from the base of her thumb to her wrist.

Gwen 'tsk-tsked' . 'There's a bottle of iodine in that cupboard, sir. I'll get a clean bandage.'

'Put it back under the water,' Jack ordered, scanning the shelves Gwen had indicated.

'It's stopped,' Sarah mumbled, sucking at the wound.

Gwen hurried back. 'Just there, sir.' She stepped up to the cupboard and moved several bottles of patent medicines. 'Now where's that got to?'

'Is this it,' Sarah asked, still milking the cut with vigorous sucks. 'It was on the windowsill.'

'Whatever's it doing there? Hold still, miss, this might sting.'

With quick strokes, Gwen bathed, anointed and bandaged the cut. Stamford waited until she'd finished before repeating the question he'd put to her before all the interruptions had begun.

'Who was your husband's mistress, Mrs Donald?'

'I don't know.'

Stamford's voice rose incredulously. 'You mean this Fox character never even told you who your husband was having this alleged affair with?'

126

'He was going to put it in a typed report, that's what he said in his letter.'

'But it never arrived.'

'Not yet.' Gwen plainly didn't like the implication that she'd been taken in.

'So you've no idea at all where we can find this woman?'

'Oh yes I do. Mr Fox put it in his letter.' She nodded between the two detectives. The reason for her indifference as to the possible fate of her neighbours last night suddenly became clear.

'I don't know who it is. But I know Donald was carrying on with someone from Balaclava Row.'

Chapter 8

Oblivious to the watchers above her, Lexie opened the door of the little brick outhouse and jumped backwards as a broom fell to the yard floor with a clatter, narrowly missing her right eye on its descent. She already had quite enough bruises from last night's scare. Holding one leg out in front of her, she balanced on the other and grimaced as she examined the damage.

She'd been lucky; most of the debris that had rained down had consisted of mud and soft dirt from the field. She'd got away with heavy bruising on her legs and a severe ringing in her ears which had lasted for several hours. Cupping the front of her foot, she pulled the leg up behind her and squinted backwards over her shoulder. There were circular marks on the back of her calf which were showing signs of blistering. It was funny how she hadn't even noticed them last night in the terror and exhilaration of scrambling indoors just before the blast that had destroyed the two houses in Brecknock Road.

Trying not to knock the blisters on the brickwork, she edged into the outhouse and dragged a heavy mangle clear of the rest of the rubbish that had accumulated over the past twenty years since the day the landlord had installed indoor plumbing and the outside lav had been relegated to junk store.

Stooping down, she sorted amongst the clothes in

the old tin bath, located the skirt she'd been wearing last night, and fed it carefully through the rollers. Shaking it out at the end of the operation, she saw with pleasure that it had come up good as new. It was the same with her underwear. The heavy topcoat had saved her. Poor old Rose hadn't been so lucky.

Several pieces of unidentifiable metal had plunged into Rose's skirt as she lay face down on the ground. Mercifully they had missed her legs, but in her panic she'd struggled to her feet, ripping her skirt to shreds, missed her footing on the greasy mud, and fallen backwards knocking herself out on the gatepost.

Lexie looked up at the drawn curtains above the grocer's shop. She ought to go round and see how Rose was, but Rose had been adamant that she shouldn't.

'I'll fetch yer mum, then,' Lexie had offered, applying a towel soaked in cold water as a compress across Rose's head. Both women were crouched under the heavy oak counter in the grocer's shop. Lexie had taken advantage of a lull in the bombing to dash back to the storeroom and hold the old tea-towel under the tap.

'No!' Rose had grasped her wrist and shook it. 'Promise you won't. I don't want my mum to know. She'll just try to get me to come home. And I'll have to see . . . other people.' Tears had welled into her blue eyes. 'Promise me, Lexie.'

'Yer, all right, if that's what you want. Don't carry on so.'

Rose had relaxed back against the pillow then, breathing out grateful thanks and orders not to knock tomorrow. 'I won't know if it's you or Mum come round to drag me home for my tea,' she'd explained.

'Please yerself,' Lexie had shrugged. 'It's eased off a bit out there. I'd better get back next door. But give us a tap if yer want anything.'

Looping a length of string across the yard now, she flicked the wet clothes over and gripped a mouthful of pegs between her lips. The tang of cordite and gritty dust tickled her nose briefly then the wind swept west again and brought the sooty breath of coal smuts from the railway line. Oh well, it was obviously going to be a choice of black spots or red spots. Pushing the last split wooden peg into position, she shoved the mangle away and bounced back into the house.

Her father was sewing buckles on a pair of black shoes, cursing and muttering as the silver metal slipped from his grasp. His hands became noticeably more shaky and his shoulders drooped as she passed.

Upstairs, the breakfast she'd cooked him lay untouched on his plate, congealing in grease. Ignoring it, she struggled into her coat, tied a scarf over her head, picked up her handbag and marched downstairs again. Frank looked up at her reappearance, she saw the flicker of disbelief in his eyes when he realised she was going out again. Two bright red spots glowed in his sallow cheeks; the feeble pain-racked body suddenly snapped upright, he started to splutter out, 'Where the hell, d'ya think . . .'

The rest of his sentence was cut off by the slamming back door.

Elsie Finch lived in a two-up, two-down terrace sandwiched between Chalk Farm Road in the west and Kentish Town Road in the east. As Lexie reached the door it was flung open and Albert White stepped out, threw back his head, and drew in a deep appreciative breath.

'Ah, wonderful morning. Just smell that air.'

Lexie had been smelling it ever since she turned into the street. The unmistakable scent of warm beer drifted in pungent clouds from Camden brewery. It did wonders for the trade of the two public houses at either end of the terrace.

The sound of singing, accompanied by a crashing pianoforte, rose behind him, forcing him to shout his 'hellos' at Lexie. 'Go on through, Elsie will be pleased to see you. I'm just popping down the road to see a man about me pig.'

'You got a pig?' Lexie was momentarily distracted from her main reason for coming here this morning.

Albert leant forward, and applied his whiskery lips to Lexie's ear. 'Pig club. One of the blokes gets us mash from the brewery. Reckons we can breed bitter-flavoured bacon rashers. Should be worth their weight in ration coupons.'

The choir behind him reached the final chorus of 'Rock of Ages'.

'Local chapel,' Albert explained. 'They come round once a month, seeing our Elsie can't go to them. Elsie plays the piano for them.'

The singers galloped towards the last line, with the piano determinedly leading by several notes. 'And every month the piano wins,' Albert added ruefully.

Lexie wavered. 'Look, if Elsie's got other visitors maybe it would be best if I come back later.'

'Why should you? She won't mind.'

But Lexie did. She didn't want a house full of witnesses. But she could hardly tell Albert that.

Fortunately, the meeting seemed to be breaking up. The scraping of chairs was followed by a chorus of 'goodbyes'.

Half a dozen women filed out, murmuring farewells.

'Lexie's here,' Albert called into the hall, thrusting the door flat and allowing her to edge past him into the passage. 'I'll be off now.'

'Don't be late back,' Elsie ordered, appearing from the parlour. 'I don't want me Yorkshire sinking.' The tantalising scents of roasting beef were emanating from the kitchen. Elsie excused herself to add potatoes and stuffed onions to the oven. Peeled carrots and chopped cabbage stood in pans ready to go on the rings.

'I didn't fink you could get onions for love nor money,' Lexie said enviously.

'Albert has his contacts,' Elsie admitted with the quiet confidence of one who was related to an open-handed grocer. Presumably his contacts also included a glazier since all the windows were filled with new glass and the smells of putty and linseed oil occasionally overwhelmed the delicious tang of the sizzling joint.

After she'd answered the usual queries about her own health, her father's health and the rest of Balaclava Row's health (all of which was of scant interest to Elsie, compared with her own health), Lexie approached the reason for her visit.

'One of me customers,' she said in a casually conversational tone, sipping a cup of tea and munching on a generous slice of madeira cake, 'was telling me 'ow when she 'ad 'er windows blown in, the bits went all down the floorboards in 'er bedroom. One of her

kids knelt on one weeks later and 'ad to be taken up
the casualty at St Pancras Hospital. Matter of fact,
it was the night they blew it up. Miracle 'e weren't
there when the bomb dropped. Missed him by
minutes.'

Unlike her brother, Elsie was built on tiny lines,
with thin limbs and quick darting movements that
resembled her namesake's. Now she fluttered with
the anxiety of a bird that had just spotted a large,
hungry ginger tom sniffing round the cage. Lexie
suppressed a pang of guilt and offered to take a look.
'Me eyes are younger than yours. Might see a bit you
missed.'

Half an hour later after a diligent search whilst
Elsie was busy with her pots and pans, Lexie had what
she'd come to find. Nestling safely in her handbag
was a bottle half filled with Elsie's sleeping draught,
whilst Elsie's bottle had been topped up with tap
water.

'Well 'bye then,' she said cheerfully. Twirling to
go, her skirt flew out, revealing, above her grey socks,
a portion of leg which was scarred by the blisters from
last night's bomb scare. She was forced to tell Elsie
the whole story and pass on Rose's request for no
visitors.

'But Albert will want to go round, see she's all right.'

'Best not to tell him until the morning then.'

Elsie accepted this suggestion with the alacrity of
the truly self-centred. Once she'd ascertained that
there had been no damage to the shop or its stock,
she even rewarded Lexie with a quarter of tea.

Instead of returning via Kentish Town Road, Lexie
worked her way northwards along Castlehaven Road

– still known locally as Grange and 'Toria. Just before she came out into Prince of Wales Road, she paused, and looked around her as if seeing the area for the first time. The brief spell of Indian summer was holding and, if you kept your eyes on the ground, it was almost possible to believe that this was just another normal Sunday. Lift them up though, and the illusion was shattered. Everything, from the hastily boarded-up windows to the barrage balloons floating above the rooftops and the unexpected glimpses of daylight through gaps that had once been someone's home, added to her sense of depression. She'd wanted things to change, some nights she'd lain in bed and prayed aloud to God to make something happen to jolt her life out of its familiar, well-used, tracks. And, now it had, she was frightened, not of death, but of change.

Mentally shaking herself, Lexie squared her shoulders and marched across Prince of Wales Road. She turned towards the High Street, but just before she reached it, she ducked instead through a white stone arch and into a quadrangle ringed by blocks of flats. The one she wanted was in the centre; it was the last address she had for a certain Mrs Alan Milligan. She'd already visited it once before and found it apparently empty.

This time she took the precaution of placing her ear against the panels before she knocked. But her sharp rat-tat brought no answer again, neither could she detect the sounds of anyone hastily ducking out of sight in case the unwanted visitor peered through the letter box. Satisfied she'd done all she could, she turned away – and froze.

A man was treading slowly and ponderously up the stairs. Lexie stared at his red cap like a mouse mesmerised by a stoat. By the time she'd recovered her wits, it was too late to move. Turning back to the door, she rapped again, and called, 'Hello, dear. Are you in? I'm from the local Temperance League. If I could just take a moment of your time?'

The military policeman was on her shoulder, she could feel his breath tickling her ear. 'Is she in?'

'Apparently not.' Lexie had adopted the rounded vowels of one of their posher customers. 'Although to be quite honest with you, er . . .' He had stripes. ' . . . with you, *Sergeant*, I fear that sometimes they do not open the door when they know that I have come to save them from the evils of alcohol. Are you interested in purifying your soul through abstinence from the demon drink?'

('Don't let him say yes,' she prayed silently.)

'I don't give a pig's ear about purifying me soul, miss. Do you know the woman who lives here?'

'I'm afraid, as I've explained, I haven't yet had the pleasure. Nor, apparently, am I going to get it this morning. So I'll wish you good morning and pray that you find salvation.'

She left him banging loudly with the flat of his hand against the wooden panels and made good her escape as several heads popped out to see what the row was about.

Her dad had come round by the time she arrived home. The prospect of no cooked dinner forced him into a grudging enquiry.

'I couldn't see no joint in the larder to go in the oven,' he said.

'There ain't any. I told yer, the meat ration don't go nowhere if we 'ave a Sunday joint. I done a kidney pudding. Water back on?'

'An hour ago.'

Lexie put the steamed pudding and potatoes on the gas rings, ignoring the disappointed droop of Frank's mouth. 'I'm just popping round to Alice's.'

'What again!'

'I want to check the water's come on proper.'

'Best let me do that. You don't understand about plumbing.'

'I want to get a pair of stockings as well. Alice won't want you going through her underwear. Shan't be long.' She whisked out before he could argue.

The keys were already in her bag. They'd been there for a couple of days to ensure that nobody else could use them. Letting herself in, she launched into a few snatches of 'Pack Up Your Troubles in Your Old Kit Bag'.

'You still can't carry a tune, Carrots.'

'I know. And don't call me Carrots.'

'Whatever you say – Alexandra.'

Lexie wrinkled her nose at the tall, thin-faced man with the skin the colour of tea-dyed curtains who had just emerged on to the landing.

'Brought you a present.' She extended the quarter of tea. 'You still all right for food?'

'Yer. Alice left plenty of tins in the cupboard. I been eating them cold.'

'Ugh! Isn't the gas on?'

'Smells if anyone comes in.'

'There's only me got the keys. And Alice. And she ain't going to split on yer.'

'I know. She's a good sort Alice. Thinks of me as a son.'

'She thinks of me as a daughter. I suppose that makes us related.'

'Pleased to meet you, Sis,' he responded, sticking out a hand.

Lexie shook it and gave a low laugh. For a moment, in the lined face, she'd glimpsed the sixteen-year-old boy who'd peeled spuds and gutted fish in the Wellers' shop.

'That Alan's sweet on you,' her mother had said.

'He stinks of cod,' she'd replied with a toss of the corkscrew curls that had reached to her waist. 'Anyway, I don't want to walk out with no fish fryer from Kentish Town. I'm gonna travel. To America, and Africa and China.'

'You've got ideas above your station, my girl,' her mother had warned. 'If you're not careful you'll end up on the shelf.'

At sixteen the idea had been ludicrous. She had looks, despite the awful-coloured hair. There would be plenty of time for courting once she'd seen the streets of New York, and the jungles in Africa and pagodas and temples in China.

A fortnight later, her mother had taken to her bed on Monday and been dead by Thursday, leaving Lexie to keep house for her waspish, demanding, manipulative father.

So it was the fish fryer who'd joined the Army and travelled. He'd come back a couple of times on leave, leaner and thinner each time, but still casting speculative eyes in her direction. Then, abruptly, he'd gone.

'Posted to India,' Alice had said, waving a sheet of paper redolent with strange scents. 'And met a girl from Somers Town. Fancy that now.'

She'd not seen him for years, until the other night when he'd nearly caused her to have a heart attack when he'd stepped out of the shadows of Alice's spare room.

'I wish I could have seen India,' Lexie sighed, seating herself on the floor of the spare room and hugging her knees to her chin. Alan had only allowed her to draw the curtains in the bedroom in case the sudden change in the flat's appearance attracted attention. Consequently, he had to move around the rest of the flat bent double, being careful not to bob above window height. Without realising it, she'd started to imitate him. 'Alice used to read us all your letters.'

'Used to write to me about you too,' Alan said, leaning against the wall next to her. 'Kept expecting to hear you'd got yourself wed.'

He failed to notice the slight stiffening in Lexie's attitude as she haughtily announced that she had quite enough to do looking after one bloke without taking on another one.

'Talking of being wed, did you see that lying wife of mine?' Alan said.

'No. I went round the flat again but there weren't no answer, like the last time when I went to post Alice's coat. I reckon the flat's empty.'

'The letter was right then. She's moved in with her fancy bloke.'

'Maybe she's just gone visiting.'

'Who?' he demanded, his voice rasping in the

darkness. 'Only relative she had was this aunt she's supposed to be nursing. And if Connie's gone visiting, what's she done with the old girl?'

'Buried her in East Finchley,' Lexie revealed. 'I asked one of the neighbours. Didn't like to ask about yer missus as well, in case they told . . . anyone . . . I'd been asking.'

He caught the slight hesitancy in her voice.

'Who's been nosing around?' he demanded sharply.

She told him about the military policeman.

Swearing under his breath, he asked if she was sure she hadn't been followed.

'Dead sure. I ain't stupid.'

Half to himself, Alan muttered, 'I hope you're right. I was so bloody careful coming up here. Nobody saw me, except the worst driver this side of the Thames.'

Unaware of his ride with Ethel, Lexie might have queried this remark if a sound from beyond the bedroom hadn't caught her attention. 'Hey. Ain't that the lav in the Donalds' place?'

'She's back. The wife, I suppose. Man and woman brought her late yesterday.'

'Yeah? Well, why didn't she come round, say hello. Even if we ain't exactly close, we *are* her neighbours. How'd we even know she was in there if there was a raid? I wonder if she went round one of the others. Rose maybe.'

'She all right now?'

'Fine. Gonna 'ave a rotten lump on the back of her head, but it don't show.'

'She doesn't remember it was me carried her in, does she?'

'Nah. Thinks I got coal-heaver's muscles, don't she?'

A thumb and two fingers squeezed the top of her arm playfully, then slid round her shoulder. 'Thanks for being a mate, Sis.'

"S all right.'

Lexie sat unnaturally still, unused to the intimacy of the touch.

'Do something else for us?'

'What?'

'Make us a brew while I flush the lav.'

'Eh?'

'Well I can't do it when the place is supposed to be empty. You heard yourself how it sounds next door. Then fill us up a sink of water. I'll 'ave a wash and shave while you're here.'

'You'd better get a move on, before Dad comes round to find out why it's taking me so long to fetch a pair of stockings.'

He did as she suggested, lathering and scraping away the stubble in record time. Afterwards they sat in the kitchen, elbows on the table which had been moved away from the window, sipping mugs of tea.

'You look daft in that lot,' Lexie said after a while.

He looked down at the baggy shirt and trousers. 'Blame Alice for feeding her old man too well.'

There was another uneasy silence between them.

'You got to find out where she's scarpered to, Lexie. I don't reckon she's gone far. I was still sending me letters to the flat. So she must 'ave gone back to pick 'em up.'

'I'll do me best. But it ain't easy to keep finding excuses to leave the shop. Wouldn't it be best to just go back to camp? Give yerself up. I mean, they give yer leave to sort these things out, don't they? When

141

the usherette at the Forum starting walking out wiv a porter from the hospital, they give her old man forty-eight hours' leave to come home and thump him.'

Alan ran a thick, callused thumb around the rim of the mug. He collected a few wet tea leaves and examined them with interest. 'No,' he said. 'I can't do that.'

'Oh.' The question hung over the wooden table. Unspoken and unanswered. Why not?

They were released by a furious bashing on the back door.

'Lexie. What you doing? You all right in there, girl?'

Lexie fled into the sitting room and flung open the window. 'Just coming, Dad,' she called down. 'Couldn't find the stockings nowhere.'

The pale disc of his face turned up towards her. In angry tones he informed her the potatoes had boiled and he was starving.

'I shan't be a sec.'

Rooting in the chest of drawers, she untangled a pair of thick lisle stockings and panted her goodbyes.

Halfway down the stairs, she turned back and asked the question. 'Why can't you just go back?'

'Because I hit a bloke who tried to stop me leaving,' Alan Milligan said with grim resignation. 'And I reckon I hurt him real bad. Maybe I even killed him.'

Chapter 9

The door to the flat crashed open and feet thundered up the stairs, bouncing vibrations from the uncarpeted wood. A balled fist hammered against the closed doors of the sitting room, bathroom and kitchen whilst a furious voice roared for admission.

The rumpus drew light feet on to the landing above.

'Albert? Whatever's the matter?'

Albert scowled upwards. 'What's the matter? Pretty obvious, ain't it? Elsie only just told me. I pedalled up here fast as I could. Why didn't you send a message to the house? I could 'ave come yesterday.'

'There was no need. The shop's perfectly all right. You can see for yourself. Most of the blast went the other way; it didn't even crack the windows.'

'Damn the shop! What about you? Elsie said you was hurt.'

'Just a bit of a bump.' Rose touched the tender spot on the back of her head and winced. 'No lasting damage. Lexie dragged me inside.'

Albert refused to be pacified. His big face glowing red from indignation and the exertions of pedalling up Kentish Town Road on the bone-shaking bicycle he used for transport, he tramped into the kitchen feeling the kettle, examining the frying pan and peering into the cupboard. 'You 'aven't had breakfast. I'll get you something from the shop.'

'I ate hours ago. Stop fussing, Albert.' She took the

143

sting from this instruction by planting a kiss on his glowing cheek. 'Now let me make you a cup of tea before we open up.'

Grumbling and protesting, Albert allowed himself to be pushed into a chair.

'Once the first rush is over, Albert,' Rose said, adding fresh water to the used leaves in the pot, 'would it be all right if I had a couple of hours off?'

'Of course it would. In fact, don't come down at all. I can manage. You have a lie down.'

'I don't want a rest. I need to go out for a while.'

'Oh?' Albert mulled this idea over, and concluded she wanted to go round to her mum's.

Rose didn't disillusion him.

Riley Street School hadn't changed. Like most public buildings in the area, it had been built of the inevitable London yellow brick. The designer had included a pattern of red bricks round each of the tall sash windows in an attempt to provide some kind of aesthetic decoration to an otherwise ugly structure. Unfortunately, he hadn't reckoned on the proximity of the railway. Forty years of coal smuts and soot-laden fogs had deposited a patina of dirt over the walls and reduced all the colours underneath to a uniformly grubby shade of greyish-black.

Stepping back a few paces, Rose squinted against the bright sky and saw that the wire caging enclosing the rooftop playground was still there.

She walked through a small archway entrance and mounted the stairs to the door marked 'Boys' since it led directly to the corridor containing the head-master's office. Pushing it open, she stepped through and was instantly transported back twenty years by the familiar smells: chalk dust, sweaty feet, musty books and – for some strange reason since the school had no canteen – mashed potatoes.

The secretary reacted to Rose's request for an interview with an assumption.

'He really likes parents to make an appointment, Mrs . . . ?'

'Goodwin. Mrs Rose Goodwin.'

'Take a seat, Mrs Goodwin. And I'll see if he's prepared to see you.'

Rose perched on an old wooden chair, the centre of its seat rubbed to a paler shade by the fidgeting backsides of generations of children who'd been despatched to 'sit outside the headmaster's office until the bell rings'.

She had to stifle an impulse to polish the front of her shoes on the back of her calves before the secretary returned.

Ushered into the headmaster's office, she found him poring over a large ledger. 'Goodwin?' he said, running a finger down the lists of names in the register. 'I'm so sorry, Mrs Goodwin, I don't seem to be able to find a Goodwin. What Christian name is it?'

'I'm not a parent,' Rose admitted. She took a deep breath, feeling the air pushing down the nausea gurgling in her stomach. 'I understand that you've recently lost two teachers: Mr Perkins and Miss Gilbert.'

'Well yes that's correct, but I don't see . . .'

'In that case,' Rose rushed on, 'I'd like to apply for one of the jobs. I've brought my Teacher's Certificate. And a reference from my last school.'

Clicking open her bag, she thrust the documents at the bemused headmaster before he had time to formulate a refusal.

Whilst he was trying to think of some way to get this forceful young woman out of his office, the headmaster was automatically smoothing out the sheets of paper. His eyes dropped to the date on the reference.

'This is nearly five years old. If you don't have any more recent experience . . .' Relieved to have found such an easy escape route, the headmaster started to stand.

Rose kept her seat. 'I was asked to leave when I married.'

'Well, yes, of course. We have the same policy here. I'm afraid we don't employ married women either.' He tried to give the documents back to her. Rose ignored them.

'I'm a widow. My husband was wounded at Dunkirk and died shortly afterwards.'

The headmaster's seat sank reluctantly back towards his chair. He still had no intention of employing her, but the circumstances clearly called for a tactful refusal. He made a pretence of reading the reference whilst he sought for the right words. As he scanned the lines, he felt his interest quicken; it was very complimentary about Miss Rose Tammie's teaching skills; very complimentary indeed.

Refolding the letter, he drummed his fingers consideringly.

'Posh' Perkins's call-up had been expected – and not entirely regretted. The man had always acted as if teaching in Kentish Town was akin to missionary work in Matabelee land. But Miss Gilbert was a different matter.

On the wall behind his desk was a picture of the school's first infant class. In those days they'd segregated the sexes. Behind the rows of cross-legged little girls stood Miss Gilbert, her face grim beneath the hair bun, her chin resting firmly on the high-necked starched blouse, her hands folded over the waistband of the tight ankle-length skirt. In her hand was the famous cane; a long thin length of willow, tapering to one end, that was nearly as tall as she was.

For forty years, Miss Gilbert had stalked between the rows of desks, first in the female infants, and in later years in the mixed. At the first sign of transgression, the cane would whip down, with an accuracy that a fly-fisher would have envied, and catch the offender a swift and painful crack on the soft flesh of his or her ear lobe. The headmaster had seen middle-aged women cross the street, one hand cupped over their right ear, whenever they saw Miss Gilbert approaching.

And now she was dead. He'd pieced together what had happened later that day by questioning the children. Miss Gilbert had written a list of spelling words on the blackboard and ordered the class to copy them on to their slates.

'Once you have finished writing,' she'd announced with crisp authority, 'you will put your chalk down, fold your arms neatly on the desk, and remain in that position until I tell you you may move.'

Having issued her orders, Miss Gilbert had then clutched her chest with considerably less drama than Sammy O'Day's performance, quietly slid to the floor – and died.

It was only when the playground teacher realised that the mixed infants were absent from the morning break that the headmaster had gone to investigate and found forty small children sitting with folded arms, eyes fixed on the blackboard, whilst Miss Gilbert lay dead behind her desk.

'She was so small,' he said speaking to himself. He'd thought of Miss Gilbert as seven feet tall. It had come as a shock to see the way she'd shrunk in death; like looking at a piece of elastic that had always been at full stretch and now had sprung back to its original length. 'She was only . . .' He indicated a position just over his shoulder. 'Not much bigger than the children.'

He saw from the way she rubbed her right earlobe that Rose knew to whom he was referring.

'Do you think you are capable of stepping into Miss Gilbert's shoes, Mrs Goodwin? Of carrying on in her tradition.'

'I wouldn't want to. Frankly, I've always thought she was a dreadful bully.'

The headmaster blinked. His mouth dropped open. To speak ill of the dead was not customary. To speak ill of Miss Gilbert (alive or dead) was equivalent to sacrilege.

He thought about what she'd just said – and realised with some surprise that he agreed with her. 'I wonder if you would mind waiting in my secretary's office whilst I make a couple of telephone calls, Mrs Goodwin.'

The headmistress of Rose's previous school did indeed remember Miss Tammie. Her casual enquiry as to Miss Tammie's current address confirmed his suspicions that his wasn't the only school suffering from a staff shortage now that male teachers were no longer exempt from conscription and females under twenty-six could (and were) joining up.

The chairman of the School Board had lost his only son at Dunkirk. Providing employment for a Dunkirk widow healed a minuscule part of his grief.

Rose left Riley Street with a temporary appointment to be reviewed at the end of three months – and the seemingly insurmountable problem of explaining to Albert that she had to start tomorrow.

To her surprise, he was delighted. 'That's the spirit, love. You want to get out in the world, not go hiding yourself away in this shop with old Albert.'

'I thought it would take weeks to check my references,' she explained, one eye on the shopwindow in case a customer came in. 'I'm so sorry. But you did say you'd be giving up the shop, so I thought I'd better find another job. If you'd like me to leave the flat, I'll quite understand.'

'Leave! Course I don't want you to leave. I can have a schoolteacher as a tenant, can't I?'

'I'll still do the books in the evenings. And I'm sure there are plenty of women who'd be pleased to help out in the shop.'

'I'm sure too. It's finding one who ain't going to help herself that's the problem. But don't you worry, leave that to me.' Seizing her shoulders, he planted a wet kiss on either cheek.

'Oi, oi,' Lexie said, coming in to the accompaniment of the jangling bell. 'When's the banns going up then?'

Rose flushed and Albert beamed. Before she could stop him, he'd told her the news.

'Fancy you taking Miss Gilbert's place,' Lexie

marvelled. 'Got yer throat cutter.' Her fingers described a collar round her throat. 'And yer hobble skirt.'

Rose caught her bottom lip. 'My clothes. I'd forgotten. My skirt, Saturday night. It's only fit for the rag cart.'

'Well, ain't you got another one? You must 'ave more clothes than yer best and that old dress and cardy you wear in the shop?'

'I've a skirt Auntie Mabel gave me last month. But it's right down to my ankles. She must have had it for forty years.'

Albert pressed down the 'No Sale' on the massive cash register. Extracting five pound notes from the clip, he placed them on the counter. 'Here, love, you go round to Daniel's. Get yourself something nice.'

'No. No.' Rose's blue eyes widened in genuine distress. 'I can't do that, Albert. I can't take your money.'

'Why not?'

'Yeah. Why not?' Lexie echoed. She couldn't remember a time when her father had ever dipped into the till on her account for anything more than the bare essentials.

'I just can't.' Rose knew they'd never understand even if she attempted to explain. The blast on Saturday night had shaken her in more ways than one. Lying in bed on the Sunday it had dawned on her that she might never have seen this day. That yesterday could have been the last day of her life.

For a long time now she'd had the sensation that she was standing on a station platform whilst the train, with everyone else on board – Albert, Lexie, even Molly Winslow – was slowly gathering speed with each whoosh and shunt of its massive steam engine and drawing away from her. She'd been content to see it go. But this morning, unexpectedly, she'd found herself taking a few tentative steps down the platform. She wanted to catch the train after all. There was still a long way to go but she knew she couldn't do it if she started accepting handouts, even from a sweetie like Albert.

'It was a very generous thought but you keep it, Albert,' she said, tucking the notes back into his big hand. 'There's nothing wrong with my old skirt that a pair of scissors and some hemming won't cure.'

'I'll run it up on Alice's machine for you if you like,' Lexie said eagerly.

'Are you sure?'

'Dead sure. No trouble at all. Mind if we pop up and 'ave a look now, Albert? I can take it back wiv me.'

'Please yourself.' Crestfallen, Albert replaced the notes.

'Did you know Gwen was back?' Lexie mumbled through a mouthful of pins. 'Turn round and hang on to that waistband. You've lost weight. I'll take the button over a couple of inches.'

Rose twirled on the kitchen chair. 'When did she come back? Is she all right? I'll go round soon as you've finished this.'

'Wouldn't bother. I went yesterday. Acted like I'd come to pinch the silver.'

'She's upset, Lexie. Did she say anything about James?'

'Co-op are doing the funeral.'

'Is the body . . . ?' Rose nodded, in the general direction of the Donalds' shop.

'No. Police say she can't have it until they've found out what done him in. Finished.' Lexie sat back on her heels. 'You can step out now.'

'I think I'll go round anyway. I mean, it's not very nice, is it? Not paying your respects,' Rose said, pulling the old cotton dress over her head.

'Don't say I didn't warn you.' Lexie folded the skirt over her arm. 'I'll do this after tea. See ya later.'

Gwen Donald received Rose's condolences with calm thanks and immediately excused herself so that she could continue to check the stock and accounts.

Apparently, everyone else from Balaclava Row was met with the same reception.

'She's not the emotional type,' Helen Fortune said when she slipped into the grocer's to change a pound note. 'I told that policeman that.'

'Did 'e say anything. About what happened?' Albert asked, counting out piles of silver. 'There yer are. Ten shillings, twenty tanners, that do you?'

Helen scooped up the change gratefully. 'Thanks. No, he didn't say anything. But then he's hardly likely to tell me, is he? Must dash, I've left a permanent wave setting.'

But she wasn't allowed to go until Albert, beaming proudly as if it was all his idea, had told her about Rose's new job.

'That's wonderful, Rose. Congratulations,' Helen fumbled for the door catch, with visions of a half-bald customer floating before her. 'Come round after work. I'll give you a cut and set it – on the house.'

'That's not . . . necessary,' Rose said to the empty door.

She would have preferred to keep her plans secret until she was established at Riley Street. But she knew it was pointless asking Albert to be discreet. Most of the neighbourhood knew about Rose Goodwin's new job by the time she turned the shop sign round to 'Closed' that evening.

Everyone it seemed wanted to help. Matthew Fortune came downstairs, whilst his sister was mixing up shampoo powder and massaging it into Rose's hair, to offer a briefcase.

'Helen bought me a new one, so I don't need this any more.' He twisted it, dangling it over her nose as she leant backwards over the basin for the rinse. 'I thought you could carry books in it.'

A towel shot over her head and her hair was squeezed into a damp ponytail. 'Thank you, Matt. It's smashing.' She tweaked a corner of the towel up to smile at him, just in time to see his right hand disappearing into his jacket pocket. 'You shouldn't mind you know. No one else does.'

'I don't. It's just a stupid habit I got as a kid. See.' He whisked her towel away with the deformed hand in the manner of a matador working a cape and dodged a sisterly clout.

Helen flicked an expert comb through the damp locks, parting, dividing and instructing Rose to put her head forward. ' I suppose,' she remarked, 'you had to find something else, now that Albert's leaving.'

'How did you know about that?'

'He mentioned it a few weeks ago. When we were discussing the leases.'

Rose was surprised and a little aggrieved to find

that she didn't always have first place in Albert's confidences.

'Three down eh?' Matthew said, sitting in the other styling chair and thrusting his long legs out in front of him. 'The Wellers aren't coming back, did you know?'

'Lexie said. How do you mean three down?'

He touched his thumb against the little finger of his strong hand. 'The Wellers.' The thumb moved to the index finger. 'Albert. And the Donalds.' The thumb scored off the Donalds on the middle finger.

Her chin on her chest, Rose said indistinctly, 'What do you mean, Gwen hasn't left for good?'

'I don't suppose she'll come back now, will she? I mean, it was James who was the jeweller. Did all the repairs and alterations and making up bits and pieces. She won't want all the bother of finding an assistant to do all that, will she? I reckon she'll sell the stock and stay down on this farm.'

It hadn't occurred to Rose before. But once he said it, she could see it made sense.

'There you are then. As I said: three down. Only two more to go, Sis.'

The damp fringe hung down in front of her eyes like prison bars. Looking up quickly now, Rose glanced through the dark gold strands and saw Helen catch her brother's eye in the mirror and shake her head slightly before telling him to get out from under her feet.

Cold steel slid over her damp skin, sending chills down the back of her neck, as Helen snipped expertly. An hour later, she'd been curled, dried and combed out. 'Thank heavens for that,' Helen said, bending the last strand over her fingers and pushing it into place. 'I'm always afraid they'll cut the water or the electricity whilst I'm in the middle of doing a customer.'

Pulling towels and overall off Rose, she shook them vigorously, flung them on a pile of dirty laundry and fetched a broom from the back room.

Rose admired her reflection the mirror. 'It's lovely, Helen. Thanks. Are you sure I can't pay you for it?'

'I'll be offended if you try. It's nice to see someone getting what they want out of life before it's too late.'

Rose looked at Helen's dark cap of hair as it bobbed with each vigorous pass of the broom. A glint of light caught a solitary grey hair in the black. She wasn't the only person that time was passing by.

As if she was aware of the scrutiny, Helen straightened up, leant on her broom – and smiled. 'There. All finished. I'll just let you out before I put a mop over the floor. Then I'd better get on with the tea. Matthew will be starving.'

'Can't he cook it?'

Helen gave a hollow laugh as she snapped the light off and released the door bolts. 'Could Peter?'

The approaching dampness of the evening after the warm shop sent a shiver over Rose's body. At least, that's what she told herself. She was saved the bother of replying by the arrival of Josepha who thrust her way into the opening door.

'Good. You still open. I need hair-grips. This hair it won't stay up. See?'

Pulling the door out of Helen's hand, she shut it, put the light back on, and twirled to give them the full effect of her new hairstyle: it had been piled and twisted in loops on top of her head and insecurely fixed by pins that were already sliding out.

'I haven't got—' Helen began. She was cut off by the door hurtling open again. 'The blackout!' she called warningly.

Maria slammed the door shut again with a crash that rattled the windows. 'Where you goin'?' she demanded.

'I got a date,' Josepha said. 'He's waiting for me.' She slid complacent hands over a jumper and skirt that clung like paint.

'You're not going out dressed like that, you look like a whore.'

'You should know.'

'Come here.' Twisting her hands in her sister's rapidly descending curls, Maria attempted to drag her from the shop to the accompaniment of loud squeals.

Calmly, Helen picked up the fire bucket and emptied the contents over the fighting girls.

Rose fled.

The flat felt cold and unwelcoming after the company of the hairdresser's.

Running a hot bath, she wrapped a towel carefully round the newly set hair, made herself a cup of cocoa, and luxuriated in the soapy water, enjoying the forgotten sensation of self-indulgence. It was a long time since she'd been kind to herself.

Even the Luftwaffe seemed to be on her side today; the alarms stayed silent, allowing her to close her eyes and float away on daydreams.

Suddenly she sat bolt upright, her heart thudding violently.

Straining her ears, she listened intently, certain

that she'd heard the creak of floorboards somewhere in the flat.

She'd undressed in the bedroom, so she had no choice but to wrap the inadequate towel around herself and tiptoe cautiously on to the landing.

'Hello?' she called, her voice scarcely audible even to herself. 'Albert? Is that you?'

Only the violent thudding of her own heart answered her. She took a couple more steps, leaving damp prints on the strip of carpet in the hall. 'Hello?'

'Hello! I finished it. All right if I come up.' Brandishing the skirt, Lexie took the stairs two at time, arriving at the top wreathed in smiles which faded when she saw Rose's face. 'What's the matter?'

'I thought you were . . . Oh, never mind.' The wet towel was slipping. 'I'll just get dry.'

Lexie followed her into the bathroom, and sat on the edge of the bath whilst she towelled herself. 'It's come up nice,' she said, turning over the hem to display her stitching. 'I've been thinking. You used to 'ave a lovely beige costume suit, I remember saying to Alice that I wouldn't mind one like that. What 'appened to that?'

'It wore out. Lexie, how did you get in?'

'What yer mean? I come in the back, same as usual.'

'But it was locked. I always lock the doors after Albert goes.'

'You must have forgotten.'

Rose struggled to remember. She'd been busy trying to stop her new hairstyle blowing around in the gusting wind. Just after she'd stepped into the stockroom, she'd turned to twist the key and caught a glimpse of her reflection in the window. And then

. . . She experienced a chill of horror as she realised that, for the first time, she'd forgotten to lock herself in.

Lexie, who had been complacently admiring her own sewing, straightened up suddenly. 'What was that?'

'What?'

'Thought I heard someone.' A knowing look suffused Lexie's freckled features. 'Heh I ain't in the way, am I? You should have said if I was being a goosegog.'

'No. Of course you're not. There's no one else here.'

She'd scarcely said it, when the protesting creak of a badly warped floorboard sounded from somewhere. Rose's instinct would have been to lock the bathroom door, but Lexie had sprung across the room and whipped it open before she could move.

Clasping the damp towel, Rose went after her.

Lexie had disappeared when she reached the stockroom. Padding barefoot into the dark yard, Rose peered around.

'Lexie?'

'Lost 'im,' Lexie said disconsolately, slouching back through the gate. 'He scarpered over the field. Let's 'ope he falls in the bomb 'ole. Didn't even get a decent look at him.'

'Everything all right, miss?' The sudden appearance of a third shape, looming in the gateway took them both by surprise. In the pale starlight, they saw the blue and white striped band on the man's right wrist.

The weak beam of the policeman's torch slid past Lexie and played up and down Rose. It lingered rather longer than was necessary to establish her identity.

Possibly the young constable was trying to work out why she was standing in the backyard wearing nothing but a towel which not only started halfway down her breasts and ended before the curve of her bottom, but was also so wet that it left nothing to the imagination regarding what was beneath it.

"Ad a good eyeful?' Lexie demanded.

'Yes thanks,' he grinned, unabashed.

'Well when you finished gawping, me friend's had someone broke in her place.'

The constable's knowing look was instantly replaced by a square-shouldered alertness. 'Which way did he go?'

'Over there.' Lexie jerked a thumb over her shoulder at the crater-potted field. 'It ain't no good chasing him though, he's good and gone by now.'

'What did he look like?'

'Dunno. Never got a decent look. Smallish and thinnish I fink.'

The constable disappeared in the indicated direction anyway, much to Rose's relief since it gave her the chance to skip back upstairs without the torch beam playing on the exposed portion of her backside.

By the time he returned to confirm there was no sign of the intruder, she'd pulled on her old dress and cardigan and was able to face him with a reasonable degree of composure despite the cheeky wink he bestowed on her when Lexie's back was turned.

'Anything missing?' he asked.

'Not that I can see. I haven't anything worth stealing and Albert – Mr White – always banks the takings each night.'

'Probably some tealeaf out to make 'imself a few

quid on the black market. I'll 'ave a look round, see you're all right.'

He did so thoroughly, climbing to check the attic and scrambling down a rickety ladder to shine his torch around the damp cellar, as well as searching in all possible hiding places in the other rooms before leaving them with a cheery 'goodnight, ladies' and another wink.

'He's a cheeky blighter, but I expect 'e's right,' Lexie remarked, preparing to go herself. 'It was just someone wanting a dip in Albert's private stocks. You can come and stop round our place if yer nervous about bein' on yer own.'

'There's no need. In fact, I think it was probably all your imagination, Lexie. After all, I never saw anyone.'

Indignantly, Lexie started to argue, but Rose seemed strangely insistent on denying the burglar's existence.

Chapter 10

Stamford had had a very frustrating couple of days. He'd assumed that it would be a simple matter to trace James Donald's mistress. He'd a shrewd suspicion that none of the potential candidates in Balaclava Row was going to volunteer the information, but that didn't matter since they had the private investigator's evidence.

'There's no definite evidence that she's connected to Donald's murder. In fact, until we get the post mortem results, we can't even be sure it *was* murder. But even if she isn't involved, there's a chance that she saw something – or Donald confided in her – so let's go track the fox to his lair, Sergeant,' he'd remarked with breezy confidence as they left Gwen Donald to her checking once more and made their way back to the police station.

The newspaper advertisement for the French Investigation Agency had directed clients to reply to a box number c/o the paper. Gwen Donald had confirmed that all her correspondence with Mr Fox had come and gone via the same box number. Therefore it was obviously going to be a few minutes' work to obtain the mailing address for that particular box from the paper.

Wrong!

After the telephone had rung fruitlessly for five minutes, Sarah had diffidently suggested that since

161

the paper normally came out once a week on Thursdays, there was really no need for them to be working on Sunday.

'Damn, I forgot it was Sunday. Is there a copy of the paper in the station by any chance?'

'I'll ask.'

She returned five minutes later with two spots of colour burning brightly in her cheeks having discovered that the supposed affair between herself and Stamford was still a prime piece of canteen gossip. Grimly sticking to her resolve to let the whole thing blow over rather than possibly adding fuel to the flames by involving Stamford, she merely told him that the station copy of the paper was at the bottom of the cook's daughter's rabbit hutch. 'It might still be readable, I suppose. Do you want me to go round there?'

'No. I've seen a copy somewhere else recently. Now where was it?' A picture clicked into place: himself seated in the O'Days' kitchen idly reading the back of an outstretched newspaper. 'Maury, that's it. Maury had one. Come on. Let's pray this one isn't under the chickens.'

It wasn't, although several pages were now festooned over Eileen's clotheshorse in the shape of linked rows of dancing dolls.

'Maury was cross,' Annaliese informed Sarah, in a voice husky with approaching cold.

'Was he? Well I'm sure your daddy will get him another paper.' She gave the little girl a hug and Annaliese didn't resist.

Stamford noted that once again, she'd placed another grown-up between herself and him. He scanned through the flimsy dolls, pretending he didn't mind. 'Here it is. Editor: George Stanhangar. Thank heavens he's not called Smith. We can telephone from my house.'

Mrs Stanhangar confirmed that they had the right man. She also informed them that her husband had left early that morning to take part in a training exercise in Epping Forest with the renamed Home Guard.

'They've given him a gun,' she said in a tone of resignation. 'He couldn't wait to go and play with it.'

'Does he have an assistant?'

'Oh yes. He's in the Guard too.'

'What about the staff?'

The office staff consisted of 'Old Ben' and 'the girl'. Mrs Stanhangar couldn't supply a surname or address for the girl, but had heard that Ben usually drank in the Bull and Gate. Today was no exception. Ben *had* drunk in the Bull and Gate. In fact, he'd drunk so much that they eventually located him in the cells at Agar Street. One look at the slack mouth and a lungful of the overwhelming stench of beer-laden breath that erupted every time a snore spluttered from whiskered nostrils told them that there was no chance of getting any sense from him until Monday morning.

They were forced to await Mr Stanhangar's return from manoeuvres in Epping Forest on Sunday evening. In answer to Stamford's query he blithely informed them that he had no idea where the classified ads information was filed. 'I always leave all that side of thing to the girl. She'll know. You ask her.'

'We'd love too. But your wife didn't know her name, or her address.'

The click of exasperation erupted from the earpiece. 'Her name's Mary Smith, how can anyone forget a name like that?'

Without bothering to move the mouthpiece, he bawled the same question at his wife, half deafening Stamford before he could hold the receiver at arm's length.

'What about the address?' Jack found himself shouting too.

Mary Smith lived in Raglan Street. If they'd stood on the station roof at Agar Street, they could have thrown a stone into her garden.

It was then that Jack began to get an uneasy feeling. 'This is going to be a bugger of a case,' he murmured.

'Pardon, sir?'

'Er, never mind. I'll tell you some other time.' Belatedly Jack remembered that his current assistant was female. Despite knowing her for six months, he still wasn't sure quite where Sergeant McNeill's modesty level lay. She seemed unshockable, but perhaps that was just in her job. For all he knew, she had other standards for her personal life.

The Smiths, predictably, insisted on ushering the two officers into a small cold parlour, and seating them on two overstuffed armchairs which had been untouched by human bottoms since the vicar last called.

'Why can't we ever talk in kitchens?' Jack whispered.

From the side of her mouth, Sarah murmured back: 'You could if you were a sergeant, sir. It's what wiv you being a nob and all,' she added, relapsing briefly into her childhood dialect with a twinkle in her blue eyes.

Mary smelt strongly of fish and salt. Scrubbing at her hands with a dish cloth she explained apologetically that she'd been helping her mum to shell shrimps for their supper. 'The bits stick.'

Not until she was satisfied her hands were clean, would she accept the cutting Sarah was holding out to her.

'We need the forwarding address for this agency. Will you come back to the office and open up the files please? Mr Stanhangar has given his permission.'

Mary scorned any suggestion that she needed files. 'Forty-nine Waterman's Lane, Stepney, that's where I forwarded the letters.'

'Are you certain?'

'Dead certain. I'm going to be a journalist. You need to have a good memory for facts. Besides,' she added with a burst of candour, 'I always used to hope some of the letters might be open a bit. I bet they were really interesting. Stands to reason they'd have to be, if they wanted to hire a private investigator.'

Sarah couldn't resist asking, 'And were they? Unstuck I mean.'

'No. You wouldn't believe how well stuck down they were.'

Jack said, 'Did you ever meet Mr Fox?'

'Who?'

He tapped the cutting. 'The man who placed this advertisement. I take it it *was* a regular placement?'

'First Thursday of the month. But I never met him. Didn't even know he was called Fox. He just sent a postal order through every month and I had a stack of big stamped envelopes that I put the replies in and posted off to Stepney. When I got to the last one, I put

165

a note in and he sent me some more.'

'Is that usual?'

'Well . . . no, I suppose not. But we never had any complaints about the service.' Whilst she'd been talking, Mary had, with what she obviously imagined to be a casual manner, taken a small notebook from her skirt pocket and started jotting down brief sentences. 'Did you say you were a chief inspector, Inspector?'

'That's right.'

'I daresay that means you only work on the really important cases. Like that suspicious death in Balaclava Row?'

'No comment.'

Mary shot him a look of annoyance, then her expression changed to one of pleading. It made her look about thirteen. 'Oh, please give me a statement. He, Mr Stanhangar, never lets me do anything but make the tea and do the weddings and funerals. In fact, ever since I got two mixed up and buried the chief bridesmaid by mistake, he doesn't even trust me to do those. If I could get a really good story he'd have to print it. And then maybe I could get a proper job on a real paper in Fleet Street.' She turned a determined little face in Sarah's direction. 'You tell him. I bet they don't let you do any of the good jobs in the police, do they?'

Sarah temporized, 'Well, they're letting me work on this case, aren't they?'

'What case?' Mary shot back quickly.

Stamford stood up. 'We'll give you a statement when the case is closed. Is that fair enough?'

She supposed it would have to be and showed them

out with a plea that they solve it by Wednesday before the paper went to print.

'She's as bad as Dunn,' Jack said as they hurried back towards the station. The sirens had blasted out their nightly warning as they stepped out on to the pavement. Now as they trotted quickly across Agar Street, the air was full of a 'plopping' sound, like gigantic peas being dropped on a sheet of metal.

Clapping her hand on to a non-existent metal helmet, Sarah sprinted across the road and up the station steps, beating Stamford by several paces.

'You're fit,' he called as she whisked away from him down the corridor.

'No, I'm a coward,' she shouted back over her shoulder. A few moments later she was back with the steel helmet safely in place and clutching a stirrup pump.

Jack fished his own helmet out of a filing cabinet and joined the rest of the fire-fighting squad in extinguishing the incendiary bombs that clattered down in the street and station yard. Eventually, the only ones left were smouldering in the guttering. The youngest constable was despatched with a billhook and a bucket of sand to sort them out and Jack was finally free to check his desk for messages.

'Oh damn.'

'Sir?' Sarah turned from the fly-blown mirror that she was using to scrub away smuts from her face.

'I've got to be in court tomorrow. An old blackmail case I was working on; it's taken a year to get to trial and now they've gone and rescheduled it to start tomorrow.'

'Will it take long?'

'Who knows? I could be hanging around for days until they get to my testimony. I'll have to go in tomorrow and see if the prosecution have any idea when I'll be called.'

'What about Fox?'

'You go over to Stepney tomorrow, have a word with him. If he gives you any nonsense tell him we'll get a court order to seize his records.'

'Can we do that?'

'If you don't know, the chances are he won't either.'

Stamford scribbled a note and pinned it to DC Bell's desk with his helmet. 'In the meantime, Ding Dong can have another talk with Mrs Donald and see what he can do about tracking down the "special" that was collected last week. My guess is, the widow knows more than she's telling.'

'What shall I do with the information from Fox?'

'Come back here. I'll try to get back after the court rises. Although no doubt you'll be back long before me.'

The next day, and unable to believe what she was seeing, Sarah picked her way cautiously over the rubble and dust of Stepney, relieved that she'd put on her flat uniform shoes with her plain coat. They enabled her to avoid too many slithers into the streams of water and sewage that were gushing unchecked from broken pipes, before seeping through piles of debris and running into whatever was left of the gutters. They'd read the reports coming through to the station, but she didn't think anyone there had really appreciated just how badly the East End had been hit.

The smell of cordite and brick dust which hung

heavily in the air, stinging her eyes and clogging her nose, told her this was the result of last night's raid.

A group of heavy rescue workers were dragging stone and timber from the top of a pile to her left. Balancing on wobbling chunks of stone, Sarah made her way cautiously forward. 'Excuse me!'

One of the men looked round and shouted to her to get away. 'We ain't cleared this area yet. Get out 'til we tell you it's safe.'

For a moment Sarah was taken aback. She'd been to plenty of incidents in the St Pancras area and no one had ever ordered her out. In fact, she'd usually been the one doing the ordering. Then it dawned on her; she'd always been in uniform. Now she was just another civilian getting under the rescue services' feet.

It was easier to obey than launch into an explanation for her presence. Stepping delicately, she negotiated a path back to the centre of the road where it was just about possible to pick a route through the mess of shattered buildings and bomb craters.

Her map was useless. She'd drawn it from a locked cupboard at Agar Street where all maps were now kept as a precaution against possible spy activities. Sarah wished she could find a fifth columnist to give this one to; it was leaving her in a state of total confusion.

It wasn't just that the street names had been obliterated; whole roads had gone, disintegrating into heaps of so much brick, timber and glass and collapsing in ways that made it impossible to tell where one street had ended and another had begun.

The logical thing to do was to locate the local police station and ask for assistance. But she was reluctant to take that path. In her heart, she could admit to herself that it was because she knew that a male CID officer would take over the enquiry and expect her to trail along behind him.

She turned into another road, where the shells of the houses remained, their fronts reduced to untidy piles of bricks on the pavements like collapsing curtains.

Halfway down the street, a flutter of movement through one of the glassless windows caught her attention. The remains of the front door was lying across some bricks, forming a makeshift drawbridge into what had once been the hall passage. 'Hello? Anybody there?'

'Out the back. Come through.'

With one eye on the sagging timbers of the stairwell, Sarah made her way through a hole that had once been the back door.

In the back garden, a woman was crouching over a fire constructed of four bricks and filled with slivers of timber and torn paper. Placing an iron saucepan on the top, she stirred the contents with a wooden spoon. 'Not council are you?' she said, looking Sarah up and down. 'Nor one of those useless bleeders from Public Assistance.'

'No. I'm not. Sorry.'

'Don't be sorry, ducks. I reckon if you worked for that bunch of useless blighters you'd 'ave somefing ta be sorry about. What can I do for ya?'

'I was looking for Waterman's Lane.'

'That's it. Or was it, I should say.' The porridgy spoon indicated a wavering pile of debris about eight foot high that ran along the back length of this street and stretched for some distance beyond it. 'Knocked it flat three nights ago.'

'Were there any survivors?'

'Not many I reckon. 'It the street shelter, didn't they? Fell down flatter than the 'ouses. I always knew them fings weren't safe. Me and Jimmy took our chances under the stairs.'

For the first time Sarah noticed a child of around two was sitting on a legless chair amongst the grass, dividing its attention between her and the bubbling pot. She smiled and he gave her a tentative grin in return.

'When were you hit?' she asked the woman.

'Ten days ago.'

'Ten days! Can't you get rehoused?'

The woman gave a snort of derision. 'You try it, ducks. That po-faced lot down the Assistance Board act like it was my own bleedin' fault I got 'it. Reckon they fink I stuck a big sign on the roof – 'it this one so's I can go down the Assistance and get rich on 'andouts. Well I've 'ad enough of them nosy buggers. Soon as we've 'ad our breakfasts, I'm off down to Kent. Me sister and 'er lot are living in the caves down there. Got to be better than 'aving the roof fall in on ya 'ead, ain't it?'

'I'm sorry.'

'Ain't your fault. Know someone in Waterman's did ya?'

'Not really. I'm trying to find a man called Laurence Fox. I have to talk to him.'

The woman started slopping dollops of grey porridge on to a large cracked plate.

'Fox, ya say? Can't say I know 'im.'

'He lived at number forty-nine.'

'Don't know 'im.'

'What about the ARP post? Would they know?'

'Local one was at the end of the street. They 'it that too. You could try the temporary one. Or go down the big shelter. That's where the ones that were left went.'

'Would they be there this time of day?'

'Might be, not much to choose between the shelter and the rest centres. They all stink.'

The woman hadn't exaggerated. The stench in the shelter was unbelievable – dank, water-logged and unconnected to the sewage system, it had room enough for thousands – providing they happened to be short-sighted troglodytes with low standards of personal hygiene. Since these were in short supply in the East End of London, Sarah couldn't blame the current occupants for the murmurings of anger and misery as they struggled to retain the dry patches they'd staked out.

Her first enquiry was at the temporary ARP post and turned up the information that only two occupants were listed for 49 Waterman's Lane: Pierre and Marie Duclos. Furthermore, what was left of two bodies, one male, one female, had been recovered from beneath the wreckage and were now in the temporary mortuary if she wanted to see them.

She didn't. There was little point when she had no idea what Laurence Fox looked like. That was why she was now prowling round this hellish place trying to locate someone from Waterman's Lane.

For reasons she didn't quite understand herself, she found herself not wanting to admit her identity.

Ever since she'd come into the area, she'd been aware of a vague, indefinable, resentment against all forms of authority, including the police. Instead of her warrant card, she used a packet of Players as an introduction. The cigarettes were accepted with gratitude, but brought her little luck until she was down to the last three.

'Waterman's ya say, ducks?' an old woman said, reaching in eagerly to take a cigarette. Instead of lighting it, she stuck it behind her ear, wedging it between the lobe and the edge of the scarf that was knotted over her curlers. 'Beattie, ain't you from Waterman's?'

"Oo wants to know?"

'Lady here looking for someone.'

Beattie's share of the world was defined by an old blanket on to which she'd packed her few possessions knotted into a tablecloth tied at the corners, a couple of grubby toddlers and a metal saucepan. Dipping a rag into the saucepan, she scrubbed at a sliver of soap, and started washing one of the children. 'Who'd you want in Waterman's?' she asked as Sarah came over and knelt beside her, tickling the stomach of the other child.

'A man called Laurence Fox. He lived at number forty-nine.'

'Forty nine?' The makeshift flannel slid beneath the child's clothes. 'The tobacconist's, that's it. Not Fox. Duclos that's what they were called.'

She pronounced it 'Dew-close'.

'They're dead. Saw 'em being pulled out. Never 'eard of no one called Fox there though. 'Ere yer are.'

Sarah accepted the cleaned-up child that was being

passed to her. The other was dragged on to its mother's lap.

"Ad his fun and skipped out on yer 'as 'e?'

Sarah knew instinctively that this story would earn her more sympathy from these people than the truth. 'I got to find him,' she said, cradling the squirming child in a maternal fashion. Something occurred to her. 'How old's your postman?'

'Yer wha'?'

'Old, is he?' Sarah persisted.

'Been around since I was a nipper.'

'Thanks. Thanks a lot.' Feeling in her pocket, Sarah located a couple of half-crowns, pushed them into the cigarette packet and left it casually on Beattie's blanket.

She was lucky enough to find the postman picking his way along the rubble as she arrived back in what had once been Waterman's Lane.

'Fox?' he said, rolling a plug of tobacco round his jaw. 'No. No Fox at forty-nine. That was the Dew-closes' place. Foreigners they were.'

'Perhaps he stayed with them?'

'If 'e did, 'e never got no letters. I bin on this walk for years and I ain't *never* delivered to no Fox.'

Something that Mary Smith had said niggled at the back of Sarah's mind. 'I never knew his name was Fox,' she'd declared.

'They weren't addressed to him,' she called after the postman's departing back. 'Big brown envelopes posted in Kentish Town. They'd have come once, maybe twice, a month.'

'Oh them.'

'Then you did see them?'

'His Majesty's mail, miss, is private. I ain't at liberty to discuss it.'

She had no option but to show her warrant card. The man's attitude immediately altered. A thin stream of brown liquid was spat just short of Sarah's shoes.

'Why does everyone around here hate the police?' she demanded angrily. 'What's the matter with you all?'

'Matter? I'll tell you what the matter is, copper, you're all on *their* side, that's what the matter is.' Several other people who'd been rooting amongst the ruins, trying to salvage possessions, started to collect in the circle, attracted by the postman's angry voice.

'On whose side?' Sarah queried. In Kentish Town the only hostility the police had faced since the start of the Blitz had been some grumbling by those forced to evacuate unsafe homes and a bit of lip from the odd would-be looter. There had been nothing like the hatred emanating from the faces edging closer to her at this moment.

'*Them*,' another voice called. 'The council, the ARPs, and the other useless bleeders. Bet their families aren't left swillin' in filf when they get bombed out.'

A rumbling of agreement went round the crowd.

'And what 'appens when you tell 'em you want a decent lav not a 'ole in the ground that leaks shit all over yer feet? You coppers beat us up, don't yer?'

Air raid shelters made Sarah nervous. Intimidation made her mad! She squared up to the woman who'd moaned about the toilet facilities. 'You work?'

'Laundry. What about it?'

'Goin' to take the blame for every washerwoman who shrinks a pair of socks are you?'

Whilst she was speaking Sarah had been walking forward. Startled by her attack, the crowd parted to let her through.

'You're still a copper,' the woman muttered.

'But I'm not every copper in London. Now what about the Ducloses. Did you give them the large brown envelopes?' She called the question over the crowd's head.

The postman nodded. 'Yer. I delivered them.'

'But you never heard of a Laurence Fox living at number forty-nine Waterman's?'

She included everyone in this question. And received only shrugs and puzzled head shakes. 'Nor any regular visitors to the shop?'

'Travellers,' the postman shouted back to her. 'Selling sweets and fags. Always regular they are.'

Slowly the onlookers lost interest and drifted away. Gradually, the street emptied again until Sarah was left on her own. Tilting a quizzical eye at the only other occupant, an inquisitive magpie that was exploring discarded tins, she said, 'So was Pierre Duclos really Laurence Fox? Or did they pass the letters on? Or was it all just an enormous con trick by the Ducloses?'

The magpie had no answer.

Chapter 11

Stamford started Tuesday in a fairly good mood. On Monday afternoon the defendant in his blackmail case had suddenly changed his plea to guilty, releasing Jack to return to Agar Street and pick up the threads of his casework.

The pathologist had telephoned through his preliminary report on James Donald: death by asphyxiation.

'Time?' Stamford asked.

'I wouldna swear by it on oath, but I'd say late hours of Wednesday night. Just afore the witching hour would be where my money goes. But it could ha' been a hour or so either side.'

'Any other features?'

'I daresay you noticed the marks round the wrists?'

'Rope?'

'No, nor cords. Something with a smoother texture, like a weave. Maybe an inch and a half thick.'

'How about a tie?'

'Most kind, Chief Inspector, but ma dear wife buys me one every Christmas.' In response to an impatient click of Stamford's tongue, he sighed and agreed it could indeed have been a tie.

'Any other injuries?'

'There's some bruising in the centre of the chest, about three inches in diameter.'

'Consistent with someone pushing their knee into

Donald's chest whilst they held something over his face?'

'Entirely so.'

'How about sex?'

'Once again, the dear wife at Christmas.'

'Are you drunk?'

'Alas, noo. And, since you ask, the late Mr Donald was not sexually gratified. At least, not in the hours before his death. There's a wee bit of additional bruising on the face incidentally. Lower cheeks. One mark on the right cheek, three on the left. Consistent with a hand being pressed over his mouth, afore you ask.'

The doctor had nothing else to report beyond the fact that Donald had eaten a meal of pork, peas and potatoes approximately four hours before his death and had drunk a small whisky much later, probably only half an hour before death.

Sarah came in just as Stamford was replacing the receiver. He relayed the gist of the pathologist's report to her.

Pushing a hand through her thick golden-brown hair which she'd left loose this morning, she flopped into the spare chair and said, 'It's pretty much how we thought it was then, sir. Did you think it might not be murder?'

'Not really.' Stamford rested his arms on his desk and scrutinised her with critical eyes. 'You look tired. Did the bombing keep you awake?'

'No. I hardly notice it these days, not unless one lands really close.'

'So, what is the problem?'

She told him about the conditions in Stepney. 'I

know it doesn't look like it out there, but it makes you realise we're getting off lightly.'

'Mmm, you're probably right, but I wouldn't put it about, it's not a view that's going to make you very popular in the canteen.'

'Oh I'm *very* popular in the canteen. In fact they hardly seem to talk about anything else,' Sarah said bitterly.

'Oh?'

'It doesn't matter, sir. Do you want my report?'

Stamford took the hint and shut up, letting her talk, summarising her visit yesterday.

'I've left instructions at the ARP post, the police station and the mortuary that if anyone makes enquiries about the Ducloses, we're to be informed immediately. And I've called Criminal Records to ask them to check out Duclos and Fox. I don't see what else I can do at present. Unless I ask for a check to be made for Fox on the National Identity Register.'

'He'll be dead of old age before we get the answer.'

'That's rather what I thought. Do you think he really exists? Or it was a pseudonym for the Ducloses?'

Leaning back in his chair, Stamford stretched and linked his hands behind his head. 'How old were they, did you find out?'

'Sixties, both of them.'

'Hardly likely to be lurking around behind Donald's shop in the small hours. Of course we don't know that anyone was. They could just be very good at playing on their clients' fears and confirming their worst ones. On the other hand, Mary Smith said they'd never had any complaints about the service.' He returned his chair to the upright position. 'Well our best hope is that Fox will come looking for them. The travellers aren't a bad idea. A rep would be ideally placed to pick up mail. Since Sergeant Agnew is so keen on deskwork, I think I'll get him started on telephoning the main cigarette companies, see if they had an employee called Fox who worked that area. In the meantime, let's go and see how Gwen Donald is getting on.'

He collected his hat from the stand but, before they could leave the office, a WPC opened the door, smiled a tentative hello at Sarah, and handed Jack several envelopes.

'Your mail, sir.'

'Thank you, er ... Jeannie.'

'And a note for you, Sarge.'

Stamford shuffled the letters, slit an internal one open, and gave a mutter of disbelief. 'Did you gain the impression that James Donald was an outgoing, gregarious type, Sergeant?'

'Definitely not. Quite the opposite in fact.'

'Exactly.' He held the sheet out to her. 'So how do you account for the fact that fingerprinting have identified ten separate sets of fingerprints in his bedroom. What on earth was he doing up there – holding orgies?'

'There's something else.' Sarah passed him across her own note. 'Somebody tried to break in to the grocer's in Balaclava Row last night.'

Stamford glanced at the scrawled lines. 'Whose handwriting is this?'

'Dave's. PC Wilkin's. He was on patrol on that beat last night. He thought I might be interested.'

Jack checked his watch. 'I suppose he's going to be

in bed by now if he's got any sense. We'll have to catch
up with him later. Let's get round to Balaclava Row.'

'Who first?' Sarah asked as they approached the
Row.

Stamford elected to see Gwen and break the news
that it was now confirmed that her husband's death
was murder. 'You go and speak to the woman in the
grocer's. Mrs Goodwin, isn't it? I'll meet you there.'

Gwen received his news with a calm indifference.
Presumably she'd been expecting it. She was one of
the few people he'd met who was happy to sit a chief
inspector in her kitchen.

Piles of receipts and invoices were arranged in neat
groups across the surface. Gwen sat behind them
looking like a plump cashier in her black skirt, black
shiny blouse and discreet jet jewellery. 'I've checked
everything. Nothing is missing from the stock.'

'What about the special items? Is it possible your
husband didn't record them all?'

'No. Donald was most meticulous. I've already told
that other policeman that.' Gwen's rosebud lips
tightened, deepening the tiny lines that radiated into
the upper lip with its faintest hint of a moustache,
and implying she hadn't enjoyed her interview with
Ding Dong. 'He was rude.'

'Was he? Perhaps you misunderstood him.'

'He good as said I wasn't telling the truth. About
not knowing the special customers. He said I could
tell if I really wanted to.'

'And did you? Tell him anything?' DC Bell's desk
had been empty when Stamford returned to the office
this morning. The rota had indicated he was out on
enquiries about this case.

Gwen stacked the receipts and returned them to an old shoe box. 'We had had one or two pieces in like that last item in the ledger, the gold and ruby earrings. I suppose they could have come from the same person. Not that I know him by name.'

'But you were able to point the constable in the right direction?'

'Donald did mention that he'd seen the man going into the Black Cat a few times. I think he lives down by the canal.'

'Could you describe him?'

'I told the other one. He was a little man.' She placed a flat hand level with her shoulder. 'A foreigner. And he used some terrible-smelling oil on his hair.'

'Working class would you say?'

'Oh yes. Pretending not to be though. But when I was in service I saw the real gentry. He wasn't one of 'em. I could tell he was the sort that puts the milk in the tea first.'

'Hardly the sort of person to be lawfully in possession of valuable jewellery then?'

'Like I told you, Inspector. Nothing Donald copied was ever reported stolen. Not to us in any event.'

He'd have to let it go for now and hope Ding Dong was making some progress. 'I need to look at the bedroom again. Have you moved any of your husband's clothing since you came back?'

'I've cut up one of his shirts.' She opened a basket Jack hadn't seen under the table and held up several pieces of material held together by pins. 'I'm making a blouse for Evelyn from it. He'd have liked that.'

Treading up the stairs, Jack thought that James probably *would* have liked that. The deeper he delved into the Donalds' lives, the more he had a sense of a couple who'd married solely to have children, and whose only bond was their mutual love of those children. It was very different from his own marriage which, as he viewed it with more clarity over the intervening years, he now realised had been based almost solely on sexual attraction. Annaliese had been an inevitable result of that attraction but instead of drawing them together, it had pushed them further apart. He wondered if James Donald had been lonely too. Probably, if he'd taken a mistress.

'Where did your husband keep his ties?' he asked Gwen Donald who'd followed him up the stairs.

'In the wardrobe. There's a rack inside the door.'

There were only three: black, brown and grey. The black was less smooth than its companions, the material crumpled and creased and the edges distorted instead of being pressed flat like the other two. 'I'll be taking this for a while.' Folding it carefully into a clean handkerchief, he stowed it in his pocket. 'Did your husband have any silk clothes, Mrs Donald?'

'Silk! Goodness me no, sir. Whatever would Donald be doing with fancy stuff like that? Cotton and wool that's what I bought him. And flannel next to his chest.' There was no need for her to ask why he wanted to know. She was far from stupid. 'Found silk in there did you, sir?' Her lips twisted in distaste as she regarded the site of her husband's death. 'I can't say I'm surprised. You'd not expect a woman like that to wear respectable underclothes.'

'Do you really have no idea who this woman is?' Jack demanded. He watched her face closely as she replied. Either the woman was a superb actress or her denial was genuine. Which brought him to his next question: what were upwards of ten people doing trooping around this room?

'It was at the party,' she replied calmly. 'James's birthday party the week before last. There was a big raid somewhere to the east and Lexie said that she'd never seen a raid because she was always down in the cellar. So we put the lights out and came up here to watch.'

With a sinking sensation in his stomach, Stamford asked, 'Who exactly is *we*?'

'Everybody. The whole Row came.'

'So what you're telling me is – every single person in Balaclava Row has been in this flat, and up into this room, within the past two weeks?'

'Yes.'

Jack groaned silently. So much for locating the missing mistress through her fingerprints.

He went to find out how Sarah was getting on in Albert White's shop, and encountered his next setback of the day.

'She's not here, sir,' Sarah said, as they waited for Albert to finish a hushed conversation with a thin, down-at-heel woman with dark circles beneath her eyes.

'Ta ever so much, Mr White,' she said, gathering up her basket. 'And don't you worry about our Ena, she'll do a good job scrubbing yer floors or she'll have me to answer to.'

Letting her out, Albert returned his attention to the two officers.

'Your young lady tell you our Rose has got herself another job, sir? She's a teacher you know. Got her certificates and everything.' He sounded as if he was personally responsible for coaching Rose.

'Mrs Goodwin started work this morning, sir. At Riley Street School.'

Sarah exchanged a look with her boss that said she knew exactly what he was thinking: his daughter went to Riley Street School.

'If it's about the burglar, sir, Lexie can tell you. I don't know what Rose was thinking of, leaving the door unlocked like that. Not after what happened to James.'

'Are we sure that's what happened?'

Sarah answered him. 'It must have been, sir, there's no sign of forced entry. Come and look.'

In the back room they both re-examined the stout door lock. It was old, solid and battered, with no bright tell-tale scratches to show that anyone had been trying to pick it. Stamford pushed experimentally at the two windows; the frames didn't move under his pressure. He tried to slide them open and found the wood held fast by ancient paint that flaked under his touch.

'Mr White says the windows haven't been opened for years, sir. The cats used to get in. His sister had a thing about cats. She used to work here until last September. That's when Mrs Goodwin took over.'

'What did you find out about Mrs Goodwin?'

Sarah flicked open her book. 'Moved here about two years ago with her husband, Peter. He was a teacher too. Killed at Dunkirk. Matthew Fortune,' her pencil jabbed over her shoulder in the general direction of the hairdresser's, 'went to Haverstock Central with both of them. He recommended them for the tenancy when Mr White moved in with his sister.'

Albert, bustling back through the dividing curtain, caught the last sentence. 'Best thing young Matt ever did for me,' he beamed. 'She's a marvel with the books is Rose. And all them ration coupon things. And the customers like 'er.' He blew out a regretful cloud of breath. 'I'll miss 'er.'

'Where did Mrs Goodwin work before you employed her?' Stamford asked.

'Didn't. Married woman, weren't she?'

'She was still married last September?'

'Yes, well, Peter were away, weren't 'e. No need to be keeping a home for a man who weren't coming back to it. I told 'im so.'

His relief at the jangling summons of the shop bell was plain to both of them.

'Sounds like Mrs Goodwin wasn't seeing eye to eye with Mr Goodwin, doesn't it? And according to her statement she was here, alone in the flat, when Donald died.'

'She's not first on Mrs Donald's list though, is she?'

Stamford looked at his sergeant with surprise. 'Has she said something? You didn't tell me.'

'But you were there,' Sarah protested. 'When we looked out of the window and saw Miss Emmett hanging out the washing a couple of days ago. It was pretty obvious from her tone that Mrs Donald's got it in for her. Didn't you notice?'

He hadn't, not consciously anyway. Although, now Sarah mentioned it, he acknowledged she could be right. 'Why her I wonder? Did something happen in the past she hasn't told us about?'

'Maybe it just makes sense. I mean Lexie Emmett and that woman in the hairdresser's were closer to his age. Mrs Goodwin's only twenty-six, and that other couple in the cafe are even younger.' She consulted another page of her book. 'Twenty-two and seventeen.'

'Doesn't necessarily follow. Maybe she preferred older men.'

Albert nipped back again. 'Did you want to see upstairs, sir?'

Stamford raised an enquiring eyebrow in Sarah's direction.

'I've already looked,' she confirmed. 'There's nothing worth seeing. But if you'd like to look . . . ?'

'No, I trust you. Let's go and talk to Miss Emmett.'

He had, Sarah reflected following her boss's back along the pavement, an irritating habit of getting under her skin when she least expected it. Very few senior male police officers would have trusted a female officer to assess the scene of a crime correctly.

Lexie was perched on a stool behind the counter, vigorously buffing a man's boot. As she dropped it next to its fellow, they could see the thin rim of brown polish around her forearm where the polishing rag had overshot its target.

She wore no make-up, so that the generous sprinkling of fawn freckles that often went with that shade of bright red hair, stood out clearly against her pale skin.

Her original statement to the police had put her in the cellar under the shop at the time of Donald's death. If she thought it odd that he asked to see it she recovered herself quickly and jumped down from the stall to push back a scrap of carpet behind the counter.

The squeak of the trapdoor being raised, brought a shout from the back room. 'Lexie, what you doing out there? What yer want down the cellar?'

'The police want to see it, Dad.'

'Police!' Shuffling on carpet slippers, Frank Emmett hurried from his workroom. His watery blue eyes flicked around the trio with suspicion. 'I ain't stopping sheltering down there,' he whined. 'I don't care what the council says. It's my cellar, I ain't having that jumped-up bunch of timewasters telling me what I can't do in me own place.'

'They've not come about the air raid precautions, Dad. At least . . .' Lexie paused halfway down the steps, with only her top half protruding from the floor. Craning up at Stamford she said, 'You ain't come about that? Have yer?'

'No. I was just curious.'

Lexie preceded them down the steps. The officers followed gingerly aware of the accompanying grumble emanating from above their heads.

'Bloody waste of time. Paying out taxes for coppers to be *curious*. Should be out catching murderers. Bad as that lot up at the town hall. Another bunch of jokers I'd sack if I 'ad my way . . .'

'Don't mind Dad,' Lexie said, striking a match. The cotton wick spluttered and spat, filling the confined space with the smell of paraffin.

'We seem to have really upset him,' Sarah said, feeling her way off the bottom of ladder and ignoring Stamford's proffered hand.

'No, you'd only do that if yer've come to invite me out. Brings on his 'eart condition that does. Mind yer feet, it's damp. Well, here it is then.' Lexie waved the lamp around, sending monstrous shadows dancing over the ceiling and walls.

There were two beds of the kind used in military camps with iron frames that slotted together and canvas bases. Pillows and bedclothes were folded on each. She moved the light slightly so they could see the upturned tea chest with a collection of tins that they apparently used for storage, a dilapidated deckchair and an old wooden table and stool. There was a shoemaker's last on the table and curling strips of rubber and leather in an old biscuit box beneath it.

'Your father works down here?'

'Sometimes. Light's not very good and 'e won't have the electric down here in case we get electrocuted.'

'He's probably right.' The whole place had an air of dankness. At one point Jack was certain he could hear the gurgle of water running behind one of the brick walls. 'What did he mean about the council?'

Lexie perched on the table. She had a girlish, gawky way of moving that was at odds with her age. 'They wouldn't strengthen the cellar. Said it weren't suitable for a shelter and that we should go down the street shelter.'

'So why don't you?'

'Dad don't like them.'

'What about you?'

'Me? Oh he just finks what 'e wants, I must want.'

'And you come down here every night?'

'That's right. When the daylight raids were on we were down here every day too.'

'No exceptions.'

'Just last Saturday when I went up the pictures with Rose.'

'What about the night of James Donald's party?'

'Come down here soon as we come back.'

'Was that usual? For the Donalds to have a birthday party?'

'Never known 'em do it before. 'Ad 'em for the kids, of course. But not for James. Or Gwen. Didn't even know it *was* 'is birthday 'til Gwen come round and asked us over. It weren't much of a party mind, just sherry and sandwiches and cakes. But anyfing's better than being stuck down this tomb.'

Sarah drew herself up on the table beside Lexie. 'Why don't you just stay upstairs then?'

Lexie's only response was a heartfelt snort.

'How long had you known James Donald?'

'Since we come here. They moved in about the same time as us.'

'When was that?'

Lexie screwed her eyes up and stared at the ceiling as if the answer might be written in the stones. 'I was nine. So it was twenty-eight years ago. That would be, let's see . . .'

'Nineteen twelve,' Sarah supplied.

'Oh gawd, it would, wouldn't it?'

'So James Donald would have been nineteen when he came here?'

'Suppose so. He was grown up, that's all I remember.'

'Any idea where the Donalds came here from?'

'No. Don't fink they ever said. It weren't local though, I remember the LMS carrier bringing their furniture up from the station. We pushed all our stuff up on a barrow from Somers Town. Me dad used to have a lock-up down there.'

Jack switched tack again, 'Tell me about the burglar last night.'

'Nuffing to tell really.' Lexie swung her legs as she told them about returning the skirt, hearing the disturbance and chasing the intruder down the stairs. ''E got away over the back field. It's all churned up since the bomb, I couldn't catch 'im.'

'Just as well probably. What were you going to do if you had?'

'Dunno really. Clout 'im I suppose.'

'What if he'd hit you back?'

'Didn't look like 'e could knock out a rabbit.'

'You saw him clearly then?'

'Not really,' Lexie admitted. 'Saw the top of 'is head and 'is back as he went across the bomb site.'

But by then the darkness had closed over the scoured and blasted field and she caught only a glimpse of a small, thin figure darting and dodging amongst the twisted hillocks of dying weeds and crumpling earth mounds.

Stamford looked at her speculatively: 'You're quite certain he came from the grocer's shop?'

'Well. Sort of. I mean, I never actually saw him come out the shop. He was just there in the field when I run out.'

Lexie had been thinking the matter over herself and it had belatedly occurred to her that perhaps the footsteps she'd heard had been Alan on the staircase behind the dividing wall. Her doubts communicated themselves to the officers.

Jack led the way back upstairs. The water-swollen wood of the stairs creaked painfully with each step making it clear that it would be difficult for anyone to slip out of the cellar unheard.

There were no customers in the shop but Frank

Emmett had chosen to stay in there rather than return
to his workbench out the back. Leaning both elbows
on the counter, he tucked and pulled a miserly plug
of tobacco into a sausage shape and pushed it into a
roller. The tip of his thin tongue emerged from tight
lips and teased the edge of the cigarette paper. Frank
pushed the machine shut, twiddled the metal rollers
with long fingers disjointed by nodular joints, and
disgorged a cigarette as thin as a match. 'Bugger!' he
swore as machine and fag both sprung from his hand
and clattered to the floor.

Jack retrieved both and produced his lighter.

'Ta.' Frank sucked greedily trying to draw air
through the tightly packed tobacco.

'Your daughter tells me you spend every night down
in the cellar.'

'Wha' of it?'

'I was just thinking it must be nice and quiet down
there. Bet you can hardly hear the bombing at all?'

The barely glowing tube of paper stuck to his bottom
lip, wriggling in time to his indignant tirade that he
never got a wink of sleep. 'I can 'ear everything.
Bombs, fire engines, ambulances, even bleedin' street
sweepers. Why the 'ell the council can't sweep the
streets when everybody's awake, instead of . . .'

'He wakes up at every sound.' Lexie interrupted
the flow by simply stepping between her father and
Stamford and leaving him grumbling at her back.
'Wakes me up to listen to it too.'

'Including the night of Donald's death?'

'Course. There wasn't nuffing funny though. We
didn't hear no screams or anyfing or we'd 'ave said.'

Either it genuinely hadn't occurred to her that she

might be a suspect, or she'd decided on disingenuous ignorance as a good defence.

Jack put the question about the Donalds' parents previous address to Frank. And he also denied any knowledge. 'Kept themselves to themselves. Especially 'er. 'Ardly ever talked to anyone. Helen, 'er in the 'airdresser's, might know where they come from.'

'Is it important?' Sarah queried as they stepped back on to the pavement once more.

'Probably not. I was just curious. If James was nineteen, they must have been getting on a bit. I wondered why they uprooted themselves to come here.'

'Will you ask Miss Fortune?'

They'd drifted down to the hairdresser's shop and could clearly see several customers in various stages of shampooing, curling and combing through the steamed-up window.

'Not now. I think I'll leave it until she's less busy. Let's go have a word with our chief burglary suspect.'

'Have we got one?'

'Don't tell me that description didn't ring any bells, Sergeant? Smallish, thinnish, quick on his feet?'

He was mucking out the stable when they found him shovelling a mixture of muck and trodden straw into a wheelbarrow. Just out of kicking distance, Kitchener was tethered to a metal ring in the yard wall.

Jack didn't waste time on subtlety. 'Morning, Felonious. Know anything about a burglary in Balaclava Row?'

Felonious produced his standard defence in such situations. 'I never dun it,' he yelled, backing away from them.

A second later he catapulted forward into Jack's arms propelled by a muscular thump from Kitchener's rump between his shoulder blades.

Struggling free, Felonious pleaded with Sarah. 'You tell him. I was wiv yer. The whole time. I couldn't 'ave nicked it.'

'With me where?'

'In Donald's place. And when yer went to phone. I didn't nick it!'

Stamford raised expressive eyebrows at his sergeant. This line of enquiry was proving far more promising than he'd anticipated. 'And what exactly didn't you nick, Fel?'

But that was the problem. Felonious couldn't remember. He just knew that something that had been amongst James Donald's property in the sitting room when he first discovered the body, had been missing when he went back there again the next day with Sarah.

Chapter 12

Everybody – with the exception of Gwen Donald and Matthew Fortune – had turned out to see Rose off for her first day at Riley Street. Even Maria and Josepha had taken a break from hostilities to bring round a pile of freshly cut tongue sandwiches and a slab of current cake. 'For your dinner,' Maria had explained, offering the food which was wrapped in a clean tea-cloth.

Blinking back tears, Rose had tucked the parcel inside Matthew's briefcase and given the Maltese girl a quick hug.

'And I told Dad he can sole yer shoes for free. Bound to wear out quicker now you got more walking to do,' Lexie said.

Helen gave the blond bob a professional twitch. 'Matt said to wish you all the luck in the world. He had to leave to catch the bus.'

'Thanks. Thank you all,' Rose gulped. 'I'd better go before I start crying my eyes out. It wouldn't do for the children to think it's the teacher who doesn't want to go to school!'

'You'll find the class is full. A few of them were evacuated but they were all back by Christmas,' the headmaster said, walking her along to the classroom after morning assembly. 'There are no special problems. There's one little Dutch girl, Annaliese

Stamford. Well, half Dutch to be exact. She should be in the second year, but I've kept her down because she still has trouble with English. And then there's Starkey, of course. But every teacher has their cross to bear, don't they?'

There was something distinctly shifty about the way he suddenly scuttled ahead of her along the corridor. But before she could ask any further questions, he'd reached the classroom door and flung it open.

Forty pairs of heels made contact with forty iron chair struts. With a crash, forty chairs were thrust back and eighty feet hit the wooden floor.

'Good morning, class.'

'Good morning, sir.'

'This is Mrs Goodwin, your new teacher.'

They'd already seen her sitting with the rest of the staff in a semi-circle behind the headmaster at assembly. Now they regarded her with the interest of a pride of lions sizing up the latest line in Christian snacks.

'Well,' the headmaster snapped, 'where are your manners? Say good morning.'

'Good morning, miss,' they chorused obediently.

'Right, I'll leave you to it, Mrs Goodwin. Any problems and you know where my office is.'

'Thank you, sir. I'm sure everything will be fine. You may sit down, class.' With a simultaneous 'thwack', bottoms were plumped down and chairs scraped noisily back into position against desks. Trying to control her shaking legs, Rose sat down at the high teacher's desk, opened the lid, and removed the register. She found the names were listed alphabetically by surname. But their first names were represented by a simple initial.

As she pored over the lined sheets, she was aware of a shuffling and whispering amongst the class as it tried to work up enough courage to challenge her. Most of the disturbance came from the left side of the class where the boys were sitting. It was them she faced as she raised her head quickly and said loudly and firmly, 'Now, class, pay attention.'

Several nervous hands flew to ear lobes. Forty pairs of eyes jerked to the front; although many were fixed on the willow cane that still lay against the board rather than on Rose.

'Now, class,' she repeated, smiling to soften her words. 'When I call the register I want you to put your hand up and answer with your first name, not "here". Do you understand?'

'Hssmiss.'

'Good. Abbott.'

'Peggy, miss.' A plump pig-tailed blonde semaphored vigorously.

'Adams.'

'Sidney, miss.'

They progressed smoothly through the alphabet, via several Peggys, a couple of Joans and Williams, assorted Georges, Marys, Mildreds, Jimmys, Johns, Stanleys, Kittys, Shirleys, Davids, Charlies and Dorothys. Rose discovered that, with due deference for the segregation of the sexes, Miss Gilbert had seated them alphabetically.

'Scannell.'

'Ginger, miss.'

'I beg your pardon?' Lifting her head, Rose gazed

at a small, thin girl with mousy ear-length hair
secured by a drooping pink ribbon who was holding
aloft a straight arm supported beneath her armpit by
her other hand.

'Ginger, miss. Me name's Ginger.'

The register gave her initial as 'V'. But Ginger was
having none of it. She insisted her name was Ginger.
'Me mum says so,' she produced as a final argument.

There was a buzz of agreement round the class.

'Tis, miss.'

''Er sisters say so too, miss.'

'Headmaster calls her Ginger, miss.'

'They 'ad a murder done in her 'ouse, miss.'

'Not when we was livin' there though, miss,' Ginger
assured her earnestly. 'It was me Auntie Edie's 'ouse
then. She lives next door wiv me gran and granddad
now.'

'Thank you!' Rose pencilled the name in. 'You can
put your arm down now, Ginger. Stamford.'

Ginger spoke up again. 'She's sick, miss.' She waved
one hand across the empty portion of her double desk
to demonstrate that her classmate hadn't acquired
the secret of invisibility. ''Er brother brung a note.'
She pointed to a folded sheet of paper on the front of
Rose's table.

'Sammy ain't 'er brother,' called one of the Williams.

'Good as,' yelled back Ginger swivelling round in
her seat. 'Lives wiv 'is mum, don't she?'

'Don't make him 'er brother,' chipped in Peggy
Abbott.

'Thank you, class, I don't think we need to go into
Miss Stamford's relations now.' Refolding the note
from someone called 'E. O'Day' informing the school

that Annaliese was being kept home with a cold, Rose annotated her register. Writing against the girl's surname something niggled at the back of her mind. She'd heard the name Stamford somewhere else recently. But where?

'Starkey?'

A dead silence greeted her call. Looking up quickly she caught several of the boys nudging each other and suppressing smirks.

'Is Starkey away too?'

Her question brought an instant barrage of cat-calls and pretended disgust.

'Cor no. Wish he was!'

'Can't you smell 'im, miss. Phew!'

'Gawd, I fink I felt somefing jump on me.'

The whole performance was accompanied by a pantomime of held noses, simulated gagging and vigorous scratching of heads and bodies.

'Be quiet!' Rose slammed her palm down hard on the desk top. The spirit of Miss Gilbert fell over a class hushed into dead silence. 'Now then, which is Starkey?'

The two boys in the front double desk slid down in their seats. Several rigid arms shot out at right angles to shoulders pointing at the second desk in the row. In all his glory, Starkey was revealed.

For a brief moment, Rose experienced a feeling of sympathy with the rest of the class.

Beneath a head which appeared to have had clumps of hair ripped from it, Starkey scowled. It didn't improve the appearance of a face already covered in scabs.

Despite Rose's warning, the boy in front of him

gagged noisily and dug his deskmate in the ribs. 'Be quiet,' Rose ordered, deliberately keeping her own voice low and controlled. 'Now, Starkey, what is your first name?'

The child's scowl deepened. She thought he was going to ignore her, then he muttered something.

'I'm sorry, Starkey. I didn't hear that. Say it again please.'

He did. It sounded like 'Narnel'.

Getting up Rose made her way down the row. She saw Starkey brace himself, his lips locking tightly together as he obviously prepared himself for a whack.

Reaching his chair, Rose squatted down and took one of his hands gently. Out of the corner of her eye, she caught the surreptitious nudging from the front row again.

Now she was this close, her eyes and nose were telling her that the class were not being entirely unfair. The boy's clothes were covered in smears of mud, food and other stains she'd rather not think about. The tattered jumper that covered his thin chest had sprouted enormous holes in the arms through which his scarred and dirty elbows protruded. All other areas of skin that were visible were overlaid with a rime of encrusted dirt and, in large patches, violent red rashes.

'Now, Starkey,' she said gently. 'I can hear better. Tell me your first name again.'

'Naf-nel.' His teeth were coated with yellow fur and his breath stank.

'Are you sure? I've never heard of anyone called that before.'

His head nodded. Rose could have sworn that

something winged and many-legged flew out of it. 'All right, Nafnel. Thank you.'

She pencilled the name in lightly with a question mark against it and dealt with the final two boys in the front row who proved to be called Roger Veeney and Philip Wright.

By break she'd started to sort them out: Wright was, she suspected, the class bully, with Roger Veeney as his chief lieutenant; Ginger was the helpful one; Peggy Abbott was the class know-it-all; one of the Stanleys was the clown, and Starkey was the class leper.

'Who is he?' she asked in the staff room at break.

Mr Jenkins, who taught the fifth form, scratched a hairy ear and admitted no one really knew.

'Turned up about three weeks ago. Comes from East Ham or West Ham or somewhere like that. Mother killed in the bombing, father unspecified. Starkey lives with his grandmother in Warden Road.'

'What's his first name. All I can get out of him is "Nafnel".'

'Haven't the faintest idea. It's all anyone can get out of him. He's down in the books as "Anon" Starkey.'

'But surely his grandmother must have said, when she registered him?'

'Turned up one morning, shoved him into the playground, told the teacher on duty to hang on to the little bleeder because she wasn't going to no court on his account. I rather think,' Mr Jenkins said sipping his tea, 'that Grandma Starkey had had a visit from the School Board Inspector.'

'Couldn't somebody have written, or gone round, and asked what the child's Christian name was?'

'I believe the headmaster did send a note. But he never received any reply. No doubt Mrs Starkey was too busy indulging in her hobby of studying the forms of wildlife indigenous to English rain water.' Seeing the bewilderment on Rose's face, he elaborated further. 'She spends an enormous amount of time face down in the gutters getting close to her subject.'

'Oh, I see. You mean she's . . .'

'As educated as a newt most of the time,' Jenkins agreed cheerfully. 'You'll need to keep an eye on Starkey. He has a habit of attempting to make a dash for freedom in the break periods. We've had him returned several times by the costers up Queens Market. He steals from the stalls. Miss Gilbert used to lock him in the boiler room. Where have you left him?'

She'd left him lining up with the others for milk in the hall. But when she hurried in, nervously envisaging losing a pupil on her first morning, Rose couldn't see him anywhere. She grabbed Peggy Abbott. 'Where's Starkey?'

Peggy sipped daintily. 'Out there, miss. He knows it's not allowed. I told him.'

The door to the hall opened on to a minute area that was used as a secondary playground in addition to those on the roof. 'I told him you're not allowed to take bottles out there, miss,' Peggy said virtuously. 'You have to finish your milk in here then you can go play.'

'Yes. Thank you, Peggy.' Rose hurried across to the partially open door.

'D'ya want it then?' she heard a wheedling voice enquire. 'Go on, take it, Stinky. I don' wan' it.'

202

Through the gap, Rose saw Phil Wright extending his bottle of milk. Starkey hovered uncertainly, his left hand clutching an empty bottle, his right moving slowly outwards. As his fingers touched Phil's bottle, the other boy let go. Glass and liquid crashed into the grille beneath a drainpipe.

'Oops. I dropped it. Go on, Stinky, lap it up. Go on get down on your knees.' Phil seized one of Starkey's arms and attempted to twist it behind his back, whilst Roger Veeney got hold of the other shoulder and tried to yank him down. He didn't get very far; Starkey's teeth sank into the ball of his thumb.

Roger's shriek of agony was cut short by Rose's appearance.

"E frew me milk away, miss,' Wright yelled, full of righteous indignation.

Rose faced Starkey: 'Put that bottle back in the crate, then go to the classroom and wait for me. Do you understand?'

She waited until she was certain he was moving back into the school rather than bolting out of it, then she turned her attention to the smirking Wright and Veeney. A minute later they were both slinking away, Veeney to fetch the caretaker to clear up the glass and Wright to work out how he was going to explain to his dad why he had to write 'Wasting food helps the Germans' so that his son and heir could copy it out fifty times.

Starkey was curled into a ball in the corner of the class, picking at the hard skin exposed by a gaping hole in one of his plimsolls. 'Here you are,' Rose said, handing him a full bottle of milk. 'It's Annaliese's. She won't be wanting it today.'

He approached it warily, obviously expecting another trick. When his fingers were in reach, he snatched it quickly from her hand, ripped off the top, and tipped the whole third of a pint down his throat in one gulp.

Returning to her desk, Rose took out the packet of sandwiches and offered him one. 'Eat it quickly,' she urged when he hesitated. 'Break will be over soon.'

The food went the same way as the milk. He scarcely bothered to chew it, instead snatching off great chunks with his yellow teeth and gulping them down with convulsive swallows that sent his Adam's apple bobbing violently.

The notes of the brass handbell announced the end of break. 'Go back to your desk now, and you can have the rest of the sandwiches and some cake at dinner time.'

She had his full attention for the rest of the morning; even if it was fixed on her desk rather than her blackboard.

At midday most of the children streamed home for their dinners. One, charging down the corridor and struggling to find his coat sleeves at the same time, said hello to her.

He'd gone past and pounded out of the front door before she recognised him as Sammy O'Day. Recollecting his performance of 'The death of Miss Gilbert' the other day clarified an elusive memory that had been nibbling at the corner of her mind all morning: the 'E O'Day' who'd signed Annaliese Stamford's sick note must be Pat and Sammy's mother. One memory brought with it another: Stamford was the name of that detective who was investigating James Donald's death.

Returning to the classroom, she thought for a moment that it was empty. 'Nafnel?' she called, praying he hadn't slipped out amongst the other children.

A furtive scuffle came from the raised platform containing her desk and the blackboard. It sounded like a large rat scrabbling for food. Except that this rat had already found it. Cross-legged beneath her desk, he had a sandwich in one hand and the currant cake in the other, and was snatching bites from both with frantic haste, the partially eaten food falling from his mouth as he attempted to pile in more.

'Y'sa'd,' he mumbled defensively, clutching his remaining scraps so tightly that they started to disintegrate between his fingers.

Rose sat on the floor, tucking her skirt modestly against the back of her legs and crossing her arms on top of her bent knees. 'I know I said. But you should have waited for me to give them to you. Not opened my desk without permission. Did you think I might change my mind?'

'Might,' he agreed, licking his grubby palms to sweep up the last of the crumbs.

'Doesn't your grandmother cook you dinner at home?'

'She don' cook.'

'What do you eat at home then?'

A wary look settled over the little boy's face, deepening the purple shadows beneath his eyes. 'Gotta go now.'

He attempted to push past her, but Rose got a firm grip on one wrist. 'You can go and play on the roof. We'll both go.'

'Wanna drink.'

'All right.' She stood by whilst he twisted sideways to gulp water from the drinking tap in the lower playground then escorted him to the roof.

There were only about twenty children in the wire caged area but they were making enough noise for sixty as they ran, shrieked, skipped, kicked balls and delivered the odd punch, slap and pinch when they thought Mr Jenkins, who was on playground duty, didn't notice.

'Had your dinner already?' he said, drifting across to join her.

Rose huddled inside her cardigan. Up here, unprotected by the buildings, the approaching winter was more apparent in the vicious nip of the wind. 'I wasn't hungry,' she said. Which was true; although Albert had always insisted that she take half an hour for lunch, she'd generally done no more than sip a cup of tea in the flat.

'I see you're keeping Starkey under guard. I can get you the key to the boiler room if you want to lock him up 'til the bell.'

Rose opened her mouth to give him a piece of her mind, then closed it again. She was the new girl. She couldn't start throwing her weight around – just yet. 'I'll stay up here, thanks. I feel like some fresh air. I'll do your duty if you like?'

'Splendid. I can see you're going to be an enormous asset to this school, Miss Goodwin.'

'Mrs.'

'Beg pardon?'

'I'm Mrs Goodwin, not Miss.'

'Ah yes. Of course. Well that's going to take a bit of

getting used to, married teachers. Well now, just time to get one of those excellent meat pies from the stall in the Crescent I think.'

Rubbing his hands together in delighted anticipation, Mr Jenkins bounced off.

Rose hurried across the playground to separate a group of screaming, yelling boys who were piled in a heap on top of something. With resignation, she uncovered a tattered body, curled into a defensive huddle.

"'E's got me ball, miss!'

'Have you, Nafnel?'

'Nar. Sod orf.'

Rose glared down at the curved back, the knobs of the child's backbone clearly visible beneath the woollen material. 'Stand up, Starkey. *Now*.'

Reluctantly, with Rose's fingers locked into the back of his jumper, he did so, revealing a pregnant bulge over his stomach.

'What's that?'

In reply Starkey withdrew the ball and flung it across the playground. 'Don' wan' it anyhow.'

Waiting until the other children had resumed their game, Rose released her grip on Starkey's jumper and slid the hand along the back of his thin shoulders. Turning him to face her she admonished him: 'You mustn't take other children's things, Nafnel. It's stealing. Do you understand?'

'Yeah.' He scuffed the ground refusing to meet her eye.

'Good. Go and play then.'

It was a useless instruction. She soon discovered that none of the others wanted to play with him. And

Starkey didn't seem able to stop stealing. By the end of the day she'd retrieved the ball twice at dinner time, a skipping rope in the afternoon break, and Ginger's pencil box from his desk just as she was about to dismiss the class at the end of the day. She was too shattered to do more than tell the class they could go and follow them to the door to see them all safely off the premises.

Yelling and whooping they streamed away.

Ginger rushed over to an elderly woman pushing a pram laden with bags, blankets and a toddler. Praying that she wasn't complaining about the pencil box, Rose drifted nearer.

'I 'ope they ain't been kept in. Yer Auntie Edie will never be able to save all them places if we ain't up there soon,' the woman said scanning the school with an anxious frown over her well-worn face.

'This is me new teacher,' Ginger piped up as Rose came within speaking distance.

'Pleased to meet yer, I'm sure.'

Rose shook the offered hand. 'How do you do, Mrs Scannell?'

'Meeks, love. Mrs Meeks. I'm their nan. Their mum's at work.' She peered round Rose, searching for someone. 'They ain't kept 'er sisters in, 'ave they, miss? Only if we don't get up Hampstead Tube soon all the places will be gone.'

'You shelter in Hampstead. It's a long way to push this lot, isn't it?'

'Oh you get used to it, miss. And it's lovely and deep. You don't 'ear the bombs at all. Come on quick, you two, we ain't got time to dawdle.'

Two older girls flew out of the school gate gasping

apologies. Irene Meeks released the pram brake and flung her weight behind the handle.

'Mrs Meeks,' Rose called as the woman started to move away.

'Yes, miss?'

'I was just wondering ... Why is your grand-daughter called Ginger? Her hair isn't red.'

Irene's face lit up with a smile. 'Why, it's after the film star, miss. Ginger Rogers. Our Pearl loves the pictures. She called 'em all after film stars. There's Marlene and Greta, and this one ...' She drew the pram back to give Rose a clearer view of the runny-nosed toddler. ''E's Tyrone. After that Tyrone Powell.'

Rose was stunned into silence. Rarely had she seen a collection of children who looked less like their Hollywood namesakes. She was still standing with her mouth open as Ginger called back that her mum was going to call their next baby Clark if it was a boy or Tallulah if it was a girl.

'Let's hope for the poor little devil's sake that it's a boy then,' remarked someone at Rose's elbow.

Startled she swung round and found herself looking into Pat O'Day's dancing brown eyes.

'Oh, er. Hello. I think Sammy's already left.'

'Charged in five minutes ago. I came to see you, not him.'

'Why?' It came out with an abruptness that bordered on rudeness. But his direct approach had jolted her out of her normal reserve.

'Oh you know. I fancied a chat.'

It would have been ridiculous to hide in the school until he went away. All she could do was collect her coat and set off down Malden Crescent with him. To her relief, he made no attempt to take her arm.

'How was the dance?' she asked when the silence was becoming embarrassing.

'What dance?'

'When you were in the shop you said you were having a dance to raise money for a Spitfire.'

'Oh that. That's this Friday.'

'Oh.' She'd assumed it was to have been that Saturday evening, now she saw that she'd given him the opening he needed. Desperately looking round for something, anything, to distract him, she found that a small, smelly figure was dogging her footsteps.

'Nafnel, shouldn't you be going home? Won't your grandmother wonder where you are?'

'Nah.'

Now they'd stopped, Starkey halted too, one foot on the kerb the other in the gutter.

'What did you call him?' Pat demanded.

'Nafnel. I know it sounds unlikely, but he insists it's his name,' Rose murmured from the corner of her mouth.

'Tis. 'Oo's he?'

'Don't be rude, Nafnel. This is Mr O'Day. A . . . friend, of mine.'

If Pat noticed the hesitation before she decided on his status, he gave no sign. Instead he extended a hand and invited Nafnel to shake. 'You call me Pat and I'll call you Nafnel, deal?'

'Fair nuff.' The niceties out of the way, Starkey turned his attention to his main obsession: 'You got any more of them sandwiches?'

'I'm afraid not. Won't your grandmother be getting your tea for you?'

210

'Nah. She ain't in.'

Inspiration struck Rose. If she couldn't shake off Pat, then at least she could have a chaperon. 'Would you like me to cook your tea for you, Nafnel?'

'Yeah!'

'Good. Come on then.' Suppressing a shudder, Rose took his hand. Pat fell in beside them.

It wasn't until she turned into Balaclava Row that she started to experience a niggling doubt. Images of Albert's scrupulously scrubbed shop with its open barrels of oat flakes, flour, sugar, rice and beans and its gleaming marble slabs holding lumps of fresh butter and cheese started to dance in front of her eyes. Through clenched teeth, she hissed to Pat over the child's head: 'It's a food shop. Albert will have a fit if I take him past the customers.'

'Take him round the back then. Tell you what, if you like I'll slip back to the chemist's. Get you a few things to clean him up a bit.'

'Would you? Oh, thanks Pat.' Rose accepted his suggestion with alacrity. How to explain why she was sneaking down the back entrance with Pat O'Day had been worrying her even more than Albert's possible reaction when he laid eyes on Starkey.

Chapter 13

'Gawd, what the hell's *that*?' was Albert's reaction. He stood in the back of the stockroom gazing in disbelief at Starkey.

'A pupil. I'm just going to give him his tea. Up there, Nafnel.' She pushed the boy through the door to the flat stairs. 'Everything all right in the shop, Albert?'

'Oh, yer, fine. Got Mrs Tracy 'elping out mornings. And 'er Ena coming in when we shut to scrub down the floors and counters.' Rousing himself from the shock that Starkey's appearance had caused, he went on to tell her that Ena had strict instructions to call up when she was leaving. 'So you can come down and lock up proper. Don't want no more burglars getting in.'

'There wasn't a burglar, Albert. It was just Lexie's imagination.'

'That's as may be, but I don't want you ending up like poor old James.'

'Is there any news on that? I feel dreadful not doing more for Gwen, but she's acting so funny. I felt really uncomfortable talking to her. And Lexie said she was downright rude when she went round. Wouldn't even let her in the flat.'

'Best leave her if that's what she wants. Some folks like to be on their own. The police must be on to something, they come round this afternoon to . . .'

He never finished, the door bell and the imperious

shout of 'shop' sent him hurrying back out front.

Rose walked upstairs to find all the flat doors open and Starkey descending the upper staircase.

'Where's all the other people then?'

'What other people?'

'All the other bleeders what live here?'

'There isn't anybody else. I live here alone, since my husband died. And please don't use that word, Nafnel.'

'What word?'

'Bleeders.'

'Why not?'

'Because I say so.'

Nafnel swaggered down the last few steps in a manner that clearly said, 'Oh yeah? And who are you when yer at home?'

'Let's see what's in the kitchen?' Rose suggested.

He was happy to fall in with that idea, following her around snatching biscuits and dipping fingers into jars as soon as she took her eyes off him.

'That fat geezer yer fancy man?'

Rose didn't feel up to any more grammar lessons today. She contented herself with informing Nafnel that Albert was the landlord and was relieved when the self-same landlord called up the stairs: 'Rose? Visitor for you.'

Pat bounded up the stairs with a brown paper bag that clinked of glass clutched to his chest.

'Got them. This one.' He handed her a bottle of violet liquid. 'You put on the rash. And this stuff, you mix with water and paint on all over his body. And the little bottle . . .'

'I know,' Rose interrupted, uncorking the small

brown flask and recoiling from the pungent smell that hit her nostrils. 'I remember – the Nit Lady.'

'Exactly. Here yer are.' He untangled a large steel comb from the parcel. 'And I got a bottle of Lysol too. Thought you might want to wash things down here after you've done him.'

She did. Ever since she'd taken Nafnel's hand, she had been repressing a strong desire to scratch. It was all in her mind, of course. At least, she prayed it was.

'You gonna cook me tea now?' Nafnel enquired, wandering back into the hall.

'As soon as you've had your bath.'

'Barf? I don't want no barf.'

'Yes you do,' Pat said firmly. 'Tell you what. I'll scrub him while you do the tea. Where's the bath?'

'In here.' Rose threw open the door.

Nafnel pushed past them both and demonstrated that he'd already been in. 'Yer turn the taps on like this, see?' he announced spinning both full on. 'And yer don' 'ave to wait for nobody to send the water, it comes right out.'

Pat deduced from this description that his experience of bathing hadn't been confined to a scrub in front of the fire. 'You've been to the public baths then, have you, Nafnel?'

'Yeah. Me mum took me once.'

'*Once!*' Rose mouthed.

Thrusting the bottles at Pat, she fled back to the kitchen to discover that the only thing she had in for tea was a tin of jellied veal that Albert had insisted on giving her months ago. She didn't even know whether she liked veal, but it would have to do, providing she could scrounge something to cook with it.

Ignoring the screams and yells that were emanating through the closed bathroom door, she hurried downstairs again and nearly collided with Albert who was hovering outside the bottom door.

'Everything all right, love?' he asked, blushing to the tips of his ears that she'd caught him eavesdropping.

'Fine. Pat's just giving Nafnel a bath. I need a few things for tea.'

'Jam, that's the thing. Kids like that. And I got some boxes of cakes in. And a bit of butter, eh?'

'I need vegetables, I'm just slipping down to the cafe to see if they'll loan me some. And I've had my butter ration for this week. Albert, have you been giving out things without asking for the coupons again?'

Albert shuffled. 'Aah ... em ... well you know, some of the regulars just can't manage.'

'Well they'll just have to try,' Rose said sternly. 'For heaven's sake, Albert. What if one of them turns out to be a food inspector? You'll end up in court – or jail.' She relented and gave his thick arm a playful punch. 'I've a good mind to give you a hundred lines. Go on, get back to your bacon slicer.'

Maria provided cold boiled potatoes.

'Are you sure you can spare them,' Rose said, taking the dish gratefully.

'Sure. Tomorrow I make littler shepherd's pie and maybe some rissoles. You cook for your boyfriend, yes?'

'What boyfriend?'

'The one who go in the back just now. The nice-looking fireman.'

'Pat isn't my boyfriend. He's just a friend.'

'Sure. I understand. Your husband not dead for long. Best people don' know yet.'

Rose gave up. 'I don't suppose you've got any onions?'

'No. No onions for weeks. Me, I don't mind, I put 'erbs in the meat. But the customers they complain, what's all these little green bits doing in the meat? So I go back to plain stew and cabbage like the English like.'

Removing one of the heavy iron saucepans from the cooker, she whipped off the lid and proudly showed Rose a mess of overstewed leaves huddled in the bottom. 'You want some?'

'Please, if you can spare it.'

'Sure. Not many customers now.' The empty tables beyond the serving hatch testified to this statement. 'Is business bad?'

'Not good.' Maria tipped the soggy mass of greens into a dish. 'When Alice and Fred were open it was better. People come for fish and chips then change their minds, decide maybe to have their tea here instead. But now . . .' Her shoulders lifted and her mouth pouted in a gesture of resignation. 'No fish and chips, plenty bombs. Not worth opening in the evenings.'

'I'm sorry.'

Maria leant against the scarred wooden table that she used for preparing the food. Delving into the pocket of her apron she produced a packet of Players. 'Want one?'

'No thanks. I don't smoke.'

'You should. Keeps the damp off your chest. Papa taught me that. You need anything else?'

217

'I don't suppose you have any beef dripping?'

She could do bubble and squeak to go with the cold veal.

'Sure.' With a large, flat-bladed knife Maria scooped out a generous lump of fat and brown jelly and lobbed it in a cup. 'Albert tell you about the fingerprinting?'

The dish of gently steaming cabbage was making a damp patch on her blouse. Rose put it down and said, 'No. What fingerprinting?'

'We all been done. 'Cept you and Matt.' She held up her right hand to show Rose the faint marks on her fingertips. 'That woman policeman come with another bloke and they ask if we mind.'

'But why?'

'For the murder. 'Spect they want yours too.'

They did. When she got back to the shop, Albert was issuing stern instructions to a thin, vacant-looking thirteen year old, regarding soap, elbow-grease and the importance of scrubbing the corners. 'Oh, Rose,' he said breaking off from his lecture, 'I been meaning to tell you, the police been here getting fingerprints.'

'I know. Maria said. What's it all about?'

'Looks like it's definite that poor James was done in. They got a load of prints from his place. They want to match us up. Take away ours and I suppose the one that's left must be the murderer. Anyhow the lady sergeant asked if you'd mind popping into the station to give yours.'

'When?'

'Soon as you can I suppose. Daresay tomorrow will be soon enough. Well, get on with it. You know where the tap is.' This last remark was directed at Ena who'd been standing open mouthed, breathing in short gasps through her mouth, overcome with the excitement of mixing with the sort of sophisticated people who had murders done in their shops.

Rose reclimbed the stairs and was nearly knocked flying by Nafnel hurtling from the bathroom and rushing into the sitting room. Pat threw himself after him. 'Come here.' He succeeded in grasping one slippery wet ankle.

Nafnel seized the sofa leg. 'Gerroff.'

'Whatever's the matter?'

Pat was on his knees. He'd removed his jacket and the front of his shirt was soaked. 'He don't fancy the purple stuff.'

'I'll look like a dafty,' shrieked Nafnel, still grimly holding on to the sofa leg.

Rose put the dishes on the floor and crawled across to him. 'Look, Nafnel, you've got to have it, otherwise the red patches will never get better. How about if Pat only puts it on your body? No one will see it under your clothes. And as soon as you're done, we can have tea. I'm cooking bubble and squeak and cold meat.'

Nafnel could put up with practically anything if there was a square meal at the end of it. He allowed himself to be led back to the bathroom.

Rose mashed the potatoes, added chopped cabbage, and formed the mixture into round cakes. Before putting them on the gas, she went back to the bathroom to see how much longer the clean-up was going to take.

Huddled on the edge of the bath, with one of her towels wrapped round him like a kilt, Starkey shot her a resentful look. 'Told yer I'd look bleedin' daft.'

The gentian violet, applied over the red rash, had certainly not improved the appearance of this skinny body. On an impulse, Rose stooped and hugged him. 'It's only to make you better. It will soon fade. Have you done his hair?'

'Not yet.'

With an involuntary jerk of her neck, Rose whipped her head away. Pat gave her a malicious grin. 'I'll do it,' she said, stretching out her hand for the comb.

Evidently, Nafnel knew this routine. Hunched on the hard bath rim he muttered under his breath but gave her no trouble whilst she sprinkled the evil-smelling liquid over his hair and ran the steel teeth carefully through each section sweeping the little grey lice eggs from the wet shafts.

'What shall I do with his clothes?' Pat asked, picking up the tattered garments with two fingers. 'It's too late to light a bonfire.'

'We can't burn them. What would his grandmother say? Put them in the bath and pour some Lysol over them. I'll wash them out tomorrow.' She flung another towel round the little boy's shoulders. 'In the meantime, we can't send him home dressed like this.'

Pat span the bath taps. 'Not to worry. I'll shoot home after tea. Mum's got some of Sammy's old stuff.'

She'd been planning to cook for two, but she could hardly tell Pat to get out now. 'I'll get the bubble and squeak on.'

'Good. I'm starving.'

'Me too. 'Ow much more washing I gotta have before I get me tea?'

'Just teeth left. Have you got a spare toothbrush, Rose?'

It was in the drawer of the little table that the mirror stood on. Dried up, misshapen, the bristles pushed out of shape by the pressure of hand against enamel. 'Peter's,' she said briefly. 'There's a tube of Kolynos over there.'

Not looking at him, she practically flung the brush across the room and fled back to the kitchen.

The squeak was crisping up nicely in the bubbling dripping and she'd sliced the whole tin of veal on to three plates by the time they came trooping in, Nafnel running the tip of his tongue over his newly cleaned teeth with interest.

'Monday tea,' Pat said after a while.

'Yes.'

Nafnel paused in his attempts to shovel in the entire plateful in one go to demand, 'Why?'

It was Pat who explained that Monday was washday. 'No time to cook on washdays. You get the leftovers from Sunday.'

'Isn't that what your mum used to do, Nafnel? Do her washing on Mondays?' Rose was glad of an excuse to probe into the child's background.

Nafnel offered the fact that his mum sometimes went down the laundry but he didn't know when.

'Where was the laundry?'

'Next to the boozer.' Nafnel crammed in the last few morsels of food and pushed them into place with a couple of fingers.

Whilst he was temporarily masticating noisily, Rose asked Pat if he'd found any papers in the boy's clothes.

'Nothing but holes. And bugs.'

'But he must have an identity card. And a ration book.' Taking her own from her handbag, Rose set them on the table. 'Have you got a book like this, Nafnel? A blue one?' she asked, flicking the pages so he could see the ration coupons.

'Dunno.'

'His grandmother's probably got it. Does it matter?'

'I want to find out his name. It can't possibly be Nafnel.'

"Tis. You gonna eat that, mister?' Nafnel eyed Pat's half-finished meal.

Pat swept half on to the boy's plate with the back of his knife.

'You shouldn't do that. I could have given him something for afters.'

'The kid's starving. Look at him.'

Rose did. For the first time she looked properly and saw beyond the sores and rashes. With a thrill of horror, she realised that Pat was right: the skin had already started to collapse between his ribs on his chest; the cheeks had sunk in, emphasising the high cheekbones and the deep smudges of purple beneath his eyes weren't due to tiredness but lack of food.

'You'd better do him that afters while I go home and get them clothes,' Pat said pushing back his seat.

'I've been thinking. I'll have to take him home, I can't just send him all washed and dressed in new clothes. His grandmother will think I'm trying to be all la-di-da and patronising.'

'I shouldn't worry about hurting his gran's feelings. Anyone who leaves a kid in that state deserves to hear a few home truths.'

But Rose was adamant. She wanted to take Nafnel back to Warden Road. 'There's no sense in you going all the way home and back and then me having to take Nafnel the same way. If you don't think your mum would mind, we could all go round the Square, get some things for him, and then go on to his gran's. You could wrap him in a blanket and carry him.'

Pat fell in with her suggestion with alacrity. She knew what was in his mind. Taking her home like that, even to beg secondhand clothes, was practically an announcement that they were walking out in his mind. He'd have to find out that it wasn't what was in hers in his own good time; Pat was a nice bloke, but she had no intention of getting involved with anyone.

They had to wait whilst Nafnel slurped his way through a dish of tinned peaches and custard, before he allowed himself to be bundled up and carried out into the half-dark streets in Pat's arms.

The sirens went as they reached Kentish Town Road. There was none of the panic of the early days of the bombing. Those who intended to take cover in the public shelters and tube stations headed for them at a steady, but unhurried pace; but the majority of the pedestrians still outside simply increased their pace slightly and continued homewards.

'You gotta shelter?' Pat asked suddenly.

'I get under the counter in the shop if the bombs sound really close. Why?'

'I just wondered. It's best to be low down. Most of the survivors we've found, they've been sleeping downstairs, kitchen or under the stairs. What about you, champ?' He jiggled the half-asleep child, making him giggle. 'Where'd you go when the bombing gets really loud. Yer gran take you down the shelter?'

'Nah! She don't 'ear nuffing me gran after she's

been down the boozer. She just snores.'

'What about you? What do you do when you hear the bombs?' Pat persisted.

'I watch 'em. From me window. Some of 'em go off really good. Kaaa... boom!' Nafnel yelled his imitation of an exploding land-mine in Pat's earhole.

Fortunately for him they'd reached the O'Days' house.

Pat left them both in the kitchen and went out to the garden to fetch his mother who bustled in behind him a moment later struggling to drag out the curlers she'd just started winding in her black hair and directing even blacker looks at her eldest's back.

Muttering apologies for her appearance, she disappeared upstairs and returned with a bundle of underwear, a shirt, trousers, a jumper and a pair of boots. 'Our Sammy's only got the one pair of shoes, I'm afraid. I was saving this pair of Conn's 'til he grew into 'em. They might fit if you stuff 'em with a bit of newspaper.'

The boots, however, were far too large. Even well laced and stuffed with several sheets of paper, they flapped and banged and forced him to walk with a strange splay-toed gait.

'I'll bring your plimsolls in to school tomorrow,' Rose reassured him.

'If you're determined to take him home, we'd best be going. I'll come down the shelter when I get back, Mum.'

With Nafnel slapping along between them in his newly acquired shoes, they retraced their route up Malden and along Riley Street.

The school reminded Rose of something she'd been

meaning to ask Pat. 'Your mother looks after that policeman's little girl, doesn't she?'

'Mr Stamford? Yeah, that's right.'

'Doesn't he have a wife?'

'Sort of. She's Dutch, yer see? Left him and went home a couple of years back. Took the kid with her.'

'Where is she now? Still in Holland?'

'Don't know. Neither does Mr Stamford. Some Belgian refugees found Annie after their column was strafed by a German plane, brought her over to England with them. She was holding on to a dead woman, might have been her mum, might not. Mr Stamford ain't got no way of knowing now.'

'What does Annaliese say?'

'She don't. Won't talk about it. Just clams up if you try and make her.' They'd reached Warden Road by now. 'Which house is it, Nafnel?'

'Down there.' Soles slapping against the pavement, Nafnel took a hand from each of them, and led them to a tall tenement house. The sound of a baby's crying, mingled with the yowl of a cat on heat, drifted from an open window.

'Which floor, Nafnel?'

'Up 'ere.'

He led them up three flights of bare wooden stairs; dirt crunched beneath their shoes and exploded in tiny clouds of grit. Voices rumbled and whinged behind the closed doors on the unlit landings. A woman's voice, resentful and accusing, was swiftly silenced by a man's reply and the slap of bone against flesh.

They'd reached the top landing. In the pale moonlight that was fighting to get past the grime and sticky tape on the window they saw the stained sink with

its solitary cold water tap and the ancient gas cooker.
Green slime, deep brown limescale, and baked black
grease decorated them like camouflage paint.

'In 'ere.'

The room was in darkness. Pat cautiously swung a
torch. Its shaded beam picked out the rubbish-strewn
floor, ankle deep in greasy, crumpled newspapers from
the local fish and chip shop. He moved the light beam
upwards, to reveal the table. Open tins, dirty dishes,
and a burnt-out saucepan huddled together. Pat's light
darted around, on the wardrobe one moment, sliding
across the armchair, stuffing exploding from ripped
holes, the next. And finally coming to rest on the bed.
The heap of blankets murmured and moaned at the
intrusion, then turned away from the probing beam.

'Come on.'

Pat's boots stuck to the linoleum as he made his
way across to the bed and shone the light full on the
recumbent figure.

'Ger orf. Leave 's alon'.'

Her coat hung half on, half off, draping over the
side of the bed. A dress, once pale pink, was rucked
up round her waist, revealing white legs riddled with
rivers of blue veins, each well supplied with tributaries. In the space between her legs the blankets were
stained a darker grey. The stink of stale urine carried
to their nostrils, together with the overwhelming smell
of alcohol.

Pat played the light over her face. Eyes opened and
regarded him unseeingly.

'Ask her where Nafnel's papers are?' Rose whispered.

The question brought a mumbled curse. Gingerly,

Rose felt in the woman's pockets. They were empty. A handbag, thrown to the ground, its contents half strewn out, contained nothing of interest either.

'Try the floor,' Pat advised, swinging his torch downwards. 'I can't put the lights on, she's got no blackout curtains.'

'Lights don't work,' Nafnel piped up. 'The geezer downstairs bust into the meters.'

Despite scrabbling through all the rubbish, hindered rather than helped by Nafnel who was enjoying the game, they could find no sign of the child's identity card or ration book. 'I don't like to look through the wardrobe or cupboards. But I've got to find out his name. Mr Jenkins, at school, said East Ham or West Ham. Maybe they've got records there,' Rose said brushing off her hands in disgust, glad that she couldn't see what was on them.

'Which is it, Nafnel? East or West Ham?'

'East, I fink.'

He obviously wasn't too sure, but Pat offered to make a start there on Friday. 'I'm off again then.'

'You don't have to. He's my problem, Pat.'

'I want to. Where'd you sleep, champ?'

'On the bed wiv 'er if she ain't too stinky. Or under the table if she is. Reckon I'll sleep there tonight.'

So saying he curled up on the floor. 'Oi, watcha doin'?'

What Pat was doing was scooping him up under one arm and running lightly downstairs again. When he reached the bottom, he opened the cupboard beneath the stairs. It smelt damp and dirty, like the rest of the house. 'See this cupboard?' He swung Nafnel so that his head went into the dark cavity.

'Next time the bombs sound really close, you don't kneel up there watching 'em, you come down here and sleep in here. Understand?'

When Nafnel agreed that he did, he was told he could go back upstairs again.

Alone in the passage with Pat, the feeling of panic swept over Rose again. He was too close; she could smell the scents of his skin and sweat.

'Rose, I was wondering . . .'

'Let's get back.'

She was practically running down the road, forcing him to sprint to keep up with her. Ahead of her, the skyline lit up with the flash of exploding bombs.

'City's getting it again,' Pat said, catching her up and taking her arm. 'You could stay in our Anderson tonight, if you like.'

'No. Thank you. I want to go home.' She tore herself free from his light grasp. 'I'll pay you back for the disinfectants and things when I get paid, if that's all right?'

'Don't be daft. I don't want paying. Tell you what though, you could go to the dance with me Friday. How about it?'

'I can't.'

'Look, if it's on account of Peter . . .'

'No. It's not that. It's . . . I haven't got anything to wear.'

The clouds parted momentarily to allow her to see his face. The rejection and disappointment etched into his eyes, made her relent and explain more than she'd planned. 'I haven't, honest, Pat. All I've got is what I've got on, and that old dress I wore in the shop. And it's too late to make anything. Goodbye, thanks for everything.'

She was gone before he could respond.

Halfway along Prince of Wales Road she started to imagine he'd followed her. The echoing footsteps in the blacked-out street impinged on her subconscious, their light, steady rhythm acting as counterpoint to the sticks of bombs crashing far to the south.

Once she stopped, ears straining for a movement behind her, but the footsteps had ceased too. Imagination, she told herself, crossing and retracing the route she'd taken with Lexie on Saturday night. It was quieter once she'd left the High Street. The first onslaught of bombers on the City had passed and the ack-ack guns had ceased their booming response. The air was suddenly still again.

This time there was no mistaking the sound; footsteps, moving when she did, stopping when she did.

'Hello? Pat, is that you?'

Someone moved. It was no more than the shifting of a patch of blackness, disengaging and splitting into two separate shadows: one was ragged, a bush overhanging someone's garden, the other angular, the outline of a shoulder and cheek visible for a brief moment.

'Who's there?'

The reply, hissed between clenched teeth, was half lost in the next furious assault of the anti-aircraft guns.

'Whore.'

Stifling a half-scream, Rose ran.

Chapter 14

The day hadn't started well. In the misery of her cold, Annaliese had clung harder to Eileen, refusing even to kiss her father.

'She's poorly,' Eileen had said, excusing the rejection once more. 'Little ones want their mums when they're poorly. Mine always did. Still do, in fact.'

'You aren't her mother, Eileen.'

'Closer to it than you are, love. Don't fret. Soon as she's up and around again, she'll be wanting to play with daddy.'

'She hasn't shown any sign of wanting to so far.'

'You try too hard. Just ignore her for a bit. Let her get used to living with you again.'

But that was the problem; he didn't think she'd ever lived with him. The more he saw of this child, the more convinced he was becoming that, no matter how much she might look like her, this wasn't Annaliese. He nearly said as much to Eileen, but once again something stopped him. Instead he'd watched her spooning an evil-smelling brown liquid down the little girl's throat.

'What's that?'

Eileen's thin face lit up with pride. 'Sliced onion sprinkled with brown sugar and left to seep overnight. Best thing for a cough. Didn't think I'd be able to get 'em now. But our Maury come up trumps. You should see the onion he got me. Must be all of three pounds.

231

I'm saving most in case Pat decides to invite his young lady round for her tea.'

She then proceeded to inform Jack that Pat was courting a girl who was one of the suspects in his current murder case.

By the time he arrived at Agar Street Station, he was already thoroughly depressed and his mood wasn't improved by the sight of Detective Sergeant Agnew and Detective Constable Bell both peering mournfully at him through the depths of a smoke-screen that could have blanketed most of north London.

'Someone to see you,' the DS said, his voice flattened by his attempt to keep his pipe stem clamped between his teeth.

Eyes watering, Jack managed to make out Matthew Fortune sitting against the wall. He made to rise, but Stamford waved him down. 'There's more oxygen nearer the floor.' Agnew didn't take the hint. Irritably, Stamford slammed a window open.

With a look that made it clear he suspected his superior of attempting to save on his police pension by inducing a bout of pneumonia, Agnew slunk out muttering that the gentleman was here about finger-prints.

'Helen said you wanted to take mine,' Matthew said eagerly. Oddly enough Stamford's fears that the inhabitants of Balaclava Row might be offended at being asked to provide fingerprints had been unfounded. In fact, the opposite had proved to be true.

'They seem to quite enjoy it, sir,' Sarah had reported. 'I suppose it's something different.'

It looked like Matthew was viewing the procedure

with much the same enthusiasm. Despite Stamford's instruction, he'd stood up and only reseated himself when Jack took a chair.

'Thanks for coming in. I've not caused you any problems at work, have I?'

'None at all. I'd hardly call deciding what the public can be allowed to be told is essential war work. Or do you agree with censorship, Chief Inspector? Perhaps you think the ignorant masses need to be protected from unpleasant truths, just in case they decide that if this land is greener and pleasanter for some than others, then the recipients of all that greenery and pleasure should be doing rather more of their share of protecting it.'

The speech was delivered in the light-hearted mocking tone that he'd used when excusing his deformity, but the green flecks in the hazel eyes glittered with a suppressed rage. It confirmed Stamford's first impression that Matthew Fortune was a young man with a great deal of inner anger. Before he could answer, however, Ding Dong spoke up.

'You a communist then, sir?'

Matthew's expression relaxed into (as far as Jack could tell) genuine amusement. 'Me? Good heavens, no! I couldn't be bothered to belong to an organised political party. I'm a Liberal.'

Jack said, 'But a Liberal who doesn't like his job?'

'Yes. As a matter of fact, I was quite glad to come in, because there's something I wanted to ask you . . .' The brown eyes slid in Ding Dong's direction in a clear request for privacy.

Ding Dong rose: 'I'll be getting on. Got a bit of a lead on the gent what ordered the ruby ear-rings special.'

Stamford didn't press for further details whilst Matthew was in the room. Instead he sent for an officer to take the prints. There was a slight hiatus when the man finished rolling the fingers on Matthew's left hand across the ink pad and held out his own hand again. 'Right now, please, sir.'

He'd kept it casually draped in the suit pocket. It would have looked effeminate if Jack hadn't known the real reason. Now he pulled it reluctantly into the light and laid it out for inspection.

'Not much doubt if you find fingerprints from that, is there?'

The officer responded with a tight-lipped smile but his hesitation before he touched each deformed finger was painfully obvious. With each digit Matthew Fortune's expression became more neutral. It was hard to say which of them was the more relieved when the ordeal was over.

'Thank you,' Stamford nodded at the other officer, wishing now that he'd done the job himself. 'Get those over to the Yard for checking against the Donald file. Have you had breakfast,' he asked as the man collected together his cards and inks and backed out.

'Ages ago.' Matthew was trying to match his casual approach and almost succeeding, apart from a slight tic that jerked against the corner of one eye.

'I'll get us some tea then.'

It was one of those odd periods when all the officers in sight were either engaged with members of the public or speaking on the telephone. Eventually, Jack found himself so close to the canteen, it was simplest to collect two cups of tea himself.

The sudden silencing of the buzz of conversation

told him that he'd been the main subject of said conversation. But in what context, he wondered? He must remember to ask Sarah.

'You understand,' he said, returning to Matthew, 'that we only want your prints for elimination. We shan't keep them on file.'

'Helen said. How are things going? Apart from ...' He waggled the fingers with their staining of pale grey that always took a while to wear off. 'Any other leads?'

'We're following up several lines of enquiry at present, Mr Fortune.'

'You mean you're not going to tell me. I don't know that this lark is going to help you much. You do know that we've all been in the flat recently? For James's birthday do.'

'We know. Did it surprise you? The invitation, I mean?'

Matthew sipped slowly, apparently weighing his reply. 'Yes, I suppose it did, really. It had never happened before. Gwen was, is, very involved with her children, but I don't remember her ever putting herself to any trouble on James's behalf. Have you noticed the way she always calls him "Donald", never "James"?'

Jack had, but he'd imagined that perhaps it was because she was talking to strangers.

'No. She always did it,' Matthew assured him.

'And what about him? Was James fond of his wife?'

'Not especially. I mean, he didn't talk about that sort of thing.'

'Did you know him well?'

'Not really. We got to know him better this past

year. He used to invite us round for a drink or a game of cards occasionally.'

'Us?'

'Helen and me.'

'Together?'

'Sorry?'

Jack elaborated. 'Did you and your sister always go to James Donald's flat together?'

'Not always, no. Why?' Matthew shifted restlessly in his seat, the direction of the questions making him not exactly suspicious, but on his guard.

'Sometimes people will confide more on a one to one basis than to a group of people. Did James ever suggest to you he was lonely? That he missed his wife?'

Some men, Stamford had found, couldn't resist boasting a little about their extra-marital affairs.

'No. He often said he missed the girls. But he never talked about Gwen. Not in that way anyway.'

'Do you think he ever spoke to your sister about her?'

'I shouldn't think so. She never said he did.'

'You seem very close, you and your sister.'

Matthew's face softened. 'Yes. She's the best. My sis.'

'Have you always lived in Balaclava?'

'I have. She hasn't. She had her own business. In Watford.'

'What brought her back?'

'I did.'

Matthew drained the last of his tea and replaced the cup. His touch with the withered hand was light and deft. 'When Mother died she came home to look after me. She won't admit it, but she also broke off her engagement for the same reason.'

'When was this?'

'Oh years ago. I was ten.'

Old enough surely, Stamford thought, for his father to cope alone. Unless he'd died before his wife?

'Dad? He died about five years ago. Why?'

'No reason. It's just one of the penalties of being a copper. You become incurably nosy about other people's lives.'

Matthew glanced at the expensive watch on his left wrist.

'I won't keep you any further. Thank you for coming in.'

He offered a hand. This time it was Matt who hesitated before reaching forward. 'Some people,' he explained in response to Jack's raised eyebrow, 'think they have to make a grand gesture by shaking it.'

'Perhaps if you worried less about it, other people would too.'

'That's what Rose said. But it's always easier to give advice than to take it, isn't it?'

His remark about Rose Goodwin reminded Jack of something that had been niggling at the back of his mind for some days. 'You were a friend of Peter Goodwin's weren't you?'

'We went to school together, yes. Rose too.'

'Was Peter ever in the Territorial Army? Or some sort of Cadet Corps?'

'Not that I know of. In fact, no. I'm sure he wasn't. Why do you ask?'

'I rather gained the impression from something Albert White said that Peter was called up last September. It struck me as rather odd that a young man of twenty-six, and in a reserved occupation, should be conscripted so early. He was a teacher wasn't he?'

'Elementary school, same as Rose. But Peter wasn't conscripted, Chief Inspector. He joined up last summer.'

It probably had nothing at all to do with the case, but like he'd told Matthew, over the years he'd acquired a habit of noting odd quirks in other people's behaviour and worrying at them until he found the answer.

Like where James Donald's family had originated from. Gwen Donald was the person most likely to supply the answer to that one; but he'd sensed a reserve when she spoke to him. So he'd despatched Sarah to see her this morning to probe a little under the guise of checking up on Mrs Donald's general welfare. She was, after all, recently widowed, if not exactly grief-stricken.

He'd also deputised one other little task to his sergeant which he felt she might be able to undertake with rather more success than himself, given her particular relationship with a certain sticky-fingered milkman.

Irked at the necessity to sit and wait for information to be brought to him, Jack decided to stroll round to Balaclava Row, and intercept Sarah on her way back.

It was a fine autumn morning again. The pale blue sky was overlaid with a fine gauze of cloud but it showed every sign of burning off later and turning into another bright Indian summer day. The golds and burnished coppers of the trees and bushes along Islip Street added to the impression of peaceful normality. For some reason, Jack found it all infinitely depressing. It occurred to him that if the whole population of this island was wiped out tonight, the plants would still go on growing, the sun would keep shining, and in a few centuries all traces of humankind would be obliterated.

He gave a half-shiver and tried to shake off these morbid fancies. This business with Annaliese was affecting him more than he cared to admit to himself. It was almost a relief to breathe in a sudden pungent cloud of chlorine. Eyes watering, he stopped for a moment to mop away the tears and watch one of the council's decontamination squads spreading bleach paste over the kerbs.

Across the road, a military policeman had stopped, apparently for the same purpose. Catching his eye, Jack nodded a brief professional greeting, forgetting for the moment that there was nothing about him to distinguish him as a colleague. However, the man seemed to take it as an invitation.

'Fine morning,' he called, crossing to join Stamford.

'Very fine.' Jack cast an appraising eye over the man's demeanour. It didn't entirely suggest someone out to enjoy an autumn stroll. 'Are you out on duty or pleasure, Sergeant?'

'Oh a policeman's never what you might call off duty, sir.'

'Really?' It was a silly game. Hiding his own identity. But he took a childish pleasure in doing it. 'So what are you investigating today then?'

'Fish and chip shops, sir. Do you know of any round here?'

That was a new one even on Jack. For a moment

he suspected a leg-pull, but the man's pugnacious jawline was set firm.

'There're a couple in Kentish Town Road,' he offered.

'I've tried them. Anywhere else?'

He'd also sampled those in Camden Road, Queen's Crescent, Fortess Road, Dartmouth Park Road, several in Somers Town and one in Highgate. Jack was forced to admit defeat.

'Blimey,' one of the workmen hissed as the soldier strolled towards the high street with a stiff-necked stance that advertised his profession even more clearly than the khaki uniform. 'My missus always complains I'm a fussy eater. She should have that one.'

'Reckon she would, Joe, given half a chance,' one of the others called.

Jack left them squaring up to each other, bristle brushes raised like lances, and continued on his walk to Balaclava Row, his mood unaccountably lightened by the encounter.

Sarah was standing at the front window of the Donalds' flat. Glancing up, he caught the almost imperceptible shake of her head and nodded his understanding. His first impulse was to go into the cafe, but at the last moment he crossed opposite the hairdresser's.

He was in luck; the salon was empty except for Helen Fortune, who emerged from the back at the sound of the shop bell. Her welcoming smile faded briefly when she saw him, then returned, lighting up her tired face.

'Sorry. Did you think I was a customer?'

'I did. Mind you, I don't know whether I'm glad or

sorry that you're not.' She tried to stifle an enormous yawn behind a slim hand tipped with scarlet nails. 'Excuse me. Thank heavens it's half-day closing.'

'Rough night?'

'ARP duties. I do every fourth night.'

Jack remembered that she'd been out on them the night James Donald had been killed.

'What do you do exactly?' he asked.

'A bit of everything. Taking messages, spotting fires, digging out casualties. Riding down to the morgue.'

She saw the question in Stamford's eyes. 'Sometimes,' she explained, 'we get a casualty that has to go to hospital, but they don't want a dead relative to go to the morgue on their own. So I go. It's not logical. But if it's someone you've loved . . .' She shrugged, and he thought she wasn't going to finish the sentence. But then she added softly. 'The children are the worst.'

They were both lost in their own thoughts for a moment, then she took one of the styling seats and gestured him to the other. 'Did you see Matthew?'

'Yes. Thank you.'

'Did he ask you?'

'Sorry? Ask me what?'

'He was going to ask you about joining the Auxiliary Police Force. Didn't he?'

'No.' Stamford recalled that Matthew had said he wanted to ask him something when he'd first entered the office.

'He must have changed his mind.'

'Yes.' He didn't tell her about the fingerprint officer's attitude, but Stamford guessed it was what lay behind Matthew's second thoughts. 'I could,' he said hesitantly, 'give you an address he could contact . . .'

'But you don't think it would do any good, once they'd seen his arm? It's all right,' she reassured him, seeing him struggling for the right words. 'I know. So does Matt really. He's already tried to join the Armed Forces and the Auxiliary Fire Service. And failed the medical for both. It's always been the same. Really the arm doesn't handicap him at all but he has to fight to prove it.'

She sat back in her seat, arms folded across her stomach, moodily staring into the darkened mirror. She was waiting for him to speak. He had, after all, called on her. Out of the blue, and without knowing he was going to say it, Jack blurted out, 'He said you'd broken off your engagement because of him. Is that true?'

Colour flooded into her creamy cheeks, but she answered with cool composure. 'Yes. I suppose so. I didn't realise he knew that. He was very young when it happened.'

'Ten. Old enough for your father to cope with surely?'

It was none of his business and he could see the memories were hurting her, but he had to keep niggling. It was irresistible; like the way the tongue always returned to an aching tooth.

'My father,' she paused for a moment, biting at her lip, then tried again. 'My father was one of those men who had a disgust of anything deformed. He couldn't bear to touch, or even look at, Matt's arm.' Her hazel eyes turned to Jack's brown ones. 'He wasn't deliberately cruel. He tried to hide his revulsion, but he couldn't. I couldn't leave Matt alone in that situation.'

'And your fiancé wasn't prepared to take him on?'

'No. Jamie – he was a James too strangely enough – Jamie didn't want me to have the responsibility of someone else's son.'

'Couldn't you have had him to live with you in Watford?'

She smiled ruefully. 'Matthew has been chatting, hasn't he? No, I couldn't. Jamie had put up half the money for the shop you see. When we split up, he wanted it back, so I had to close the shop. But please don't think it a great sacrifice or anything, Inspector. That incident made me see Jamie in a new light. I was glad to come back here and help out in Dad's business.'

'Your father was a woman's hairdresser!'

Her peal of laughter was warm and clear. 'No. Of course he wasn't. My dad was a barber, Inspector. And so was I for ten years until he died and I converted the business.'

Springing to her feet, she unhooked a framed photograph from the wall and passed it to Stamford. 'That's Dad.'

It had probably been taken as an advertisement. A heavily moustached Mr Fortune, resplendent in his best suit and his Sunday gold watch-chain and tie-pin, posed self-consciously beneath his striped barber's pole, one hand raised to point to the script message on his window pronouncing him to be 'Joshua Fortune; Gentleman Barber'. Behind him, in the doorway, a little girl in a smocked frock and lace-up boots, peeked from the shadows.

'Is that you?'

'Yes. I got a terrible telling off for spoiling the photograph. They had to take it again.'

'How old are you there?'

'About ten. Mind I could give a fair back and sides even then. Dad always said I was the best apprentice he ever had.' A mischievous twinkle lit up her eyes and pulled up the corners of her mouth. 'Would you like me to prove it?'

Before he could answer, she'd whipped a fresh white cloth across his chest and tucked it securely into his collar. 'This could do with a trim.'

Stamford didn't answer. He was having trouble coping with the sudden surge of emotions that had swept through him. There was something oddly erotic about the feel of her fingers lifting a section of his dark auburn hair and letting it fall back into careless clumps.

With professional grace, she combed it briskly into place, scooped up a section, and snipped with tidy movements. A cloud of downy ends spotted the pristine white sheet. This close he could smell the delicate rose perfume of her soap.

'What about you, Inspector? Are you married?'

'I don't know.'

The reflected Helen's eyebrows rose at this bizarre statement. He found himself telling her about his Dutch wife and the changeling child that claimed to be his daughter.

'I didn't recognise any of the clothes she was wearing you see. And they had Belgian labels, not Dutch.'

The snipping scissors slowed. 'But surely, in all the

panic of an evacuation, they might have dressed her in whatever came to hand.'

'Yes. But it's not just that. There are other things. English words that she used to know, and now she doesn't.'

'How long since you'd seen her?'

'I was in Holland at Christmas. She shouldn't have forgotten that much in six months.'

'Maybe there are things she doesn't want to remember.'

Or maybe, Jack acknowledged to himself, he was just looking for reasons to excuse her rejection of him. After all, children change quickly at that age. And she'd have only heard Dutch spoken at home.

Helen started to cut, using the scissors with skill on the nape of his neck rather than resorting to a razor to get a close cut. He deliberately forced his mind into a detached, analytical mode. And once more a strange fact about these shops struck him; the interiors, although battered and shabby now, had the hallmarks of opulence and were in odd contrast to the rather shabby street outside. It appeared that at one time the shops must have been far more prosperous than their current scanty custom suggested.

'Do you have any staff in the shop?' he asked.

'Not now,' Helen replied. She was stooped slightly behind him now, her breath gentle on the nape of his neck. Her assistant, time-served and eager for the bright lights of the West End, had left at Christmas. 'It just wasn't worth taking on anyone else. There's not the trade.'

'That must make things difficult for you.'

'Oh we manage quite well on Matthew's salary.'

The soft brush bristles whisked lightly over his skin, tickling gently. 'Mind you, I'm not sure how much longer that will last. I've a feeling I'm shortly to be presented with a future sister-in-law.'

'Someone you like?'

'Someone I've never met. Yet. It's just a feeling.'

'Will you mind? Being on your own?'

'Perhaps I shan't be. I haven't quite decided to resign myself to being "spinster of this parish".' She rubbed a globule of Brylcreem lightly into the palms of her hands. Standing behind Jack's chair, she placed them flat against his temples then moved them deliberately back, allowing the freshly cut hair to ripple through her long, slim fingers.

There was no mistaking the invitation this time, or the flicker of rejection in her eyes when Stamford said, 'What were James Donald's parents like?'

But she replied with composure: 'A bit like him really: dull, ordinary, kept themselves to themselves. Mrs Donald, especially, hardly ever went out.'

'Have you any idea where the three of them came here from?'

'No. I don't think they ever said. Some other part of London I'd always assumed.'

'Miss Emmett thinks they came from somewhere north of here. She remembers the three of them arriving on the LMS carrier's cart.'

'Well she may be right. But she's wrong about them coming together. James didn't come with his parents. He joined them about a year later.'

'Are you sure?'

'Quite certain.' Refolding the covering sheet, Helen fetched a broom.

Jack felt for a handful of coins.

'Please don't,' she said quietly. 'It was, after all, my idea.'

He knew he could retrieve the situation by a simple invitation. For a drink perhaps?

She scooped up the last of the cuttings and straightened up to face him. 'Were there any other questions, Inspector?'

He hadn't intended to approach the matter head on, but since the subtle approach seemed to be getting them nowhere, he put the question. Which of the women in Balaclava Row had spent most time with James Donald?

Her answer amazed him.

'Josepha,' she replied promptly. 'She was always round there sweet-talking him into letting her try on the jewellery. She liked parading around in it. I think he let her borrow it sometimes.'

They'd been standing opposite each other, so close that they were almost touching, Helen's head tilted back to look into Stamford's face. The door bell made them both jump apart.

'Sorry to interrupt, sir,' Sarah said. 'I'm finished at Mrs Donald's. I'm just on my way back to the station.'

'I'll walk with you.'

He put his hat on, but not before Sarah's blue eyes had slid critically over the newly shorn hair. She made no comment but he felt the freeze of disapproval.

'Felonious come up with anything useful?'

'No, sir. I had him wandering around that flat for an hour. Mrs Donald wasn't too pleased at all. But it's no good. He knows something was moved between the time he first found the body and the time he came back with me, but he just can't remember what it was. I told him to keep thinking.'

'How's Mrs Donald bearing up?'

'Quite well. She's already made arrangements for someone to come and make an offer for the stock. And she has absolutely no idea where her husband lived prior to Kentish Town. He never said.'

'A bit odd that, isn't it?'

'It seems to have been a fairly odd marriage, sir. But she did tell me a couple of interesting things.'

Stamford waited. She continued to keep pace with him, her face partially hidden by the black hat she'd worn to Aldbury. He had the distinct feeling she was enjoying keeping him waiting. 'Leo Bowler made an offer for Balaclava Row. About a month ago.'

Stamford digested the fact that the instigator of most of the villainy on the patch was extending his real estate holdings. 'You said two things. What's the other?'

'Guess who owns the freehold on the Row, sir? Your new barber: Helen Fortune.'

Chapter 15

'I'm going crazy stuck in here. You've got to find her for me.'

Lexie thrust the knitting needles that she'd used as an excuse for her latest trip round to the Wellers' shop into her cardigan pocket, and informed Alan Milligan roundly that she was doing her best and if he didn't think it was good enough maybe he should give himself up.

'That wouldn't be good for you, Carrots. Aiding and abetting a deserter is an offence. I wouldn't be the only one who'd end up in jail.'

'Don't you try and blackmail me, Alan Milligan.'

She was standing over him as he sat with his back against the kitchen wall, his forearms resting on his knees. One foot tapped warningly.

Alan instantly switched to a conciliatory tone. 'Sorry. It's just that I've read every flaming bit of paper in this place, I'm sick of playing patience, and I daren't turn the radio on. It's not even as if there's much to see out the windows if I risk sticking me 'ead up. I don't know how you keep going, amount of customers you get.'

It was something that had been bothering Lexie as well lately. Her dad had slowed down over the past few years. And just recently they'd had more and more complaints that work wasn't ready on time. She suspected that only the fact that they'd still got some of their monthly leather allocation left had brought most of the customers in this week.

Her worried expression told Alan that he was in even greater danger of alienating his only friend at present. He hurried into speech again, trying to undo the damage. 'I just want to speak to Connie, then I'll turn meself in and you won't be involved, promise, Carrots.' He reached up and captured one of her hands, squeezing lightly. 'Don't give up on me now, eh?'

'I ain't goin' to.' Reclaiming her hand, Lexie made for the stairs. 'It's half-day closing and I got an idea. Might have some good news for yer tonight. See ya then.'

The news that she was going out that afternoon, brought a predictable response from her father. Hands shaking, he whispered that he really didn't think he could manage his dinner. 'Bit of a pain in me chest,' he explained, rubbing a balled fist over the central portion of his pullover where a well-worn patch showed it had received many such treatments.

'Leave it for later,' Lexie said, slapping a plate over the hastily fried liver. 'You'll probably fancy it then seeing we ain't got any cheese in for you to pig when me back's turned.'

Two hot spots of anger flared in the parchment white of her father's cheeks. 'Don't you talk to me like that. I'm your father. I deserve respect. I don't know what's got into you lately. And you can't go out. There's cleaning and washing to be done here.'

'Well they ain't going away, worse luck.'

Halfway along Leighton she slowed her hip-swinging, head-high gait and drew a breath of relief.

She'd been frightened that, on this occasion, just because she wanted him to start an argument, her dad would be in one of his rare periods of good humour. And that really wouldn't have done at all. Because then his eyes would have been all over her and he'd have noticed the heavy lumpish shape in her supposedly empty shopping bag.

At the junction with Kentish Town Road she'd almost put one foot in the road, when a flash of red to her left caught her eye. Glancing round was a mistake. Her eyes were staring into the grim grey ones of the military policeman she'd attempted to convert to temperance on her way back from Elsie Finch's. The damn man seemed to be haunting her; every time she stepped out to find Connie Milligan, there he was.

Imagination, she told herself. Or a guilty conscience. There was no reason to suppose he was watching her. She made herself walk past him as he hovered in the sandbagged entrance to the railway station. Rescuing a scrap of paper from her pocket, she ran a finger down it, as if it were a shopping list, squared her shoulders and headed with apparent purpose for the fishmonger. Glassy eyes stared back at her as she perused slabs of white cod, kippers smoked to the colour of red mahogany, silvered mackerel and herring, piles of rosy shrimps and frilly-lipped oysters.

Something about the last heap caught her attention. She leant closer, inhaling the gluey smell. The fishmonger sidled down behind the marbled counters. 'Papier mâché, madam. The girl did 'em.' He indicated the cashier in the wooden cage. The budding sculptor blushed. 'Something else I can serve you with? The kippers are real.' He prodded one to demonstrate.

Whilst appearing to be weighing the relative merits of kippers or cod, Lexie looked over the man's shoulder. A familiar figure was in deep contemplation of the mustard-coloured patch that had been painted on the pillar box to warn of gas attack.

'Just one kipper, please.'

'Eight pence, thank you, madam.'

The smelly parcel was consigned to her bag and Lexie passed the coppers into the cashier's cubicle and received her receipt.

She was across the road before the MP could move, leaving him caught on the kerb as a bus blocked his view for a moment.

When it cleared, Lexie had disappeared.

She spent quarter of an hour wandering round Daniel's Department Store and left, convinced she'd shaken off the military policeman.

He was standing not ten yards from the front door.

Taking advantage of the fact his back was towards her, Lexie clipped off. Her route lay up the road, but she didn't dare pass him; she'd just have to cut in and work her way back by the side roads. She was aware of a tingle of excitement flowing through her body: the idea of outwitting the police was acting as a kind of drug on her nerves. Suddenly, after years of boredom, when one predictable week had followed the next until the pattern had become so entrenched that she no longer had the will to try to change it, her life contained a secret. She could almost have hugged herself with glee and danced down the road, if it wouldn't have attracted the kind of attention that she was desperately trying to avoid.

Taking a firmer grip on the shopping bag, she continued to walk with a slow, steady pace, the 'shopping list' conspicuously consulted at each likely shop. After a few minutes, she threw a quick look over her shoulder to check the MP had lost interest and it was safe to turn right. The shock of finding him still within a few yards, made her catch her heel in a loose paving stone and lose her balance.

'Steady, miss.' Straightening, she murmured her apologies to the lugubrious man who'd caught her arm and only afterwards realised that it was the detective who'd taken her statement about the night of James Donald's death.

She was nearly at the old underground station. At this rate she'd have walked all the way to Camden. Just as she was toying with the idea of calling on Elsie Finch again, she came opposite the Castle pub and was nearly knocked flying by a fat, sweat-flushed man who flew out of the door, dispersing equal amounts of beer-laden breath and curses.

'Come 'ere.' A uniformed police constable flew after him, followed by the potman, his swelling nose dribbling a chain of bright red drops which had already stained the white cloth knotted around his waist.

The two men circled the drunk, who milled his fists threateningly, screaming at them to stay back or he'd lay them out. 'I'll say what I like,' he bawled. 'This Government's useless. And the Army couldn't fight their way out of a paper bag.'

'See what I mean, officer,' panted the potman. 'Defeatist talk. Been at it since we opened, 'e 'as. You arrest him.'

'Stay back, get 'way from me. I'll do for yer, I'm telling yer.' The whirling fists spun out indiscriminately. One thumped backwards and made contact with a khaki-covered chest. Next moment its owner was sprawled on the ground with a size fourteen boot pinning his right fist to the paving stones.

Lexie didn't wait for the outcome. Whisking around, she ran and didn't stop until she reached the quadrangle of flats in Prince of Wales Road which Alan's elusive wife had once called home.

Leaning against the white archway, her heart thumping as she fought to regain her breath, she was forced to step aside to allow a battered pram, its interior piled high with a tattered velvet curtain knotted to resemble an enormous pudding cloth, to bump out into the street.

A white ARP helmet was swinging from the pram's handle. Glancing inside, Lexie saw a brush, soap and a bottle of disinfectant. 'Goin' down the laundry?' she asked brightly.

'No, love. I'm taking the bugs in these blankets down the baths for a swimming lesson.'

Lexie sniffed. 'I only asked, I'm sure.'

The woman wasn't to be shamed into an apology. After a night of sleeping down the tube, she'd found her bedding crawling with infestation. 'I'm sleeping up in me flat from now on. To hell with the bombs.'

'I think yer right, we always sleep at home too. 'Ang on,' she called as the woman made to move away. 'Yer the warden, ain't yer?'

'One of 'em,' the woman admitted reluctantly.

'Then maybe you know who I want.' Removing a newspaper-wrapped parcel from her bag, Lexie displayed a pair of her own shoes, newly soled with rubber. 'Woman left these up our shop six months ago. I lost 'er name and address and she ain't come back. Ought to sell 'em by rights, but I don't like to when I know she come from these flats. Thing is,' she lowered her voice confidentially, 'couple of the other customers were talking about 'er when she went out. Said she were a terrible tattle-tongue. Always poking 'er nose in where it weren't wanted.'

Abandoning her pram, the woman took Lexie's arm and led her back inside. 'See that flat,' she said, pointing to one of the centre blocks. 'Third floor. Green door. Grey nets. She'll be the one you want.'

Lexie tried to keep the satisfied grin from her face. The flat was only three doors away from the one Connie Milligan had shared with her aunt.

'She denied she'd written the letters at first. Even when I said I was from the Troops Welfare Committee.'

Alan Milligan asked, 'Is there such a thing?'

'No idea. Should think you'd know better than me. Just thought it sounded good. I told 'er sending letters like that was good as sedition. What is sedition, by the way?'

'Never mind. What she say about Connie?'

But Lexie was enjoying her big moment and had no intention of being hurried. She'd even brought the props with her. Daringly buying two bottles of beer with some money she'd hidden from her dad in a tin of starch (calculating that he'd never use it) and splashing out another one and sixpence on a Tangee lipstick. She slid an exploratory tongue over her lips now, savouring the way the perfumed cosmetic mingled with the malty flavours of the bitter.

'Dinner all right?' she said.

'Yer. It's great. Really great.' They were sitting on
the bedroom floor, the Wellers' double bed serving as
a table.

'We can have a bit of light in here,' Lexie had
remarked, taking charge and spreading a clean tea-
towel over the bedspread to prevent gravy splashes.
'Seeing as how you let me draw the blackout.'

Alan scooped up a few more forkfuls of the stew.
He appeared to be enjoying it. But then so he should.
She'd put their whole week's meat ration in it. Her
father had gobbled down his share with gusto and
didn't notice that she hadn't touched hers. 'Go on,
what did this snoop say? She admit she wrote me them
letters?'

'Good as. Mind I had to drop the official act, and
pretend I liked a bit of juicy gossip much as her.'

After that the woman had been only too happy to
spend half an hour pulling her neighbour's character
to pieces.

Lexie imitated the waspish, pseudo-concerned
voice: 'Went out at all hours she did. Tarted up to the
nines. Leaving that poor old woman on her own. Of
course I knew soon as I set eyes on her, she was no
better than she should be.'

Alan muttered a curse under his breath. 'Go on.'

'Well, apparently the bloke never come to the flat.
But a week after the aunt dies, Connie goes off with a
couple of suitcases. Returned to 'er loving husband,
old Nosy Parker thought. Until Connie come back to
pick up her letters. Nosy figured she'd 'ave 'ad 'em
redirected if she'd gone back home, so she thought

she'd drop you a nod like. She says the council have requisitioned the flat. They're coming round to clear it out next week. They wanna put a bombed-out family in there.'

Alan swigged from the bottle. 'Looks like I'm going to have to break in and see if Connie left any clue to who this fancy bloke is. I just hope the MPs ain't still watching it.'

'Still?'

'Be the first place they'd have looked. They'd have a record of where me mail went, see?'

'Oh.' Lexie thought about this. 'Just as well old Nosy didn't find out where Connie was until yesterday then, ain't it?'

'What!' He was on his knees, gripping her shoulders so hard that she cried out in pain.

He let go. 'Sorry, Carrots. Only don't tease me, there's a good girl.'

'I ain't a girl. I'm a woman, case you ain't noticed. And I weren't teasing. If you want to know, yer precious Connie's in Tufnell Park.'

Having blurted out the location, she told him the rest. How the woman had been visiting a friend up there yesterday. 'Got lodgings in the house by the station. Not what she's used to, but 'er place got bombed clean out. Anyway I was helping her get her curtains up and I just happened to look out the window. And there she was opposite. Connie Milligan, bold as brass, pegging out nappies like she owned the place.'

'Nappies!'

'The bloke she's taken up with is a widower seemingly. Got two kids.'

'That would have been the attraction then. She's been moping for a kid for years.'

'How come you never had any then?'

Alan scowled. 'Never 'appened, did it? Not that I can't. Don't go thinking there's anything wrong with me. It was her fault I reckon.'

'Maybe you're better off without her then. I mean you could start again with someone else. 'Ave kids.'

'You reckon?' He took another swig of the beer. 'Think I could find another woman to fancy me, Carrots?'

'Course you could.'

He cleared the plates and bottles, pushing them carelessly on to the Wellers' dressing table, and returned to sit by her. This time his arm slipped round her waist. Despite the fact this was pretty much what she'd planned, Lexie still jumped.

Apologising, he removed his arm. She put it back. Moving the hair lying across one shoulder, he started to nuzzle at her neck. She turned, feeling the roughness of his skin as her lips sought for his.

The fastness of his response startled her.

Rolling on top of her, Alan groped for the waistband of her blouse. She barely had time to thank heaven that she'd put her decent bra (without the mended straps) on before he'd whipped it off. Sliding one hand behind his neck, she pulled his mouth to one of her nipples.

'What about your dad?' he panted, his tongue and teeth licking and nibbling as they explored the soft swellings and hard tips. 'Won't he be round seeing where you are?'

'Don't worry, I've fixed it.' Her body arched and

she seized his buttocks, forcing their stomachs and flanks together.

Groaning, Alan fumbled with his trousers. Lexie reached round to unfasten her skirt, but he couldn't wait. Jerking it roughly to waist level, he ripped down her pants and thrust himself urgently inside her.

Her backside thumping up and down against the Wellers' bedside rug, she was aware only of an incredible building crescendo of need that hadn't peaked when he gave a sudden cry of triumph and fell heavily on top of her.

'No. Don't stop, go on.'

'I can't. I'm done.'

'Oh.'

'Didn't you enjoy it?'

'Oh, yes. It was lovely.' But far too short, she wanted to add. She looked consideringly at the underside of the Wellers' bed which was still looming over them. She'd have to wash the sheets afterwards of course. 'Come on,' she pulled at Alan's hand.

'Where we going?'

'Let's get into bed. It's more comfortable than the floor.'

'Is it all right? You sure you can stay?'

'Course. I told you. I fixed it.' Shedding her skirt and stockings, Lexie leapt quickly between the sheets and held up one corner invitingly.

Alan tumbled in beside her, turned away, and promptly fell asleep. Frustrated, Lexie slid her arms round his chest, curved her body to fit against his back, and lay in the darkness listening to his stentorious breathing.

He didn't wake until the bombing started.

'You want to go home? Take shelter?'

'No.' Locking her lips fiercely on his, she ignored the crash and roar outside and pushed herself aggressively against him.

'Blimey, Carrots,' he said when they'd rolled apart into two panting heaps again. 'You'll wear me out. You're a natural, Carrots.'

She didn't know whether to be pleased or offended. In the end she decided on pleasure. After all, she could be dead tomorrow.

As if to confirm this statement, another explosion rocked the building. Lexie started laughing.

'You all right?' Alan rolled up on one elbow and peered into her face. 'You ain't getting hysterical on me, are yer?'

'No.' Lexie drew in a deep breath in an effort to control her voice. 'I was just thinking,' she quavered. 'Do you believe in life after death?'

'Eh?' Alan sat up alarmed by this further evidence of instability. 'No. I mean, well, yes. Of course, I do. There's no need to be scared, Carrots.'

'I ain't scared.' Lexie giggled. 'I was just thinking. If we get hit tonight, I'd really like to come back and watch their faces when staid, old-maidish, Lexie Emmett is pulled out of bed with a naked man.' She finished on a squeal as another bomb dropped somewhere to the south, and dived under the eiderdown, pulling Alan with her.

Despite the bombing, they drifted into a warm, cosy sleep until dawn when the cold draught of Lexie slipping out of bed awoke Alan. He seized her wrist.

'I got to go, Alan. I'll try and come back this evening.'

He pulled her down for a kiss. 'Do something for me?'

Lexie's mouth curved in a wicked smile. 'Thought I just had.'

'Something else?'

'What?' She pouted and dragged her wrist free sharply, guessing that it was something connected with Connie.

'Go see Connie for me. Ask her to meet me tonight.'

Lexie dragged her underclothes on. 'Don't know if I can. It ain't half day. I can't keep leaving the shop.'

Her sharpness was a mixture of annoyance and pique. She still didn't love the fish fryer, but she'd slept with him, and in her mind that gave her a right to object to this obsession with his wife. After all, he'd just done what he was accusing Connie of – so they were even. Why not just leave it at that and get on with his life?

She said none of that to Alan, but muttered that maybe she could pretend to have a toothache if the shop didn't get too busy. 'But I ain't promising nothing, mind.'

'I knew I could count on you, Carrots.'

He was still sprawled in bed, the sheets protecting his modesty.

'You'd better make that, case anyone comes in,' Lexie instructed.

She half thought he might suggest she slip back in again but he merely begged her, once more, to try to see Connie.

'Said I will, haven't I?'

She made to kiss him goodbye; but he didn't notice her. His grey eyes had gone blank and seemed to be seeing something far away, beyond the bedroom walls. There was something about his expression that sent a chill down her spine.

'Alan,' she said sharply, reclaiming his attention, 'you do just want to talk to Connie, don't you? I mean, you ain't thinking of doing anything else?'

He smiled. ''Course I ain't, Carrots. I've never lifted me fists to a woman. Don't intend to start now, I promise.'

'That's all right then. See you later.'

He waited until he heard the door close quietly, then he swung his legs out of bed and sat, naked, on the edge. Holding his fists out in front of him he balled them until the knuckles gleamed white against the brown skin. 'No. Never lifted 'em to a woman,' he said into the still, slightly sour-smelling room.

Standing with a quick reflex jerk of his powerful knees, he padded into the kitchen, careless for once of the undrawn curtains, and opened Alice's cutlery drawer. Rummaging amongst the knives, he slid several blades over the skin of his stomach before he found one that's sharpness pleased him.

Chapter 16

'Wish this weather would make up its mind,' Mr Jenkins remarked, snuffling noisily into a large white handkerchief. 'How are you getting on with the little monsters?'

'Very well. I think,' Rose said prudently. 'It's difficult to tell what they're thinking at that age.'

'It's impossible at any age if you ask me,' Jenkins grumbled, knocking out his pipe and tucking a woollen scarf out of sight beneath his jacket. 'The trouble is they're so *resilient*. Don't seem bothered by the bombing at all most of them. Just bounce back next morning full of life and raring to go. Suppose it comes from believing you're immortal at that age. Ah, well. Back to the Mongol hordes.'

Rose followed him down the corridor, where the buzz and clatter of chattering and laughter was silenced abruptly as each teacher entered their classroom. Stifling a yawn, Rose entered hers to a crash of chairs and a chorus of 'Good morning, miss.'

'Good morning, class. You may sit.'

Under cover of removing the register from her desk, she gave another enormous yawn. For the past three days she'd alternated between exhilaration and dog-tiredness. ·

Scrubbing out the flat and disinfecting Nafnel's old clothes had taken most of Tuesday night. She'd attempted to return them to his grandmother after school on Wednesday, and found the room deserted.

'See. Told ya,' Nafnel had crowed. 'She'll be out boozing.'

The door across the landing opened and an unshaven man, dressed in trousers and a ripped vest, leant on the door jamb running a speculative eye over Rose. 'Want something, love?'

'I wanted to speak to Mrs Starkey but she appears to be out.'

Hitching up his trousers, he lounged closer, blocking her route to the stairs. 'Don't suppose she'll be long. Want to come in and wait?'

'No. Thank you. I'll try some other time.'

'Don't be like that. Come and wait. I got a couple of bottles of beer in.'

She could smell the stale sweat from his armpits as he reached one arm across the banister, forming a barrier to the stairs.

'You a mate of Ma Starkey's then?'

'No. I'm her grandson's teacher. Now I'd like to pass, please.'

'No hurry is there?'

A door opened on the landing below. The man leant backwards over the banister to see who'd come out. Taking advantage of the distraction, Rose had knocked his arm down and clattered down the stairs.

Nafnel had insisted on following her home again, but this time she'd packed him off as soon as he'd had his tea, declining his offer to take another bath if he could stay a bit longer.

'I'll see you at school tomorrow,' she promised him. 'With some more sandwiches.'

The bribe had had the desired effect. She could

make out the top of his head behind Roger Veeny out of the corner of her eye as she started to run down the register.

The unpredictable weather, warm one day, blustery the next, was having its effect on the class: several more names were met with the information (mostly from Peggy Abbott) that: 'He's off sick with a bad chest, miss.'

'Starkey.'

'Yeah.'

Her eyes sought him automatically. Only the smirk on Phil Wright's face made her choke off the exclamation that arose to her lips. Once she'd set the class a list of arithmetic problems on the board, she called him to her desk.

'Where are your new clothes, Nafnel?' she said quietly.

Nafnel scowled down at the ripped jumper and trousers. 'She told me to stick these on today.'

'But why?' A thought struck Rose. 'She wasn't offended, was she? By me giving you new clothes?'

'What's 'fended?'

'Angry,' Rose translated. 'Was your grandmother angry?'

'Na. She was dead pleased, miss.'

Rose gave up and sent him back to his seat. She'd have to try to see the woman again after school. And hopefully sort out the mystery of the clothes and Nafnel's real name.

Mentioning the matter to Mr Jenkins at break, she was startled by his bark of laughter. 'Offended! She'll have popped them, my dear, or sold 'em off at the secondhand clothes stall. And thanked you very much as she poured them down her throat! What are you doing?' His slightly patronising tone changed to amazement as Rose shrugged her coat on.

'I shan't be long.'

She flew along Malden Road and up to Queen's Crescent. Perhaps she was already too late, but she was damned if she was going to let the woman get away with it.

As it turned out, her luck was in. Pushing her way through to the secondhand clothes stall she saw Grandma Starkey picking over a familiar bundle of clothes.

'It's good stuff, plenty of wear in it. See for yerself. Give us anuver bob, eh?'

Rose flung herself forward and grabbed the clothes. 'Don't you dare pay her for them. They don't belong to her.'

'What yer saying. Yer calling me a thief. I'll 'ave the law on yer.'

The woman was as unattractive sober as she had been drunk; worse in a way, since the sharp-faced pasty skin with its tracery of purple veins was further marred by yellowing eyes and a whining voice.

'They're not yours,' Rose panted. 'I gave them to Nafnel.'

'Oh, yer "Miss" are yer?' The woman's predatory expression sharpened. A thin hand, its emaciated fingers like talons, fastened over Rose's wrist. 'I'm grateful. That grateful, miss. It's 'ard yer know, losing yer only daughter and 'aving to bring up 'er kid on me own.'

'Yes. It must be.' Rose fought the inclination to snatch her wrist back from the hot, dry fingers. 'I was wondering, Mrs Starkey. What's Nafnel's real Christian name?'

'Real? Well it's Nafnel, ain't it?'

'But it can't be! I mean, what does it say on his ration book. Could I see it?'

'I ain't got it.' Thrusting Rose away abruptly, Mrs Starkey stretched out a claw to the stallholder. 'All right, three bob and yer can 'ave the clothes.'

'No you can't. I told you. They don't belong to her.'

'What that kid's got is mine. I'm 'is gran.' The clothes were roughly yanked from Rose's arms and pushed back at the stallholder. 'Free bob.'

Help arrived from an unexpected quarter. 'Don't you pay 'er. Them's our Sammy's clothes. I only loaned 'em.'

Eileen thrust her way forward to stare down Mrs Starkey.

' 'E never said they was loaned.'

'Well I'm telling you now. Stealing that is. Selling what don't belong to you.'

The stallholder promptly announced he ran a respectable business and he weren't interested in no stolen property.

Mrs Starkey wasn't going to give up so easily. It was nearly twelve hours since she'd had a drink and desperation was gnawing at her nerve ends, setting them on fire as they screamed for the deadening comfort of the first drink. 'Just two bob,' she pleaded. 'She's lying. The clothes are my boy's.'

It must be nearly the end of break. And she shouldn't have left the school premises anyway. Fumbling in her coat pocket, Rose hauled out her purse and scrabbled inside. 'Here. Take this.'

The talon uncoiled eagerly.

Desperate to get rid of the stinking old woman, Rose upended the purse and shot its entire contents into the grasping hand. It didn't amount to much; about two shillings and sixpence in coppers.

'That all? Ain't you got a bit more in yer pockets?'

'Oh look,' Eileen exclaimed. 'There's Sergeant McNeill. Maybe we'd better have a word with her. See if she can sort out this business of who owns our Sammy's clothes.'

The sight of a tall figure striding towards her clad in Metropolitan blue had the desired effect on Ma Starkey. Fingers closed tightly over the precious money and she slid quickly away through the market crowds.

'Morning,' Eileen called. 'You not helping Jack any more?' she asked alluding to Sarah's return to uniform.'

'Just a temporary diversion, Eileen. Ja . . . I mean, Mr Stamford is at the coroner's inquest this morning. Good morning, Mrs Goodwin.'

Rose murmured her hellos, conscious once more of a puzzling reserve in the police's attitude, that she'd first been aware of when she'd called at the station to give her fingerprints.

Before she could say anything more, however, a short, dark-haired young man shouldered his way across the market, planted himself in front of Sarah and said baldly: 'Tell Mr Stamford it's OK if they put the right drainage pipes in. Not critical. When you got half a mo. Morning, Mum. Got to go, business.'

'I'd best be off too,' Eileen said, inured to the strange behaviour of her second youngest. 'I've got to get this dress along to the dry cleaner's. It's for the firemen's dance.' She displayed the black frock. Mostly for Sarah's benefit since it had belatedly occurred to her that the sergeant might have got the wrong impression seeing her hanging around a secondhand clothes stall with a dress over her arm. 'As a matter of fact, Rose, I was going to ask . . . '

Rose never found out what she'd intended to ask. The faint tones of the playground bell tolled through one of those brief moments when everyone and everything in the market was silent at the same second.

Hugging the clothes to her chest, Rose reached the playground just as the last of the children was being marched in from break.

She bundled Nafnel back into the clothes at dinnertime. 'Here,' she gave him a packet. 'Pilchard sandwiches. Eat them in the playground.'

Slipping into her own coat, she prepared to make a visit she'd been putting off since Tuesday.

The Tammies occupied two floors of the house in St James's Gardens. The basement housed one of her father's unmarried sisters and a great aunt. Rose felt her way down the narrow metal steps to the area.

'Are you in trouble, young lady,' was Great Aunt Mabel's frank greeting.

'I thought I might be.' Rose bent over and kissed the old woman's papery cheek which smelt of camphor, lavender cachous and wintergreen.

Mabel had been bedridden for some years, but her mind was as sharp as ever. Huddled in a pink fluffy shawl she watched as Rose crossed the room and bestowed a kiss on a middle-aged woman who sat rocking in a chair by the coal fire. The woman gave her a vague smile and went back to cooing over a tattered rag doll that she cradled tenderly in her arms.

'She'll 'ave seen you come down,' Mabel said, jerking a nearly hairless head towards the ceiling.

'Is Dad home for his dinner?'

'Not yet. Best get it over quick. That with you?'

Rose looked round and found a familiar figure investigating the china fairings on the whatnot.

'Nafnel, how did you get in here?'

'Frew the door, same as you. She your gran?'

'No. I'm her great aunt. Who are you?'

'This is Starkey. He's a pupil.'

He'd moved across to examine the occupant of the rocker, twisting his head sideways to peer up into her face. 'What's up with 'er.'

Mabel had never been one to mince her words. 'She's barmy.' She crooked a finger at the little boy. 'You know how to play gin rummy?'

'Nah.'

'Bring them cards over and I'll learn you then. You'd best get upstairs, Rose.'

Rose used the internal staircase. She knew what was coming. And it did.

'Oh, it's you,' Marge said, banging a pie plate on to the table with unnecessary force. 'Kind of you to spare us the time I'm sure.'

Thursday had always been her mother's baking day. Rationing of fats and sugar had curbed her normal routine, but Marge wasn't one to give up without a fight; as the aromas of warm baking that were drifting round the cluttered kitchen testified. Scooping sliced apple into the plate, she crushed a couple of saccharin tablets into hot water, sprinkled the fruit, and dumped a pastry sheet over the lot. The precision with which she trimmed the edges of the spinning pastry would have done credit to a Harley Street surgeon.

From habit, Rose started to twist the pastry scraps into lopsided loops and bows. Her mother's mouth tightened into a thin line, forming a mean gash in her oven-reddened face. She dragged the back of her hand across her forehead, leaving a floury smear.

Rose still refused to speak.

Finally Marge cracked. 'Well,' she said, her voice high with effort of trying to control her anger, 'a new job *and* courting as well. Don't bother to tell me. I don't know why you should really. After all, I'm only yer mother.'

'They had to get confirmation from the Board before I was certain about the job,' Rose lied. 'And I'm not courting anyone.'

'That's not what I heard up the market. You've been seen out walking with Pat O'Day. And cooking his tea for him. It's coming to something when I have to hear that from complete strangers.'

'Well the complete strangers have got it wrong,' Rose said hotly. 'Pat was just helping out with a pupil. He's downstairs with Auntie Mabel now.'

'What!' Marge attempted to unknot her apron whilst thrusting strands of damp hair behind her ears. 'Why didn't you say so. Tell him to come up for his dinner.'

'Not Pat, Mum. The pupil, Nafnel.'

'Nafnel?' Marge repeated, disappointment plain on her face. 'What kind of stupid name is that?'

'I don't know. And I can't get a straight answer out of Mrs Starkey.'

'Ma Starkey. What's she got to do with it?'

'She's his gran. Do you remember her daughter, Mum?'

'Flighty bit. No better than she ought to be. Mind you what can you expect with a mother like that. A good mother,' Marge said with heavy emphasis on the 'good', 'takes an interest in who her daughter's going with. Always assuming she's allowed to, of course.'

Extracting cake tins and a baked suet roll from the oven, Marge flicked the gas up and inserted the pies. Slicing along the pale brown sausage, she released the scent of sage and bacon into the room. 'Lay up your aunties' trays, and put out a place for yourself.'

'I'm not hungry, Mum.'

Ignoring her, Marge tipped boiled carrots and potatoes on to the plates and covered the lot with gravy. Carrying the trays downstairs, Rose found Nafnel deep in a game with Aunt Mabel.

'Don't let him gamble for money,' she wailed, seeing the piles of halfpennies and pennies lurking in the folds of the eiderdown.

'Mind your own business,' snapped Auntie Mabel. 'I'll raise you a penny ha'penny.'

Giving up, Rose removed Auntie Beryl's doll, tied a napkin round her neck and saw that she was safely eating before returning to round two with her mother.

'And another thing,' Marge said, sweeping the remains of flour and pastry off the table as Rose ate, 'what if I'd run into the Goodwins? What sort of upbringing would they think my girls had had? Not

272

even having the decency to tell them you're courting again.'

'I'm *not* courting anyone. And I don't know why you set such great store on what the Goodwins think. He only works for the council, same as Dad.'

'It's not the same. Mr Goodwin's in Building. Your dad's in Sewage.'

'You mean they think Peter married into muck,' Rose said, with a tinge of bitterness.

Marge missed it and took her words at face value. 'Well, there's no denying they always made it clear they thought Peter could have done better for himself; him nearly getting to university and all. But still they paid up handsomely for the wedding when they saw how set Peter was on it.'

'Why shouldn't they? He was their son.'

'Exactly!' Marge dished up her husband's dinner and set it on the gas to keep warm. 'That's what I'm saying, ain't it? You ought to go round and see them. Explain about how you're courting Pat. They shouldn't hear it from total strangers.'

'I'm not courting anyone. And if I was, it wouldn't be any business of theirs. I'm going back to school.'

She had to remove Nafnel forcibly from the card game.

'Sharp little snapper, ain't he?' Mabel said, tying a collection of coppers into a handkerchief.

'Is he?' Nafnel had never volunteered answers in class, and she'd never picked him out because of an unacknowledged fear that she'd embarrass him in front of the rest of the children. It had never occurred to her that he might be bright.

* * *

The inquest verdict was predictable: James Donald had been unlawfully killed by person(s) unknown.

'I'm sorry it's taken so long, Mrs Donald. But even with the Emergency Regulations meaning they don't have to hold inquests on death resulting from War Action, the pressure on the mortuaries and all the relocating of the Coroner's Court because of the bomb damage means they've built up a backlog of inquests.'

'It doesn't matter, sir. I'm sure these things have to be done properly. Will it be all right for the undertakers to get on with the funeral arrangements now?'

'Yes, they've released the body.' Once again, Jack had a sense of a marriage being neatly and efficiently packed away.

Gwen Donald had 'done her duty' as a wife. Now she was embracing widowhood with the same calm efficiency. She was already dressed for the part in the black skirt and blouse she'd been wearing since her return from Aldbury, plus a serviceable black coat and a tiny, veiled pillbox hat, which perched on top of her plain, thick locks and looked rather absurd.

She must have been aware of this too, because as soon as they were safely seated in the back of the police car, she unclipped it and laid it carefully on her knees. 'Helen was kind enough to lend me a hat, since I didn't have a black one of my own. I think I'll have to buy something a bit more decent for the funeral though, don't you, sir?'

Jack muttered something about it being a very attractive hat.

'That's what I mean, sir. It won't do for a funeral. I can't be seen to be wearing fripperies at the graveside.

It won't look respectable. I shall 'ave a small do for the mourners at the flat after the funeral I think.' She gnawed at her bottom lip, brow furrowed, as she planned her last duties towards her husband. 'Nothing too grand. He wouldn't have wanted no fuss. It's too late for salad, even supposing you could still get it, but I shall do it right, I'll bury him with ham.'

She was thinking aloud rather than talking to Stamford, but it gave him the opportunity he'd been wanting. 'Mrs Donald, why did you hold a birthday party for your husband this year? It wasn't your usual custom, was it?'

Gwen turned to face him, but her eyes flickered sideways as she murmured that she felt she ought, what with him not having the girls with him this year.

He was sure it wasn't the truth. But he was equally certain she wasn't going to tell him the real reason behind the party.

Escorting her back into the flat, he deliberately lingered until she was forced to invite him to sit down.

'Should I make tea?'

'That would be very nice, thank you.'

Her attempt to fill the kettle was met with a violent coughing and banging from the water pipes. 'Darn. I thought they'd fixed that.' Grabbing the kettle, she marched along to the bathroom. 'I keep the bath full,' she explained, returning a moment later. 'The water keeps going off.'

'Probably a leak out back. You've had a lot of bomb damage out there.' Casually, Jack drifted into the sitting room, ostensibly to raise the curtains and peer out at the raw and blasted earth of the field behind the shops. He took the opportunity to glance around

the room again. The furniture was of the heavy
durable type that had been made to provide value for
money and years of irritation by outlasting its owners
and proving a source of annoyance to their heirs who
hated the sight of it but felt obliged to give it house
room for sentimental reasons.

All surfaces, whether wood, upholstery or marble,
were protected by lace runners and doilies wherever
possible. The ornaments, likewise, lacked any taste.
They were solid, unimaginative, and decorated in
predictable colours. The walls displayed framed
pictures of the two daughters, an ugly oil painting of
winsome spaniels, and a sepia-tinted portrait of a stiff-
faced couple, dressed in Edwardian clothes. The piano
looked new, so did the sheet music lying on the top of
it. He guessed that the Donald daughters had been
pressed into music lessons. The only possible
indication of the family's quirks and individual
preferences lay in the small collection of books in the
case.

Letting the curtains drop again, he stepped across
to read the titles. The bottom shelf were the children's:
Black Beauty, *What Katy Did*, *The Red Fairy Book*,
Kipling's *Puck of Pook's Hill* and *The Just So Stories*.
The other three shelves contained classics such as
Dickens, Wordsworth's poetry, the Brontës' works, a
couple of Tolstoys, Proust and Gibbon's *The Decline
and Fall of the Roman Empire*. Stamford knew,
without knowing how, that these had all belonged to
James Donald. The only sign of Mrs Donald was a
battered and stained copy of *Warne's Model Cookery*.

His perusal up the various shelves had brought his
eyes almost level with the sepia portrait. He'd passed

it on his first examination of the room, assuming it to be just another example of Mrs Donald's bad taste in interior decorating. Now he looked closer, and realised that what he'd taken for a print, was actually a photograph. Slipping it from its hook, he extracted a penknife from his pocket and levered off the clips holding the backing. The frame and glass came away in his hands, leaving him holding an oval photograph. Running one finger round the edging he confirmed what his eyes were telling him; the picture had been inexpertly clipped from a larger one.

'What are you doing?' Gwen's black-clad frame vibrated indignation.

'Who are the people in this portrait, Mrs Donald?'

'My husband's parents.'

Jack turned the back of the picture to the window, angling it to catch the best of the light. There it was; very faint, but distinct, an ink imprint, similar to that stamped by photographers on the back of their work. He moved it nearer to the window. And could have cried with frustration: whoever had trimmed the print to fit the frame had removed the name and address leaving only the corner of the border and the beginning of a letter that might have been a capital 'B' or 'P'.

Sighing, he let his arms fall and started to reassemble the frame.

'Don't bother with that, sir. I'll give the picture to our Evelyn for her scrapbook. The frame can go to the secondhand dealers same as the rest of the furniture. I shan't need it down at the cottage. It's furnished already.'

'You won't be coming back to London then?'

'No point, sir. I'm not a jeweller. I thought with the money I get from the stock and the other bits and pieces I might open a little tea-shop. Tring or Berkhamstead maybe. Somewhere with a bit of life, but handy for our Ruby's place.'

Her eyes were already sparkling in anticipation of her return to her country roots. James was dead: rest in peace.

For a moment, Stamford was almost tempted to believe that she'd engineered her husband's death herself. Except they'd already checked that she'd been at a knitting circle on the relevant night. And anyway, if she'd had the steel to commit murder, then she'd undoubtedly have had the necessary resolve to tell James she was leaving him and taking the girls with her. From what little Stamford had gleaned, the late Mr Donald wouldn't have had the backbone to stand in her way.

And that was the problem really: he was such a remarkably colourless, dull, *negative* sort of person that it was difficult to see why anyone would want to kill him.

'Why do you think Lexie Emmett was your husband's mistress?' he said, reaching for his tea-cup and putting Sarah's theory to the test.

The china rattled violently before he could take it.

'I'm sure I don't know what you mean! I never said that!'

'Implied it though. You do think it, don't you?'

Gwen pressed her lips together. 'I never said. But since you ask, sir.' Linking both hands, she leant forward confidentially. 'Donald did happen to mention that his parents were keen on a match between them.'

'When was this?'

'Oh, just before they both passed on. Nothing came of it.'

'If nothing came of it when he was free, why assume he'd take up with her now?'

'More likely it was her taking up with *him*. I mean she's eleven years older now, isn't she. There's not that many men around when you reach that age. I know. Not that I'd have ever stooped to taking someone else's.'

'So your husband did talk about his past sometimes.'

'Of course he did.'

'But he never mentioned where he came from originally?'

'I told you. I don't know why it's so important.'

Stamford didn't either really. He was aware that he was clutching at straws in an attempt to find some kind of thread that he could follow to this damned, elusive victim. 'What about the census returns. He must have put place of birth on those.'

'Donald filled in the forms. He was the head of the household.'

Somehow Stamford doubted that. 'And you never glanced over his shoulder?'

'Once.' She seized his cup before there could be any suggestion of a second cup. 'He put London.'

'But I thought they came from the Midlands somewhere.'

Gwen shrugged. 'Maybe they moved twice. Once away, once back. If you'll excuse me, sir. I've got the man coming to make me an offer for the stock.'

'One more thing, Mrs Donald. Are you sure you haven't noticed anything missing from this flat? Fel,

Mr Monk, the milkman, is certain something was moved in the time between his discovering the body and alerting the police.'

'Well if it has been, I can't think what it could be. Of course Donald might have bought something since I went to the country. But unless I know what I'm looking for, I can't say that it's missing, can I, sir?'

Jack was forced to leave the matter there. Emerging on to the pavement, he set off back to Leighton Road. Passing the cafe, however, he was startled out of his reverie by a violent banging on the glass.

Ding Dong Bell wiped a porthole in the condensation-covered window and mouthed something at him. Jack shook his head; unable to lip-read the words.

Flapping an excited hand in the manner of someone telling a dog to 'sit', Ding Dong whisked the door open and hurried outside. 'I been waiting for you to come down, sir. Thought you'd want to know straight away. I found him.'

'Found who?'

'Him, sir. The gold and ruby ear-ring bloke. The last "special" that Mr Donald did before he snuffed it.'

Chapter 17

'You not want yer dinner, mister?'

Turning back, Jack and the DC found Josepha standing in the cafe doorway, a steaming plate balanced carefully on a folded cloth. A wistful expression passed across Ding Dong's face: 'Thought you might be spending a bit of time with Mrs Donald, sir.'

Stamford saw his DC brace his shoulders, preparing to bid a manful farewell to his dinner. He came to a quick decision.

'Will your "special" wait?'

Ding Dong's mournful face twisted into what would have been mild depression in anyone else's, but probably counted as a smile on him. 'Oh yes. In fact, probably do him good to simmer for a bit.'

'I'll join you for dinner then. What's that?' Jack asked, seating himself opposite the DC but speaking to Josepha.

'It's tripe. Is disgusting.'

'What else is there?'

'Rabbit stew.'

'Is that any good?'

Josepha lifted indifferent shoulders, making it clear the decision was Jack's alone.

'I'll try it.'

Contrary to their waitress's bizarre selling technique, the stew proved to be excellent.

281

'Your sister does the cooking, does she?' Jack asked as Josepha returned to slam two glasses of water on the chequered tablecloth.

'*Si*. Ordering, cooking, *banking*.' The angry clash of metal on metal from beyond the ordering hatch showed the words had been overheard and understood.

'Number three's ready.' Two plates were shoved on to the ledge of the open hatch. Stamford caught a glimpse of Maria's agitated face, red and sweaty beneath the knotted scarf, before she retreated back into the clouds of steam.

Josepha snatched up the plates, made a rude face, and stomped back to table three. Despite her angry posture, there was still the hint of a provocative wriggle in her rear. Two workmen, their boots caked with drying yellow clay, gave her an appreciative once-over before tucking into tripe with enthusiasm.

Whilst he ate, Stamford glanced around the rest of the tables. Only about half were taken, yet it was the middle of the dinner time, and presumably could be counted as the cafe's busiest time. There was nothing wrong with the food; he wondered if the lack of trade could be attributed to the fact the waitress appeared to have been trained by Attila the Hun.

'Shouldn't think that's got anything to do with it, sir,' Ding Dong said, unearthing a small sliver of onion with obvious pleasure. 'Look at that. The lady wife ain't been able to find none of them for weeks. No,' he said, returning to his theme, 'it's the same as all these 'ere shops, ain't it? You don't 'ave to go nowhere to get *to* 'em. And you ain't *coming* from nowhere when you comes across 'em.'

Unravelling this sentence, Stamford suggested, 'You mean there's no passing trade.'

'And precious little fixed, sir.'

'Hmm.' Stamford covertly examined the rest of the diners and realised what his DC meant. Most of the eaters were men, and their clothing suggested they were manual workers from the clearance and demolition teams dealing with the bomb damage in the next street rather than regulars.

Josepha started to clear a vacated table. Something was stuck to the bottom of a plate. She peeled it off and smoothed out a ten shilling note.

'He leave,' she said. 'For a tip you think?'

'Seems a bit steep for a tip, miss,' Ding Dong pointed out. 'The bloke's probably left it by mistake.'

It wasn't a view Josepha wanted to entertain. But eventually she compromised. 'I leave it under counter. If he not come back by the time we close, then it is tip. *My* tip,' she yelled at the hatch.

A draught of cold air from the door across the back of Stamford's neck announced the arrival of another customer. He looked behind him, expecting to see another dust-engrimed road mender, and experienced a mild surprise at finding the new customer was Sarah McNeill.

He'd half smiled a greeting, assuming she'd come to find him, before he realised that his sergeant wasn't too pleased to find him there.

'Problems?' he enquired.

'No, sir. There was something I wanted to check.'

'Join us.' He pushed a chair out.

'I got your message, Ding Dong. Jeannie's gone down to collect the lady.'

Stamford raised an enquiring eyebrow in the DC's direction.

'A connection of the "special", sir. I reckon it's her . . .' He flicked a lobe, indicating an ear-ring.

'Tell me more when we meet the gentleman. Have you taken a meal break yet, Sergeant? The stew's good. I don't know about the tripe.'

'Yuck,' Sarah said frankly. She slipped the striped band from her wrist and put herself 'off duty'. 'Can I have another plate of the stew, please,' she accosted the passing Josepha. 'And I'd like a word with your sister, when she can spare a minute.'

'Why?' Stamford asked as soon as Josepha had accepted the order with her usual charm.

Sarah bit her lip. 'It's just something that occurred to me, sir. I'd like to see if I'm correct before I say anything.'

'All right, ask. But then come back to the station and give me a report. I can't have officers following separate leads all over the place. It just leads to duplicated work and possible foul ups on the case.'

'I intended to, sir,' Sarah assured him, sweeping him with the same cool, distant expression she'd been in the habit of using when they'd first met and she wished to put him firmly in his place. 'How did the inquest go?'

Stamford told her. 'Did your 18B go off all right?'

He'd lost her services back to uniform that morning due to the necessity of taking into custody a female anti-war agitator under the Emergency Defence Regulations.

'Waste of time. She wasn't there. Special Branch are chasing north after her. I see the Battle of Malta is still raging,' she remarked calmly as a jumble of swearwords burst from the kitchen and were abruptly cut off by the slamming of the hatch covers.

'What the devil's the matter with those two?' Jack demanded.

'You mean you don't know?' Both his junior officers stared at him with surprise.

'Promotion tends to cut down the opportunities for snooping,' he apologised. 'And by the time you reach chief inspector, they don't even tell you the canteen gossip.'

A slight pinkness stained Sarah's cheeks; her gaze challenged Ding Dong to say something. Prudently he dived into his pudding instead.

'Their father,' she explained, waving her fork at the noisy argument in the kitchen.

'The ship's cook?'

'The ship's cook,' Sarah agreed, 'wanted to marry Josepha's mother, but he got Maria's mother pregnant, so the family made him marry her instead.'

'But he went on, er, associating with Josepha's mother?'

'You know what they say about sailors, sir,' Ding Dong chipped in, 'a girl in every port. This one was daft enough to have 'em all in the same one – Valletta.'

'Anyway,' Sarah continued, 'it seems that Maria's mum died about five years ago, and instead of marrying Old Man Browne, Josepha's mum married another bloke who didn't want an illegitimate stepdaughter hanging around. He and the rest of the family told Dad to sling his hook or whatever nautical expression they use in these circumstances, and to take his daughters with him.'

'Why Kentish Town? Sailors usually settle in sight of the sea, don't they?' Stamford queried, one eye on Josepha who was drifting closer, ostensibly tidying away dirty cutlery.

'The last owner of the cafe was a distant cousin, let him have the lease cheap. But you're right about him missing the briny, sir. He ran off to sea again a couple of years later.'

'Probably floating at the bottom of the Pacific, weighed down by a couple of his own suet puddings,' Ding Dong suggested. In answer to Jack's look of incomprehension, he explained. 'By all accounts he was the sort of cook who'd have been hard pushed to flog a cheese sandwich to Ben Gunn, sir. The grub's been much better since Miss Maria took over the kitchen. Pity she ain't got a better place, she could make a nice little packet, I reckon.'

'She make plenty of money,' Josepha burst out, giving up her pretence of polishing the smeared forks and dragging a chair to their table. 'And half of it is mine. That right, isn't it? Just because her mama is so ugly she have to trick Papa into marrying her, don't mean business is all hers, does it?'

Jack thought it might well do, if their father was truly dead. He compromised by suggesting it depended on who Mr Browne had left in charge of the business.

'Papa didn't leave no one. We just get up one morning, find note: Shipping out. Keep cafe afloat until I dock again.'

'When was this?'

'Three year ago. Three years she put all the money in bank in her name, so I cannot go home.'

'Back to Malta, yer mean, miss? I don't reckon you

ought to be thinking of going there. They're bombing it.'

'They bomb here.'

'But you couldn't get there, Josepha,' Sarah explained.

'Not now, no. But after the war, when we beat the Germans, I go home. To my mama. She wants me really, you know?'

For a moment her pretty face twisted, and all three officers glimpsed the little girl beneath the cheap make-up.

'Miss, can I pay yer?' One of the workmen waved the bill.

Josepha slouched over, her mouth drooping once more into a pout.

'We'd better go too, Constable. I'll leave you to your enquiries, Sergeant.' He dropped his voice lower, and bent across to murmur in her ear. 'When you speak to Maria, ask her about her sister's relationship with James Donald.'

The day had a notable chill to it. Leaves, dried to the colours of russet and gold, whispered along the gutters in front of them, blowing in the gusts of breeze that crept around corners and sped through the occasional blasted building. Here and there wisps of blue smoke drifted from chimneys in a solid pillar, to be grabbed by the same breeze and ripped into ragged fragments. Occasionally, the raw, dry, smell of brick dust tickled their noses.

'Know what I miss most, sir?' Ding Dong said suddenly. 'Church bells. Made you feel all was right with the world, sitting in yer shirt sleeves, mopping up the fried egg with a bit of the lady wife's fried bread, and hearing the bells sort of calling to each other all over the city. Sundays just ain't the same now they banned the bells.'

Jack, who'd never suspected that his DC's lugubrious expression might hide a poet's soul, said, 'You a bit of a campanologist then, Constable?'

'Me? Oh no, sir. The lady wife and I always stop in me sister's boarding house for our 'olidays.'

Luckily for Jack's future relationship with his DC, his chuckle was lost in the gasp of Ding Dong's protest as a woman cannoned into him.

'Here. Steady on, miss. This is getting to be quite a habit.'

The collision had partially dislodged her headscarf, revealing Lexie Emmett's shock of bright red hair. 'Habit. What do you mean?' she said, her voice high and tight.

'Running into each other like this, miss.'

'Oh that. Yes. Sorry. I was in a bit of a hurry to get back. Me dad's in the shop on 'is tod. Toothache,' she garbled, clutching the left side of her face. 'Just 'ad to get it fixed. Bye.'

They stood for a moment, watching her scurrying away, jumping skittishly sideways to avoid the debris from a mechanical street sweeper. When she regained her balance again, the fist was once more applied to the side of her face. But this time it was the right side.

'I wonder what she's really been up to?' Jack mused.

'Probably wanted a couple of hours away from that dad of hers. They reckon he keeps her on a tight rein.'

Stamford grunted in a non-committal fashion. 'Tell me about the ruby ear-ring customer. What's he called?'

Ding Dong fished out his notebook and read slowly and ponderously, 'Ray-zoo-moves-key. Lives in one of them cottages along the towpath.'

It wasn't an address that Jack would have automatically associated with the little man who faced him in the interview room. From the tips of his well-polished patent shoes to the top of his oiled hair, he exuded all the charm of a professional lounge lizard. Springing to his feet on Stamford's entrance he squeaked in a surprisingly girlish voice, 'Count.'

'Count what?' Jack enquired.

The head twitched. The cloying perfume from the hair oil drifted into the officers' disgusted noses. 'I do not invite you to do arithmetic, Inspector. I introduce myself. Count Andrei Razumovsky. At your service.'

'Russian?'

'Of course.'

Jack guessed that the man was one of the many thousands of Russians who'd drifted westwards into Europe and the United States following the 1917 Revolution.

'So, er, Count, I believe my constable has already asked you certain questions about a jeweller in Balaclava Row?'

'The man had a certain skill. He could not, of course, emulate the work of the great craftsmen who worked for the imperial courts, but . . .' The count shrugged magnanimously, obviously prepared to overlook James Donald's shortcomings which were presumably compensated for by his ability to keep his mouth shut. When Jack suggested as much to the count, the little man swelled like an indignant blowfish.

'You suggest that I am a criminal, yes? But this is

not so, what I brought to the jeweller was mine.'

'And I gather you've brought several pieces to him over the years, isn't that so?'

The count graciously inclined his head. 'He gave satisfactory service. I continued to give him my patronage.'

'You've heard he's dead?'

'Your officer told me. It is most inconvenient. I shall have to find someone else. Perhaps you can recommend?'

'It's hardly my line, sir.' The words had hardly left Stamford's mouth, when it occurred to him that if you were looking for a bent jeweller, it probably *was* a good idea to ask a policeman. He wondered whether that was what the count had been implying, but the man's smooth face remained blandly non-committal. 'Why did you want copies of your jewellery, sir?'

'Surely that is my business, Inspector. It is not against the law.'

'Well it might be, sir. If you wanted them in order to commit a fraud, say.'

'The count does not commit fraud. I require capital for certain investments.'

Keeping his hands beneath the table where the count couldn't see them, Ding Dong dealt an imaginary hand of cards. Jack raised an understanding eyebrow. 'When did you . . .?' he began, then swung towards the door as a tentative tap claimed his attention. 'Come in.'

The young WPC, Jeannie, peeped into the room. 'She's here, Mr Bell. I put her in Matron's room.'

'Ta, Jeannie. It's the lady, sir. The one who's tom I reckon he's been selling.'

If the count didn't understand the slang, he

certainly grasped the gist of Ding Dong's statement.

'No. You should not have disturbed the countess. She is not to be bothered with such matters.'

'The countess? Your wife, sir?' Jack enquired.

'His auntie, sir. According to him,' Ding Dong interjected.

'What do you mean "according to him"?' Jack asked, leaving the fuming count in the interview room, whilst they made their way down to the matron's room.

'Well, sir. I'd 'ave said the lady was the real McCoy. But him, well he's just like them bits of jewellery Donald made – gilt pretending to be gold, sir. Gawd!'

A step behind his DC, Jack peered over his shoulder into the matron's room and beheld the bizarre spectacle that had jolted this exclamation out of Ding Dong.

In the centre of the station matron's room stood one of the fattest women he'd ever seen in his life. The sight was all the more fantastic because, apart from a large floppy velvet hat decorated with a well-chewed feather, she was wearing only a corset; a garment which stretched from her armpits to her knees and appeared to have been constructed by Brunel as a bit of light relief.

The sudden appearance of two strange men whilst she was disrobing had no discernible effect on the countess at all. She was in the process of extracting a gold chain from her cleavage and she continued to do so; drawing it slowly forth in the manner of a conjuror producing yards of chiffon scarves.

'I asked the lady if she had any jewellery, like Constable Bell requested, and she is being kind enough to show me, sir,' Matron explained.

'Er, fine. We'll er, be outside, when you're finished.'

'I shan't be long, sir,' Matron said calmly. She was a police sergeant's widow, and had been known to knock out a roaring female drunk twice her size with one swift uppercut. But her tiny delicate features and genteel manners were reminiscent of a high-class lady's maid. Perhaps that had reassured the countess. In any event, she had no qualms about disgorging the contents of her underwear at Matron's request.

'I think that's the lot,' she assured Stamford a few moments later, passing over a cardboard box.

'Thank you, Matron. I wonder whether you'd be kind enough to entertain the countess whilst I have a word with her so-called nephew?'

'Certainly, Inspector.'

'What did you make of her?'

'A lady,' Matron said promptly. 'Doesn't care what anyone thinks of her. That's always a sign you know, sir. Of course she's a bit . . .' Matron tapped a slim finger against her fair hair.

The countess surged into the corridor. Her formidable figure had now been clad in a velvet dress that had probably been high fashion thirty years ago. But her head was now bald apart from a few wisps of white hair. 'I forget this one,' she said, extracting a brooch from the base of the dark wig, and flicking it accurately into the box Jack was holding to his chest.

He grinned. 'You should play alleys, Countess. You'd clean up.'

The countess banged her wig back on and pulled it into place. 'What is alleys please?'

'Marbles, Countess,' Matron replied. 'A children's game with small glass balls.'

'Who is this person, please?'

'Chief Inspector Stamford, Countess,' Matron made the introductions. 'The Countess Tatiana Maria Korsakov, sir.'

She extended a hand, palm downwards. It was surprisingly small. Jack took it and touched his lips to the fingers.

The countess beamed with childish pleasure. Despite her age, her face was smooth and unlined. 'You have beautiful eyes,' she announced as Jack straightened up. 'You have eyes like my son, Alexander.' Her own eyes lost their innocent sparkle for a second and clouded with some adult memory. The small hand in Jack's tightened convulsively. Gently, he untangled the fingers and passed her to Matron, who nodded her understanding.

Placing one hand on the countess's elbow, Matron steered her back into the room. Stamford was reminded of a dragonfly darting against a huge milch cow. Slowly but surely the countess turned the way the fly wanted her to go.

'Let's see what her nephew's got to say about this lot.'

'They are the countess's property,' is what he said, the red cheeks puffed once more with indignation.

'I don't doubt it,' Jack replied. He slid his fingers into the pile and drew up brooches, rings, amulets, lockets, chokers and chains. 'But how much of it is genuine, eh, Count? And how many are copies?'

The count lifted his shoulders. 'One must live.'

'When did you leave Russia, Count?'

'Nineteen nineteen.'

'And you came directly to England?'

'At first no. I travel. Berlin. Vienna. Paris. In Paris

the countess and I rediscover each other. We see each other across the restaurant. We recognise each other. We embrace.' The count swept up several cubic yards of air in an imaginary hug. 'We are a family again.'

'I see. And how long had it been . . . since your previous reunion with the countess?'

'Perhaps ten years.'

Stamford judged the count to be about forty. 'So,' he clarified, 'you were a child last time the countess saw you. And a young man when you met again. Yet she recognised you immediately?'

'Of course. We are a most distinguished family.' The count puffed out his very undistinguished features. His eyes had taken on a combative gleam which plainly said, 'Go on, try to prove I'm an imposter.'

Jack would have bet a year's pay he was; but he also knew he'd never prove it now. Anyway, it scarcely mattered, apart from the fraud which they suspected he'd been perpetrating on his 'aunt'.

Jack stirred the glittering pile with one finger. 'Do you sell the original, or the copy?' he said abruptly.

'The original naturally.'

'And the copy?'

'A small deception. To spare the countess's feelings.'

'So she is the legal owner of the jewellery?'

The count spread dismissive hands.

'And is she aware that you've been selling it off over the years? I don't imagine there is much left if you've been playing this game for what . . . fifteen, sixteen years?'

'She would not believe you. And if you truly wish to be of service to the countess you will say nothing.'

'Will I indeed?'

'Of course. You have seen the countess, yes? She is not like others.' Plump fingers described circles in front of the count's temporal lobes. 'If I were to be sent to prison, who would take care of her?'

Whilst Jack was swallowing this outrageous statement, a gentle scratching on the door was answered by Ding Dong. He murmured something to the constable outside, then called back over his shoulder. 'You ain't got a posh newspaper 'ave you, sir? The ladyship wants one and the lads 'ave only got the *Daily Mirror*.'

'No. I didn't buy one this morning. Tell them to try the superintendent's office. He gets *The Times*.'

Ding Dong relayed this message and returned to the table.

'How long have you been using James Donald to make copies, Count?' Stamford demanded abruptly.

'Perhaps five, six years.'

'The last item, the ear-rings, which day did you collect them?'

'Wednesday.'

Jack looked up quickly. '*Last* Wednesday?'

'Yes.'

'What time?'

'It was late. Perhaps eight o'clock, perhaps just before. I do not know. Is it important?'

'Are you absolutely certain it was the Wednesday night?'

'Of course. I had arranged with an acquaintance to make certain investments on Friday.' (A card game, Stamford translated silently.) 'I required the ear-rings to sell on the Thursday. Why?' For the first time, the count started to look uneasy. Moistening his red lips, he smoothed back his hair. The palm came away gleaming with oil.

'Go on. You called on Donald, by the back entrance I assume since the shop was shut?'

The count nodded.

'And then what?'

'He took the pieces from the safe for me to see and we went upstairs, to his apartments.'

'Why?'

'The light. I wished to examine the work but he had not put his blackout board up.'

'Go on.'

'There is nothing to tell. I look carefully. The work is good. I pay him and go.'

'Was there anyone else in the flat?'

'No. His family had gone to the country.'

'And he had no visitors there?'

'I saw no one.'

'Did anything strike you as odd that night?'

'No. Why do you ask me all these questions?'

'Because you were probably the last person to see Mr Donald alive.'

'Yes?' The idea appeared to please the count.

'Apart from the murderer. Unless, of course, you were the murderer?'

'Me! Why should I wish to kill the man? He was most useful.'

'Maybe he'd threatened to tell the countess what you were doing.'

'He did not know the countess. And what would it matter if he had spoken to her? She would not believe him.'

The quiet confidence with which he uttered this statement made Stamford's gall rise, but he was inclined to agree with the smug little bastard.

'You have finished your interrogation, Inspector? May I go now?'

'Just a couple more questions, sir. When you left Donald's shop that night, did you see anyone hanging around?'

'No.'

Whilst he'd been talking, the count had been drawing one finger along the top of the box containing the jewellery. Now he nudged it slightly closer to his chest.

Jack moved it back. 'And after you left the shop, where did you go?'

'Home. To dine with the countess.'

'And you stayed in all night, did you, sir?'

'Not all. At perhaps eleven o'clock I go out. Some friends invite me to join them on *The Saucy Sally*.'

'The what?'

Ding Dong interjected, explaining, 'It's a barge, sir. Moored down on the canal.'

'We drink a little,' the count said airily. 'Play a little cards.'

'Until when?'

'Perhaps two, three o'clock.'

Stamford slid a notebook across the table at him. 'Write down the names and addresses of these other men.'

Bending forward revealed the bald spot, carefully concealed by strands of hair plastered from the side, on the count's pate. 'They live on the barge,' he explained, writing in bold but fairly illegible strokes.

'You are going to charge me, Inspector? The countess she will say I have the right to sell the family's property. It is my inheritance.'

Stamford kept him in suspense for a few more long minutes, then pushed the box violently across the table surface. The count grunted in surprise as it hit him full in the chest.

'I'll have to ask you to provide your fingerprints for elimination purposes. After that you can go. However, I'll be telling the local patrols to keep an eye on the countess in future.'

Stamford didn't really imagine the count had any evil plans for his 'aunt'; if he had, he'd have made a more determined effort to prosecute the man and put him safely out of harm's way. But as it was, he privately agreed with the count that there was little chance of getting a coherent statement from the countess which would stand up in a court of law.

Anyway, in a strange way, he did seem genuinely fond of the old girl. And she, in turn, greeted him as if they'd been parted for years, flinging his arms round her rotund shape with pleasurable cries.

'Come, Countess. I shall escort you home.'

Clutching his arm, the countess sailed forward: an ungainly tanker guided by a solid little tug boat. At the desk, she paused briefly to return the super-intendent's paper with her gracious thanks for the loan.

'Our pleasure, madam,' the desk officer said. 'Afternoon, Sarge.'

'Good afternoon,' Sarah replied. 'Who on earth was *that*?'

'One of James Donald's "special" customers,' Jack

called through from the corridor. 'Come down to my office and I'll bring you up to date. What's the matter?' he added as Sarah squealed in amusement.

Stepping further along the corridor, Jack poked his head into the front office and had to choke back a shout of laughter.

The desk officer held up the superintendent's *Times* and peered at it with consternation. Or to be exact, he peered through the hole in the centre that had been neatly punched out in the shape of a lavatory seat.

Still chuckling they moved back into Jack's office where he gave her a quick briefing on 'the count'.

'So you don't think he's a possible, sir?'

'Anything's possible, I suppose. Ding Dong can check out his alibi with the bargees. But somehow I doubt if he was involved in the murder. Donald was more use to him alive than dead. Despite his assurances to the contrary, I rather suspect he's actually working a scam and selling off several copies before he gets rid of the original. Unfortunately, we can't do anything about it until someone complains. As things stand, we're still pretty thin on motives for this murder.'

'Not necessarily, sir.' Sarah's eyes sparkled in triumph. 'That's what I've been doing. I think I've found one.'

Chapter 18

'All right,' Stamford invited. 'Tell me.'

Sarah perched herself on the edge of a desk.

'Well,' she said. 'It's about the buildings . . . Oh damn!'

'Pardon?'

'Sorry, sir. I just remembered. I saw Mrs O'Day's son up the market this morning. The short one.'

'Maury. Although he wouldn't thank you for that description.'

'Everyone tends to look short when you're a beanpole, sir.'

'I know, my head's up there too, remember. And why have you taken to calling me "sir" every other sentence again?'

She was doing it because she was nervous, sensing that he wasn't going to like the theory that she'd been developing. Which was one reason she'd seized on Maury's message as a welcome diversion. 'I assume you understand it, si . . .?'

'Mm. It's about Leo Bowler wanting to buy the freehold of Balaclava Row.'

He'd been wondering aloud the previous evening why anyone would want to invest in London property at the present time. Unexpectedly, it was Maury who'd spoken up.

'Best time, Mr Stamford,' he'd said, looking up from the paper he'd been studying, his normally taciturn face lit up with enthusiasm.

Sitting in a rocker by his mother's cooking range, his feet braced to the floor to prevent the chair moving, he'd delivered a lecture on economics at Jack. A lot of people, he'd pointed out, who'd left the city at the beginning of the war had drifted back and showed no sign of leaving again despite the current bombing. 'If 'itler keeps knocking down houses at this rate, Mr Stamford, then pretty soon there's going to be a shortage of places for people to live. I 'eard the council's already started looking for places to put them that's been bombed out. And even if they take 'em off yer, they got to pay you rent or something.'

'The property I'm thinking of is shops, not houses.'

'Good bit of land is there?'

'I suppose so. There's a field at the back.'

'Cor, just perfect, Mr Stamford. Plenty of room to build see? In fact, 'itler could be doing yer a favour if 'e knocks the shops down. You can build more 'ouses or flats then. Flats would be best. You get four or five times rent for the same bit of land, see?'

His hands moved one on top of the other, like a child building blocks. Stamford had watched him with fascination. Eileen's four older boys were all tall and muscular like Pat. And Sammy, with his over-large hands and feet, was already showing signs of growing into a typical O'Day. Only Maurice had inherited his mother's dark looks and short stature. Normally when he spoke to Jack, his black eyes tended to focus away over the policeman's shoulder, lending credence to his mother's fears that whatever he was up to, he'd rather the law didn't know. But for once he was looking Stamford full in the face, his enthusiasm for his subject overwhelming his natural caution.

'You take my advice, Mr Stamford, don't go for all them middle-class 'ouses. Buy up cheap stuff wiv plenty of land to stick more on if you can get it. That's where the money's going to be made after the war. Soon as I get a bit more capital, that's what I'm going to do.'

'Where's the money going to be made whilst the war's still going on?' Jack had asked, more from a desire to keep Maury talking than any real interest. It was the longest conversation he'd ever had with the boy, and he was partially hypnotised by the depth of the differences between Maury and the other O'Days.

'Food,' Maury had responded promptly. 'Course engineering is good too, if you can get 'old of a Government contract. But it takes too much capital to start up. No, food's yer best bet. People always gotta eat. Put yer money in food. That's what I done. I gotta couple of hot food stalls going up the markets and I got me eye on a few more prime sites.'

Maury had been seduced from his normal reserve by the stimulus of his subject; neither his mother nor his brothers had ever taken his ambitions seriously. Now he remembered Jack wasn't just any other neighbour. Just before the shutters closed again, Jack said quickly, 'I don't know that your development theory can be right about these particular shops. The land's waterlogged.'

'Oh.' Maury thought about this. 'Can't be that bad if they already built these shops on it, can it? 'Spect it just takes a bit of nous to know what yer doing. Tell you what, Mr Stamford. I'll ask round if you like. I gotta contact in that line of business.'

Stamford had solemnly said he'd be grateful for Maury's assistance.

'So Maury's contact says it's all right to build over Balaclava if they lay the correct drainage pipes first,' Sarah said, as Stamford came to the end of his explanation. 'You think Maury's theory is right, and that's what Bowler is up to?'

'Well, I can't imagine that he sees much future in half a dozen businesses that are scarcely keeping their heads above water.' He winced as Sarah laughed. 'Sorry, no pun intended.'

'It would fit in with what I've found out.'

'Which is?'

'Well . . .' Sarah slid into the chair opposite. 'You know I've been talking to Maria?'

'Did you manage to ask her about Josepha's relationship with Donald?'

Sarah could have screamed with frustration; didn't this wretched man *want* to hear her theory? Controlling her voice with deliberately deep breaths, she said in an even tone, 'Yes. I did. According to Maria it was a sort of father-daughter thing. He used to let her dress herself up in the jewellery. Maria says Josepha tried to pretend it was something more at first, but Maria didn't believe her. And to tell you the truth, sir, neither do I. From what I can gather, that vamp act of Josepha's is just that – an act, to annoy Maria. If her sister told her to date every man north of Charing Cross, I reckon Josepha would be out the next day applying to join the sisters at St Joseph's.' This whole speech had come out in a breathless rush. Now she stared Stamford down and asked if it would be all right if she went on with her report.

'Yes. Sorry I interrupted,' Jack responded with mock meekness.

Sarah considered replying in kind, decided she'd be pushing her luck and continued: 'Right. Well, I asked Maria if I could see the cafe's lease, and guess what – it's in the father's name: Aloysius Browne.'

'If I say that leaves me all at sea, you're going to get annoyed, aren't you?'

'Yes.' Sarah knew she was being teased, but found herself glad about it. It somehow put their relationship back on to the close, easy-going path that it had been following towards the end of their last investigation together. It was a pity she had to spoil it really. 'It means, sir, that the girls have no legal right to be in the cafe. You see the money for the ground rent is paid to Miss Fortune. And she's not obliged to take it from anyone else. If Aloysius isn't there to pay it, then that's it, end of lease. She's only been accepting it from the girls on sufferance. Miss Fortune could turf them out any time.'

'What's all this got to do with James Donald?'

'Don't you see?' Holding up her right hand, she ticked off the shops on her slim fingers. 'The cafe can be cleared at any time. The Wellers have already gone. According to rumour, Albert White's giving up the grocer's shop.'

'Haven't you forgotten the cobbler?' Stamford said, beginning to see the direction of her argument, and not liking it at all.

'I doubt if he'll be working much longer. Didn't you notice? He's got terrible arthritis in his fingers. And sleeping down in that cellar will bring it on even quicker. No, the only person in that row who wasn't going to shift, was Donald. After all, he didn't really rely on the shop trade for his profits, most of them came from the "specials", and 'e had no reason to give up a cheap workroom and shift somewhere else. And the lease was in his name alone, Gwen ain't, isn't, on it. I checked.'

She knew from Stamford's expression that he was annoyed, and that in turn made her garble and allow her commoner childhood accent to creep into her voice.

'So to sum up, Sergeant. You think Miss Fortune murdered James Donald in order to secure the vacant possession of Balaclava Row. Always assuming, of course, she could somehow accelerate Frank Emmett's arthritis. Or do you think we should expect him to be our next victim?'

Stamford hated himself for allowing an edge of sarcasm to frost his response. But Helen's pale face with its curtain of raven hair had swum into his mind as Sarah talked and the idea of her killing any other creature was ... He meant to tell himself it was ludicrous, but an innate truthfulness made him admit he found the idea unbearable.

Gritting her teeth, Sarah ground out that people had been murdered for a lot less than the profit on a lucrative land deal.

'Maybe they have. But I don't think it's the case this time.'

'Don't you? Or is it just that you don't like to think of Miss Fortune as a murderess?'

She hadn't meant to say it, and once it was out she'd have given anything to snatch it back. But it was too late. If she hadn't been sitting on the opposite side of the room, she would have fallen on the uniformed sergeant who opened the door and kissed him for interrupting at that point.

'Sorry, sir,' he said. 'But we've got a bit of a problem with staff tonight.'

Briefly he explained that if the WPCs were to patrol all the streets and tube stations, they had no one to cover for the female police officer that they were supposed to have on duty in the station throughout the night. 'They're sending me a girl over from Arbour Square, but she won't be on until ten. So I was just wondering . . .' He nodded at Sarah.

She checked her watch. It was nearly five. 'All right, I'll cover until she arrives. If that's all right with you, sir?'

'It's fine with me. But you should take a meal break.'

Sarah knew he wanted to get rid of her before they had a row. 'How about if I take an hour now and come back on duty at six?'

'Great, thanks,' the uniform sergeant breathed, relieved to have got his rotas sorted out so easily.

Once outside the CID office, Sarah found herself dithering again. It wasn't like her, and the mere fact she could get into this state, only served to exacerbate her nerves even further. 'Food or walk?' she said aloud. 'Come on, make up your mind.'

'Walk,' her mind decided. Or, to be exact, it decided it had had enough of pretending to ignore the speculative whispers in the canteen for one week.

Without consciously meaning to, she found herself walking at a slow, patrol pace, towards Balaclava Row. The autumn wind had slackened and the fire smoke now tumbled down the sides of the brick chimneys in grey billows interspersed with the occasional spit and

sparkle of igniting soot, betraying those houses where
the flues hadn't been swept since the previous spring's
fires. Avoiding the chalked hopscotch lines on the
pavements and the goal posts marked by piles of
discarded jumpers, Sarah moved automatically
through the groups of playing children, without really
seeing them.

She'd got what her family had always referred to
as 'the Thursday blues'. After Thursday came
Friday and Saturday; paydays for her dad if he'd
managed to get any work that week. And after that
came the hours of roaring drunkenness when he
hadn't known, or cared, who he was hitting. But
the worse bit had come later, with the maudlin
apologies and whingeing promises that it would
never happen again.

Half lost in her own memories, it took her a few
seconds to disentangle the whining female voice from
that of her dad's which was still pleading inside her
head.

'Just another five bob, miss. Yer can spare that,
can't you? Young lady in a good job like you got.'

'I haven't got any more. I gave you everything this
morning, Mrs Starkey.'

Blinking, Sarah discovered that she'd arrived in
Balaclava Row. Rose Goodwin was outside the grocer's
shop facing a small, scruffy boy and a pasty-faced,
middle-aged woman who, Sarah thought, she'd seen
in the market that morning.

'But I ain't got no food in for 'im. You wouldn't want
Nafnel to go 'ungry would ya?' An affectionate claw
squeezed the bony shoulder in front of her.

Her grateful grandson responded with a snarled,

'Gerroff!' and a violent twist of his body to release himself.

'Look, he can eat with me. You both can.'

'Oh I couldn't be putting yer to that trouble, miss. You give it to me, and I'll cook it. Maybe yer grocer friend could spare a bit of bacon or sugar, eh? And a packet of tea. 'E does love a drop of milky tea out of me saucer before 'e goes to sleep, bless him.'

'I don't, I ain't a bleedin' cat.'

'Nafnel! Language.'

Albert surged from his shop to join the little trio on the pavement. 'I heard what your friend was saying, Rose. How about a few nice lean back rashers, eh?'

Ma Starkey's ravaged face shone with the anticipation of drink money to come. Reaching out to take the greasy parcel, she found her way blocked.

'That food is on ration, madam. Have you taken the correct coupons off her, Mr White?'

Ma Starkey could see her next glass of gin fading back into the ether. 'Why can't you mind yer own business, yer nosy cow. You ain't a food inspector.'

'Would you like me to send for one?'

Thwarted, Ma Starkey backed away. 'I should 'ave let them stick you in an orphanage,' was her parting blessing on her flesh and blood.

'You shouldn't give a drunk money, or anything they can sell to get it, Mrs Goodwin,' Sarah admonished, the spectre of her own dad hovering on her shoulder. 'It's just helping them to kill themselves in the end.'

Nafnel tugged on his teacher's skirt. 'Giv me gran a quid quick, miss. I'll pay yer back when I get big.'

'You won't get much bigger if you keep talking like

that,' Rose scolded. 'Come on, I'll see what I've got in to cook for your tea.'

Nafnel allowed himself to be led through the shop. His piping voice carried back to the front door. 'Miss, if me gran does snuff it, you'll take care of me, won't yer?'

'Poor little tyke,' Albert said to no one in particular.

'I take it, that was one of Mrs Goodwin's pupils. How's she getting on with the new job?'

'Oh lovely, thanks, miss. She's a way with kids, has Rose. Always got on a treat with the customers' little ones.'

'I'm surprised she gave up teaching then. There are some schools that take married women, aren't there?'

'I couldn't say, miss. Never 'aving 'ad the need to call on their services meself. Anyhow it wouldn't have made no difference if they was begging for 'em. Not with that husband of 'ers. Not a bloke to take kindly to his missus doing anything better than him that one, for all his fancy manners.'

'Oh?' Despite the fact she'd cast Helen Fortune in the role of chief villainess, Sarah's instincts still prompted her to ferret out any gossip relating to possible marriage problems for another female in the Row. But before she could delve further, the front door of the jeweller's shop opened and Gwen Donald appeared.

'I thought it was you,' she called, turning the key in the front door. 'It saves me a call.'

A small spark of hope that Gwen had finally worked out what it was that Felonious had noticed was missing from the flat was dispelled by an invitation to the funeral.

'There's to be a service at St Luke's at twelve, miss. Then on to the cemetery. And then back here for the funeral tea. It won't be anything fancy, but I thought you and the inspector might want to come. Not that other one though.'

Sarah promised she'd try to attend.

Satisfied, Gwen issued the same invitation to Albert and his sister.

'I'll be pleased. Don't know about our Elsie. Funerals make her come over queer.'

The tightening of Gwen Donald's lips told Sarah what she thought of Elsie Finch's fads. 'As you wish. Perhaps you'd pass the message to Mrs Goodwin for me?'

Gwen moved back to the cafe. Curious, Sarah followed and saw Josepha receive the invitation with her usual pouting disinterest.

It would have been logical to step into the cobbler's next, but Gwen walked past and entered the hairdresser's instead. Loitering on the pavement, Sarah saw the message issued and accepted again. The windows were covered in condensation, Helen's face was no more than a fuzzy pink blur framed by the dark cap of her hair; but Sarah was certain that for a heart's beat, Helen looked directly into her own eyes and her mouth curved slightly in a challenging smile.

There was no time to do more than respond with a stare of chilly indifference, before Gwen came out and marched purposefully into Emmetts' shop.

Obviously; whatever the police might think, she still had Lexie cast in the role of scarlet woman.

'She's out back,' Frank Emmett spat through a mouthful of tacks. He'd moved his last on to the serving counter and was struggling to revive a boot that had been ground into virtual oblivion by its owner. 'Lexie! Missus Donald and that lady copper want to see yer.'

'There's no need to trouble her. I've come about the funeral. Twelve tomorrow, if that suits?'

'Have to I suppose. Means shutting the shop for a half day. You hear that, Lexie? More trade lost.'

Lexie was folding a pair of men's long johns against her chest. The smell of slightly burnt flannel joined the scents of fresh leather and wax polish. 'Been catching up on me ironing out back,' she explained. 'I'm all behind these days.'

'It's 'cos you gad about too much.'

'It's because I spend all flaming day in this shop and all flaming night down that cellar. When d'ya expect me to clean and iron?'

An expression of deepest self-pity settled over Frank Emmett's sour features. His hand moved to his middle chest in an automatic rubbing motion. 'Yer don't have no call to speak to me like that. You'll be sorry when yer old dad's gone,' he quavered.

'I wish,' snapped Lexie.

They'd both forgotten their audience. Gwen's mouth had once more pursed in disapproval. She came from a world where the man of the house was always shown respect in public whatever the private position might be.

'We'll be there,' Lexie said. 'Is it cars or carriages?'

'Cars. I'd have liked carriages but it would take too long for East Finchley if the girls are to go back home that evening.'

Sarah noted her use of the word 'home'. Once again,

Gwen gave the impression of tidying her husband's corpse away in the same way that she was disposing of the unwanted furniture.

'Will there be room for us?' Frank queried. 'We can't go paying out for taxis.'

'There'll be room. It's just the Row to come to the cemetery. I'm having two cars, separate wreaths from me and the girls and our Ruby's lot, and a proper marble headstone with gilding. He'll have a good send-off. I always done my duty by him as a wife and no one will be able to say I never done it as his widow.'

Gwen left the shop first. With her sharper ears, Sarah heard Frank's hissed instructions to his daughter to ask what she'd be doing with Donald's clothes.

'Ask yerself, I ain't robbing graves.'

Sarah shut the door on the simmering row. On an impulse she nipped back to the grocer's shop and found Albert alone.

'Do you have any chocolate?' she asked. There was none on the shelves.

Albert rubbed his jaw. 'Well I might have a bit put by, miss. How much did you want?'

'I don't want any at all.' She put sixpence on the counter. 'Give the little boy who went in with Mrs Goodwin some, will you?'

After all, she reasoned, leaving the shop again, us drunks' kids have to stick together. The gesture made her feel a bit better over the row with Stamford.

She started back towards Agar Street Station, but had barely reached the corner of the Row when a police Wolseley drew alongside her and Stamford leant across and flicked open the passenger door.

'All right, you win,' he said. 'Get in. According to Miss Fortune's statement she was on duty at her ARP post in Montpelier Road on the night of Donald's death. Let's check it out.'

Her watch said quarter to six.

'That WPC, Jeannie something, is standing in for you. I said we'd be back by seven.'

'Crimmond,' Sarah said happily. 'Jeannie's surname is Crimmond.'

She knew her theory was far-fetched but she didn't really care. Even if she fell flat on her face with this one, her opinions had been taken seriously.

'Thank you, sir.'

'You're welcome.'

Stamford flicked a sideways glance. 'Is it that important?' he said suddenly.

'Yes.'

She took a deep breath and said, 'I'm sick of being sent out to chaperon evacuees around station platforms or lecturing wayward girls on the perils of loose living. I mean, by the time we get them, they've usually found out the hard way what the perils are, and they either want their mum or they've opened their own savings account and are doing very nicely thank you. Either way, they want a social worker, not me. I want, I want . . . I want to be taken seriously.'

She could feel her insides cringing with embarrassment. It sounded so smug when she put it into words. Mercifully by that time they were drawing up outside a three-storey terraced house with a heavily sandbagged basement area and a large handpainted sign announcing 'ARP POST'.

'This is it.'

Surprisingly enough in an area where most houses contained several families or, at the very least, several generations of the same one, the full-time ARP warden lived alone in this one.

'To tell you the truth,' she admitted, preceding them down the basement steps. 'I was quite glad of the war. It gives me something to do.'

Sarah exchanged an amused look with her boss behind the woman's back.

'Well here we are. The post.'

It was well furnished with large scale maps of the area on the walls, a telephone, first aid cupboard, folding camp beds, easy chairs, gas cooker, desk and large table around which two women, a young boy and an elderly man were playing dominoes.

Under their curious stares, Stamford was invited to check the log book.

'Everyone's logged in and out. Just in case, you know . . .?'

Stamford nodded his understanding. On the relevant night, Warden Fortune had left the post at twenty-two thirty hours. Destination: Pratt Street Control Room. She'd returned to the post at twelve twenty.

He showed the ARP Warden the entry. 'Do you remember this?'

'Let's see. Wednesday night. That's the night the phones packed up, isn't it?'

There was a general murmur of agreement.

'Is that why Miss Fortune left the post? To report the phones?'

'Only partly. We'd had a couple of incidents. An Anderson partially buried with people trapped inside.

And then some parachute mines that had caught up on a rooftop and could have come down any minute.'

'Why didn't you contact the police station? We could have relayed the incident.'

'We tried. The first box we got to didn't work either. In the end Helen volunteered to ride round to Pratt Street. She had all the details of what was needed.'

'She was gone rather a long time, wasn't she?'

The boy at the table piped up. 'She saw some incendiaries drop in Brecknock Road. Went round to see if they'd done much damage.'

'And had they?' Sarah enquired.

'Dunno. Don't think she ever found 'em. Sometimes see, yer get bits of shells bursting and they look like incendiaries. 'Appens all the time,' he announced with the airy confidence of a veteran. 'Great, 'ere we go,' he crowed as the eerie wail of a siren announced the beginning of this night's bombardment. 'They're early tonight.'

The two woman buckled on white helmets and picked up torches. The boy grabbed a pair of Navy-issue binoculars and bounded out of the room.

'We'll get out of your way. Thank you,' Stamford said.

'Where now?' Sarah asked, standing with one hand on her car door, the other shielding her eyes as she scanned the planeless evening skies.

'Pratt Street. Let's see if they can tell us what time Miss Fortune left them that night.'

The pedestrians and few vehicles in the dusk-lit streets were moving in a calm, unhurried fashion as their police car bowled past them. Straining against the noise of the engine, Sarah's ears could not detect the deep, powerful far-off throbbing that heralded the approach of the bombers.

'Do you think it's a false alarm,' she said, cramming forward to peer through the windscreen.

'Shouldn't think so. They're raising the barrage.'

Silhouetted against the dull, overcast sky, the balloons had lost their silvery gleam. In their blackness they looked like monstrously misshapen tadpoles anchored to the earth by ever-lengthening umbilical cords.

'I can't see anything up there.'

Rolling down the window, Sarah tried to get a better view. 'There's still nothi— Yes! There they are!'

Jack risked taking his eyes off the road for a second and squinted against the fading light. Three dark shapes were diving through the low clouds, their outlines becoming more distinct as they left the frozen crystals behind.

'They're too small for bombers. Must be fighters.'

'There's two more up there. Look.'

The newcomers were sweeping downwards with a clear purpose. The flashes from their guns could clearly be seen on the ground.

The original three planes seemed to accelerate, turning in a tight arc and heading west into the sun.

Sarah, who'd been half standing in her seat in order to get a better view, flopped back as all five fighters disappeared over the horizon. 'Phew. Well that's that. No bombers after all. What on earth's the matter with . . .'

She had been intending to say, 'What on earth's the matter with that shop?'

The building in front of them had suddenly

expanded, its walls bulging outwards as if they were made of elastic. Her confused senses registered that the bricks returned to their normal shape before collapsing in a cloud of masonry dust and that the window panes had sailed out of their frames intact; before a tremendous roaring sound filled her ears and the world disappeared as suddenly as if someone had snapped a camera shutter over her eyelids.

Chapter 19

Returning to consciousness, she was drowsily aware of the warmth of another human body pressing against her legs. Her instinct was to scream and kick out, but fright froze her for a moment; long enough for the rest of her senses to catch up with her flustered brain and remind her of last night's events.

Easing her cramped limbs against the hard floor, she sat up cautiously. The other end of the blankets stirred immediately.

'Morning, miss,' Nafnel beamed.

'Good morning, Nafnel,' Rose said. 'Are you all right?'

'Course I is.' Kicking away the coverings, he scrambled out from beneath the shop counter and shot over to the door to lift up the blind a crack and peer out. 'Everyfing's still there, miss. I don't reckon they 'it nuffing.'

'Anything,' Rose corrected automatically, folding the blankets. 'I don't think they hit *anything*, Nafnel.'

'Anything,' he repeated, bouncing back to her. 'We gonna 'ave any breakfast?'

'In a minute. Help me carry these pillows back to the flat. I just hope your grandmother hasn't reported you missing.'

'What 'er! She don't know if I'm 'ome or not.'

'I hope not.' Rose knew she could be in trouble with

the school authorities if his grandmother did complain. But the earliness of last night's air raid alert had meant she hadn't been able to send him home after tea.

Nafnel scratched his back against a tub of oats. 'Don't do that. What's the matter, have you got an itch?'

Rose smoothed her fingers over her dressing gown, her senses alert for the crawling of tiny legs beneath her pyjamas.

Nafnel had slept in his clothes. Now he dragged the shirt and vest from his trouser band and peered down at the patches of gentian violet that Rose had applied over his red sores last night. 'I fink they're getting smaller. They don' alf itch though. What's the matter, miss?'

The bedding clasped to her chest, Rose was staring in space, a worried frown creeping between her blue eyes. 'Can you hear anything, Nafnel?'

'Milkman, miss. And cars. And there's a train. See there's its whistle.'

The mournful blast of a goods train approaching Kentish Town Station drifted across the wakening streets.

'No. I don't think it's out there. It seems to be coming from in here.'

Obediently Nafnel copied his teacher's frowning pose. 'I can't hear nuffing, miss.'

'It's stopped.'

They both strained, waiting to hear if the sound would start again.

'It's stopped. Come on. Bring the pillows and I'll get breakfast.'

Nafnel needed no further invitation. He scuttled eagerly in front of her and was halfway up the stairs when a sharp rapping reverberated against the panels of the back door.

Rose paused, one foot on the bottom tread. The first unwelcome thought that came into her mind was that Mrs Starkey had arrived to make a scene about her missing grandson.

Taking a few steps back into the stockroom, she called, 'Who is it?'

'It's Eileen O'Day, love.'

She had a shopping bag in one hand and a dress folded over the other. 'Sorry to call so early. But I wanted to catch you before you went to the school.'

'Yes. Of course. Come in.' Bewildered, Rose ushered her unexpected caller to the stairs. Nafnel was crouched on the middle treads.

'Well that's lucky,' Eileen said, holding up the dress to avoid tripping. 'I've got something for you. From our Pat.'

'Me?' Scrambling to his feet, Nafnel preceded her to the landing on all fours like a dog.

Rose rescued the abandoned pillows and followed them.

'Go through to the kitchen, Mrs O'Day. I was just about to put the kettle on.'

'What you got for me?' Nafnel demanded.

'Don't be so rude,' Rose ordered. 'Here. Fill this kettle.'

Striking a Vesta, she lit the gas ring. Nafnel spun the taps fruitlessly.

'They don't work.'

'Oh dear, it's off again.'

A saucepan yielded enough water for three cups of tea. Eileen refused breakfast.

'Had it, thanks. Jack came home with the dawn. Poor Sarah, his lady sergeant, caught one last night. So 'course he had to stop with her.'

'It is serious?' Rose asked.

'Walking wounded,' Eileen said succinctly. Delving into her bag, she produced two parcels. 'Here you are, love. These are for you.'

The tip of a pink tongue protruded from the corner of Nafnel's mouth as he ripped the paper from the bigger bundle and revealed a pair of new leather boots.

'I brought some of Sammy's socks.' Eileen offered an assorted bundle. 'He should grow into them.'

Ignoring this boring present, Nafnel dived into the next parcel and emerged with a pocket torch. 'For me, honest?'

'Our Pat said you was to take it when you go down to the cupboard under the stairs when the bombs start. I went all over for that,' she confided to Rose as Nafnel stared into the light, flicking it on and off in a game of 'shadows'.

'I suppose they all got snapped up when the black-out started. I know I bought one.' Rose sensed they hadn't got to the real reason for Eileen's visit yet. She tipped out a cup of water from the kettle. 'We'll have to have a lick and spit this morning, Nafnel. Take this down to the bathroom and wash your neck and face. And make sure you use the soap.'

'What about me breakfast?'

'It will be ready when you get back. Now go on.'

Carrying his precious torch, Nafnel went.

Pushing a strand of fair hair behind her ear, Rose asked, 'Is Pat all right?'

'Fine. He's getting the kids off to school for me this morning. He's the reason I come round really.'

Rose had been afraid it was.

'He told me what you said about not having nothing to wear for the dance tonight.'

'Oh.'

'That true? Or were you just trying to let him down light?' Despite her friendliness, Eileen's tone took on the sharp defensiveness of a mother who thought her first-born should be irresistible to any woman in her right mind.

'Yes. No. I mean, I really haven't got anything.'

Both women's eyes turned to the dress Eileen had hung behind the kitchen door.

'I had it cleaned yesterday. I know it ain't really fashionable. But it's only a shelter dance. People will be dressed any old how.'

'But I couldn't take your dress, Mrs O'Day.'

'Why not? Nobody's going to notice if I'm dressed in a potato sack. And our Pat's dead set on taking you, love.' She laid one hand over Rose's. 'It's not like proper courting. You could help me with the food. Nobody could say anything against that. Yer husband wouldn't 'ave wanted you to sit home and mope, would he? Not if 'e really loved you.'

Rose stared across the table, aware of her mouth twisting and a burning aching in her throat which became unbearable as she fought to hold back the tears. She was saved from making a complete fool of herself by Nafnel who sauntered back and informed her he could hear the funny noise now. 'It's coming from downstairs, miss.'

The three of them trooped back to the landing and stood at the top of the stairs. It was clearer this time; a low rhythmic tapping, like skeletal fingers against stone.

'Maybe you got a ghost, miss,' Nafnel whispered.

'Rubbish.'

Lifting up her dressing gown, Rose made her way downstairs, hoping she looked braver than she felt. Once back in the stockroom, the sound seemed to be all around her.

'I think it's coming from the cellar,' Eileen said, her voice low and hushed. 'Shall I fetch a policeman?'

'No. We can manage. Pass me that mop.' Taking a firm grip on the wooden handle, Rose tried to raise the trap. It was too heavy for her to manage one-handed.

'Here,' Eileen took the mop. 'Give me that. You get it open and I'll bash 'em if they try to come up. You hear that down there,' she shouted. 'I'll bash yer head if yer stick it up.'

Raising the mop over her shoulder like a sledge-hammer, she waited.

Rose twisted both hands into the metal ring and heaved.

It took a second for her eyes to become accustomed to the dark cellar and make sense of what they were seeing.

'Well look at that,' Eileen said, edging forward for a clearer view.

Years ago when this area had been built over, the Victorian builders had, as Maury's contact suggested, laid the right drainage pipes, and confined some of the River Fleet's numerous tributaries within their stone sheathing. Their calculations, however, had been made before the advent of aerial bombing. Over the past few months the pipes had shifted and cracked and finally, last night, released the tributaries to find their own paths through the subsoil. One had joyfully bubbled into the cellars of Balaclava Row.

Kneeling, Rose cautiously peeped into the dark openings and identified the knocking sound as a metal-edged packing case that had been left down there for some reason. It was now bobbing on the water's surface, one of its metal corners banging at regular intervals against the brick walls.

' 'Spect the rest of 'em along here have flooded too,' Eileen remarked, replacing the mop. 'There'll be some mopping up needed today I reckon.'

Rose gave a half scream and jumped up, nearly pitching head first into the trap-opening as her foot caught on the dressing gown hem. 'Lexie! Oh God, Lexie. She sleeps down the cellar.'

'Well she'd have got out soon as the water come in surely?'

'Then where is she? Why hasn't she come round to tell me we've been flooded?' Rose rushed for the back door. 'Perhaps it came in too fast for them to escape.'

She fled out into the backyard and stumbled on to the path at the same time as Matthew Fortune erupted from his own gate, tucking his shirt into his trousers. 'The cellar,' she called.

'I know, we've just found it. Are you all right?'

'Yes. But what about Lexie and Frank? They always sleep down there.'

The Emmetts' back door was locked. Banging frantically with the flat of her hand, Rose shouted, 'Lexie? Can you hear me? Open the door!'

Standing a few feet behind her, Matt scanned the upstairs windows. 'Can't see any movement. Here, get back.'

Using his good shoulder as a battering ram, he flung himself against the door.

Eileen and Nafnel added their voices to Rose's.

'Lexie! Lexie!'

The solid wooden door bounced Matt back three times. 'Sod it. Get something from the outhouse to sling through the window.'

'Frank! Lexie!'

'What?'

The four of them swung round. Hugging her coat round her, Lexie repeated, 'What? What are you all yelling for?'

Rose gasped, 'Lexie! Where did you come from?'

'I been round Alice's. Why? What's going on?'

It was Matthew who asked where her father was.

'Down that flaming cellar, I suppose.' Lexie produced her key from her coat pocket and inserted it in the lock. 'If you ain't all woken him up by now.'

'Don't.' Matt lay his good hand on Lexie's. 'How long were you round Alice's, Lexie?'

'Why? What's the *matter* with you all. Why you looking at me like that?'

Her question was answered by Josepha, who arrived in a rush, hopping on one foot as she attempted to drag a shoe on. 'You seen? Maria she send me to ask Helen to telephone fire brigade before we all get drowned.'

'It won't come to that,' Matt said, opening the cobbler's back door. 'Once it reaches floor level, it will just pour out into the street.'

Enlightenment hit Lexie. With a cry she thrust Matt aside and rushed for the trapdoor. 'Dad!'

'Let me.'

Between them, Lexie and Matt heaved the trap open. The greedy slosh and suck of water against the steps told its own story.

Laying on his stomach, Matt wriggled the top half of his body over the gap, lowered his head down and squinted into the darkness.

'Is he there?'

'Can't see.' Matt rolled on to his hip. 'Give me that torch.'

The probing beam of Nafnel's torch slid over the dark water like an oil slick. Sodden knitting wool, its yarn unravelling in streamers, drifted past like a gaily coloured jelly fish. A magazine bobbed like a raft, nudging amongst a forlorn flotilla of shoes. In the centre of the cellar, the water swelled, bulged and fell in on itself again in a half dozen bubbling springs.

'It looks like it's coming up from below.'

'What about Dad?'

'I can't . . . Yes. There!'

They all fell to their knees, except Eileen.

Only the pale disc of his face was visible. Green and eerie in the torch's light, it floated against the cellar wall farthest from the steps. Matthew eased himself down on to the top step. 'Have you got a rope and something hooked? I'll try to pull him across.'

Josepha squeezed down beside him, dipped a hand into the water and scooped a palmful. 'Just water,' she said, sniffing cautiously. 'I get him.' Whipping off her dress and shoes, she pushed herself off the steps, swam across the cellar in a steady breaststroke, and dragged Frank Emmett back to the steps.

With Josepha pushing and Matt dragging on the waterlogged pyjama jacket, they managed to haul the body on to the shop floor.

'Dad?' Crouching, Lexie brushed her fingers over the dead white cheek. 'Dad!' Grasping his jawbone, she shook the head violently. The eyes, fixed and unseeing, turned first to the workroom where he'd spent so many years of his life and then back to the counter stool where Lexie had perched for the past twenty-one years. 'Dad. Wake up!'

Placing an arm round Lexie's shoulders, Rose drew her gently to her feet. 'He's gone, Lexie. Leave him.'

'You'd better take her upstairs,' Matt decided. 'And her.' He nodded at Josepha who was now shivering in near transparent underwear. 'I'll get back to Helen, get her to call the ARP post. We'll need the fire brigade to pump this lot out. And the water will need to be turned off. Electricity too, I shouldn't wonder. Don't use it even if it's still working. It's too dangerous.'

For once he was no longer the careless young man, hiding his hurt behind a self-mocking banter. Instead he was very much in control, organising and calming the situation.

'We'll need someone to move the corpse . . . To move Frank. The post will fix that too. I shan't be long.'

Eileen took the unusually subdued Nafnel's hand.

'You come with me, love. I'll get you that breakfast before you go to school.'

'Ain't miss coming?' Nafnel enquired in a small voice.

'She'll be along in a minute.'

'No, she can go now.' Lexie shrugged off the comforting arm. 'Go on, Rose. You'll be late for school. There's no sense losing yer job for Dad. It ain't as if he was family to you.'

Despite Rose's protests, Lexie insisted she go back to the grocer's.

'I don't feel right about leaving Lexie,' Rose said, dressing in the half-darkened flat. 'I felt bad enough having to tell Gwen I couldn't ask for time off to go to the funeral. I'm beginning to wish I'd never taken this job.'

'There's no call for you to be feeling like that,' Eileen replied. 'There's people dying all over the place. It's bad enough when you're close to 'em. If you start feeling bad about all the ones you said "good morning" to, you'll go barmy I reckon.' She was attempting to slick down Nafnel's hair with a comb and spit. A probing finger was run around the inside of the boy's shirt collar. 'That could do with a change. I'll see if I got another one I can cut down. Now you get along, love. I'll stop here until Mr White arrives and give yer friend next door a bit of a hand if she needs it.'

It put her further into Eileen's debt, and would make it even harder to keep Pat at arm's length. But Rose couldn't see any alternative.

She made one last trip to the cobbler's shop before she left and found that Matthew had disappeared but Helen and Gwen were now staring down at Frank

Emmett's blanket-covered body.

'This is too bad,' Gwen wailed. 'How can I do Donald's funeral tea without the gas or electric?'

'I'm sure we can manage, Gwen,' Helen murmured, keeping her voice low in case it carried upstairs to Lexie. 'I'll give you a hand.'

Ungraciously Gwen remarked that she supposed Helen wouldn't be able to do the hairdressing without water. 'I expect the cafe will have to stay closed as well,' she said as Josepha rejoined them wrapped in a blanket which left her shoulders and arms bare.

'Is Lexie all right?' Rose asked Helen.

'A bit shaken up. I think it's shock. Don't worry about her, Rose. I'll stay as long as she needs me.'

There was nothing more to be done here; she wasn't wanted or needed in the present crisis. The best thing she could do was take herself off to Riley Street where she *could* do something useful.

The register that morning had several fresh 'absents' as colds and sniffles claimed more children, but the original absentees were now drifting back, including that policeman's daughter, Annaliese. Ginger Scannell led her to the teacher's desk and insisted on making an introduction; 'This 'ere's Annie, miss. She's 'alf foreign but she don't sound it most of the time. She speaks proper just like you and me. This is the new "miss", Annie. She's a "missus" really but me granddad says that's all right if she gives 'er job back when a bloke wants it.'

Flicking back plaits the colour of barley-sugar twists, Annaliese whispered her 'G'ning, miss', and retreated behind her stronger-minded deskmate.

She spent the rest of morning on sums and spelling

with the promise of painting and stories for the afternoon. It was Roger Veeney's turn to go round with the huge bottle of diluted brownish ink refilling the inkwells. In doing so he managed to splash some over Nafnel's new boots. With a scream, his fists windmilling frantically, Nafnel launched himself out of his seat, sent Roger flying one way and the ink bottle the other.

The cacophony of wails, giggles and shouting, as splashes were discovered, wiped and smeared to worse messes over clothes, desks and slates were cut off abruptly by the rising wail of the air raid alarm.

Forty desk lids were raised instantly. Books, knitting, pencils and gas masks were gathered up. With their arms full, the children sat quietly, looking expectantly at Rose.

She realised that this was a drill that they'd practised. Unfortunately, nobody had told her about it. There was no sound beyond that of several hundred children moving in various parts of the building, but if the alarm was genuine the raid could start at any minute. She couldn't leave them all sitting here whilst she went for advice.

'Peggy,' she said, 'do you remember what you have to do next?'

Peggy Abbott swelled, delighted at this chance to show off her knowledge. 'Oh *yes*, miss.' She chanted her litany confidently. 'When you say, we line up in twos and walk to our seats in the shelter. And we mustn't talk or run, but we have to walk fast.'

'Very well,' Rose said, one ear straining beyond the brown-paper-covered windows, trying to detect any approaching planes. 'Everyone go now.'

Prompted by a request from Ginger to carry the register, Rose thrust it under her arm and tagged on to the end of the children. The crocodile joined others snaking their way around the corridors. Some of the older children were filing out of the doors and into a brick shelter in the grounds, but the majority were trooping down the cellar stairs.

The first year huddled on two rows of slatted wooden benches at the far end, fitting themselves in with a good deal of thrusting and elbowing.

'Help,' Rose hissed as she passed Mr Jenkins. 'What do I do now?'

'Call the register,' he mouthed. 'Then do something to keep their minds off it. Stories or songs or something.'

Most of the girls were already disentangling bundles of needles, wool and half-finished, amorphous, knitted shapes in navy and khaki.

'We do socks in the shelter,' Peggy explained. 'For the soldiers and sailors. We do pairs. I'm doing a left foot. And Maggie's doing the right.' She proudly held up her own effort and jerked her deskmate's aloft at the same time. 'Everyone show miss what you done.'

Needles were waved triumphantly all along the forms. Prudently Rose raised the register to eye level to hide her mouth. If His Majesty's Army and Navy weren't full of personnel with odd-sized club-feet now, they certainly would be if they ever wore Riley Street first year's efforts.

'Yes. Very good, Peggy. Er, pay attention everyone and answer to your name.'

She'd hardly reached the Cs when the head appeared on the stairs to announce it was another false alarm. 'The all clear's gone now. Everyone back to your classroom quick as you can. Mrs Goodwin, there appears to be a mess in your room.'

'I was just about to get it cleared up, sir. Nafnel, go to the caretaker and ask to borrow a mop.'

Phil Wright's sibilant, 'Teacher's pet', carried clearly above the pushing, shuffling children.

She ignored it, but it bothered her.

'It's not fair for a teacher to appear to have favourites,' she said to Great Aunt Mabel when she revisited the Tammie house at lunchtime. 'But I don't know what else to do. His grandmother isn't a fit person to look after him, and nobody else seems to care.'

'Report Ma Starkey to the cruelty man,' Mabel advised, turning her face to catch the sun struggling through the basement window as the weather, following the pattern of the past few days, suddenly shrugged off the approaching winter and burst once more into a glorious Indian summer day. 'Put a bit of elbow-grease into it, girl.'

The middle-aged woman by the fireside obediently buffed harder with the scrap of Brasso-laden rag, smearing the liquid over a pair of Marge Tammie's brass candlesticks and humming a tuneless song to the rhythm of the buffing.

'Give me that drying cloth, Rose.'

Friday was the day that the house was swept, cleaned and polished in anticipation of visitors over the weekend. With an old tablecloth spread over her bed and an enamel bowl of soapy water in her lap, Mabel rinsed and polished the collection of china ornaments that Marge had carried down that morning.

'I know I ought to report her,' Rose said, returning to the subject of Ma Starkey, 'but I'm scared they'll take Nafnel away and put him in a home.'

'Don't sound like he'd be worse off. Ain't 'e got no one else to take him in?'

'I don't know. He's never mentioned anyone. His dad seems to have disappeared years ago.'

Rose gnawed her lip. Mabel finished her china, took out a box of silver teaspoons and selected another rag. 'If you want a kid, Rose, 'ave one of yer own, don't go taking on someone else's. You know what they say: What's bred in the bone comes out in the blood. 'E may be a taking little snapper now, but he's got his dad's blood in him and you don't know nothing about him. Much better to get yerself a family by a steady local bloke.'

'Like Pat O'Day you mean?'

'If 'e's your fancy.'

'He's not. And I wish people would stop marrying us off. Pat's just a friend.'

Mabel clucked. It was a cluck of pure scepticism. But before the conversation could develop into a full blown row, Nafnel burst in from the basement door.

'Got 'em, miss.' He extended a newspaper bundle which was exuding a delicious smell of hot fat, vinegar and salt.

'Open 'em on here,' Mabel instructed, shoving the ornaments out of the way. 'She,' she announced, jerking her head upwards to indicate Marge, 'never lets me eat 'em out of the newspaper. Chips don't taste the same off a plate.'

Nafnel and Mabel dived in enthusiastically. Rose

nibbled one thick finger, her ear half turned for the sound of her mother's feet on the internal stairs. She just knew she was going to get the blame for allowing Mabel to spoil her dinner.

'Where's me change?' Mabel mumbled through a mouthful of chips. 'I give you a half-crown.'

Nafnel wriggled. 'Dropped it.'

Rose looked at him sharply. He was sitting cross-legged on the bed, his head bent over the golden pile. Reaching over, she put one finger under his chin and forced his head up. 'Give Auntie Mabel her money back, Nafnel.'

'Can't.'

'Why not.'

He smeared the back of his hand over greasy lips. 'Weren't my fault.'

'What wasn't?'

'She took it. Didn't see her 'til she grabbed me. I tried biting her, honest.'

'Your gran?'

Nafnel nodded.

'I'm sorry, Auntie Mabel. I'll give you the money back soon as I get paid. Finish your chips, Nafnel, we have to get back to school.'

Scooping up a handful, Nafnel scampered into the area.

'Remember,' Mabel called after Rose. 'Bred in the bone. There's Ma Starkey's bones in 'im too. Don't get stuck with 'im.'

But she had no choice. She couldn't bear the idea of the little boy wandering the streets in an air raid, hungry and afraid. What if he was injured? What if he was lying somewhere? How long would it be before his grandmother even realised he was missing? She just had to allow him to follow her home again that afternoon.

'Cor look at that, miss. What a mess.'

It was an understatement. The escaping springs had forced their way up through the drainage covers in the street. A thin layer of sludge and dirt had been deposited over the pavement and road surfaces and was being joined by clumps of thick clay from the boots of the workmen excavating both in front of and behind the shops.

Albert was perched on a stool in the stockroom; his normally good-natured face sunk into lines of worry. He looked old. 'Hello, Rose. I shifted the tubs of dry goods and the cheese and bacon and stuff up to your flat. Hope you don't mind.'

'Oh, Albert, of course I don't. And don't look so miserable. We'll soon get this lot scrubbed out.' The sound of sloshing liquid still sounded clearly from below her feet. 'Aren't they going to pump the cellar?'

'No point until they seal the leaks. Don't worry. The level's stopped rising. You'll need these.' He gave her a bundle of candles and matches. 'And they've put up a standpipe at the end of the street for water. Course you could always come and stop with me and Elsie if you like.'

'No thank you, Albert. I'm sure we'll manage.' Rose had a shrewd idea that Elsie Finch wouldn't welcome Nafnel at all. 'I'd like to stay close to Lexie, in case she needs me. How is she?'

Albert blinked and seemed to have trouble focusing. 'You don't know then.'

'Know what?'

'Lexie's been arrested. They reckon she killed Frank.'

Chapter 20

Her father's death had meant that Lexie hadn't felt able to attend Donald's funeral. Refusing all offers of company, she'd lashed all her carefully hoarded ration butter on two slices of bread, spread it thickly with the last of the jam, and sat huddled in her flat gorging away her guilt at *not* feeling more upset. Through the window she'd heard James Donald set out on his last journey from St Luke's to East Finchley.

Stamford had excused himself from the actual burial since the cemetery was some distance from the church, but had felt obliged to put in an appearance at the funeral tea.

'Don't reckon old James 'as ever been so popular,' Albert remarked munching on a tongue sandwich and trying to balance a tea-cup that looked like a child's toy in his ham-like hand.

'It's certainly a good turnout,' Stamford agreed, scanning the chattering crowd in the Donalds' flat. 'Who are all these people?'

'Neighbours mostly,' Helen explained. 'We asked them to help because of the flood and losing the power. People like to feel needed, don't they?'

'Is that why you joined the ARP?'

'One of them I suppose. That and I was sick of perm lotions, curlers and scissors. I just wanted to do something useful. I'd have liked to do it full-time, but it would have meant closing the shop, and I just couldn't afford to lose the trade.'

It was the opening he needed to ask her about reclaiming the leases and selling Balaclava Row, but once again he found himself avoiding the subject. Looking across the room, he was relieved to see that Sarah was out of earshot talking to Maria. She was wearing the black, beribboned hat that she'd worn to Aldbury. Tilted over her left eye it partially hid the deep purple bruise and gauze dressing on her forehead. Helen followed the direction of his gaze.

'What happened to your sergeant? Assaulted by a crook?'

'Not exactly. She was assaulted by a brick.'

'I beg your pardon?' Helen's hazel eyes sparkled beneath the veil of the pillbox hat that she'd reclaimed from Gwen Donald.

For the first time, Jack noticed that hats suited some women and not others. Sarah looked good in whatever style she wore; Maria suited the sailor's hat with the improbable velvet butterfly; Josepha was vividly exotic in a mantilla made from black lace and secured with a golden-coloured brooch with her initial in the centre. Even Gwen looked reasonably dignified in the plain turban she'd sewn up; but Helen's simple classical beauty was diminished by the round pork pie and netting.

'An unexploded bomb chose to explode just as we were driving past,' he explained. 'Fortunately, most of the blast went the other way. And the car took the rest.'

'Except for the brick.'

'Except for the brick,' he agreed.

The open window had probably saved Sarah from

a faceful of glass fragments. Instead, the airborne brick had hit her forehead with a crack that had scared the life out of Stamford.

Hauling her limp body back into the passenger seat, he'd driven at speed to the first aid station in Plender Street, one hand holding a handkerchief against the spurting wound, the other trying to steer along the debris-strewn road.

'Mild concussion and a nasty headache,' had been the doctor's verdict. He'd ordered her to bed for twenty-four hours. So Stamford had been shocked to find her already at the flat helping to lay out the food when the funeral party returned from the cemetery.

'What are you doing here?' he'd hissed, dragging her into a corner. 'You're on sick leave.'

'I felt better.' She probed the bruise and winced. 'I've had worse.'

'Go home. I hate martyrs.'

'Me too, sir. They're so uncomfortable to live with. Why don't you just .put me down as bloody-minded instead. How are *things*,' Sarah asked, her intonation making it clear she was referring to the case rather than the events of the morning.

'Ding Dong's checked out the count's alibi. His card players confirm he didn't leave the boat until gone two. So it looks like he's in the clear. And fingerprinting have confirmed that, with the exception of Felonious and the police personnel, all the other fingerprints in this flat belong to the family and the inhabitants of Balaclava Row.'

'And Pratt Street Control? Did you manage to speak with them after you'd carted me home?'

He had. With the raid in full progress he'd had to

wait for a lull in the bombing before he could claim the attention of the subcontroller and explain what he wanted. The log clerk had been delegated to find the relevant incident in her log and retrieve the top copy of the message form from the filing cabinet in the message room.

'It was timed at eleven-twenty,' Stamford told his sergeant.

'Time enough for Miss Fortune to pedal back up to Balaclava Row and murder James before reporting back to her post that she hadn't found these supposed bombs in Brecknock Road.'

'Yes. But why should she want to?'

'If you don't care for my lease theory, what about the good old-fashioned woman scorned? He was dumping her to go back to Gwen.'

'Have you seen the papers this morning?' Stamford asked in an apparent change of subject.

'No. Why?'

Jack waved a half-eaten sandwich at the chattering funeral party. 'There's nothing in any of them about this. I thought perhaps the lack of press interest was due to the fact the cause of death wasn't generally known. But now we have the inquest, and still nobody cares. Even his in-laws couldn't be bothered to turn up for the burial.'

The two little Donald girls had arrived on the early morning train escorted by the land girl, Aggie Kemp. They, at least, had been red-eyed and noisily tearful throughout the ceremony. But certainly the only other emotions being demonstrated at present were greed, curiosity and embarrassment as several mourners beginning to feel the effects of numerous cups of tea edged nearer to the door of the bathroom and wondered whether they dare . . . ?

'Sudden death isn't as strange as it once was, is it?' Sarah murmured. 'Anyway, we know someone cared for Donald, if he had a mistress. What did you expect her to do, fling herself into the grave as they lowered the coffin?'

'Well it would certainly have solved one problem. Although not necessarily the murder.'

'Why not?'

'Because even if Donald was jumping into bed with every woman in the street, it still doesn't prove they killed him.'

Oh, damn subtlety, Sarah chided herself silently. Go straight to it. 'Have you asked Miss Fortune about the leases, sir? Or would you like me to do it?'

'No I wouldn't. Go and mingle and keep your ears open.'

He was tempted to reprimand her for her tone. It wasn't one that he'd have accepted from any other sergeant that had ever been under his command. On the other hand, her ability to hang on to her own beliefs and not be swayed by possible censure from above was one of the things he valued in her. He supposed if he wanted one, he'd have to put up with the other. At least until he found out what had put her in such a strange mood recently.

Edging round the room himself, he listened to snatches of conversation.

'Have you noticed the way the only person who seems out of place here is Gwen?' murmured a voice in Stamford's ear.

Turning, he found Matthew Fortune nibbling on a

slice of pie. It was, Jack admitted, fair comment. With most of the tea preparations taken from her, the grieving widow had nothing to do but accept the condolences of her husband's family and friends. But since he appeared to have neither, she was reduced to standing in the centre of her own living room, watching acquaintances examining the furnishings, ornaments and books as if they might be planning to outbid the dealer.

'Have you taken the day off?' Jack asked.

'No such luck, we're too busy. I went in for a couple of hours this morning and I'll have to make this time up this evening. Preventing the British public from finding out how the war's going is a full-time job, Inspector.'

'Do you think you should be speaking like that in public?'

'Are you going to arrest me for spreading defeatist talk?'

'I doubt you'd get into uniform, Mr Fortune, even if you did get dismissed from your present job.'

Matthew gave a disarming grin. 'Didn't realise I was that obvious.' He popped the last morsel of pie into his mouth and used the free hand to tap on the arm of a woman squinting at the base of one of the mantelpiece vases. 'Five bob to you, ma'am. I can see yer a lady what knows a bargain when she sees it.'

Flushing, the women hastily replaced the ornament and plunged into a comforting group of her neighbours who'd congregated at the piano.

'Has Mrs Donald appointed you her auctioneer?'

'No. But it's an idea. What do you think? Shall I get on a chair and invite bids? Ladies and gentlemen, what am I offered for this remarkable example of excruciating bad taste?' He seized an ornament in the shape of a cow, garishly painted in white and bronze, its brilliant scarlet tongue suggesting it was the world's first carnivorous bovine. Matthew spun it in his good hand, the other predictably was thrust into his coat pocket. His normally deft fingers fumbled the spin; Jack fielded the ornament just as it tumbled towards the floor.

'Whoops. Nearly smashed the adorable Evelyn's and Mavis's inheritance. Sorry,' he said catching Jack's eye. 'It's funerals, they always have this effect on me.'

'Why come? You could have used work as an excuse, surely?'

'Helen wanted me to; for Gwen's sake. She's a bit like that, my sis. Gets sort of mother hennish to the other tenants.'

There was no ignoring the opening this time. 'I hadn't realised your sister owned the freehold on the Row until recently. Or do you hold it jointly?'

'Good lord, no. Dad left it solely to Helen. I got one hundred pounds and a few personal bits and pieces: pocket watch, fountain pen, that sort of thing. He used his will to say what he could never admit to my face, that he despised me.'

His voice had risen enough to reach his sister's ears. 'That's not true, Matt. Dad never despised you. He just couldn't cope with your arm, in the same way some people can't stand heights, or spiders or . . .'

'Cripples. Why go on protecting him, Sis? We both know what he really thought. Fifteen years of waiting for a son to end up with a dead wife and a cripple.

345

Hardly a great deal from Dad's point of view. I need a drink.'

His sister's anxious eyes followed him across the room. Stamford felt her taut body relax as, rather than slam out of the flat, Matt slumped on to the sofa next to Josepha.

She was standing so close to him that the top of her arm was pressed against his bent elbow. He could smell the shampoo and perming lotions that had become permeated into her skin over the years. 'He's got to come to terms with it himself you know. You can't cocoon him through life for ever.'

'I know.' She was cradling her cup as if her hands were cold. 'I offered to sign over half the freehold to him, you know? But he wouldn't take it because Dad hadn't left it to him. In some ways he was his own worst enemy; as soon as he was old enough to realise how Dad felt, Matt would deliberately put himself in situations where Dad had to touch, or at least look at, the arm. Once he put it through a window when I was out, so that Dad would have to bandage it up. He said he fell; but he didn't.'

'Your father's business must have done well for him to be able to buy the freehold of the Row.'

'Buy it!' She gave that low musical laugh at the back of her throat again, the tone suitably hushed in deference to the occasion. 'Dad couldn't have afforded the freehold on a hen coop. Can you fill the cups on the draining board please, Mrs Tracey?' The last instruction was directed at a thin woman in a pinafore and clay-covered wellington boots who'd just bustled in from the street bearing a massive tin teapot stamped 'Property of Lyndhurst Street Mission'.

'You were saying,' Jack prompted before someone else could claim her attention. 'Your dad was not a financial genius.'

'I'll say he wasn't, otherwise I'd be a richer woman today. Do you really not know the story? I thought you were a local man.'

'I bought a house here eleven years ago. I take it this happened before that?'

'Long before. Nineteen nineteen to be exact. It's quite a sad story. The man who owned the Row was a well-known local builder. His three sons all died on the Somme and his only daughter committed suicide after her fiancé was killed at Passchendaele. The builder died a couple of years later – of a broken heart according to local folklore – leaving all his property to people who'd been kind to him or done him some service: the car went to his chauffeur; the house to the housekeeper; that sort of thing. My dad was his barber.'

'So he left him the barber's shop.'

'And the other four for good measure. And some money. Which Dad promptly spent on the shops and flats. You must have noticed how ridiculously over-decorated they are.'

'Well now you mention it, yes.'

'That was Dad. He wanted to make this the grandest barber's shop in north London; but he didn't want to hurt his neighbours' feelings. So he had all their shops refurbished as well. He squandered the lot. We were the talk of Kentish Town: marble tiles, indoor baths with plumbing, parquet flooring. We were the first people in the district to get rid of the gas mantles and get the electric in. The grand opening was quite an event. We got a whole page in the local paper.'

'I remember that!' Gradually, without either of them being aware of the intrusion, other mourners had attached themselves to the group like pins to a magnet. Now one of them pushed her way into the conversation. 'You remember the Balaclava Party, don't yer, Ada?'

'I'll say. They 'ad all them flags from the Toc H Club strung across the street. The ones they 'ad from Armistice Day.'

'That's right. And they 'ad the trestle tables set up outside too. Remember? With free tea and buns. And lemonade for the kids.'

'And there were presents as well, remember,' the woman who'd been addressed as Ada said, drawing in her listeners with a waving slice of madeira cake.

'That's right. Something extra for every customer. Your dad give out shaving brushes and mugs wiv a picture of Primrose Hill on 'em, didn't he, love? My Charlie still uses his.'

Notes were compared on the boxes of chocolates from the grocer's ('Alway's open-handed, Albert'); the cakes and puddings from the cafe and extra portions from the fish and chip shop.

'What did the Emmetts give out, anyone remember?'

'Shoe polish and cloths. Mind, it were that small I give it to our Mildred for her dollies' shoes. That Frank always was a mean devil, God rest his soul.'

'Frank Emmett is dead?' Stamford said. 'Since when?'

'Last night, sir. Ain't you heard?' A babble of voices told him with ghoulish glee of Frank's end in the flooded cellar.

'I'm surprised nobody mentioned it to you at the service,' Helen said.

But, as he'd told Ding Dong and Sarah, his rank tended to discourage people from gossiping to him. He'd certainly noticed the Emmetts were missing from the church service but had simply assumed that the old man had decided Donald's burial wasn't worth losing half a day's takings. And of course nobody would have reported the death to the police station; Frank would simply have been logged as another air raid casualty.

'What about Miss Emmett? How did she escape?'

'Lexie's all right,' Helen assured him. 'Luckily she'd gone round to the Wellers' shop and fallen asleep.'

'I see. I had no idea. Excuse me.'

He was accosted by his sergeant in the kitchen. 'Sir, I've just heard, Mr Emmett . . .'

'I know, I've just heard too.'

'A complete hand of empty properties then, sir. Miss Fortune must be pleased.'

'If she is, she's concealing it very well. I think Miss Emmett might prove to be more enlightening than her landlord. Do you know where she is?'

'Maria said she was lying down in her flat. Shock, you know?'

'Let's find out.'

All the doors were wide open, presumably to admit the fire and repair crews, but there was no sign of Lexie in the flat over the cobbler's shop.

'Hello? Anybody up there?'

Stamford returned to the head of the stairs and called back, 'Yes. Who's that?'

A plumpish round-faced man, dressed in the uniform of an auxiliary fire officer bounced up the stairs. 'I say,' he gasped in an accent that had come straight from Knightsbridge, 'I'm so sorry to intrude, but we're ready to pump. I understand that this young lady has a key to the fish and chip establishment.' He raised his helmet to Sarah.

'Me? No. I think you must want Miss Emmett. We're looking for her ourselves.'

'I think,' Stamford remarked, starting back down the stairs, 'the chip shop might be an excellent idea. It seems to be her bolt-hole.'

Banging and rattling the back door had no effect. It wasn't until Stamford asked the fire officer, in a loud voice, to bring an axe so they could smash off the locks, that there was a scuffle of movement inside and they heard the key being turned.

The crumpled dress hung in shapeless folds to her ankles and the whole effect of dowdiness was only relieved by her distinctive hair which hung in loose folds around her white and drawn face.

'Fire service, miss,' the auxiliary introduced himself as if she couldn't see his uniform. 'Please forgive the intrusion, but would you be kind enough to open the front door of these premises so that we can get the hose through into the cellar.'

Reaching into her pocket, Lexie passed over a keyring with a request that they replace it in the cobbler's shop when they'd finished.

Stamford waited until the fireman had moved out of earshot and then said quietly; 'I've just heard about your father. I think we need to talk, don't you, Miss Emmett?'

Tears spilled down Lexie's cheeks. 'I didn't mean to do it, honest I didn't.'

'Didn't mean to do what, Miss Emmett?'

Lexie choked and gasped a frightened sob. 'Kill him. I didn't mean to kill him.'

They took her back in the police car, escorting her through the tides of yellow water being pumped out by the auxiliary engine. Any hope of slipping away casually was dashed by the fact that the funeral party had grown bored with pricing up Gwen's furniture and were now drifting outside to watch the pumping operation.

It was Helen who stepped forward and asked if she could help. 'Is she ill? Do you want to bring her into the shop?'

Sarah had been guiding Lexie into the back seat with a discreet but firm pressure on her forearm. Now Lexie twisted free and grabbed Helen's hand. 'I killed him, Helen. I killed Dad.'

'Nonsense. Of course you didn't.' Helen looked at Stamford for support. 'Of course she didn't kill Frank. She's upset, you can see that. She doesn't know what she's saying, You can't question her in that state, it's not fair. I'll come with her.'

'I'm afraid that's not possible. Miss Emmett will be fairly treated, I assure you.'

Using both hands this time, Sarah manoeuvred the weeping woman into the car and got in beside her.

'I didn't mean it,' Lexie repeated like a chant all the way back to the police station. 'It was a mistake.'

'Get her to the Matron's room,' Stamford instructed. 'And let her tidy herself up a bit. And then bring her down to the interview room.'

He rearranged the chair that the count had occupied with such arrogant assurance two days ago. Unlike that gentleman, Lexie Emmett had no doubts about her guilt. In fact, she continually protested it; coupled with the assurance that she 'didn't mean it'.

'Yes, all right, we understand that you didn't mean to do it,' Stamford said, passing across his own handkerchief to help with the free-flowing tears. 'But what I want to know, is *how* did you do it?'

Lexie gave a convulsive gulp, blew vigorously into the handkerchief and sat up, determined to *tell all*. 'I took some of Mrs Finch's sleeping draught,' she said. 'In fact,' she admitted, caught up in this orgy of unburdening her guilt, 'I stole it.'

'And gave it to your father?' Stamford prompted.

'Yes. In his cocoa.'

'How much did you give him?'

'Six drops each time. The bottle said two, but I wanted to make really sure he'd not wake up while I was out.'

'Why? Where did you go?'

Lexie's red eyes widened innocently. 'Only next door to Alice's. I used to read or listen to the radio. I just couldn't stand being stuck down that flaming cellar.' Her mouth twisted again choking back a sob. 'I didn't know,' her voice rose in a wail, 'I didn't *know* it was gonna get flooded, did I?'

'Is there any of the sleeping draught left?' Stamford asked, raising his voice sharply to quell the rising hysteria.

It worked. 'Yes,' Lexie admitted in her normal tone. Thrusting a hand into the deep pocket of her coat, she drew out the bottle she'd filled in Elsie Finch's. 'I 'ave to carry it with me. Dad is, *was*, so nosy.'

Stamford passed it across to Sarah. 'Get the police surgeon to let me have his opinion. He's in the station somewhere, I saw his car parked out back as we came in. And then come back. We need to question Miss Emmett about another matter.'

By the time Sarah returned with a tray and three cups of tea, Lexie's expression bore an even stronger resemblance to a rabbit caught in a car's headlights. The tremble in her voice caused it to rise and fall in a frightened squeak as she asked, 'What did the doctor say?'

'He's carrying out an examination at present, Miss Emmett. He'll get round to us as soon as he can.'

Stamford said, 'How long have you been doping your father with this mixture, Miss Emmett?'

'Only since last Sunday, honest. You can ask Mrs Finch. I went down to visit last Sunday.'

'Have you ever visited Mrs Finch's house before?'

'A couple of times. She don't go out no more. She's got nerves.'

'So how do I know this is the first time you've stolen her sleeping draught?'

Lexie looked bewildered. 'Well course it is. Why'd I want to do it before?'

'Why did you want to do it now?'

'I told yer. I was fed up with sleeping down that damn cellar.'

'Tell me, Miss Emmett. When you both slept upstairs, could your father have heard you if you got up and went out?'

'Course he could. He was always listening for sounds. Even in his sleep. And then he'd wake me up to listen to 'em too. I told yer that.'

'You did indeed. But you see, Miss Emmett, my problem is that when you told me before I took the view that it would be impossible for you to get out of that cellar at night without waking your father up. Now I know it wasn't. Which effectively means that you have no alibi for the time James Donald was killed.'

Incredulity flooded Lexie's face; adding colour once more to her pale cheeks and putting a sparkle back in her eyes. 'James! What would I want to kill James for?'

'His wife seemed to think there was a certain affection between you once; before their marriage. Apparently his parents were quite keen to welcome you as Mrs Donald.'

'Well, they were the only ones that were. I wouldn't 'ave got into bed with James for a thousand quid. The whole idea gives me the shudders.' She demonstrated the fact by giving a convulsive heave.

'Could I ask something?' Sarah interjected.

'Go ahead,' Stamford invited.

'Will you go on with the cobbler's business now, Miss Emmett?'

'Eh? What you mean I ain't under arrest?'

'I think what the sergeant means is, assuming we don't bring charges in connection with your father's death, will you continue with the shop in Balaclava Row?'

'No. I can't, can I? I never did any of the mending. Dad would never teach me. 'E always reckoned it was quicker to do it himself than show me. I just took the money. Don't know what I'll do now,' she finished forlornly. 'Can I go 'ome yet?'

'No. I think it would be best if you stay in the cells until we've heard what the doctor has to say.'

'We can't charge her with murder, can we?' Sarah asked as Lexie was led away by the station matron.

'No. She'd have had to know the cellar was going to flood for us to prove intention. If things really occurred the way she says, it's not even manslaughter. Wanting to give someone a good night's sleep doesn't amount to intention to harm. How long do we have to wait for the doc?'

'Half an hour or so, I'd guess.'

'Let's walk then.'

'Where?'

'Anywhere. I just need some air while I get my thoughts in order.'

Positioning the hat with tender care over the swelling bruise, Sarah followed him to the front lobby. A car slid to a stop next to kerb as they emerged from the building, and Helen Fortune scrambled from the back ignoring the assistance offered by the uniformed chauffeur.

Neither officer paid her much notice; their attention fixed on the other passenger in the back seat. Leaning forward the man graciously dipped his silver head. 'Chief Inspector, how pleasant to see you again. And your charming sergeant; I see the general public have been assisting you with your enquiries, my dear.'

Gritting her teeth to prevent herself rising to that 'my dear', Sarah said calmly, 'Good afternoon, Mr Bowler. We don't often have the pleasure of seeing you at the police station – unfortunately.'

Leo Bowler wiped an imaginary smear from his

ebony cane. 'Oh, I fear I do not feel entirely welcome in constabulary premises.'

Stamford leant one arm on the open window and addressed the area's biggest villain. 'You mustn't feel that way, Mr Bowler. We'd love to welcome you to Agar Street. For an extended stay preferably.'

'So kind. But I fear I must decline your invitation, Inspector. I have business to attend to. I merely made this slight diversion in order to convey the delightful Miss Fortune to you.'

'Mr Bowler called to discuss ... some possible business,' Helen explained as the car slid away. 'I asked him for a lift because I wanted to find out what's happening to Lexie.'

'She's still assisting us with our enquiries.'

'That could mean anything. Should I get her a solicitor? I have one.'

'Helping you to flog off Balaclava to Bowler, is he?'

Helen turned to face Sarah. 'If I choose to do so, yes.'

'Frank Emmett's death must have been quite a stroke of luck for you, Miss Fortune.'

'What?'

'The Wellers and Donalds gone. The cafe girls with no proper lease. Albert White planning to leave. There was really only Frank Emmett between you and a nice little profit from Bowler.'

There was a tangible silence caught in the triangle of space between the three of them. Stamford wanted to find excuses for Sarah's behaviour; to diffuse the situation before it became impossible to retrieve. But he couldn't do it because Sarah was his sergeant and, if he wanted to preserve their working relationship, he had to back her up in public and reprimand her in private.

Helen Fortune was an astute woman; she grasped the significance of Sarah's outburst immediately. 'I think,' she said in a quiet, controlled voice, 'it would be better if I didn't come into the station. I'll contact my solicitor and ask him to bring you copies of all the leases on Balaclava Row.' She took a few steps away from them, then stopped and spun round. Her hazel eyes glittered dangerously beneath the veil. 'And I think you'll see very clearly that I really had no need to murder my tenants. *Any* of my tenants.'

Chapter 21

They let Lexie go two hours later.

'You mean you ain't going to charge me?' Lexie gasped, caught halfway between relief and anticlimax.

'Not at present, Miss Emmett. We've checked with Mrs Finch's doctor and the draught he prescribed for her was a mild sedative. A triple dose wouldn't have had a serious effect on a healthy adult. Our police surgeon is of the opinion that your father would have woken as soon as the cellar started flooding.'

What he'd actually said was, 'You knock yourself out with this jollop, Chief Inspector, then get somebody to shove your head in a bucket of water. See how fast you come round. The human instinct for survival is a wonderful thing.'

'Then why'd he drown?' wailed Lexie.

'We don't know at present. Perhaps he panicked and slipped trying to get out. The autopsy will tell us.'

'And I can really go 'ome?'

'For now. However, we shall probably want to question you further. So please don't leave Balaclava Row.'

'I won't.' Grabbing up her bag and clutching her flapping coat around her, Lexie fled before they could change their minds.

It was the beginning of the weekend and, war or

no war, most of the inhabitants of Kentish Town were still sticking to their old routines as far as they could. Hurrying home, she found the streets busy with housewives making their way up the market to pounce on whatever stallholders were soon going to have to sell off at cut-prices. Further down the High Street the cinema queues were already starting to form, whilst the public houses were releasing bursts of laughter and beer fumes in equal parts every time someone pushed open the doors. It was only the queues at the tube entrances, with prams and bags piled with blankets, thermos flasks, and kids, that betrayed the fact that life had been turned upside down. That, and the unexpected encounters with uniforms.

The sight of khaki as she approached Balaclava Row caused Lexie's stomach to turn several somersaults before she registered the fact that they weren't red caps but a small contingent of the Home Guard marching in smart formation to take over weekend guard duties at the steam-line stations.

'Lexie!'

The scream jolted her from her own preoccupations with such force that she actually let out a frightened yelp of her own. Tilting her head upwards, she found Rose leaning out of the flat window.

'Are you all right? I was going to come to the police station but Helen had already gone.'

'I'm fine, thanks.'

For the first time it occurred to Lexie to wonder what sort of reception her neighbours were going to give to a self-confessed murderess.

She needn't have worried. They flocked around her

with welcoming squeezes and kisses.

'See, I told 'em it was all a big mistake,' Albert boomed, catching her in a bear hug.

'What you still doing here?' Lexie said when she could struggle free.

Rose gestured to the mud-covered pavements; the doors of the shops wide open displaying the filthy floors covered in drying dirt and muddy footprints. 'Clearing up. Water's back on, but the gas and electricity are still off. We're trying to get this lot cleaned while there's still daylight to see it.'

A whoosh of water from the cafe doorway was followed by Maria wielding a stiff broom. A brown arm was raised in salute to Lexie before she sped back inside screeching instructions at Josepha to 'stop messing about with the hair and get on with scouring the floor.'

'Give us a sec,' Lexie said. 'I'll just check Alice's is all right then I'll get me bucket and brush and giv yer a hand here before I do our place.'

'No need for that, love. You should lie down after what you been through. Tell you what, you pop upstairs and Rose can bring you some hot, sweet tea.'

'Don't be daft Albert. I ain't had a shock. Well, I 'ave. But it ain't like when you 'ear about someone dying . . .' Lexie stopped again, growing confused, since that was exactly what her father had done.

That funny-looking kid who always seemed to be trailing Rose around these days, rescued the situation for her. 'We gonna 'ave our dinner before you go to the dance, miss?'

Interest puckered the corners of Albert's eyes. 'Dance. You never said nothing about no dance, Rose.

You go up and fix yourself up. Me and Ena can finish up 'ere, can't we, love?'

The rapid increase in Ena's nasal breathing might have meant, 'yes', 'no' or 'how about some extra wages'.

Rose denied she was going to any dance.

'What that lady leave you that dress for then?' Nafnel demanded. 'The one,' he continued revealing his own interest, 'who said you could give her an 'and with the food.'

'Mrs O'Day,' Rose was forced to explain to her audience. 'But I'm not going. I can't. Oh no! Don't move, Lexie. And don't turn around.'

'Why? What is it?' Lexie's neck muscles tensed and knotted with the strain of *not* turning when all her instincts were crying out for her to do just that. 'What is it?' she pleaded.

Rose had now taken up a strange position, with her legs partially bent and her elbows hugged into her waist as if she was trying to keep a slipping skirt up. 'I don't think she's seen me.'

'*Who?*'

'Nafnel, get under the counter quick. Say I'm out,' Rose instructed, shuffling backwards in her peculiar pose, then spinning quickly as soon as she was inside the shop and diving under the oak flap.

Lexie turned to face a pasty-faced middle-aged woman whose breath stank of stale alcohol and rotting teeth.

'Just popping up to see the young lady,' Ma Starkey croaked, attempting to slip past Albert.

'She ain't in.' Albert's bulk wasn't easy to slip past if he didn't choose to let you.

'Not there?'

'She's gone to a dance with her young man. Ain't that right, Lexie?'

'You missed 'er by minutes,' agreed Lexie readily.

Various emotions flitted across Ma's grey face. The instinct to shout and demand admittance fought with the suspicion that she'd get a better result by employing a few manners. Manners won, but they didn't get her as much as she'd hoped.

'That all?' Two bob didn't go far when you had a need like hers. She'd long ago ceased to get any enjoyment from alcohol; it was a beast inside her that burned and twisted and fed on her insides unless she fed it what it really wanted.

'Tell you what,' Albert confided, 'Rose weren't expecting this dance to go on late. Daresay if you popped back in a couple of hours, she'd 'ave something for you.'

'I'll do that then, ta,' she added as an afterthought, her lips already drying in anticipation.

'What did you say that for?' Rose clambered out from her hiding place. 'I don't want her round here causing a disturbance.'

'You don't 'ave to answer the door,' Lexie pointed out. 'I'll sling a bucket of water over 'er if she gets too loud.'

'You could do that,' Albert mused. 'Course the best thing would be if Rose weren't in. Be no point in her hollering the street down then.'

'She wouldn't know whether I'm here or not once she's paralytic,' Rose said in exasperation. She could see where his transparent guile was leading. But she was determined not to be led. 'Anyway, Lexie shouldn't be left, not after what she's gone through. Her dad's just died remember?'

'Oh, yes. But . . .' Albert shuffled his feet, increasing his resemblance to a fat, bashful, bear. 'You'll not mind me saying will you, Lexie, love? Me having known you since you was a nipper. But, well, I can't 'elp thinking maybe you'll be better off without yer dad. Once you get over the shock.'

'No, I don't mind yer saying.' Sitting alone in that cell, wondering what was going to become of her, she'd tried to grieve for her dad and found herself unable to do so. Instead a wonderful sensation of freedom had crept over her, swiftly followed by a desolate loneliness. 'I been finking the same meself. It's just, I wish I 'ad someone else. Not 'aving Dad would be all right if I weren't all on me tod now.'

'There you are then!' Albert beamed, his problem solved. 'You go to this dance with Rose and find yourself a nice steady fellow.'

'Albert!' Rose protested. 'Even if she wasn't that fond of her dad, she's got to pretend, I mean, she ought to show, I er . . .' It was Rose's turn to become tangled in her sentences. Whichever way she phrased it, it was going to sound like she was advocating hypocrisy.

'Where is this dance?' Lexie broke in.

'In the big shelter near Carker's Lane.'

'Well I don't see nobody can say nothing about me going to an air raid shelter even if me dad is dead. I'll go fix me face while there's still light to see it. I'll come round for yer when I'm done.'

She left Albert shooing Rose upstairs and made her way through the cobbler's shop, relieved to see that the firemen had closed the trap to the cellar. The keys to the Wellers' shop had been tidily hung from a protruding nail on her dad's workbench. A few workmen clearing equipment from the back field glanced up incuriously as she made her way round into the backyard of the fish and chip shop.

At least they'd relocked the door. Thrusting it back, she stepped in and wrinkled her nose at the raw, damp smell that was rising from Alice's normally spotless floors.

The tuneless rendition of 'Pack Up Your Troubles' was answered from way above her head.

'Alan?'

'Yeah.' A pair of Fred Weller's boots emerged from the attic trap. 'What happened? The police let you go?'

She told him what the inspector had said.

'Told you it would be all right, didn't I? They can't prove you intended to kill him just 'cos you give him a few knock-out drops. Told you there was nothing to worry about.'

She was stung by his casual tone. The main reason she'd opened the door to the police and confessed what she'd done was to get them away from here before they started a search and found him. 'They've not finished with me yet,' she snapped.

He gave her a casual hug and kiss; very much a taken-for-granted gesture.

Angrily, she shrugged him off. 'What time yer goin'?'

'Now.'

'It's too early. Nine she said. And there's still people outside.'

'That's why I'm off now. If anyone's looking out,

they won't notice one extra bloke coming from the back. I'll 'ave to risk hanging around the streets for a couple of hours. You seen any more sign of that MP?'

'No.' Lexie leant back against the wall, folding her arms against her chest; she watched him shrugging his way into the old mackintosh he'd worn when he first came here, and pulling one of Fred Weller's caps well down over his eyes. 'There's nothing in the papers about a soldier being killed, or even hurt bad. Maybe they ain't looking for yer. I mean, maybe you ain't as important as you think you are.'

'Don't you believe it. Some regiments don't like hanging out their dirty washing in public, see?'

Lexie sniffed. She'd slept with him again last night and he'd spent most of his time talking about his wife; or his wife's lover; or his wife's lover's kids. 'She wasn't like I thought she'd be, your Connie.'

'What you expect then?'

'Dunno.' Someone hard-faced and out for herself, she supposed.

But Connie Milligan's slightly buck-toothed thin face had worn a mingled expression of love and exasperation as she'd struggled to pin a nappy on to a giggling, squealing baby whose fat legs waved in semaphored happiness at this funny game. Tucking a strand of dark hair behind her ear, she'd said simply, 'I knew he'd turn up sooner or later. You his girl?'

'No,' Lexie had said truthfully, knowing that wasn't how Alan regarded her. 'Just a friend. He wants to see you. Can he come round tonight?'

But Connie wouldn't have that. 'This is my bloke's place. I'm not having Alan here. It ain't fair. I'll meet him up the Mitre pub.'

'Tonight?'

'No. It's my bloke's night off. I don't want him knowing. He'll try and come along and it'll all end in a fight. I know Alan's temper.'

Heaving the baby into her arms, she dumped it back in the cot that was standing in one corner of the cluttered room. Underneath the table on which she'd been changing the baby an older toddler was playing with a string of cardboard boxes that had been painted over and strung together to resemble a train and carriages.

'I'll meet him tomorrow, Friday. Nine o'clock. I'll get the old girl downstairs to sit with these two,' she'd said.

'She said she weren't coming if there was a bad raid on,' Lexie warned.

'She'll be there.'

His quiet confidence annoyed her even more. She was tempted to tell him he weren't that irresistible. But she did the next best thing and told him she had to be off. 'I'm going to a dance with Rose. Up the shelter. Albert reckons I should be able to find meself a nice, steady bloke up there.'

She wanted him to ask her not to do that. Instead he said, 'Good idea. About time you did, Carrots.'

Tears stung her eyes. She could have hit him.

'You'd best take a blanket if you're planning to stop up there all night. Some of them shelters can get damp.'

'Who said anything about stopping.'

'Might as well. I mean, no sense in coming home through a raid, is there?'

Lexie flounced into the bedroom and stripped the

sheets. 'I'll stick these into soak before I go up the shelter. Don't suppose you'll be coming back after you've seen her, will you?'

'I guess not. I don't rightly know what I will do. Don't fancy living as a deserter. Reckon maybe I'll try to get to Ireland.'

'See ya then. Give me regards to yer wife.' With linen bundled up to her chest, Lexie clattered away down the stairs without a backward look.

Alan gave her a moment to get clear, then wrapped a muffler round his throat, partially obscuring the lower part of his face, hefted an old shovel that had once done duty on Fred's allotment over his shoulder, picked up a tablecloth that had been tied into a bundle by its four corners, and stepped out back. As far as he could tell nobody was taking any notice of him as he made his way along the back path, slipped through the gap into Leighton Street and set off towards the High Street.

He hadn't wanted to take any more of the Wellers' possessions than was strictly necessary, so he'd stuck with the old mackintosh that he'd stolen from someone's back shed after he'd cleared the camp. The bundle contained his uniform. He cursed himself for not thinking to get rid of it earlier. It couldn't be left to be discovered in the Wellers' shop and perhaps bring trouble on Lexie. He'd just have to dump it once he got clear of Kentish Town. Shifting his grip, he checked that the sticks of wood and dirt-encrusted flower pot were still protruding conspicuously. Hopefully, to the casual observer he'd just be an ordinary citizen on his way to put in a bit of work on his allotment while there was still some dusk left.

It was strange to be out in the world again, part of
the everyday bustle of normal living that you took so
much for granted until it was taken away from you.
He'd been cooped up in the Wellers' place for just over
a week, snatching the occasional breath of air late at
night, but it had made him realise how blokes in clink
must feel, locked up in a brick box for years on end.
He knew he couldn't face it. Soon as he'd done what
he had to do with Connie, he'd make his way up to
Liverpool and try to get a ship; to Ireland preferably,
or the States.

Striding along, his thoughts slipped inexorably back
to Lexie. He'd been surprised to discover how much
of his old sixteen-year old's crush was still alive and
kicking in his heart. True she wasn't the girl she'd
been back then, but even if the red hair had faded a
bit and the face had acquired a few more lines, they
enhanced her appearance in Alan's opinion. Made her
look like a grown woman who knew a thing or two,
rather than a bright-eyed little girl. He could just
picture her in a classy dress, face made up nicely,
gliding around the floor at a regimental dance.
Roughly, he shook such thoughts from his head and
strode out with more determination for the pub.

The Mitre lay to the north of Kentish Town, within
spitting distance of the railway tracks. Ordering a
pint, he squeezed into a corner and tucked the spade
and bundle beneath his seat. Nobody paid him any
attention. Conscription hadn't caught up with men of
his age group yet and there were plenty of men in the
civil rescue and repair service still out of uniform.

He sipped slowly, nursing the bitter. A clear head
was important for what he had in mind; he didn't want

the drink to start talking before he had a chance. Being slung in the cells for drunk and disorderly when he'd got so close would be the final irony. Flexing his left leg, he felt the cool steel of the knife blade that he'd strapped there before retreating to the Wellers' attic.

A burst of shrill, raucous laughter at the bar brought several groups of heads around. Squinting through the thickening fug of smoke, Alan made out a saucy froth of white netting topping a curtain of red hair. For a moment he thought Lexie had followed him; then the woman turned to run a scarlet nail down her companion's cheek and he saw she was much older than Lexie; the grey roots of her hennaed locks showed clearly round the top of the heavily ear-ringed ears. He stared at those lobes, partially hypnotised by the bar lights sparkling in the swaying crystal drops which were big as pear drops, until he was recalled to the present by a tap on his arm.

'You play?'

Blinking, he discovered the next seat had been taken by a bewhiskered old bloke who was shuffling and rearranging dominoes on the table's stained surface. 'Want a game, mate? Loser buys the drinks, eh?'

The sly nudges and grins around the spectators warned him that this was a regular occurrence. It was probably the way the old boy financed his drinking. 'No,' he said, thinking quickly. No doubt if they expected him to be fleeced, he'd have their full attention. And the last thing he wanted was to be noticed and remembered. 'Can't say I do.'

He wriggled back into his seat and buried his face in the pint glass; an anti-social, unfriendly, miserable sod who didn't want to pass time with his neighbour.

They knew the sort.

The domino player turned his attention to the couple on his other hand. Alan settled down to watch quietly; his eyes scanning the entrance curtain without appearing to do so.

The pub filled up. Blokes coming in after work; others whiling away time before reporting for shifts on the repairs parties, ARP rotas and first aid stations. A couple of soldiers pushed through to the bar, leant across, and spoke to the barman. Two pints disappeared down their throats in one swift movement and they disappeared into the night again. Probably, Alan reflected, part of the barrage balloon detail; he'd spotted the silvery fish dancing above the railway tracks behind the pub as he came in.

A half circle of empty beer glasses collected around the domino player as all-comers were soundly beaten and urged to put their hands in their pockets. The bark of guns in Hampstead followed by the roar of a bomb which wasn't quite so distant as the previous explosions caused several drinkers to make their goodbyes and head for the shelters, but most customers remained behind to laugh, chat, play darts and cuddle in a quiet corner if they could get one.

The redhead seemed to be having a good time. Balancing a sheet of lavatory paper over the top of her empty port-and-lemon glass, she placed sixpence in the centre and offered round her lighted cigarette. 'Go on, 'ave a go. If yer drop the tanner, yer buy the next round.'

Several men standing round the bar took up her invitation, crowding round and draping hands over

her bottom and back as they pressed the glowing tip
to the paper. Each attempt was greeted by raucous
squeals from the redhead. Her laughter was shrill and
giggly, more appropriate to a schoolgirl than a middle-
aged woman. Listening to it brought a picture of Lexie
into Alan's mind.

He took a longer, deeper, draught of the bitter, half
draining his glass. Lexie made him feel bad. He should
never have taken what was on offer, even if it had
been freely given. He'd always liked her; had had
hopes there even. He'd had a fancy sometimes; seen
himself sweeping back in his uniform, a few stripes
sewn on the sleeve; a very different proposition from
the spotty, awkward kid that had gutted cod and
peeled spuds in the chip shop.

Then one afternoon he'd gone to some regimental
brat's christening and been introduced to a pretty,
dark-haired lady's maid who'd come out to India with
the lady who was to marry the adjutant. Offering a
cool white hand, she'd said, 'Hello, Alan.'

It took him a second to register the fact that she
wasn't in his memory any more. Instead, the same
woman was standing before him here and now, and
saying 'hello' like this was a perfectly normal meeting.

She was thinner than he remembered; maybe the
rationing was biting harder here, or perhaps those
kids were running her ragged.

He moved further along the bench seat, intending
that she should sit next to him, but she perched on a
low stall instead.

'Didn't think you were coming.'

'The baby's teething. I couldn't leave until he was
settled.'

He didn't want to hear about her fancy man's kids. 'Want a drink?'

'Half of mild.'

She sipped delicately, rather like a cat lapping milk. That first afternoon he'd thought the sight of her pink tongue dipping into the lemonade rather endearing. For many years now, he'd just found it damn irritating.

'How you been, Con?'

'I'm very well. Didn't your girlfriend tell you?'

'She ain't me girl. Just an old mate.'

'It don't make no difference to me if she's your girl or not. None of my business is it?'

'You're still me wife.'

'That's all over. It's been over for years, you know that, Alan. You just won't let go. I got Edgar and the kids now.'

'Oh it's "Edgar" is it?' Despite his resolution to stay calm, the edges of sarcasm crept around his words.

Beneath the narrow brim of her straw hat, Connie's eyes glittered. 'Yes. It's Edgar. He's a good man. A widower.'

'So what's he do, this "Edgar" of yours? Not in uniform I notice. Not a conchie, is he?'

'No. He's too old for the call-up. And he's a chef.'

'A chef! A bleeding cook! What sort of a job's that for a man.'

Despite the fact they were both whispering, or perhaps because of it, the domino players were starting to glance in their direction, their eyes sliding quickly away whenever Alan or Connie met them stare for stare.

'Let's get out of here.'

'And go where?'

'Just along the road. Where no one can hear us. You don't want the whole world knowing your business do you?'

The room had become so crowded that Alan was forced to use his shoulder to thrust a clear path to the door. Unaccustomed to the darkened street, he collided with something warm and squashy on the step and drew a hurt yelp.

'Sorry, son. Out the way, eh?'

Several small bottoms shuffled sideways to allow them to pass.

Connie dipped in her bag and passed down a coin. 'Here, pet. Go round the back door and ask the barman if he's got a bottle of pop for you. That's terrible,' she murmured in a lower voice to Alan as they moved away. 'You'll never catch me letting my kids sit outside the boozer.'

'You and "Edgar" planning to add to the litter are you? Or you just planning to string him along a bit?'

They'd moved to their left, huddling against the wall that separated the road from the railway cutting. The noisy clanking rush of goods trains belting out of St Pancras before it became caught up in the nightly raids almost drowned out her words. 'I was pregnant, Alan. I lost the kid, how many more times you need telling.'

'Pretty damn odd the way you lost it two days after the wedding, weren't it? And no sign of a kid since.'

'That's not my fault.'

'You saying it's mine.'

They were going down the same old road; giving voice to the old arguments; the words were so familiar that they could have voiced each other's lines; answered each other before the other one had spoken. Another couple came out of the pub, their bodies huddled close together, their heads touching. Giggling and muttering, they hurried towards the wall where Alan and Connie were standing.

'Oh sorry, mate, didn't know anyone was here.'

The couple stopped, a brief shaft of moonlight glancing through the thickening clouds illuminating their faces.

Alan ducked his head, pulling his cap down further. 'We're going. Come on, love.'

He stepped around them, dragging on Connie's arm so tightly that she protested. 'What's the matter? Let go, you're hurting me.'

'Sorry. Didn't want them to see me.'

'Why not? You in trouble again, Alan?'

A snort of derisive laughter, muffled by the scarf, exploded into her ear. 'You could say that.'

They were approaching the churchyard. The dark bulk of St Martin's loomed up, its massive tower stretching upwards in a visibly ostentatious affirmation of Victorian faith. 'Let's go in here.'

'What for?'

'It's more private.'

Steering her inside, he led the way round the side where they were deep in the denser shadow cast by the tower. 'Sit here.'

'It's wet.'

'Don't be daft. Sit down.'

He pulled her down roughly, retaining his grip on her arm.

A violent shiver pulsated through the muscles

under his hand. Although, whether it was fright or the strange, dank, loneliness of the churchyard he couldn't tell. He was beginning to get a bit spooked by the atmosphere himself. Best get it over with quickly. Bending his left leg quietly, he started to work the fastening on the knife free whilst he spoke.

'I done a lot for you, Con. Got myself a transfer back to England 'cos some old biddies told you it was the heat stopping you falling for a baby. Lost me first set of stripes on account of you.'

She stirred in protest. 'I didn't ask you to thump that bloke.'

'Couldn't let him talk about me missus like that, could I? Mind, you've proved him right this time, ain't you, girl? And you didn't have the decency to tell me. I 'ad to find it out from some poisonous old bat writing me letters.'

Twisting in his grip, she faced him. 'Well, now you know, don't you?' Her free hand slid up his chest until it rested on his collar bone. He could smell the beer tang on her breath. 'Let me go, Alan. Give us a divorce. Don't go thumping someone and losing your stripes again.'

His fingers tightened convulsively. 'I've lost more than that this time.'

'What d'you mean?' Her voice had lost its softness.

'I belted Tolly. He tried to stop me jumping camp.' He'd slung the punch blindly, feeling it make contact with the other man's knobbly jaw. The smack of his knuckles making contact had been followed by a grunt of expelling air and a sickening crack.

Groping over the prone body for signs of life, his fingers had come away from the back of the skull wet and sticky. It had been too dark to see properly, but the sweet salty smell had been unmistakable.

'He weren't breathing,' he told Connie flatly. 'I'd done for him. Me best mate, Connie. And I done him in on account of some whore.'

'Here, don't you call me . . .' Connie caught back the rest of the sentence on a gasp as she saw what was in his hand. The indrawn breath she gathered for a scream was muffled by the tussock of wet grass she slammed into as he knocked her face down on to the ground.

'Know what they do to whores, Con? Cut their hair off.'

Chapter 22

The firemen's dance was an enormous success. Entertainment in air raid shelters was still something of a novelty and the queues had started forming outside in mid-afternoon. By early evening the shelter was full.

'Sorry, ladies,' the shelter marshal said wearily, 'I can't let any more in. The sirens haven't sounded yet. You got time to get down to another shelter.'

'But we don't want to go nowhere else,' Lexie said, standing her ground. 'Anyhow, this lady was invited here, by one of the firemen. You got to let her in. It's their dance.'

'Well it's my shelter. I haven't to do anything of the sort, miss.'

'It's all right. She's with us. We saved 'er a place.'

'But you aren't supposed to . . .' The marshal found himself addressing a stack of sandbags.

'It's down here. Mind your feet.' Eileen clasped one of Rose's hands, guiding her down the stairs and leaving Lexie and Nafnel to grope their own way.

The shelter was one single, narrow, high-roofed basement room, its ceiling supported at intervals by round metal pillars and the light provided by single bulbs hanging between the metal columns. The volunteers had attempted to alleviate its rather bleak atmosphere by stringing flags around the walls, draping swaths of material in Arabian-style festoons across the roof, and adding paper shades to the lights so that they glowed like precious jewels suspended against the grimy metal rafters.

'Ooh, ain't you got it nice,' Lexie admired, stepping delicately over fingers, legs, and feet. 'Where's the dancing?'

'Down the front. They got a bit roped off for the band and the dancers. Here we are, you can get up now, Sammy.'

Sammy had been guarding the O'Days' patch by the expedient of laying diagonally flat on his back, arms crossed over his chest, eyes closed, in the manner of a corpse. Jack-knifing his knees into his chest, he sprung up in one smooth movement.

'There you are, girls. You fit yourself in here. Best leave the blankets folded for now,' Eileen instructed. She looked over the heads encircling the space. 'Where's Annie?' she said sharply. 'You haven't let her wander off 'ave you, Sammy?'

'Mr Stamford's takin' 'er to the toilet, Mum.'

'Oh. That's all right then. Ah, here's Pat.'

Pat struggled through the seated shelterers, a welcoming smile on his face and a tearful auxiliary firewoman attached to his shoulder.

'Hello, Rose. Glad you could come.'

Rose flushed, smoothing open fingers over the dress skirt. 'Couldn't let your mum's dress go to waste, could I?'

It was a bit too long and the styling was decorous to the point of dullness, but Pat's brown eyes held nothing but admiration. To cover her confusion she pushed Lexie forward. 'This is my friend Lexie Emmett. She's from the cobbler's next door.'

'The one mum told us about,' Sammy asked, eyes glowing. 'With the dead 'un in the cellar.'

'Shut it,' Pat growled, shaking Lexie's hand.

'It don't matter. I ain't upset. I know I'm supposed to be an' everything. But I ain't.'

'Takes a while to go in sometimes,' Eileen said. 'What's this your auxiliary lady's saying about the food?'

'It's true, Mum. Sorry. I never thought to ask. The wardens say we can't sell it in the shelter without a licence from the Ministry of Food.'

'But I been baking for days. There's people given rations. What are we supposed to do with all them pies and buns and things?'

Nafnel immediately volunteered his assistance.

'Watcha, champ,' Pat grinned. 'Didn't notice you down there. You sleeping with us tonight?'

'He ain't sleeping with *me*,' Sammy protested. 'He stinks.'

'No, I don't. Miss washed me. Smell.' An arm was thrust under Sammy's nose.

Pat lowered his voice and murmured to Rose. 'I went over to East Ham today. I've got some news about the kid.'

Before he could go on, his mother called across him. 'Is that right, Jack? We need a licence to sell the food.'

'Yes, I'm afraid it is. I thought the fire service would have fixed it.'

It would be hard to say who was more embarrassed. Lexie at finding herself face to face with the detective who'd just released her (temporarily) from jail, or Stamford at finding he was expected to spend the evening with two of his suspects in the James Donald

381

murder. He should never have allowed Eileen to talk him into this.

He hoped his real feelings didn't show on his face, as he wished them both good evening. Annaliese didn't help the situation by twisting out of his grasp and shooting after Eileen who was now stomping towards the warden's post, muttering dark threats about wasted rations and unpatriotic, unfeeling officers who didn't know when they were well off.

Someone down the front shouted for Pat to come and lend a hand with the drums, leaving Jack alone with the two women and two small boys who'd formed a temporary truce so Sammy could get all the lurid details about Frank Emmett's drowning.

'Er . . .' They were standing in a triangle, facing each other like characters in a Greek tragedy. It seemed absurd to suggest they all sit on the floor, but he couldn't think of anything else to say.

Obediently, the women squatted on folded blankets, as if it were an order rather than an invitation. For once, Jack found himself really pleased to see Maury O'Day.

Stumbling out of one group of shelterers, he stared at Jack, said, 'Oh, I thought ya'd gone to the lavs,' scrabbled under the blankets, found a full bottle of cream soda, thrust it inside the long, loose raincoat he was wearing, and plunged into the further group of shelterers.

'Who on earth was that?' Lexie demanded.

'Another one of Mrs O'Day's sons,' Rose replied.

'Maury,' Jack agreed. The short one, he added silently, his mind recalling his sergeant's description. The thought of Sarah caused another jerk of despair in his chest. She was another problem to which he had no answer; mainly because he didn't know what the question was. Something seemed to be bothering her; she was untypically bad tempered on occasions; but he couldn't discover what was behind her behaviour.

Rose leant forward, her legs curling behind her. 'I think you're supposed to ask us if we come here often.'

'All right,' Jack said, going along with her attempt to lighten the situation. 'Do you come here often?'

'Only during wars. You just don't get the atmosphere without a good air raid.'

'I know what you mean.'

They lapsed into an uneasy silence again which lasted until Eileen pushed her way back. 'I've fixed it. We'll give it away. Can't stop us doing that, can they?'

'No,' Jack agreed, assuming this question was directed at him.

'Good.' Eileen nodded her approval. 'And if people want to put a bit in the bucket for the Spitfire fund, that's their business too.' Under her breath, she muttered. 'I don't know why Maury's wasting his time with food. Might as well go into paper forms and make a flaming fortune.'

'I'll give you a hand,' Rose said, grateful for the excuse to move.

'If you like, love. Pat's down the front. 'Spect they'll be starting the dancing soon.'

They started it as soon as the Auxiliary Fire Service makeshift band managed to sort themselves out. It had been formed by press-ganging any officer who admitted they could play an instrument, with no regard to balance. Consequently they'd ended up with a pianist, a drummer, two violinists, one clarinettist, two trumpeters, one cellist and a chap who could play a range of glass tumblers filled with water.

As many couples as they could fit packed into the little dance area to shuffle round, in turns, to a fast and then a slow foxtrot as the band tried to play at the same tempo.

Rose grabbed the metal bucket and followed Eileen as she made her way round the seated shelterers, a wooden tray purloined from the cigarette girl at the Bedford hung round her neck.

'Slice of cold rabbit pie; cornbeef sandwich; potato and onion pasty.'

'Onion?' A voice queried.

'Had one in the water the taters were boiled in,' Eileen explained, stopping and handing out the pasty. 'We *was* going to sell 'em for the Spitfire fund, but certain people,' she looked significantly at a hovering warden, 'certain people say that's breaking the law. Of course if you should 'appen to want to put something in the bucket . . . ?'

She had already taken the precaution of throwing a handful of coppers into Rose's bucket. Shaken vigorously it gave out the sort of rattle that was hard to ignore if you were munching on its owner's home cooking.

The pile of food melted away and Rose's arms started to ache with the weight of the coins. Weaving amongst the seated families she found herself frequently being pointed out as 'the new miss'.

'We're getting more than I'd have dared ask for,' Eileen crowed quietly, as they refilled the tray for the third time. Two AFS women who were working the other side of the shelter were having similar success. Together with the 'voluntary' contribution for admission to the dance 'floor', the pile of copper and silver was reaching a respectable level. 'Why don't you go dance with Pat? I can manage. One of the WVS ladies will give me a hand with the bucket.'

Rose hesitated. She could hardly refuse to dance with Eileen's son outright. Especially when she knew, in her heart, that the reason she'd come tonight had nothing to do with cheering Lexie up or avoiding a possible visit from Nafnel's grandmother.

She was relieved that Pat had had the tact not to hang around waiting for her. Instead he'd danced with several other women, a couple of whom she'd recognised as old playmates of them both. At present he and Lexie were bumping round the floor in a mad version of the popular dance craze 'The Lambeth Walk'. It came to an end with the final shouted 'Oi' and the pair came off the floor giggling and breathless.

A roll of drums quietened the chatter nearest the stage. 'And now,' the pianist announced, 'Adele is going to give us a solo.'

The polite ripple of applause stilled into a hushed appreciation as the notes of 'We'll Meet Again' sang sweetly and poignantly from the single violin and drifted over the heads of the quietened shelterers.

Rose felt tears pricking at her eyes and heard the convulsive gulp as Eileen swallowed hers. To prevent herself from crying she whispered quickly to Pat, 'She's very good.'

'She's a professional. Played in a proper orchestra before the war. Will you dance with me, Rose?'

The force of the contact when he took her hand was as potent as an electrical shock; it was like being out on her first date again.

He held her loosely to begin with, but, as more dancers joined in the waltz, they were forced to move closer together until her cheek was leaning against the rough material of his uniform jacket. The scent of smoke still clung faintly to it.

'I know,' he said ruefully when she remarked on it. 'There just ain't time to get it out these days.'

They swayed a few more steps; both caught up in the violinist's performance.

'You don't have to go on duty tonight, do you?'

'Six tomorrow morning. Unless there's a big raid. They'll send a messenger across from the station if we're needed.'

Rose gestured across the tightly packed groups. 'There's Lexie. I hope that soldier isn't making any funny suggestions. She looks really peculiar.'

Pat looked. Lexie was clasped in the arms of a burly military policeman. The expression on her pale face resembled a rabbit that had just stumbled on a ferrets' convention.

Taking a firmer grip on Rose, Pat forced his way through the crush to dance beside her friend.

'Yes indeed, miss,' the policeman was saying. 'I've always been *very* partial to redheads. I don't suppose you remember me?'

The smoky atmosphere seemed to have affected Lexie's voice. 'No,' she squeaked.

'Thought not. Spoke to you the other Sunday, when you was trying to get converts to the temperance. Course I don't hold with giving up the drink altogether. But I want you to know I ain't a heavy drinking man.'

'Oh. Oh good.'

'Saw you the other day as well. In the High Street. I was going to ask if you'd let me buy you a drin . . . cup of tea, but I was distracted by a bloke who didn't have my moderate tastes in beer.'

Faintly, Lexie said, 'Oh really.'

'She seems all right,' Pat murmured into Rose's hair. 'Look, it doesn't sound like the raid's over Kentish Town. Do you fancy stepping outside for a minute? Get some air? I can tell you what I've found out about Nafnel.'

The night air was deliciously cool after the fug of cigarette smoke, sweaty bodies and cheap perfume below.

'Come over here,' Pat said, steering her around the side of the shelter.

Her eyes hadn't adjusted to the starlight yet, so she had to cling hard to him with one hand and use the other to feel her way along the packed sandbags and on to the rough brick wall.

In the soft darkness of the night, murmurs of endearment and muffled giggles of pleasure and squeals of mock indignation drifted back to them. Evidently they weren't the only couple to find the shelter too stuffy.

Pat stopped. 'You're not cold are you?'

'No. I'm fine.'

They stood side by side, their backs to the wall, looking up at the pale stars. The air had the taint of coal dust which was unavoidable in this area. As was the shunt, rumble and rhythmic clattering of the trains which had become so familiar to the inhabitants that they scarcely noticed it. The bricks under their shoulder blades vibrated with the powerful rush of an engine thundering down the tracks beyond the shelter.

'Do you like being a fireman, Pat?'

'Yeah, I do, now. It was tough going the first year, until this lot started. People thought we were scroungers and layabouts; especially after Dunkirk. But it's different now. Everyone's dead matey. I can go anywhere in this uniform and I'm very welcome thank you.'

Distant thunder to the south east reminded them both of the reason for the firemen's sudden popularity.

'East End's getting it again,' Pat said.

'Poor things. What's it like over there?'

'Terrible. There's whole streets gone, not just one or two houses at a time.'

'What about Nafnel? You said you'd found out something? Is it another relative?'

Half of her hoped it was, so that he could be removed from his grandmother. And the other half, she had to admit, didn't want to lose him.

'No. I don't reckon he's got any other family. He lived with his mum. Sometimes there was a bloke on the scene, and sometimes there weren't. But none of 'em ever claimed to be his dad. His mum got it in the first week of the Blitz; she was in the pub with the latest bloke when it got a direct hit. Luckily she'd left Nafnel back in their room.'

'How did you find all this out?'

'Sally Army. The local lot knew Nafnel and his mum quite well. Seems they'd had a couple of goes at getting

Nafnel to the Sunday School. It was them took him in when his mum bought it. They'd just got him fixed up to go to a Barnado's Place when his gran turned up and took him.'

'But why? She doesn't seem to care about him at all.'

'No, but she cares about his ration book.'

'Oh.' The implications of what he'd said sunk in. 'You mean she's been selling the coupons?'

'Or the food. It doesn't make much difference. She's not feeding it to the kid, that's obvious. Mind you, by all accounts his mum was a stranger to the gas cooker too. It's probably why he's a bit of a runt.'

'He's *not*.'

'He is, you know. According to the Sally Army captain you've got him in the wrong class. They reckon he's nearer seven than five. Tell you something else; I've found out his name: he's down on the Sunday School list as "Nathaniel".'

Rose tried it out under her breath; turning the 'th' into 'f' and cutting short the tail end of the word. 'Oh yes. I can see.' There was a small silence, then she sighed. 'Mind, I don't think I can ever think of him as anything but "Nafnel" now.'

'What are you going to do about him?'

Rose admitted she didn't know. 'My Aunt Mabel says I should report his gran to the cruelty man. But I don't like to, in case they put Nafnel in a home. I wouldn't want that for him. Do you think they'd let me keep him?'

'Wouldn't know. I 'spect you'd have to ask a solicitor or something. Don't you have to be married before they let you adopt a kid?'

He heard the air catch in her throat and stumbled on, frightened that he'd spoilt the moment by pushing too hard when he'd intended to let her set the pace for their courtship. 'Sorry, that was clumsy. I didn't mean you ought to get married again just for the sake of the kid. I mean, I know it's only a few months since you lost Peter, and I don't expect . . . We could just be friends to start, I wouldn't expect you to love me, not like you loved Peter. If you just thought you could get fond of me, sometime, maybe? Rose?'

He was gabbling because she wasn't reacting. They were still standing side by side and now his eyes were accustomed to the dark, he could make out the fair curtain of her hair and the gleam of pale flesh that marked the oval of her face. She wasn't moving. It was unnerving. He'd almost rather she slapped his face and stormed back into the shelter. He could cope with that. 'Rose?' Tentatively he brushed her shoulder.

Her response, when it came, was whispered, the words almost lost in the roar of a passing train. Thinking he'd misheard, he bent to bring his ear closer to her lips. 'Pardon?'

'I hated him,' Rose repeated. 'Peter, I hated him. And I killed him.'

Beneath his fingers he felt her shoulder start to shake as sobs rattled her body. 'Rose, don't!'

Clumsily, he gathered her into his arms, tucking her head on to his shoulder. 'How can you have killed him, Rose? That's rubbish. He copped it at Dunkirk, didn't he?'

Muffled by his jacket, she hiccuped out her story.

Their marriage, the one they'd both been so insistent upon, despite the opposition from his parents who thought he could do better for himself, and from hers who saw all the education they'd scraped to provide for her going to waste, had been a disaster.

'He was no good, as a schoolmaster,' Rose gasped out. 'Do you remember Miss Maynard at Riley Street?'

'The one we played all the jokes on?'

'She had no confidence in herself. And we knew it. Children do. That's how it was with Peter. When he got his first job, he was full of it. To listen to him, you'd have thought he was going to be headmaster in a year. But then it all started to go wrong. I could see it, when he came home. He wouldn't talk to me for hours; he'd just prowl around, the rage festering and building up inside.'

It had been like a torrent of hate racing through his veins and swelling them from within until he looked like he'd burst. And then he'd release it. 'At first, it was just the ornaments, or the furniture. And then, and then . . .'

And then he'd started on her.

'You mean he hit you?' Pat demanded incredulously.

A sob caught in her throat. 'I was so scared. I didn't know what to do. After it was all over he'd be so different, like the old Peter. And he'd beg me not to tell in case the school heard. I just used to stay in our old flat until the bruises had gone down enough for me to put make-up over them.'

She'd turned people away from her flat, earning herself a reputation for being a bit toffee-nosed since she'd got herself educated.

'Didn't you tell your mum?'

'How could I? I'd made such a fuss about marrying

391

him. Anyway I was too ashamed.'

'Don't see why. Weren't your fault. You should have got your dad to come round an' sort him out. I'd 'ave done it, if I'd 'ave known.'

Unconsciously, in his anger, he'd tightened his grip. She didn't protest. In fact, she slid her arms around his chest.

'So how come you reckon you killed him?'

Her hiccups were less violent now, he could feel their gentle jerks against his jacket as she explained that eventually things had become so bad at school that they'd warned Peter he'd be sacked unless his performance improved.

'He gave his notice. I said I'd get a job, not teaching, something in an office. But he just exploded. He said he wasn't having people thinking he couldn't support his own wife. We had to live on our savings; but there wasn't much, and he just spent like he was still in work.'

More in fact. He'd bought expensive clothes and put down a deposit on a car, arguing it was an investment since it enabled him to look for better work further afield.

'I had to sell things. Wedding presents and furniture. And that made things even worse because I couldn't let anyone in the flat in case they saw. But he just seemed to spend more and more, it was like he couldn't stop.'

The rent arrears had started to build up until the landlord had told her bluntly she either paid up in full or he'd put her furniture on the street next rent day. And then, thankfully, Peter had got another position at a private academy in Hampstead.

'And Matthew told us that there was a furnished flat going in the Row because Albert was moving in with his sister. It was an absolute godsend. I really thought everything was going to be all right.' After the first week at the academy, she'd seen it wasn't. 'He said the children were stuck-up little prigs. And the parents treated him like a servant. And then one day he just came home and said he'd left.'

It had been in the middle of the spring term. By early summer he still hadn't managed to find another job. 'He wrote for positions all over the country, but he couldn't get any interviews. He hadn't any references you see.'

The Labour Exchange offered clerking jobs. He'd joined the Army instead, casually assuming that she'd go along with his plans.

The Army had been a repetition of his scholastic career. Unrealistic ambitions had collided with his basic lack of self-worth. 'He was full of it before he left. A general in ten years. Going to apply for an officer's course soon as he finished basic training.'

'Did he?'

'I don't know. I expect so. He never said. He never told me about the failures. In the end we had very little to talk about.' The bitterness put a sharp edge on her normally soft voice. 'It sounds a dreadfully wicked thing to say, but I was almost relieved when the war started and they sent him to France. Albert was wonderful. I don't know what I'd have done without him. He let me stay in the flat and pay the rent off by working in the shop.'

Together with a small wage and the deduction from Peter's Army pay, she'd managed to get by. 'Peter thought he'd leave at Christmas, since he'd joined up instead of being a conscript. But he didn't.'

It had been her happiest Christmas for several years. She'd even started thinking about getting a proper job. 'Unfortunately, I told the Goodwins. And they told Peter.'

He'd finally been given seven days' leave at Easter. 'He was in a state.'

'About you wanting to work?'

'He blamed it on that. But I think things were just going badly in the Army. He wasn't any more suited to it than he had been to teaching. He was weak and spiteful.' A judder went through her body, causing her arms to tighten again around his chest.

Gently stroking her hair, he murmured, 'Easy now, I'm here. Go on, what happened on this leave of his?'

'I told him I wanted us to split up.' She'd left it until the last night of his leave. 'I know that was cowardly, but I was frightened of what he might do.'

She'd told him as they were walking back to the flat after tea at his parents' house.

'He tried to laugh it off as a joke. Then he cried.' Then he'd taken her arm, urging her back home, where they could 'talk properly'.

'I wouldn't go. I knew he wouldn't hit me in the street. He never did it in front of anyone else.' In the end, she'd twisted free and ran from him. 'I sat in Waterlow Park all night. I was scared stiff to go home.'

Only when she was certain Albert would be in the shop, had she dared creep back to the flat. 'At first it seemed all right. I mean, he hadn't smashed anything. I thought perhaps he'd not been there.' Then she'd found her clothes. 'He'd put them all in the bath and

poured paraffin over them and tried to burn them.
There was nothing left except the best stuff I was
wearing and an old dress and cardy I wore for the
dirty housework.'

He'd taken the Post Office savings book too, with
the few spare pounds that she'd managed to hang on
to. Even the gas and electricity meters had been
broken open and raided. The car had long gone and
the furniture belonged to Albert. She'd been left to
fend as best she could.

'Here.' Pat handed her his own handkerchief.

'Thanks.'

'I don't see how you reckon you killed him though,
Rose, not that anyone could have blamed you if you
had done for the bastard, if you'll excuse the language.
It was the Germans got him, weren't it?'

It was actually a British frigate. Peter had been
amongst the walking wounded. They'd been trans-
ferring from a smaller boat which had carried them
out from the beach, when Peter had lost his grip and
slipped. 'The boat swung, his legs were crushed between the hulls before he dropped into the water.'
Broken bones had protruded through his flesh,
dipping into the thick black oil floating on the sea
surface. 'The wounds became infected, in the end they
amputated to stop the poison spreading any further.'

They'd left it too late. He'd died four days later.

'So how was that your fault?'

'He said he hadn't been able to concentrate when
he got back to France. Thinking about what I'd said.
That was why he'd been wounded and slipped.'

'Blaming someone else to the end, eh?' Gripping
her shoulders, he forced her back until he could look

into her face. 'Look, Rose, I've had blokes like that on the tender. Every mistake was someone else's fault, never theirs. Nothing was ever down to them. Basically, they're pathetic. There's no call for you to blame yourself for Peter's death.'

'The Goodwins blame me.'

'Well they're bound to be upset. He was their only one, weren't he? They wouldn't if they knew how he'd been treating you.'

'They don't believe me.' She slid forward into the comforting solidness of his arms. 'He, Mr Goodwin, said I'd made it up to excuse my killing Peter. He called me a whore. And he said . . . he said . . .'

'Yeah, he said what?'

The words poured from her in a rush, tumbling over each other now that they'd been released from the dam she'd built across the memory of that terrible day in the hospital when Jonas Goodwin had pinned her to the wall outside Peter's ward and spat out his hate into her face.

'He said he'd be keeping an eye on me from now on. That if Peter couldn't have a life, then I wasn't going to either. And that I needn't think I was ever going to take up with another bloke, because if I tried . . . he'd, he'd . . . kill me.' She tilted her head back, so that her face was very close to his. 'He's been following me. I know he has. I'm sure it was him Lexie chased from the flat the other evening.'

Pat's tone was grim. 'Have you told the coppers?'

'No.'

'Why not?'

'I can't prove any of this, Pat. I mean, he's cunning, like Peter. He never says any of it in front of witnesses.

And I'd have to tell, wouldn't I? About what Peter did. I couldn't bear to have it all written down. In a statement. For everyone to see. I just want to forget it. Promise you won't tell anyone, Pat? *Please*.'

'If that's the way you want it, Rose, I promise.'

Privately, Pat promised himself a few words with Mr Goodwin Senior as soon as he got his next twenty-four off.

The thunder and crack of the guns in Hampstead took them both by surprise. Subconsciously they'd heard the heavy drone of plane engines coming closer. Now they realised they were practically overhead. Several pairs of feet fled past them in the dark.

'We'd better get inside too.'

Rose resisted. 'You promise?'

'I promise.'

'Thanks, Pat.'

The touch of her lips on his was so slight he couldn't even be sure they were there, and then she was feeling her way back to the whitewashed outline of the shelter entrance.

In the darkness, he saw her collide with another body and cry out in fear.

'Sorry, miss. Didn't see yer.'

The little figure scuttled into the entrance in front of her. In the dim light of the single shaded bulb dangling at the head of the stairs, they could make out his ferret-like features.

'Mr Monk,' Rose said. 'Hello.'

Felonious beamed recognition. 'Evening, Missus Goodwin.'

'Have you come for the dance?'

'Dance? Nah. I'm looking for Miss Sarah. The lady

copper who came up your place. She ain't at the police station. You seen her?'

'I don't think so. Pat?'

Pat was behind them on the stairs. 'She's not here. Is it important? Mr Stamford's down there.'

Felonious blew a doubtful breath through pursed lips. 'Suppose it'll 'ave to be 'im then. I remembered, you see.'

'Remembered what?'

Fel dropped one eye in a wink and tapped a nicotine-stained forefinger against his nose. 'Remembered what was nicked from that jeweller's shop, ain't I?'

Chapter 23

Jack wasn't enjoying the dance. Not that he'd expected to. He'd only come because Eileen had asked him.

'It's years since a gentleman took me to a dance,' she'd said wistfully. 'You wouldn't mind escorting an old friend to a knees-up, would you, Jack? As a special favour?'

How could he refuse?

He'd intended to stay in the background, leaving the rest of them to get on with enjoying themselves. But Eileen would have none of it. Applying a bit more emotional blackmail, she'd dragged him on to the dance floor.

Holding her now, as they swayed with difficulty in the cramped space, he realised that he hadn't held a woman that intimately for over two years. Not since Neelie had walked out in fact.

It felt strange to be thinking of Eileen in that way. Despite her grown-up family, she was actually only a few years older than him. Looking down at her in the dim light, he saw her afresh as it were. She'd kept her soft Irish complexion and there were no grey strands in the dark brown hair that was tickling his nose. Taken out of her apron, and temporarily released from the worry of what to buy, cook, and clean up, she was still an attractive woman.

'Do you miss your husband, Eileen?' he said abruptly.

She looked up into his face. 'Every day, love.'

'Haven't you ever thought of finding someone else?'

'Sometimes. But whoever takes me on, would have to take on six boys as well, wouldn't they? You never really lose 'em, even when they're grown up and starting families of their own. That's asking a lot of a bloke. Different for a woman, of course. I daresay there's plenty be pleased to mother one little girl.'

Jack moved more determinedly into the dancers. The band had struck into a quickstep and his broad shoulders were an advantage as the dance started to resemble a rugby scrum. 'If Annaliese is getting too much for you, I could always find a housekeeper.'

'Don't you dare. I ain't complaining. I like looking after her. I always wanted a little girl. Had one once. My first. She died.'

Jack held her slightly away from him. 'I'm sorry. You never said.'

'Water under the bridge now. Pat come along six months later. And then the others. It's not that I don't love my boys. I do. Course I do. I'm their mum, aren't I? But every time I pushed them out, I kept hoping this time the nurse would say "It's a girl, Eileen". So you see, Annie ain't the problem. It's you, love. You ought to get yourself a nice lady.'

'I can hardly do that, when I don't know if Neelie is alive or dead.'

'I shouldn't let that bother you. Don't suppose it will bother her, if you find the right one.'

Jack blinked.

Eileen smiled up at him. 'Shocked you, haven't I? Suggesting you live over the brush?'

'Well, yes.'

'Thought I might. I don't hold with it most times, you understand. I mean I'd box my Pat's ears, big as he is, if he were planning that with that Rose. But it's different for you. It ain't your fault that Dutch madam walked out, and there's no reason for you to live like a monk. Best get yourself a young lady; like that nice Miss McNeill.'

She'd managed to knock the breath out of Stamford. Firstly, because it would never have occurred to him that Eileen would have approved of anyone living in sin; secondly, because it was the first time he'd ever heard her speak disparagingly about Neelie; but mostly because it had never occurred to him to think of Sarah in a sexual way, any more than he would have thought of Ding Dong or Sergeant Agnew.

When he attempted to convey this fact to Eileen, she simply tutted impatiently and said, 'Well find someone else then. A good-looking fellow like you shouldn't have any problems. There's plenty of pretty girls here. Want me to get Pat to introduce you?'

'No!' He caught the twitch at the corner of her mouth and knew he was being teased. 'Shall we sit down?'

'Might as well,' she agreed. 'I can't work out what this dance is supposed to be.'

Neither could a lot of other people, judging by the variations being practised on the floor. The problem lay with the percussion section, where the chap with the water-filled jars and bottles was determinedly beating out his own rhythm with a total disregard to whatever his fellow band members were trying to play. His single-mindedness was gradually having an effect on the rest of the players who were giving up the struggle and trailing to a halt.

Threading their way back to their space, they found the three children engaged in a game of 'fives', using spent bullet cartridges in place of stones.

'How many, Annie?' Sammy said, catching four cases on the back of his hand.

Pouting with concentration, she counted, 'Five?'

'Four, silly. I dunno why you can't count proper. I showed you lots of times.'

And so did I, Jack thought. He remembered sitting in her bedroom high up in the narrow house in the square, piling up building blocks whilst she solemnly counted for him. She'd been quick for her age; easily learning her numbers from one to ten. Was it possible she'd forgotten?

'Eileen, have you ever . . . ?'

But Eileen's attention had been caught by her second youngest, who had suddenly materialised in the disconcerting way he had of appearing out of nowhere. 'Oh, you're back again.'

'We are. Why? What are you up to, Maury?'

'Nothing.'

The combination of bodies and dancing had pushed the temperature in the shelter up. Maury's dark hair hung in limp locks over his pale face which gleamed greenish-white in the overheated atmosphere.

Eileen thrust a motherly hand beneath his fringe. 'You're sweating. Take that old raincoat off before you overheat your blood.'

'In a minute, Mum. Er, shall I fetch you and Mr Stamford a cup of tea from the WVS ladies?'

Eileen retrieved some coppers from her pocket. 'There's a good boy. I'm parched after all that dancing.

And give the children a sip of lemonade from that bottle of yours.'

'It's finished.'

'You rotten liar. You still got a full one under there. I saw it.' Sammy whipped back his brother's coat skirt to reveal a couple of lemonade bottles and one cream soda stuffed into makeshift poacher's pockets in the lining.

Snatching up the coppers, Maury hissed a warning at his younger brother and dived back into the crowd.

'Whatever . . . ? Pat, what's Maury up to?'

'Couldn't say, Mum,' Pat said, pushing his way back into the circle. 'This bloke's looking for you, Mr Stam . . . Er, Jack.'

Like an anxious ferret, Felonious's sharp nose tested the air in the circle. Finding nothing in there to alarm him, he stepped forward. 'I remembered,' he announced.

'Remembered what?' Stamford asked, the Donald case having been temporarily pushed into a corner of his mind by the puzzle of Annaliese's identity.

'He says he's remembered what was missing from Mr Donald's flat,' Rose offered, seating herself by the children and modestly tucking her dress behind her legs.

Stamford cursed silently under his breath. It was one of the penalties of working and living on top of the job. Now one of his chief witnesses was discussing the case in front of one of his suspects. 'Come over here, Felonious.'

He towed the milkman back towards the shelter entrance where it was possible to get a little privacy. 'Now tell me.'

'It just come to me in the Mother Shipton. I was

watching this bloke sinking a pint of best and thinking that 'is gold tie-pin looked a bit loose, and if a cove was to lean over the bar and sort of brush against him, he could find it in his own pocket. Not, of course, that I do that sort of thing any more. And it come to me. That Mr Donald's tie-pin was with 'is watch and stuff when I went in first. But when I come back with Miss Sarah, someone had half-inched it. Nice piece it was; gold, this big.' His forefinger and thumb were held two inches apart. 'And it had a big gold J in the middle.'

Even as Felonious came to the end of the description, Jack knew he'd seen the pin somewhere quite recently. But where? His memory strained to find the right picture and his subconscious stubbornly refused to let it go.

Fel was examining the shelter with a distinct lack of enthusiasm. 'I 'ate these places. It's like the clink; only it smells worse. Don't suppose you can get a drink at this dance?'

'Tea.'

Felonious pushed his hand inside his waistcoat and dragged out a large pocket watch on a chain. Seeing Jack's speculative expression, he said firmly, 'Won it in a card game, Mr Stamford.' He turned it to catch the dim light on its face. 'It's nearly closing time. No point going back to the pub. Might as well go home I suppose. 'Ave to be up soon to hitch up the 'orse from 'ell. Work's a bleedin' pain, ain't it?'

He reminded Jack of something he'd been meaning to ask Felonious for some time. 'It sounds like the raid's getting closer up there. Best hang on for a while. Have a cup of tea.'

He didn't give Fel a chance to refuse but steered him once more by the elbow. An ingrained habit of moving in whichever way the law wanted (thereby minimising any unpleasant misunderstandings about resisting arrest), made Fel come quietly – at least as far as the tea urn.

Jack found himself in the queue behind a couple of familiar backs.

'Hello. Find your fish and chip shop?'

The MP smiled his own recognition. 'Can't say I have. Still there's compensations in looking.' He slapped one hand across the khaki straining over his stomach. 'Can't beat cod and threepenny worth, can you?'

The hot, smoky atmosphere didn't seem to be agreeing with Lexie at all. Heat had melted her panstick, allowing the pale brown of her freckles to stand out like a dusting of faded confetti against the deathly white of her face. Now she swayed and would have fallen if Jack hadn't caught her.

'You'd better sit down.'

The WVS worker was already pushing a chair forward, but Lexie stood upright again. 'No. It's all right. It was just the fish and chips. Made me feel a bit sick thinking about them.'

'I'd have thought you'd be used to them,' Jack remarked. 'After all, you're li—'

Lexie saw with horrible clarity that he was about to tell a red cap who was looking for a fish and chip shop that there was a shuttered one in Balaclava Row.

'I need some air.' She grabbed the MP's arm. 'Take me near the door.'

'My pleasure. Here we'll take a cup of tea with us,

eh? You have a few sips. Be just the ticket.'

'Brandy, that's what she needs,' Felonious announced, tipping his tea into the saucer and blowing. 'You ought to keep some down here for medicinal purposes.'

'Alcohol is not permitted,' the WVS worker snapped. 'Next.'

Stamford nudged Felonious into a handy space by one of the pillars. 'Tell me something, Fel. What made you decide to go straight?'

Felonious looked around cautiously to see if anyone could overhear them. By some feat of muscular control he seemed to shrink until he was totally concealed behind the narrow pillar. 'I was tipped off,' he whispered hoarsely. ''Bout the conscripting.'

'What about it?' Jack found himself whispering as well.

Fel dropped one eye in a conspiratorial wink. 'Take them from the jails, don't they?'

'Take who?'

'The lags of course. This professor what got done for embezzlement told me. He was saying about how if there was a war they took the prisoners and stuck 'em in the Army wivout so much as a "d'ya mind, mate". So soon as I got out I got meself a regular job wiv Mr Bowler, *which* I'd still 'ave if you and Miss Sarah 'adn't made me look like a copper's nark and got me the sack. It was lucky Missus Thomas's regular bloke turned up his toes when 'e did. Otherwise I might have been tempted to backslide and they'd 'ave got me. The poor old Prof weren't so lucky.'

'No?' Jack queried, trying hard not to laugh.

'Nah. Still 'ad two years to do when I come out. I reckon them generals must have got him, don' you?'

'Actually, Fel, I think you'll find they gave up pressing prisoners into the Army around Waterloo.'

'Yeah? Didn't know they 'ad a clink down that way.'

Jack gave up.

A girl of about fourteen tottered past in unfamiliar high heels. A ricked ankle and an uneven floor sent her wobbling into him. 'Oops, sorry, mister. Mustn't throw meself at the fellers me mum says.' The statement was accompanied by a shrill giggle that ended in a violent hiccup. The belch of her perfumed breath carried the unmistakable tang of gin.

'I thought you said there weren't no drink,' Fel protested.

'I said they weren't selling it. Perhaps the young lady has her own source.' Still gripping her, Jack beckoned to the WVS worker.

'Not another one,' she sighed, taking the girl's other arm. 'I don't know where they're getting it from. Come on, dear, I think you'd better have a little lie down.'

The shelter marshal was moving amongst the crowd with a torch.

'Problems?' Jack asked as he passed.

'I reckon someone's selling drink down here. Either that or they're buying their Horniman's at a different Co-op to my missus.' He flicked the beam over two elderly ladies sipping tea from a thermos brew. They raised faces of cherubic innocence.

'You ain't seen anyone at it, have you, sir?'

'No. Sorry.'

With the exception of Lexie, his own party were all seated again. 'Best start getting ourselves sorted out before all the room goes,' Eileen decided. 'You kids go along to the lavatory now. Sammy, keep an eye on Annie. Wait for her.'

'I'll go with them,' Rose offered. She extended a hand to Annaliese and it was taken without hesitation.

'Everyone but me.'

Jack wasn't aware that he'd spoken aloud until Pat said, 'It's not you specially, Mr Stamford. It's blokes. She's all right with women and other kids, but she don't like blokes. It's the same if I try to take her anywhere. Isn't that right, Mum?'

'Can't say I'd noticed. But yes, now Pat comes to mention it, she does hang back if the binmen or the milkman comes into kitchen.'

Jack mulled this over whilst Eileen arranged the children's bedding. Annaliese, *his* Annaliese had never been shy with men before. Was it more proof that this child wasn't his daughter? Or had she seen something on her flight from the advancing German Army that had made her scared of men? Despite the humid atmosphere, a chill slid down his spine at the thought of what that sight might have been.

'Where's Maury?' Eileen demanded, kneeling up and scanning the shelter.

'Don't know, Mum. He keeps darting round here like a flaming bluebottle.'

Eileen rose to her feet to the accompaniment of a drum roll.

'Ladies and gentlemen,' bawled the pianist through a megaphone, 'we'd like to thank you for your generous support this evening. And since it's lights out in fifteen minutes, we'd like to finish our little concert with "The King".'

Grumbling and muttering, the shelterers clambered

to their feet, arthritic knees cracking audibly in the relative quietness.

There was a slight hiatus while the percussionist adjusted the resonance in his jars by sipping the contents, then the band struck up 'God Save The King'. It was a memorable performance; halfway through, the percussionist's eyes rolled skywards and he fell sideways, his stiff body slicing the air like a cheese wire slipping neatly through a pound of cheddar.

Stepping across the prone body, Adele the violinist picked up one of the jars and sniffed cautiously. 'Gin,' she said succinctly. And threw the measure down her throat before anyone could protest. After a moment's stunned silence, the rest of the band toasted the audience to thunderous applause.

'So that's where you been getting it from,' the marshal's aggrieved voice boomed across the room.

Several thermos tops and tin mugs were raised in mock salute to him, accompanied by ribald laughter.

Stamford wondered whether he was the only one who'd noticed that the percussionist had been in full sight all evening and would have found it hard to sell illicit drinks without being seen.

'Well that's that,' Eileen said, as the noise died down again. 'Went well, didn't it?'

Pat gave her a quick squeeze. 'Smashing, Mum. Thanks.'

'You're welcome, love. Let's get ourselves sorted before they turn the lights off.

The rope barriers to the dance floor were removed. A general shuffling and rearranging of the front shelterers gave them just enough space to sleep nine people if two sat up.

The three children were tucked up together between a pair of blankets. Annaliese and Sammy wriggled in protest at the unfamiliar concrete floor, but Nafnel turned over and fell instantly into a deep sleep.

Rose was positioned on the other side of Eileen. Lexie wished her soldier 'good night' and cuddled up beside the other women, leaving the MP to find his own spot somewhere near the steps.

Maury, crawling back into the circle just before 'lights out', was told to sleep widthways across the foot of the children's blanket.

'Drunk all the lemonade, Maury?' Jack enquired.

Maury unhooked a worn leather bag from inside his coat. It gave out a metallic jingle as he rolled it inside his raincoat and stuck the bundle under his head to use as a pillow. 'Yes, thanks, Mr Stamford.'

There wasn't a blush or a tremor. If Maury was ever interrogated by the police, he'd be a tough nut to crack.

They'd been fortunate enough to get a spot by a wall, which meant that Jack and Pat could at least lean against it. Nonetheless, they were both forced to sit with their legs drawn up and their arms resting against their knees.

Jack didn't expect to get much sleep but, after a while, he found his eyes growing heavier, his head fell forward and then jerked backwards as he felt himself slipping. Groaning and stretching his cramped legs as far as he dared, he vowed never to spend another night in a shelter if he could help it. Around him he could just about make out the humped shapes of other parties in the dim light of the solitary lamp burning by the marshal's post.

The noise disturbed him. For some reason he could sleep quite soundly through an air raid, but the constant hum of strangers coughing, spitting, hawking and snoring was like a dripping tap that couldn't be ignored.

Others were awake too. He could hear the quiet whispers, some whining, some reassuring, some just passing the time.

Away to his left, he heard someone putting forward the generally held view that if there was to be an invasion it wouldn't come until next spring.

''E'd have come August or September if 'e was coming. You don't take ships across the Channel this late in the year,' the unknown talker asserted. 'Stands to reason they'll wait until the weather turns warmer. That's what all the bombing's for, ain't it? Crack us before next year.'

'I dunno about next year,' a second voice complained softly. 'I've 'ad enough now. Me back's killing me sleeping on this floor.'

'Sshh. Careful. There's a copper over there. He'll do you for defeatist talk if he hears you.'

It was a shock to Stamford to hear himself spoken of in that fashion. It was true that there had been some overzealous prosecutions of those supposedly indulging in 'careless talk', but he hadn't appreciated that he was seen by some members of the local community as some kind of undercover spy for the Government.

A deep feeling of isolation and loneliness swept over him: his wife had left him: his (supposed) daughter was scared of him; and his sergeant was barely on speaking terms with him since he'd torn her off a strip

411

for making her suspicions clear to Helen Fortune.

'Mister? Inspector?'

One of the lumpy shapes had levered itself up on one elbow.

'Yes, Miss Emmett?'

'When will you know? About me dad?'

'Tomorrow.' It was probably tomorrow already. He couldn't read his watch. The pathologist had promised to put the autopsy to the top of his list – after enquiring if Stamford was trying to get a discount for bulk deliveries.

'Good,' Lexie whispered back. 'I want to know,' she said. There was a touch of defiance in her voice, a sort of assertion that there was going to be nothing in the doctor's report that would incriminate her.

'You will.' Jack drifted back into sleep; the heaviness of his head dragging on the back of his neck again as gravity and tiredness fought with the shoulder muscles.

He started to fall sideways.

'Sir? Mr Stamford, sir.'

Opening his eyes in response to the shaking hand, he blinked and gasped in protest at the light in his eyes.

'Sorry, sir.' The shaded beam was redirected on to the floor.

It took a few moments for the black spots to stop dancing in Jack's retinas and then he made out the tin helmet and dark uniform with the distinctive striped band around the sleeve cuff.

'What is it, Constable?'

'They sent me to find you, sir. The sergeant thought you'd want to know they've found a woman's body in the churchyard.'

'Which churchyard?' Stamford asked, levering himself up with the help of the wall.

Lexie hadn't been able to sleep properly either. The constable's answer carried clearly to her.

'Dale Road, sir.'

Chapter 24

His mouth tasted foul and his jaw rasped audibly when he passed a weary hand over it. He wanted a wash and a shave. His watch said it was one o'clock on Saturday morning.

'Had a few hits further south, sir,' the constable said as Stamford automatically scanned the street with his eyes and the air with his nose for any telltale signs of explosives. 'Around Tottenham Court Road way. And a couple came down by King's Cross Station but there's no major damage reported. Did you want me to phone for a car, sir?'

'I'm not that decrepit. I'll walk.'

If he could have flown he'd have reached Dale Road in a couple of seconds, since it lay almost directly opposite the shelter over the wide swath of railway tracks. As it was, he had to drop down into Kentish Town again and cut up to the churchyard.

The constable fell into step beside him.

'PC Wilkins, isn't it?'

'Yes, sir.'

'Did you find her?'

'No, sir. Bloke on the last shift did. Anyway it ain't on my beat tonight.'

'The last shift? When was this body found exactly?'

'About two hours ago. Courting couple got a bit more excitement than they'd expected.'

'*Two hours*. Why's it taken so long to call me out?'

'Couldn't find you. They sent a bloke round to your house when they couldn't raise you on the phone, but there weren't no answer.'

'No. There wouldn't be.' When Eileen had persuaded him to go to the shelter, he'd forgotten to telephone his new location back into the station. 'My fault. So how did you find me?'

'I remembered Sergeant McNeill saying the lady opposite did for you. So I tried her place. One of the neighbours heard me and told us about the shelter dance, just took a chance you might be there too.'

'Full marks for initiative, Constable.'

'Thanks, sir. Maybe you could put in a good word with me sergeant.'

They'd reached Agar Street Station by now, Stamford having walked that way with no conscious recollection of doing so.

'They've got the two who found 'er inside, sir. If you wanted to see 'em first?'

Stamford thought quickly. 'Is the body still up in the churchyard?'

'Far as I know. I don't think the sarge likes to move it 'til you've had a gander.'

'Right. I'll get up there then. Can you tell them inside to keep the witnesses sweet on tea and sandwiches until I get back?'

They parted at the station door, Wilkins to deliver his message and resume his patrol and Stamford to turn northwards again.

Even in the feeble starlight, the church tower was easily visible, its high, solid blackness appearing to soar like a shaft from the roofs of the houses until Stamford turned out of Grafton Road and could approach it directly along Dale Road.

'Other side, sir,' a voice whispered hoarsely. The shaded beam of the special constable's torch wavered along the iron railings. 'Gate's round in Vicar's Road.'

Skirting the impressive church, he slipped into the small, grass-grown yard and found his way to the back where a hastily erected screen was protecting the body from a non-existent public curiosity. Once again Stamford was struck by the ordinariness that death had acquired. Before the war, the news of the body would have been transmitted along the rows of houses by the strange process of osmosis that enabled gossip to travel through brick walls with no conscious effort on the part of the houses' occupants. Now they either didn't know, or didn't care. The dead woman was just one more casualty.

Churchyard was a somewhat glorified name for what was, in effect, little more than a large garden encircling the solid grey building. The grass here was rank and lush, growing profusely in the water-logged London clay that never dried out even on the hottest summer day.

She was lying on her back, one leg bent up behind her, her arms flung wide. Beyond her, on the other side of the canvas screen, wisps of smoke arose into the chill night air, swirling and glinting like luminous silk scarves in the fitful moonlight. A lugubrious face, its planes shades of grey, its plump rounds the colour and texture of wax, arose from the other side of the screen.

'Good morning, sir,' Detective Sergeant Agnew coughed. Taking another draw on the smouldering pipe, he released a swirl of smoke around his head,

giving Jack the impression he was addressing a head-
less raincoat.

'You're the duty officer, are you, Sergeant?'

Mournfully DS Agnew agreed that he was. He
implied, without actually saying, that night duty
would undoubtedly be the major contributing factor
when he shortly (*very* shortly) died of double
pneumonia.

Stamford dismissed his irritational twinge of
disappointment. When PC Wilkins had spoken of 'the
sarge' he'd assumed he was referring to Sarah.

'Do you know where . . . No, never mind.' Saturday
was her day off. When he'd dismissed her after that
scene with Helen Fortune, he'd told her to take the
time and get some sleep, assuming that part of her
prickly temper might be due to her recent crack on
the head.

'Do you have a light, Sergeant?'

The DS struck a match.

Jack tried to stay calm. 'I don't want to smoke, I
want to see the body. Haven't you got a torch?'

'Can't say I have, sir. The special's got one. Oi!' A
shrill whistle which ended in a coughing fit summoned
the agog special constable. He directed his light in
Stamford's direction, playing it across the dead
woman's sprawled body and settling on the face.

It had been pretty once. Now, the blue-tinged lips
and staring blood-flecked eyes gave it the appearance
of a badly painted china fairground doll. Gently, Jack
brushed away some of the strands of black hair that
were trailing across the throat. 'Put the beam on here.'

The scarf had cut into the white flesh, the ridges
either side of the cloth puffy and swollen where it

had bitten deep as the murderer had choked the life from her.

Sergeant Agnew extended something. 'Found her bag next to the body, sir. Not much in it though.'

Agnew was right. There wasn't much: a cheap compact and lipstick, a chipped mirror, a hand-kerchief, crumpled and smeared with lipstick, a chain purse with a few coins, and the woman's identity card. Stamford slipped the card in his pocket. 'I'll notify the next of kin.'

He reached forward again and touched the face briefly once more. There was a tenderness in the gesture that penetrated even the disease-obsessed Agnew's brain. 'You know her then, sir?'

'Yes. I knew her.'

Straightening up, he winced as his back muscles reminded him that he wasn't in his twenties any more. Neither was the special constable, but he'd have to leave him on guard until they could make a proper search of the yard in the daylight.

'I'll send someone up as soon as possible,' he promised. 'Stay on the gate and keep everyone out. You and I had better get back to the station and speak to these witnesses, Sergeant.'

They were scarcely more than children. The boy was seventeen; grown too tall for his weight and looking lost inside his ARP coat. The girl was sixteen and sobbed continuously.

'Her dad thinks she's safely tucked up in bed at home,' the station master whispered to Stamford. 'Seems she's been sneaking out to meet the boy whenever he's on patrol around her way.'

'Oh, please let us go 'ome before he finds out,' she

begged. 'He's gonna kill me if 'e finds out.'

'I won't keep you long,' Stamford promised. He didn't add that if the girl's evidence was important, her dad was going to find out when she appeared in court. 'Now, tell me what you saw.'

It was better than he could have hoped for, given the circumstances. They'd met at the corner of the road and gone into the church because that was where they usually went.

'He was bending over her, the . . . you know. It was dead black and we didn't see him at first,' the boy explained. 'The moonshadow makes it darker round that side and he was wearing dark clothes.'

'What kind of clothes?'

'A long coat and trousers I think. Like I said, there weren't much light and I didn't think to use the torch 'til he'd run off.'

'Could you see his face?'

'Not really. He had short dark hair, I could see that.'

'No hat then?'

'No. Yes. I'm not sure.' The boy sucked in his cheeks, giving his face a drawn look, like an old man that had mislaid his dentures. 'He scooped something up from beside the body just before he started running. I think it might have been a hat, but I ain't sure, sorry.'

'Don't be. I wish all our witnesses were as clear as you.'

'Yeah?' The boy swelled visibly. 'Well I always had a good memory. I'm going in to the RAF soon as I'm old enough. You'd need a good memory to do the navigating, wouldn't you?'

'Never mind yer flaming planes, just *tell* him and let me get home!'

'Yeah, all right, Beryl. I couldn't see anything else really. I think he was youngish. Well not old, any rate.'

'Why?'

'He shifted pretty fast when he saw us, didn't he, Ber?'

'I didn't watch. I was too scared after I'd seen that . . . thing.'

Jack queried, 'The body you mean?'

'No. Not that, it was . . . You tell 'im, Colin.'

Colin obliged. 'He had a knife.'

Stamford looked at him sharply. His brief examination of the body hadn't uncovered any cuts, either on the flesh or the body. 'Are you sure?'

'Yeah. The moonlight caught the blade for a second.'

The girl gave a convulsive swallow. 'He was cutting her hair.' Her lower lip trembled uncontrollably. 'He was hacking it off in lumps.'

It took several hours to arrange for a mortuary van to remove the body and a search team to comb the churchyard as soon as it was light. After that there had been the miserable business of informing the next of kin and the inevitable shock and disbelief that had followed. Only after he'd sorted all that out had he been free to snatch an hour's sleep in the cells before making his way home, as soon as the all clear sounded, to snatch a shave and a clean shirt.

Eileen and the two children caught up with him at the corner of the street. 'Never again,' she vowed, hefting the blankets higher in her arms. 'I'll sleep in me Anderson from now on, no matter what. Don't trail that bag in the dirt, Sammy.'

Stamford took the pile of bedclothes from her and

the children. 'Sorry, I had a call-out, Eileen.'

'That friend of Rose's said. A copper came for you.'

She didn't probe any further; years of 'doing' for him had taught her that he'd tell what he could as soon as he could.

'Where's Maury?'

'No idea,' she said. 'Went off soon as the all clear sounded. Said he had something important to do.'

Banking his takings from last night, Stamford thought grimly. How much longer was it going to be before the police had to take an official interest in Maurice O'Day and he and Eileen had the inevitable falling-out?

Annaliese gave an enormous yawn.

'I think I'll put her to bed for a couple of hours after breakfast,' Eileen said stroking the tangled red hair. 'You too, Sammy.'

Sammy rejected the suggestion with scorn. 'Me and Piggy's gonna look for shrapnel.'

'Have your breakfast first,' Eileen instructed. 'Go see if the hens have laid anything.'

Jack excused himself to shave and wash. His house felt damp and unwelcoming and the water was stone cold since the boiler hadn't been lit. Shivering in the chilly atmosphere, he stripped off in the bath, lathered the soap over his face, arms and body, and shaved rapidly relying on memory rather than using a mirror. A few jugfuls of cold water tipped over his cringing skin completed his makeshift wash down.

He'd just finished buttoning a freshly ironed shirt, when the door knocker sounded. Assuming it was Sammy sent over to summon him to breakfast, he bounded downstairs and flung the door open, an assurance that he'd only be a second already on his lips. It died as he saw the bulky figure on his step.

'Morning, Stamford. May I come in?'

'Of course, sir.'

He flattened himself against the wall to allow the stout figure of his boss to enter the house.

'In here, sir.'

He led the way into the front room, which most of his neighbours designated 'the parlour' but which his wife had always insisted they call 'the dining room'.

His first thought was for Neelie. Had the Yard received some news. If Dunn had come to break it to him, then it had to be bad.

'I've just got in. Erm, some tea, or coffee?'

'No thank you. I'll not use your rations. I'm just on my way to the wife's sister's house. Daresay she'll feed me.'

'Doesn't your sister-in-law live in Oxford, sir?'

'Er. Yes.' Dunn eased a finger round his collar. They both knew he wouldn't have taken this route. 'Just thought I'd drop in and let you know Hendry's appeal has been turned down. He'll hang.'

Gus Hendry had been the perpetrator of the murder that had originally had him transferred from Scotland Yard to Agar Street. Whilst Dunn obviously regarded this as a good outcome, it hardly rated a morning visit to Jack's house.

In the street outside, the sound of children's voices screaming excitedly was followed by the crash of breaking glass as the first goal of the day soared through somebody's front window.

'You really should move, Jack. This area is so—'

Dunn fumbled for the right words. Stamford supplied them for him.

'Working class?'

'Yes.' Dunn puffed himself out. 'And don't take that tone with me. I'm not a snob. It's a question of horses for courses. This isn't a suitable area for a chief inspector. Particularly if your nick is on the doorstep too. Means you could get involved in certain, er, undesirable, er, involvements.'

Jack had been thinking much the same since he'd found himself attending a dance with Rose Goodwin and Lexie Emmett. He said as much to Dunn.

'Glad to hear you think so. Best not to get mixed up with the wrong sort of woman if you can help it.'

'How did you know?' Stamford was bewildered by the speed with which Dunn had heard about the occupants of the Carker Lane shelter.

'Gossip travels, Jack. Even to chief superintendent's offices at the Yard. I know your wife is, well, shall we say . . . unavailable? And I wouldn't blame you if you chose to look elsewhere. But best not to do it on your own doorstep eh? Discretion, that's the key.'

'What exactly are you talking about?' As an after-thought, he tempered the edge on his question with a half-hearted, 'Sir'.

'The girl, of course. This sergeant of yours.'

'Do you mean,' Jack said slowly, 'that it's all over Scotland Yard that Sergeant McNeill and I are having an affair?'

No wonder Sarah had been in a foul temper recently.

'Well, I wouldn't say *all* over. But you know, as your immediate superior, it was felt that I should be informed.'

'Then perhaps you could go back to your inform-
ants, sir, and tell them that not only am I not having
an affair with Sergeant McNeill but I consider it
downright insulting to her to imply that *she* is having
one with *me*.'

Dunn's embarrassment increased. 'Oh. Well, of
course, if that's the case, very glad to hear it. You
know how these rumours start. Not that I really
thought there was anything in it.' He made a blatant
attempt to change the subject. 'Nearly finished with
this Donald thing are you?'

There it was again. The casual acceptance of death.
Before the war, 'this Donald thing' would have rated
a full case conference. Now it was an off-hand enquiry
en route to Oxford.

'There's another problem.' Briefly he told Dunn
about their discovery at St Martin's that morning. 'It
was the girl from the cafe in Balaclava Row. The
younger one: Josepha.'

'Good lord. What's going on in this place? Are the
deaths related?'

In Jack's opinion they were almost bound to be.
'Stretching coincidence a bit too far to have two
murderers on the patch at the same time.'

On safer ground, Dunn could resume his usual
brusquely professional manner. 'Do you need further
help?'

Jack considered. 'Give me a couple more days, sir.
I think this might be a lucky break for us. Two bodies
without any clues is pretty unlikely.'

Dunn levered himself to his feet. 'Keep me
informed. And about this other business, perhaps it
might be best if the young lady returned to uniform?'

'She never left it. You wouldn't arrange for her transfer, remember?'

But she was still in plainclothes when he found her in the CID office at Agar Street an hour later.

'I told you to stay home.'

'I left something in the desk.' She was wearing trousers; the first time he'd ever seen her in them. Presumably it was intended to indicate she was off duty rather than in plainclothes.

'Where's Agnew?'

'Supervising the search up at the church, sir.' She passed a slip of paper. 'I've just taken a call for you.'

Jack glanced at it. The pathologist wanted him to ring back immediately. Giving the number to the telephonist, he remarked ruefully, 'He probably wants to complain about the workload.'

'Actually, sir, I think he's got the results of Frank Emmett's autopsy.'

'Natural causes,' the pathologist said breezily. A damn sight too breezily for this hour of the morning. 'He was dead before the flood.'

'You're certain?'

'There was nae water in the lungs when we opened him up. It was a heart attack, pure and simple.'

'He had been complaining about chest pains for years.'

'Probably indigestion. There was nae sign of deterioration around the heart. I'd bet it was the first – and the last – attack he'd ever had.'

'What about the sleeping draught? Was it a contributory factor?'

'Only to a good night's sleep. It's like your doctor said, a dose of cold water in his face and he'd have woken fast enough – if he hadna already been making his excuses at the Pearly Gates.'

'I see. Thanks. There's another one, I'm afraid.'

'Aye, I know. She's just arrived. You'll be wanting me to put this one to the top of my list as well nae doubt?'

'Please.'

'Fair enough. Oh, by the way, Chief Inspector, ma daughter's getting wed on the last Saturday of November.'

'Congratulations.' Jack said, uncertain whether this was the prelude to an invitation.

The doctor enlightened him. 'I merely mention it so that ye could mebbe avoid finding any bodies that particular day.'

With a click, the line went dead.

'Miss Emmett's off the hook then,' Sarah remarked when Jack relayed this information to her.

'Looks like it.'

'Do you want me to go round and tell her?'

'You're off duty. Anyway I have to go to Balaclava myself. Felonious has finally remembered what was missing from Donald's flat.'

He described the tie-clip to her and she responded in the same fashion as he had: 'I've seen that somewhere quite recently.'

'Me too. Trouble is I can't for the life of me think *where*.'

'No.' Sarah gnawed her lip in the way she had when she was puzzled. She'd swept her hair up so that some of it fell over her forehead, and plastered make-up and powder over the bruise, but it still gleamed purple-black in the harsh morning light.

'Does it hurt?' Jack asked.

'Only when I touch it.' She did just that, and winced. 'I'd rather stay on duty until this investigation is finished. If that's all right with you, sir?'

He was about to refuse, and knew in his heart that it was because of what Dunn had told him. He didn't know how much she'd heard but thought it best to tackle the issue head on rather than let the constraint between them become any deeper. 'I hear we're supposed to be having an affair.'

She retained her normal cool composure. 'Yes, I heard that too. Pity they forgot to tell us, it might have been more fun.'

'We could officially deny it.'

'They'll just say no smoke without fire. Best ignore them.'

'I hope it won't affect our working relationship.'

'I hope so too, sir. We've still got one, then?'

'Well, of course.'

'Good. It's straight round to Balaclava then, is it?'

Having been outmanoeuvred, Jack allowed himself to be led towards the Row.

It was a forlorn sight. The road outside the shops had been hastily filled in by the various gangs of workman trying to repair the damage done to the water, gas and electricity services by the sudden release of the underground spring into the surrounding subsoil. The street and pavement were now pitted with large, rubble-filled pot-holes, awaiting a visit from the council's repair gangs. Only the grocer's shop was open. The cafe and hairdresser's were both displaying closed signs; the jeweller's announced 'Business Closed' in large letters across its front window; the Emmetts' place had a hand-printed sign telling customers to call next door for repairs.

Jack headed into the grocer's, past the queue that stretched on to the pavement. Surprisingly, Rose was behind the counter.

'I'm just lending a hand,' she explained. 'It's Albert's busiest morning. Did you want me?'

'We're looking for Miss Emmett.'

'She's in the back room.' Rose lowered her voice. 'I think it's just beginning to sink in, about her dad.'

Lexie certainly looked like she was in the beginnings of shock. Huddled in a spare chair amongst Albert's stock, an old cardigan flung over her dance clothes and her hands thrust into the sleeves, she was shivering as if they were in the midst of winter. When the police stepped through the dividing curtain, she looked up and gave a small moan. 'I never meant it,' she whispered. 'Honest. I never wanted anyone to die.'

Impulsively Sarah stooped and took one of her hands. 'It's all right, we know you didn't. It was natural causes.'

'Eh?'

'Your father died of a heart attack, Miss Emmett. The doctor says the sleeping potion had nothing to do with it.'

'What?' Lexie seemed unable to understand what they were saying.

Rose had slipped through the curtain in time to hear what Sarah had said. 'I'm so glad. Did you hear that, Lexie? It wasn't you. Everything's going to be fine.'

She tried to take Lexie's other hand, but it was thrust back into the cardigan sleeve. 'He was really ill?' she said blankly. 'I never believed him. I fought he was puttin' it on.'

'He probably was for years,' Sarah reassured her. 'The doc said all those other pains were most likely indigestion. He just cried wolf once too often.'

Lexie's mind seemed to be wandering. 'Where did you go last night?' she demanded of Stamford. 'What about the dead woman?'

'Nothing for you to worry about, Miss Emmett. Now if you'll both excuse us, we have to speak to Mrs Donald.'

Raising his hat, he left the grocer's and found they were just in time to speak to Gwen. A taxi was waiting at the kerb, the driver thrusting two heavy cases into the luggage area.

'I'm going back to the farm,' Gwen said without preamble, finding herself face to face with Stamford. 'I've done my duty by Donald and buried him with respect. I'll leave the keys with Helen if you need them.' She extracted the shop keys and a letter from her pocket. 'There's people coming to take the stock and furniture.'

She was squaring up to him as if she expected an argument.

He didn't give her one. After all, he knew where to find her if he ever needed her. 'Just answer me two questions, Mrs Donald.'

'Yes.' One eye was on the taxi, no doubt calculating what this interrogation session was costing her.

'Why did you hold a birthday party for your husband this year?'

Perhaps it was the thought of the mounting fare that forced her into the truth. 'I wanted to see if I

430

could guess which one *she* was. I promised myself I'd never ask, do you see? But part of me needed to know.'

'Did it work?' Sarah asked.

'No. What else did you want to know, sir?'

Jack told her about the tie-clip. 'Why didn't you mention it was missing?'

'Because it weren't. Donald never had no gold tie-pin.'

She conceded that he could have made himself one whilst she was away. But she thought it highly unlikely. 'He liked making fancy jewellery for others, sir. But he never wore none himself.'

Sarah suggested it might have been a present.

'From *her* you mean? I suppose that's possible, miss. Although I'd not have thought any of this lot had money to be throwing away on gold. More likely she was hoping he'd slip her a few presents.' Drawing on her gloves, Gwen thumped each finger into place with a determined flat-handed chop between them. 'I'll be getting on then, sir, if that's all.'

'Have your daughters already left?'

'Aggie took 'em back last night. I wanted them out of London before the raids started. Goodbye, sir, miss.'

'She didn't even ask us to let her know when we found the killer,' Sarah remarked as the taxi bumped its cautious way round the corner.

'No. James Donald is well and truly buried as far as she's concerned. But he's still our business, so let's get on with it.'

He made for the cafe, but was stopped by the arrival of another taxi, the imperious blare of its horn obviously intended to attract his attention.

'Wait,' Helen Fortune called, climbing from the back

and scrabbling a handful of silver from one pocket whilst her other arm clasped a bundle of yellowing papers to her chest.

She was dressed in her ARP uniform of long overcoat and trousers. The metal helmet and gas mask hung at her side and a white silk scarf peeped from the top of her collar, the lack of colour emphasising her own pallor.

'I was coming to see you as soon as I'd changed,' she said, addressing Stamford directly and ignoring Sarah once more.

'I didn't think you were on duty until tomorrow. Every fourth night, isn't it?'

'One of the others was sick. I changed shifts with her.' She offered him the papers. 'I went round to the solicitor's office as soon as I finished my shift. Here. The original copies of the leases for the other shops.'

'Do I need them?'

'If you'll read them, Chief Inspector, you'll see that all the leases expire at the end of this year. I don't need to murder my tenants. All I've got to do is wait a couple of months and the property reverts to me.'

He still hadn't taken the papers, so she thrust them at his chest. 'Now, if you'll excuse me, I must open up. Good morning, Lexie.'

'Morning.' Huddled in her cardigan, Lexie had crept like a ghost on to the pavement. One of the women in the queue called over to ask her if she knew whether the cafe was opening today.

'What? I don't know. I suppose so. I'll go knock Maria up.'

'No, don't do that, Miss Emmett.' Stamford took her forearm, pulling her out of the queue's earshot.

'The doctor's given her something to make her sleep. There's a WPC sitting with her.'

Lexie tried to focus on him. 'A policewoman? Why? What's 'appened?'

There had been no one around to see the comings and goings of the police cars in the early hours. So the next death to hit the little Row had gone unnoticed. Until now.

Stamford said quietly: 'I'm afraid her sister is dead. Josepha's body was found in the churchyard in Dale Road late last night.'

Lexie continued to stare blankly for a few seconds. Then she vomited violently into the gutter.

Chapter 25

Jeannie let them in and explained that the sleeping draught didn't seem to have worked.

'She drifts in and out. One minute she's asleep, next she wants to get up and scrub the cafe floor. Tell you the truth, I don't think she's quite certain whether it's Saturday or half past two most of the time, if you see what I mean, sir.'

'Is she awake now?'

'She's in her sister's room. I wasn't sure whether she was allowed or not. But every time I try and stop her, she gets hysterical. I've had to fetch her a couple of whacks already to calm her down.'

'Perhaps I'd better get up there while she's still got all her teeth left,' Sarah remarked drily.

'I never hit her that hard, Sarge,' Jeannie started to protest, then realised she was being teased. 'I was going to make her some tea. Do you think it's all right to use her rations for me?'

Stamford pointed out that it was a cafe. He passed over some change. 'Here, put the price of three cuppas in the till.'

All the flats over the shops were built on the same design. Once again they mounted the second staircase and found themselves flanked by two doors. The left-hand one was partially open. Stamford touched his fingertips to the wood and the door swung open on unoiled hinges.

Here was one Balaclava death at least that had aroused grief, anger and a sense of hopeless loss. All those emotions were lurking in Maria's raw-rimmed eyes, the dark orbs swimming with yet more unshed tears.

To give her time to collect herself, Stamford examined the room. The bed, wardrobe and dressing table were solid, dark mahogany, expensive in their day, but now scuffed and scratched. They looked like they'd been obtained as odd pieces from a secondhand dealer.

Josepha had stamped her own personality on the room. Pictures of film stars had been cut from magazines and stuck in a collage over the wall by her bed. The other walls held crudely framed views of sunny landscapes: golden flowers growing thickly over bleached soil, whitewashed churches, rocky coves where cream sea-horses rode a sea of an impossible shade of green.

Jack touched one. 'Malta?'

Maria was sitting on the dressing table stool, clutching something tightly to her breast and rocking back and forth. 'Some,' she sobbed. 'Some, they just look like Malta. But it don't matter, she say looking at them make her feel warm.'

She started to rock with more determination.

Jack completed his visual examination of the room. The bedspread was crocheted, worn but clean, as was the rag rug on the floor. The sight of several dolls propped against the pillow caused a lump to form in his throat which he hastily swallowed with his back to the two women.

He moved on to the dressing table; the surface was

covered with a fine dusting of face powder which had spilled from a partially open box. More cheap cosmetics: cold cream, lipsticks, half-used perfumes and sticky bottles of nail-varnish were huddled in forlorn groups.

'She say men give them her, as presents,' Maria sniffed. 'But it not true. She take money from till, buy them herself at the market.'

She'd relaxed sufficiently for them to see that the object in her arms was another doll; the painted features on its rag face practically worn away and the seamed head suffering from partial baldness.

Sarah touched the doll's fat, pink limb. 'Her favourite?'

Maria nodded vigorously. 'Ever since she little girl.' She gulped back more unshed tears. 'I tried to be like a mama to her, you know? I want us to be friends. One day, I think, we are a proper family. We not got anyone else; no mamas, no grandmamas and no papa; 'cos papa he not coming back; I know soon as I read his note, he not coming, but we got each other, just each other, and now I got nobody . . .' Her words were starting to garble together as she let everything out in one breathless rush. 'You catch him, you punish him the one who done this thing, you promise?'

'We promise,' Jack said, taking a seat on the bed. 'But we need your help. Tell us where Josepha went last night.'

'To the pub, she say. But perhaps not. Sometimes she say she going to dance-hall or pub, and then she go to shelter instead. I know. I follow her.'

'Why would she do that?'

Maria pulled out a crumpled hankie and scrubbed

at her face. 'To upset me. She know I don't like her doing those things.'

'What time did she go out last night?'

'Late. Half nine o'clock may be.'

'Did she have a date?'

'She say so. But she lie about that too. Always pretending the men chase her.'

'Do you know which pub? Did you follow her?'

'No. I am tired, I have to clean up after the firemen.'

Sarah put in, 'What about the man? Was it a steady boyfriend?'

'None of her men steady. All very unsteady. Bad jobs, no money. No good.'

'No, I meant, was it someone she'd been out with before?'

Maria spread her hands in a Gallic shrug. Josepha hadn't discussed her love life with her sister except as a means to irritate her.

After Josepha had flounced out despite her sister's protests, Maria had gone to bed. For several hours she'd tossed and turned, caught in that half-land between waking and sleeping. 'Sometimes the bombs sound near, and sometimes I think I hear Josepha coming in. Soon as I go to sleep, I wake up again. Then, then . . .' Her mouth trembled and the look she flashed at Stamford was one of accusation. Then, she wanted to say, you came and destroyed my world.

In response to a light scrabbling at the door, Sarah pulled it open and took the tray from Jeannie.

Maria snorted. 'Tea. Always tea. You feel faint, have a cuppa. You just had a baby, have a cuppa. Someone just kill your sister, never mind, have a cuppa.'

Stamford suggested they could move into the kitchen.

'No chairs. We not sit in there. It is storeroom, for food for the cafe. If you like we go into parlour room.'

'The parlour room' was, like so many other rooms in these flats and houses, crammed with heavy furniture from another age. It was in slightly better condition than the bedroom bits and pieces, with a polished sheen and matching patterns in its carving, suggesting that perhaps it might have been left by the previous tenant.

Here again there had been an attempt to bring a touch of the Mediterranean to north London. A fine lace tablecloth had been flung over the table, more lace adorned the backs of the chairs and protected the sideboard's surface from the knick-knacks the departed sea cook had left behind: a ship in a bottle, a scrubbed conch-shell, poker work burnt into scraps of driftwood and several vases painted in crude primary colours. Across the walls, brightly woven fringed silk shawls had been pinned like giant butterflies around a silver-gilt crucifix.

'Pretty,' Sarah remarked.

Despite her loss, a tinge of pleasure dimpled at Maria's full mouth. 'We like. Downstairs we make like proper English cafe, but up here is our home. We make it as we like it.' She ran a critical eye over the room, as if seeing it for the first time. 'It look better in the summer. In the summer, we have flowers, lots of flowers. Josepha she likes, liked . . .'

She gagged on the last words. Sarah reached across and squeezed one of the brown hands.

'I go to church,' Maria said, thrusting back her chair

decisively. 'Light a candle for Josepha and pray for you to find this man.'

Opening the sideboard drawer, she scrabbled out a black, lace mantilla, and flicked it over her head.

'I'll get the WPC to, er . . .' Stamford's voice died away.

'Donald's funeral,' Sarah breathed, touching one finger to the lace.

'What you talking about?' Maria's dark eyes swivelled in bewilderment between Jack and Sarah.

Stamford answered her. 'This scarf, your sister wore one like it to James Donald's funeral yesterday. It was secured by a gold pin with her initial in the centre. Do you remember?'

'Sure. Why?'

'Do you know where the pin came from?'

'No. I never see before. Market may be.'

'A solid gold pin?'

'Gold. No. Just polished brass. How could Josepha afford gold?'

'I don't think she bought it. I think she took it. From James Donald's flat the morning after his murder.'

'Steal! No! My sister is not a thief.'

Sarah had propped her elbows on the table and cupped her chin on her linked fingers, virtually ignoring the last interchange between Maria and her boss. Now she said abruptly, 'Have you got any iodine in the cafe, Miss Browne?'

'Iodine? You cut yourself?'

Maria had once again lost track of the conversation. But Jack flicked his sergeant an imperceptible nod of approval; he was following her reasoning, remembering, as she plainly had, the iodine bottle that had been out of place in the Donald's kitchen. 'The morning we came to examine Donald's body, your sister was standing outside your backyard. She had a large bruise on her forehead.'

'We fight,' Maria said resignedly.

'So we gathered. What about the iodine. Do you have a bottle?'

'We use it all. Weeks ago. Lots of fights,' she admitted.

'But that morning, your sister had put iodine on her bruises. We could smell it quite strongly. Now where would she go to get it?'

Maria agreed that their nearest neighbour was the logical place. 'But only for iodine,' she said hotly, 'not to steal.'

Stamford said placatingly, 'I don't suppose it was her intention to steal the pin. I suspect she went in, found the flat apparently empty, and helped herself to the iodine and the pin. Just to try on like she did with the other jewellery. She probably intended to give it back as soon as she saw James moving around.'

'But instead she saw us,' Sarah finished. 'And discovered James had been murdered. It must have given her a devil of a shock. Hang on though,' she protested, finding a flaw in the scenario they'd been building up. 'She wore it to Donald's funeral. And she didn't know Gwen wouldn't recognise it.'

'Most likely that was the idea. As Miss Browne says, her sister wasn't a thief.' He earned a warm smile from Maria for this statement. 'Remember the workman's ten bob? I think this was the same thing. If Gwen had claimed the pin, Josepha would have passed it off as a loan and handed it over at once. But since Mrs Donald didn't, I suppose Josepha reasoned she had a right to keep it.'

'Is the pin here now, Maria?' Sarah enquired.

They got the reply they were both expecting. Josepha had been wearing it in her hair when she'd gone out last night.

An unspoken question flashed from Sarah's blue eyes and was answered by a flicker of Stamford's brown ones: no, the pin hadn't been on the body when he examined it.

'Let's get back to the station,' he suggested quietly. 'They should have finished the ground search by now.'

Sarah nodded. After a quick word with Jeannie, she followed Stamford out on the pavement. It was she who vocalised what they were both thinking. 'The funeral was the first time Maria had seen the pin, so it was probably the first time Josepha had worn it in public. Which means that the murderer was almost certainly at James Donald's funeral.'

'And realised they had to retrieve the pin and silence Josepha before she told anyone where, and when, she'd "found" it. So the chances are, it is somehow traceable to whoever gave it to James.'

'Perhaps she paid by cheque? Or had it made up specially?'

'Or had it made for someone else originally,' Stamford postulated reluctantly. He didn't like where the conversation was leading, but his professional instincts over-rode his distaste at the thought of Helen being involved with Donald's murder. Or was it the thought of Helen being involved with Donald?

Taking Sarah's elbow, he steered her away from

Balaclava Row. 'Let's walk. It can't have been Mrs Goodwin or Miss Emmett at the churchyard last night,' he said, thinking aloud, 'because they have an alibi for the time.'

'Do they? What?'

'Me. Eileen dragged me along to the shelter dance. They were both there too.'

'I hope you enjoyed yourself, sir.'

'My back will be stiff for a week.'

'That good?'

Jack flicked an exasperated grin down at her. 'No it wasn't. I reckon whoever designed the public shelters has a share in a patent lumbago remedy.'

'It could have been Miss Fortune though, couldn't it? I mean she was on ARP duty last night.'

'Just like she was on the night Donald was murdered.'

'Yes. And the boy's description could have fitted her: trousers, long overcoat, short dark hair.'

'I don't recall you being at the witnesses' questioning, Sergeant.'

Sarah was relieved that the 'Sergeant' was accompanied by an amused glance. It made it easier to admit she'd scanned through the file notes before he came in that morning.

Stamford pointed out it was unlikely that Josepha would have made a date with Miss Fortune.

'Depends what the date was for. Perhaps she promised her money to keep quiet.'

They'd reached the end of the road, but the bang of a shutting door behind them caused them both to turn back. Maria and the WPC had just emerged on to the pavement. The sound of the slamming cafe door had attracted Lexie and Albert who both hurried across to the speak to the Maltese woman.

'I told Jeannie to go with Maria to the church,' Sarah said. 'Then to get one of the WVS ladies to sit with her when they get back if supervision is still necessary.'

'Fair enough. Let's get back. You can check out Miss Fortune's movements with the ARP Post; discreetly please. And I'll go through whatever they've found in the ground search.'

They left Balaclava Row behind, leaving Albert and Lexie to exclaim and sympathise over Maria.

'It's 'orrible, ain't it,' Albert bemoaned. His usual ruddy-faced good humour had disappeared; he seemed to have aged ten years overnight. 'All these people going. I mean we all been here for years and now everyone's being killed. What's happening to the place?'

Maria gave him a hug. 'Don't be scared, Albert. Everything be all right, you see.'

'I should be saying that to you, love,' Albert apologised. He shook his shaggy head sadly and said, half to himself, 'I'll not be sorry to leave. This ain't the street it once was.'

Strangely enough, his fears seemed to give Maria strength. She promised to say a prayer for him. 'And I'll light a candle for poor James, and your papa too, Lexie.'

'Probably got all the heat he needs where he is,' Lexie muttered, showing a flash of her old rebelliousness, once Maria and Jeannie were out of earshot.

'No call for that, Lexie. He is dead, when all's said

and done,' Albert remonstrated. 'He can't do you no 'arm now.'

'He's never done me much good eiver, 'as he? Look at this. Me inheritance.' She gestured at the closed shop. 'I can't even carry on the business 'cos 'e'd never trust me enough to teach me 'ow to do a proper 'eel and sole. Polishing, cooking, cleaning and washing that's all I was good for and now I ain't got . . . Oh blimey, wha' you doing 'ere?'

Her voice rose in a disbelieving shriek. Startled, Albert glanced over his shoulder.

'Hello, Albert. Good to see you again.'

Albert took the proffered hand instinctively. Balancing on the balls of his feet, he leant closer to the man shaking it, staring into the tanned face. Slowly, recognition dawned. 'Alan! It's Alan ain't it? Look at this, Lexie, it's Alan Milligan, after all these years. You remember, don't you? Used to be Fred and Alice's boy.'

Lexie continued to stand with her mouth hanging open.

'Fred and Alice are away,' Albert continued. 'Gone down to her mum in Cornwall, they'll be gutted to have missed you.' Whilst he was talking, Albert had been trying to draw Alan towards the grocer's shop. Alan stood his ground.

'I know. They wrote me. It's Lexie I want to speak to. I'll be in to say hello in a minute, Albert.'

'Course. I'll tell Rose. She'll be pleased to hear . . . No come to think of it, she ain't never met you. Still she'll want to meet you, I'm sure I . . .' His voice died away as he thrust past his customers and disappeared into the shop.

'Let's go in, shall we?' Alan said, pushing the stunned Lexie towards her own front door.

She allowed herself to be led past the racks of finished shoes and boots, through the counter flap and into her dad's workroom with its strong scents of leather, polish, stale feet and pungent rolling tobacco. He'd have taken her upstairs, but she seized the workbench and hung on. 'No.'

'What's up?'

'You know damn well what's up, Alan Milligan. That!'

A vicious jab caught Alan square in the middle of his uniform jacket with its three white stripes.

'Oh that. Yeah, well, I figured if I was going to turn myself in, might as well be properly turned out. I brought Fred's stuff back.' He swung the knotted bundle on to the bench. 'Forgot his spade though. Left it up the pub. I had a wash and brush up up the public lav. Had to use me knife to shave with.' He felt his jaw. 'It wouldn't pass parade. Couldn't borrow your dad's razor could I, Lexie?'

'Only,' Lexie hissed between clenched teeth, 'if you promise to cut yer flaming throat with it. Why didn't ya *tell* me?'

'Tell you what?'

Lexie gestured up and down his uniformed figure; from the gleaming boots to the red cap. 'That you were a military copper.'

'Thought Alice would have mentioned it.'

'Oh no ya didn't. Yer thought I wouldn't 'elp yer if I knew I was getting involved with the law. Yer a flaming *rat*, Alan Milligan. When I fink 'ow I didn't sleep a wink last night after I 'eard they'd found a woman done in up St Martin's I could take a knife to yer meself, you, you . . .' Lexie had led a sheltered life; her vocabulary of expletives was exhausted.

It gave Alan a chance to cut in. 'It weren't Connie, honest, Lexie. I walked her home.'

'I know it weren't. It was Josepha.'

'What, the goodlooker from the cafe?'

'Yes.'

'The poor little sweetheart. Who did it?'

'Dunno. Don't reckon the police do yet.' She slumped on her father's workstool, twisting shaven scraps of leather into bows. Not meeting his eye, she said, 'I thought you'd done for yer missus, Alan. I thought I'd 'elped yer. Getting 'er to the pub and all. Sorry.'

'No need to be sorry. You were half right. I weren't just planning a cosy chat.' Hitching up his trouser leg, he extracted the knife. 'I was going to shave her hair off. It's what they used to do with whores.'

'Gawd! Yer didn't, did yer?'

'No. I took her up that church. Got her down and was just going to start chopping, and you know what she said?'

'Help?' It was what Lexie herself would have said. Or screamed more like.

'Nope. She said, "I got to be back by twelve to rub salve on the baby's gums. He won't let no one but me touch them, the poor little mite." '

Suddenly the whole absurdity of the situation had struck him. The possibility of disfigurement was of less importance to Connie than her baby's teething problems. 'I know it sounds daft, but I just didn't care no more. I mean I'd been sitting up in that flat thinking about what I was going to do to her for days, and now it was like she was a stranger.' It had come to him, kneeling on that damp earth, deep in the shadow of the church, that he had no feelings at all for this woman. That he hadn't for a long time. It was only the fact that she was 'his woman' and she'd made a fool of him that had made him chase after her.

'So what happened?'

'I pulled her up, brushed her down, walked her 'ome, and told her I'd be divorcing her soon as I get the rest of my life sorted out.'

'And 'ow you planning to do that?'

'Turn meself in. Only way to do it.' With the withering of his resentment against Connie had come a clear realisation that he didn't want to spend the rest of his life as a fugitive. 'That's no kind of life, Lexie. I seen blokes who've tried it for a few months. You give up everything: your name, your past, your self respect. And what you get in return? A crick in your neck from always looking over your shoulder that's what.'

'And what about me?' Lexie demanded hotly. 'You said yerself, it's aiding an' abetting a deserter.'

'Don't worry, Carrots, I'll keep you out of it. I'll say I've been sleeping rough in a bombed-out place.'

'What you think they'll do to yer?'

Alan shrugged. 'Depends on whether I done for Tolly.'

'Who's Tolly?'

'Bloke I hit.'

'Oh. I forgot him. Are you sure he was dead?'

'I didn't exactly hang around to check his pulse but his head hit the step with a real crack and I couldn't hear no breathing.'

'Maybe it would be better then if yer . . . Oh damn.'
The front-door bell jangled loudly. 'I forgot to lock up
behind us.'

'No matter. Might as well serve 'em now you're
here.'

'I suppose. I'll lock up again soon as I've got rid of
whoever this is. Stay out of sight 'til then.'

Lexie slouched reluctantly into the shop.

'I know it says to go next door, ducks,' the customer
said, 'but they said you was round here, so I took the
liberty. 'Ope I ain't intruding on yer grief and sorrow,
it's me ole man's second best pair, please.'

The boots on the ticket hadn't been done, and she
had to go back into the workroom and sort amongst
the stack awaiting Frank's attention to find them. By
the time she returned to the shop, several other
customers had been redirected by Albert and she was
kept busy, wrapping, sorting, taking money and
fielding questions about her father. The gush of water
gurgling down her drainpipes announced that Alan
had found her dad's razor.

The brief rush finally abated. She was just about
to put the bolt on again and march upstairs to give
Alan a few more choice pieces of her mind when the
door was roughly thrust back, nearly knocking her
off her feet.

'Sorry, miss,' the young WPC apologised. 'Didn't
see you behind there.'

'No harm done,' Lexie said quickly. 'I'm just closing.
Because of me dad.' Go away, she prayed silently,
before Alan comes down.

'You wouldn't have any tins of polish, would you?'
Jeannie pleaded. 'I can't go on parade with dirty shoes

and the place near me lodgings hasn't had a delivery this month.'

'What colour?'

'Black. But if you got any others, I'll take a tin of them too.'

Lexie scooped up all her half-used tins. 'Here. 'Ave the lot. I ain't got no use for 'em any more.'

'Thanks! I shouldn't really,' Jeannie admitted, cramming her unexpected windfall into her gas mask case before anyone else came in.

'How's Maria?'

'A little better. The priest from the church came back with us. He's stopping with her for a while.'

'I'll pop round la'er then. Sorry, mister, we're closed ... Oh, it's you.'

The military police sergeant beamed and wished them both a very good day. 'Sorry to have missed you at the shelter, Miss Lexie. Got these for you.'

Amazingly, he'd managed to get a bunch of chrysanthemums from somewhere.

'Er. Thanks. A lot.' Coming round the counter, Lexie tried to edge them both back towards the door. She was sure she'd heard the creak of the stairtreads leading from the flat.

'Took me a while to find out where you're billeted. You ain't a regular up the shelter, are you?' the MP said, showing no signs of wanting to be edged. And since he was between Jeannie and the door, she couldn't get out either.

'No. Just went to the dance. Me friend Rose wanted a bit of company.'

'That would be the blonde young lady, would it? Looked a bit peaky. Hope she's feeling better.'

450

'Fine. She's next door. In the grocer's.' Inspiration struck Lexie. 'Why don't you go say hello. 'Spect she'd be pleased to see yer.' Reaching round him, she opened the street door. The bell jangled noisily once more.

Reaching back with the flat of his hand, the sergeant shut it again. 'Pay me respects in a minute. Talking of neighbours, I hear yours that way,' he indicated the wall with a jerk of his beefy thumb, 'is a fish and chip shop.'

'It's closed. Been empty for months.'

'So I see. Never know it was a chip shop to look at it, would you? What with them shutters over the window and just the name "Weller's" over the top.'

'It used to have a big fish sign hanging outside, didn't it?' Jeannie chipped in. 'I remember me mum used to bring me up here to visit one of me aunties. We used to queue up for twopenny worth and pickled onions. Me bruvver was always trying to jump up and head that sign.'

'It came down. Years ago,' Lexie garbled. Will you both *GO*, her mind screamed.

She wondered whether she dare have a good old-fashioned bout of hysterics. A bit of delayed shock and remorse over her dad perhaps. Bad enough for these two to cart her round to the local first aid station. Trouble was, if Alan heard her screaming her head off, he might come charging down to the rescue.

Alan solved her problem by strolling casually through from the back, rubbing a satisfied hand over a smooth chin. He came to an abrupt stop when he saw three figures standing in the shop. 'I thought I heard the door bell go.'

'This is, er . . .' Lexie had run out of lies. She sought

desperately for a made-up name, found her imagination had deserted, and might have introduced him as 'Fred Astaire' if the other MP hadn't said quietly, 'Hello, Alan. I've worn out a fair bit of boot leather looking for you, mate. Pity you never mentioned them old pals of yours was called "Weller".'

'Tolly. Blimey, are you a sight for sore eyes. I thought I'd done for you.'

'Tolly!' Lexie exploded. 'You mean this is the bloke yer 'it? The one you reckoned had kicked the bucket?'

Tolly gave her a familiar squeeze. 'What him! See me off? That'll be the day!'

All the worrying she'd been doing recently at the thought of Alan, or her, or both of them, ending up in prison, swept in a great wave over Lexie. And now it seemed his supposed victim had been following her all over Kentish Town. 'You're flaming useless, Alan Milligan. I dunno 'ow you ever made sergeant.'

'It's a mystery to us all, Miss Lexie. 'Specially since he's done it twice.'

'Twice?'

'Got himself reduced to the ranks. They tend to do that if you take a swing out of turn.' Tolly rubbed a reminiscent hand over the portion of his face that had taken the brunt of Alan's right hook.

'Are you here to make an arrest, Sergeant?'

They'd all temporarily forgotten Jeannie and her interruption, like her presence, was less than welcome.

'An arrest, miss? Course I'm not. I just come to give Alan this.' He handed over a folded slip of paper.

Alan twisted it tentatively. 'What is it?'

'Why your leave chit, of course, man! Ten lovely

days of freedom. Lucky you didn't get stopped without it.'

'Ten days,' Jeannie repeated. 'Blimey! You lot live well, don't you? My brother's in the engineers and he thought he was doing well getting a seven-day pass.'

'That's the old man for you, miss,' Tolly said, allowing one arm to creep casually round Lexie's waist again. 'Generous to a fault. If Milligan wants to use up ten days' leave all at once, knowing full well it could be years before his application can be considered again, he said to me, then I shall not stand in his way. Tell him to go with my blessing, the old boy said. Or words to them effect. So he signs off the chit; ten days starting twelve hundred hours on the seventeenth.'

'What!' Alan scanned the crumpled scrap. 'But this means that . . .'

'That you're due back twelve hundred hours tomorrow,' Tolly finished for him. 'Still all good things got to come to an end, eh? Nine days in London. Bet you've had a great time; dancing, drinking, pictures, bit of romancing, eh?'

'You bastard,' Alan hissed. 'I bet you found the Wellers' place days ago.'

'Language, Al. Ladies present.'

'This one has to go,' Jeannie said, catching sight of her watch. 'Pleased to have met you both.'

'And you, miss,' Tolly called over the dancing bell. He risked another squeeze of Lexie's waist since she hadn't seemed to mind the last one. 'So there's just time for us to have a nice cosy supper somewhere, Miss Lexie, before me and Alan makes an early start in the morning. I don't think we should ask him to join us, do you? I daresay he's already had all the excitement he could want on this leave.'

Which may have been true. But they were both destined to share a bit more before they left Balaclava Row for good.

Chapter 26

'Why 'ave I gotta go 'ome? The old cow don' want me.'

'Don't call your grandmother names please, Nafnel. It's not very nice. Besides you can only stay here if she says it's all right. She is your legal guardian.'

Nafnel pulled a face that made it clear what he thought of his grandmother's guardianship. He was sitting on the counter, drumming his heels against the wooden frontpiece. The socks Eileen had provided had collapsed over his new boots, displaying his skinny calves and scarred knees and there were still patches of rash peeking from his collar and spread around his mouth.

But, all in all, Rose decided complacently, he was definitely a fitter and healthier child than the one she'd found in Riley Street infants – how long ago? She took a mental count backwards. It was a shock to realise it was only five days. Last week she'd been a grocer's assistant with no ties in the world beyond a family she was avoiding; now she was a teacher, in imminent danger of becoming a foster mum, and she and Pat were . . . Were what?

She paused in her counting of the shop takings, to think about it. She liked Pat. Always had since they'd been at Riley Street together. She didn't feel the same overwhelming desire that she'd felt for Peter. But look where that had got her? Pat made her feel safe and comfortable. Perhaps that would be enough for now?

Nafnel's attempts to drum out the heels of his boots brought her wandering mind back to the present.

'Don't do that, Naf—, I mean "Nathaniel". You'll scuff the wood. Now be a good boy, just go back to the house and let your gran see you're safe, then you can come back here for tea. I'll cook it while you're gone.'

Nafnel slid to the floor with a clatter. 'Wha' ya call me that for?' he demanded suspiciously.

Losing her count for the third time, Rose said, 'Call you what?'

'That Nafanull.'

'Na-than-i-el,' Rose enunciated clearly. 'It's your proper name. I'll show you how to write it when you get back. Go along now please. Before the sirens go. Have you still got those labels I gave you?'

Delving in his pocket, Nafnel displayed a large luggage label pinned securely to the lining. Another was on a cord around his neck, pushed out of sight inside his shirt. Both had his name printed on in block capitals and the address of Rose's flat. At least now, if he was injured in the street, the hospital or first aid station would contact her. For the first time, Rose could appreciate the terrible dilemma facing mothers caught in the Blitz. Half of her wanted to arrange for Nafnel's evacuation to a safer area, and the other half knew she'd worry even more if he was far away, out of her sight and at the mercy of whoever the billeting officer could cajole into taking him.

She brought her speculation to an abrupt stop; she was running ahead of herself again. There was still the problem of his grandmother to surmount. 'Stop dawdling now, Nafnel, and get along,' she said sharply. 'I'll have the tea ready when you come back.'

'What you cookin'?' Nafnel enquired, still looking for excuses to delay his departure. He knew very well that if the sirens went whilst he was still in the shop, she wouldn't let him go outside.

'Anything you like,' Albert said, coming through from the back, and waving an expansive hand round his shelves. 'Just take what you want, love. No need to put anything in the till.'

'I couldn't do that, Albert. The takings are down again. You can't afford to give food away.'

'We lost trade on account of the flood. But it don't really matter no more, love. I been meaning to say, would you go through the orders. Cancel any we ain't had delivered yet.'

Rose raised startled eyes to his face. 'So soon?'

'I reckon so. I've 'ad a word with Helen and she's happy for me to go soon as I like. And our Elsie wrote off after a cottage in the paper; got a bit of a garden and room for a few chickens or a pig may be. It'll see us out anyway. I can't be doing with any more of these forms and coupons and allocations.'

Rose understood. The recent spate of deaths in Balaclava Row had hit Albert harder than the rest of them; perhaps because he was so much older and more aware of his mortality. 'Oh, Albert,' she whispered, wiping away the tears stinging her eyes, 'I'm going to miss you.'

He returned her bear hug with a clumsy squeeze. 'Me too, love. But you can come visit. And it ain't as if you need old Albert no more. You got yourself a good job there, and a decent young man. And I want you to have this.'

'This' was a bundle of notes.

She drew off the restraining rubber band and unfolded ten five-pound notes. 'Albert, I can't.'

Albert patted her hand. 'Yes, you can. You'll likely need to get yourself some bits and pieces. You should buy a winter coat; you ain't got natural padding like some of us.' He slapped his huge stomach complacently. 'Now I'd best be getting home before Elsie starts fretting. I wish you'd come with me, love. I don't like leaving you alone. This place ain't safe no more. You could bring the young 'un.'

'There's no need, Albert,' Rose said, brushing away the tears and trying to match his matter-of-fact manner. 'It's perfectly safe. I doubt if whoever killed poor James is going to come back and smother me. And Frank died of natural causes.'

'There was Josepha too.'

'That was miles away. Now go on,' she urged, handing him the cash satchel. 'Get this in the night safe and get on home. And don't go fretting about me. I'll probably ask Maria and Lexie to come round for the evening if that soldier friend of hers has gone. And maybe Helen and Matt too. May I really take enough to cook for everybody? I won't touch the rationed foods.'

'Take whatever you like,' Albert agreed eagerly, seizing tins at random and pushing them into her arms. Putting them back on the counter, she steered him out of door and waited until he was wobbling precariously around the pot-holes on his ancient bicycle before turning her attention to Nafnel.

'*Go.* Right now. Or I'm not cooking you anything.'

'She'll most likely be out,' he suggested, placing one

foot behind the other and moving backwards at a snail's pace. 'She were when yer made me go this mornin'.'

'You're still to go and see.'

Defeated, Nafnel turned around and slouched away, his hands thrust into his pockets. He passed that soppy stick of a girl they paid to scrub out the shop and heard Rose calling back to her that she was just going next door for a minute and then he reached the corner and was distracted by the sight of a donkey cart standing against the kerb.

It seemed to be full of food, which was always an abiding interest to him, so he wandered closer and poked around until a woman with a white armband decorated with a red cross came out and explained they were collecting for food parcels for prisoners of war.

'That's soldiers and sailors and airmen who've been captured by the nasty Germans and put in prison,' she explained. 'Do you think your mummy would like to give us a tin for the poor prisoners?'

'Shouldn't fink so, miss. She got 'erself killed, the silly cow.'

'Oh you poor mite. I expect you and Daddy miss her terribly, don't you?'

This was a tough question for Nafnel. He quite missed his mum, whom he had loved in an uncritical, careless fashion, much as she'd loved him. But he had no idea whether 'Daddy' missed her or not. Presumably not, otherwise he could have come visiting all that time before she got herself blown up.

He temporised by mumbling that he didn't know where his dad was.

'Oh dear. Is he a soldier?'

His mum had never told him. Thinking about it, he decided what he'd like his dad to be and informed the nosy woman that he was a fireman.

'Well that's a very brave thing to be,' she assured him. 'Here, I don't suppose anyone will mind.' Delving into the boxes on the cart, she found a small bar of chocolate, gave it to him, planted a wet kiss on his head and told him she'd pray for his mother.

'Ta, miss.' He didn't think praying for his mum would do much good now. The Sally Army major had done that quite often. But it had never made any difference that he could see. And whatever it was she wasn't supposed to have done, he expected God would have found out about it by now.

Thinking about the Salvation Army reminded him of their band. He'd quite enjoyed all the marching and singing behind them on Sunday mornings.

Increasing his pace to a skip and hop he tried out a few lines:

'Onward Christian soldiers, marchin' as ter war
Wiv the Tory bastards picking off the bleedin' poor.'

Fortunately, his articulation was poor enough to obscure the words and leave passers-by to smile indulgently at the tune.

The nearer he got to Warden Road, the faster he ran. As soon as he'd stuck his head in *her* room, he was going back to miss's. He found Rose's insistence that his grandmother would want to know where he was difficult to understand. Even his mum hadn't shown much interest, providing he came in for meals occasionally. And his gran didn't even want him to do that; meals for her consisted of chips with a bit of fish or meat pie if she had any cash left after the boozer. He'd been forced to prowl the foul-smelling room waiting for his chance to snatch a handful and dart away before her back-hand could land on his head.

Taking the torch Pat had bought him from his pocket, he made his way up the unlit staircase of the lodging house, playing 'big game hunter' with the shadows and a collection of cats that always seemed to be prowling the stairs and landings until he came to the greasy door handle of Ma's room.

The door slammed behind him with a rush of expelling air.

'So, yer back are yer?'

Ma Starkey leant her back to the door. 'Where yer bin?'

'Round the shop. Boozer run out, 'as it?'

'Don' you cheek me, you little . . .' Ma swung a vague clout in the direction of her nearest and dearest. Halfway through the movement, she seemed to forget where it was going, and looked at the hand attached to the end of her returning arm as if seeing it for the first.

Nafnel recognised the mood; she'd already had a skinful. Which meant that at least she wouldn't be violent. It was only when she hadn't had enough, and didn't know where the rest was coming from, that she tended to lash out.

Ma was now working the light switch.

'They turned it off after somebody bust in the meter, remember?'

'Bassterrds,' Ma slurred.

Pushing the tattered blanket harder against the nails around the window, Nafnel located a box of matches amongst the debris on the table and lit a stub of candle. It revealed an empty bottle of Gilbey's gin and another partially full one.

'Good boy.' Lurching across the rubbish-strewn floor, Ma gave him a hug. 'You're a good lad. My own flesh and blood. All I got.'

'Sod off.' Nafnel wriggled vigorously. 'Where'd you get the money for the booze?'

'Shops.' Taking a crushed packet of Players from her pocket, she stuck one to her cracked lower lip and dipped unsteadily to the candle. The flame wavered and flared in response to her gin-laden breath.

'You bin nicking?' Nafnel asked.

'Course I ain't. Nice fing to say about yer old granny, I must say. Went up that shop of yourn last night.'

'There weren't nobody there. We went down the shelter. They 'ad a dance.'

Ma wasn't really interested in the social calendar of Kentish Town. Her addled brain could only follow one line of thought at a time. Last night she'd gone to Balaclava as Albert had suggested. Her sense of outrage at discovering that Rose wasn't going to give her the promised money had been assuaged by a man pulling her away from the shop door and instructing her to stop her hollering before she woke the Row up. A crisp five-pound note had accompanied the brusque words.

'I met a gentleman,' she said, straightening up. For

an instant the raddled lines of her face smoothed, and
the younger, prettier girl who'd attracted plenty of
gentlemen years ago was vaguely aware of what
she'd become, then the moment passed. 'He gave
me a present. I like gentlemen. Glad you was a
boy. Couldn't be doing wiv a granddaughter. Grow
up into a nasty, ungrateful little slut like that
daughter of mine. You'll always stay wiv yer old gran,
won't yer?'

'No. I'm goin' back to the shop. Only come 'cos miss
said I 'ad too. See ya.'

'You come back 'ere. Yer'll stay if I say yer will.'

He was jerked back by the shirt neck and flung on
to his bottom. Ma turned the key in the lock and
dropped it into her pocket.

'Give us that.'

She won the struggle. Alcohol had given her a
temporary strength whilst it deadened the pain from
Nafnel's lashing boots.

'Go 'sleep,' she mumbled. Collecting the partially
full gin bottle and the candle, she flopped on to the
mattress, clutching the first and placing the saucer
containing the light on the floor.

Nafnel slid to the floor, clasping his legs and resting
his chin on his scarred knees. In a few minutes she'd
be sound asleep and he could get the key back.

But for once Ma seemed in no hurry to slip into the
comatose state that usually followed one of her binges.
Murmuring low protests, she tossed restlessly on the
crumpled bed. Occasionally, a louder groan was
accompanied by a convulsive spasm that arched her
shoulders back into the mattress and sent another
splash of alcohol over her clothes and bedding.

Nafnel bit his lip and stirred restlessly. He was growing hungrier. Why couldn't she get a move on and go to sleep.

Other sounds drifted up through the floorboards: people fighting, the baby crying, the cats yeowing to be fed. He didn't like this place. He wasn't coming back to it no more, no matter what miss said.

He became aware that the figure on the bed was lying still. On all fours he crept closer and edged an exploratory hand over the rucked-up dress. The pocket with the key was buried under a bony hip. Kneeling up, he traced the metal outline and sought the pocket opening.

'Waa ya doin'? Who's there?' A claw fastened on his wrist.

'Leggo. Get off.'

Ma half raised her shoulders from the bed. She stared at her grandson with feverish eyes; there was no recognition in them.

Nafnel wriggled and scrabbled at the restraining fingers. 'Get off, yer 'urting me, yer stupid old cow.'

Ma's chest jerked; something filled her mouth and, with a convulsive cough, she shot a stream of blood down his sleeve.

Shocked, Nafnel sat down heavily, freeing his wrist, but kicking over the candle with one skidding boot.

The yellowing flame flickered, twisted, nibbled at the edge of a trailing blanket, and then shot up the grease- and alcohol-soaked fabric with a triumphant 'whoosh'.

'Gran. Wake up!' With both hands dug into her skeletal ribs, Nafnel shook frantically. Even though he had no fondness for her, it didn't occur to him just to leave her.

Lost in her alcoholic unconsciousness, Ma remained oblivious to the danger.

The gin bottle which had fallen to her side was caught by the reverberations of the mattress as Nafnel continued to try to rouse her. It sprang off the bed to roll noisily across the paper-strewn floor. The dancing fire raced along its path, catching up with it as it came to rest against the table leg and exploding in a shower of flying fireballs.

Debris on the table burst into flames. Other shards hit the blackout blanket which fizzled into singed holes before adding to the dozen small blazes which were now breaking out all over the room.

Heat puckered Nafnel's skin and stung his eyes. Taking a deep breath, he choked on the thickening smoke, then plunged his fingers into Ma's clothes and managed to drag the key clear. 'Get up, get up,' he whimpered, half dragging her on to the floor.

Ma groaned. Her trailing hair was fanned out behind her across the smouldering mattress. The greedy flames found it and crackled joyously.

'Gran!' With the flat of his fingers, Nafnel smothered the blackening tendrils. He took another breath and found the blood was pounding in his ears. On hands and knees he crawled across the floor, pushed the key into the lock and managed to turn it and drag the door open.

The draught fed more oxygen into the flames. Rivulets broke off to race across the ceiling.

'Fire!' Nafnel croaked. ''Elp. Somebody 'elp.'

The greasy gas stove and brown-stained sink that

they shared stood on the landing. Seizing a dirt-encrusted saucepan from the ring, he held it under the cold tap until it became too heavy to hold. Two handed, he flung the contents into the blazing room. His pathetic offering hissed and sizzled into steam and for a moment the curtain of flame and black smoke parted. Through a porthole of clearness he saw Ma. Slumped against the roaring bed, her legs spread wide, her partially singed hair falling over her face, she was miraculously untouched by the flames.

'Gran. Wake up, yer stupid old cow.' Nafnel slung the saucepan. It whizzed past her left ear and hit the wall behind. The fierce heat was starting to singe his face. Backing away, he looked for something else to throw. There was only one thing left. Taking his precious torch from his pocket, he hurtled it overarm at the recumbent figure. He saw it bounce from her drooping head before the wall of fire closed once more with an almighty roar.

Tendrils explored the doorframe. One edged along the dirt-encrusted gap between two floorboards. Nafnel stamped a heavy boot down, snuffing it out. He started for the stairs, hesitated, then ran to the opposite door, banging loudly and shouting a warning.

There was no reply. Clattering downstairs, he found the cats had already fled. 'Fire,' he squealed, crashing both palms against the nearest door. Inside, the baby screamed in protest and a woman's whining voice cursed.

Nafnel didn't wait. Kicking vigorously at the flimsy timbers of the other room doors, he rushed towards the front entrance. Above him he could hear the other

466

tenants coming out on the landing, calling queries at each other.

'Wha' the 'ell's goin' on?'

'Dunno. It's that bleedin' Starkey kid, I fink. Wait 'til I get me 'ands on the little sod. 'E's woken the baby up.'

'What's that stink?'

''Ere it ain't gas, is it?'

'Nah, it's more like . . . Oh my God! Fire! We're on fire. Oh God, where's me ration books. The little sod's set the 'ouse on fire.'

Half falling on to the pavement, Nafnel heard that final remark and sped away into the darkened streets. He hadn't meant to kick over the candle. It was all Gran's fault, taking the key and trying to lock him in.

His one thought was to find somewhere to hide; before they caught him and put him in prison for starting the fire and killing his gran. There was only one person he could trust.

The air raid siren moaned out its warning as he sped past the police station. Startled by the sound, he looked upwards and crashed full tilt into something soft and squashy.

'Steady on, son.'

Nafnel gulped up into the grim face under the steel helmet. 'Sorry, mister. Didn't see ya.'

The policeman retained his grip on Nafnel's arm. 'Where you off to, son? Didn't you hear the warning?'

'Yeah. That's why I was running, mister. I been round me gran's, see if she was all right. I'm going home to me mum. She said I 'ad to run if the siren went.'

Diving into his pocket, he showed the label Rose
had written. 'See, that's me mum.'

'Balaclava eh?' The constable assessed the skies
with a professional ear and eye. There was no sign of
any enemy aircraft. 'Right, get along then. And do as
yer mum says, run all the way.'

Nafnel didn't need telling. Elbows pumping, he
didn't stop until he staggered breathless into the
grocer's backyard.

The back door was locked. But she always did that
after Ena left. Grabbing the handle, he twisted and
shook, shouting at her to let him in.

There was no reply.

'Miss! Miss, it's me. Let us in.' Dancing backwards
he looked up at the window. In the darkened glass, a
few pale stars were appearing in the reflected sky.
He stared at the curtains, willing her to tweak back
a corner and looked down at him. But nothing happened.

He bashed harder, setting the door rattling. 'Let
me in. The siren's gone, miss. I'll get bombed.'

There was still no response. He gave a small sob of
frustration and fright. Why wouldn't she answer?
Maybe she couldn't hear?

That was it. The kitchen overlooked the front street.
She'd be in there cooking, probably hadn't heard him
knocking out back.

He sped to the front and hurled himself against
the shop's front door. 'Miss, oi, miss. It's me, Nafnel.
Open up.'

He knocked again, until his arms ached. But the
grocer's shop remained silent and unresponsive.

Gulping back another sob, he trailed miserably

round to the back of the shop and slumped down in the yard. She didn't want him. Maybe someone had come round and told her what he'd done?'

Even as he thought it, he knew it didn't make sense. None of those miserable buggers from the lodging house could have got here quicker than him. And if they had, she'd have stood up for him, like she had done against that lot at school. She must have gone out. He'd just have to wait until she got back.

Pleased with his reasoning, he snuggled back against the unyielding brick wall. No sooner had he got comfortable, than another idea struck him. What if the one who'd done in that bloke at the jeweller's shop *had* come back?

'Miss! Miss, you in there? You all right? Oi! If the bloke what done in that uver bloke is in there, I'm going to get a copper right now. You 'ear me. You leave 'er alone.'

He accompanied his threat with a final kick at the door and then sped out on to the back path again, his own problem forgotten in his anxiety to protect Rose.

He'd barely reached the corner of the back footpath, when three other figures hurried round from the opposite direction. Even in his distress, his ever-questing nose caught the scents of beer and fish and chips.

'We should have gone down the tube, Miss Lexie. That cellar of yours isn't safe.'

'You go if you want. I ain't. It stinks. Hello, Nafnel. What you doin' out 'ere?'

Nafnel gasped out his explanation. ''E might be in

469

there now. Strangling 'er. Get a copper quick, miss.'

'I've already got two here. Come on.'

Lexie led the dash back to the grocer's yard. 'Rose. You there? Open up.'

Above their heads something hit the window and fell back into the room with a muffled tinkling of smashing china.

Alan pulled Lexie back. 'Stand clear. We'll break it down.'

In the dark living room Rose backed away from her father-in-law, her questing hand finding her way round the furniture, fingers fumbling for another ornament to hurl.

He'd appeared suddenly in the kitchen as she'd opened tinned stew for their dinner. She'd been alone. Lexie had appeared to be making up for lost time by having a date with not one but two soldiers; Maria had wanted to sleep and Helen and Matthew had declined her invitation with an abruptness that was totally unlike them.

Wishing Ena good night, she'd locked up, collected enough for herself and Nafnel from the shop and made her way upstairs. Her mind had been busy with what she had to do tomorrow. The flat would have to be cleaned; and then there was the washing, she'd have to rub out her blouse and underwear; and all Albert's returns to the food office would have to be sorted out. The tinned food drew a wrinkle of her tilted nose. Her mum would have called it slovenly, living out of tins. Next week she'd have to go up the market after school; see if she could get some fresh vegetables and fruit.

Her mind busy and happy with the minutiae of everyday living, she'd glanced up at a slight disturbance of the air against her cheek, and froze.

'I told you, didn't I, Rose?' Jonas Goodwin had said quietly. 'If our Peter can't have a life, then neither will you. I heard about the dance. About the new boyfriend.'

Reaching across he'd taken the tin-opener from her lifeless fingers.

'How . . .? How . . .' The words wouldn't come.

'How did I get in? Slipped in while that girl was scrubbing. Waited down the cellar until she'd gone. Until you were alone, Rose.'

And that was what she had been. There had been no point in screaming. She'd heard Lexie and her two escorts go out. On the other side there was only the deserted fish and chip shop. Perhaps if she could throw something through the window?

He'd twisted the tin she'd seized from her wrist. It still surprised her how much stronger even the puniest-looking man was compared with a woman. 'Oh no. We don't want anyone else coming, do we, Rose? Let's go in the back, shall we?'

It was his quiet politeness that had scared her more than his previous ranting and raving. She'd allowed herself to be led into the blacked-out living room. And for nearly two terrible hours she'd been trapped in there with him.

'Rose? Yer up there?'

'Get out the way, kid. Let us through.'

Nafnel ignored this instruction. He scampered upstairs on all fours, reaching the landing just behind the two MPs and just before Lexie.

'Hello? Anyone here? Light's on in the kitchen, Alan, check down there, mate.'

'Rose?' Lexie peeked in the bathroom. 'There's nobody in . . . Hey!'

They all spun round at the sound of the living-room door crashing back on its hinges. A slight figure sprang for the stairs.

'Rose! Oh God, what's he done to you?'

The sight of the pale face, one eye swelling in a bruise and blood pouring from the cut lip paralysed them all long enough for Jonas Goodwin to reach the bottom of the stairs. Tolly and Alan shot after him.

'What's going on in here?'

A tall figure was framed in the open doorframe. Jonas sprang at him, but missed his footing on the remains of the smashed door which was now lying across the floor and swayed off balance.

'Stop him!' Tolly snapped in a voice used to issuing orders.

Drawing back his right arm, Pat landed an upper cut on Jonas's chin. It lifted him clear off his feet and deposited him neatly into Tolly's welcoming bear hug.

'Now then, mate, there's no point you kicking like that. Get the other arm, Alan.'

Between them the two MPs pinned Jonas's arm behind his back.

'Whore,' hissed Jonas, breathing noisily through a pulped nose. 'She's a whore. She'll pay for my son.'

Pat had brushed past the struggling trio and ran lightly upstairs. The sight of Rose, her face swelling rapidly, whilst Lexie dabbed at it with a towel and cold water, made his normally healthy complexion blanch to a chalky shade beneath the veneer of smoke soot. 'I'll kill him.'

'No. Oh, please don't make trouble, Pat. I don't want everyone knowing. You promised, Pat.'

'I never promised to stand by and let that nutter half kill you. It's time somebody set him straight.'

'No, *please*. Why are you here? I thought you were on duty.'

'I am.' Pat opened his gloved hand to reveal a charred and blackened torch. 'There was a fire. Nafnel's gran's place.'

Even in her own distress, Rose could manage to ask whether anyone had been hurt. 'Only Ma, she was a goner before we got there. Everyone else got out, except we couldn't find no sign of Nafnel, just his torch. I got leave to come round and see if he was here.'

'He is. He's . . . Where is he, Lexie?'

'Dunno. He was 'ere a minute ago.'

They eventually found him crouched in Rose's wardrobe. It was only after Pat had assured him that he wouldn't be blamed for the fire that they persuaded him to come out.

'Can I stop 'ere, miss?'

'Of course you can, Naf . . . Nathaniel.'

'All the more reason not to 'ave some lunatic trying to break in,' Pat pointed out. 'Don't want him 'aving a go at Nafnel, do you?'

'He wouldn't!'

'He might. He's crazy enough. You gotta report him to the police, Rose.'

'Alan and Tolly have tied 'im up downstairs,' Lexie

chipped in. 'They wanna know what they should do with 'im?'

'Well, Rose?'

Rose licked her lips, tasting the salt blood from the punch he'd given her when he'd grown tired of the cat and mouse teasing and taunting. The guilt she felt over Peter's death was overridden by a fierce protectiveness for Nafnel. She took a determined breath. 'Could you ask them to take him to the police station in Agar Street, please? I'll follow them down.'

Kicking and protesting, Jonas Goodwin was frog-marched through the dark streets. The few people who heard his angry demands to be released soon put their heads down and hurried past when they saw his captor's uniforms. The country was at war: nobody queried the military police.

Even the Home Guard member who'd been detailed to guard the police station entrance during air raids merely snapped to a smart salute, oblivious to Jonas's assurances that he 'knew important people on the council'.

Feet skidding on the polished linoleum, Jonas was dragged between the two MPs to the desk and made to stand in line whilst the station sergeant dealt with a sombrely dressed woman.

'I'm sorry, ma'am,' the man said. 'Sergeant McNeill's not on duty. You'll 'ave to come back in the morning.'

'But her message said it was very important. I'd hardly be wandering around in an air raid if I just wanted to report a lost dog, would I?'

Ignoring the sarcasm, the sergeant asked what message that would be.

'She left one at the ARP headquarters in Stepney. Asking that I contact her as a matter of urgency. My name is Laurence Fox.'

Chapter 27

Saturday night again. Pre-war it had been a bustle of baths and early teas before the inhabitants of the Square made their way to the cinemas, pubs and dance halls. In the O'Day house, as the older boys grew up and started earning, the weekly ritual of the galvanised tub before the fire had been replaced by a trip to the public baths.

'They'd be coming back from the Prince of Wales now,' Eileen had said wistfully picturing her older sons all glowing from the hot water and brisk rub-down, their damp brown hair sleeked over newly shaven faces. Then she'd remarked philosophically that she was glad that at least three of them were out of danger.

Jack had tried not to laugh, although he could see what she meant. Judging from their recent letters the three boys who'd joined up were in far less danger than their mum and brothers who were sitting directly under the Luftwaffe's flightpaths every night.

Once the tea things had been cleared, he excused himself. He no longer bothered to ask Annaliese if she wanted to come and sleep in her own room tonight. With each day that passed she was becoming more part of the O'Day family. He sensed that if one day he didn't return to the house over the road, it would cause her little distress. She didn't want or need him.

Emerging from the O'Day's front door, he found a

uniformed policeman knocking on his own.

Dave Wilkins touched his tin helmet as Jack strode swiftly across. 'Getting to be quite an 'abit this, ain't it, sir?'

'What is it?'

'Can you give the station a ring please, sir? They been trying to raise yer.'

'Have you any idea why?'

'Dunno, sir. They don't tell the foot soldiers "why", just "what and when" me dad always used to say.' He flashed another cheeky grin at Stamford before swinging on to his bicycle. 'Sergeant McNeill's back in though, sir.'

Shrugging his way into his overcoat, Jack made his way through the dark streets, his pace quickening as his eyes became accustomed to the lack of light. He arrived at Agar Street seven minutes later, flicked his identification somewhere in the direction of the Home Guard sentry and bounded up the stairs.

Entering the CID office he reeled back with shock at the dense wall of fumes that hit his disbelieving nostrils. Somewhere amongst the stink he could detect wintergreen, goose fat, paregoric, balsam and burning tobacco. From his corner, Sergeant Agnew raised running eyes and directed a look of hatred and despair at Stamford.

'Sergeant Agnew thinks he's caught pneumonia and pleurisy from all that damp air up the churchyard,' Sarah murmured, her tones redolent with honeyed scorn.

'I take it you didn't get me back here to hold his hand?'

'Two things,' she said briskly. 'Firstly, Mrs Goodwin

478

has been assaulted by her father-in-law. He's in the cells, yelling his head off incidently, and Mrs Goodwin is coming in tomorrow to make a proper statement.'

'And the second thing?'

'Laurence Fox, the private investigator Gwen Donald hired, has turned up. She's in the interview room.'

'She?'

'She. You'd better come and meet her, sir. She's got quite a tale to tell.'

The woman who rose to greet him was unremarkable at first glance. Medium build, medium height, early forties, drab coat and a plain felt hat pulled far too low over thick eyebrows. Then she smiled, and her plain face was transformed.

'Go on, Chief Inspector, say it: you're not a man!'

Since it was exactly what he *had* been about to say, Stamford felt himself warming to the woman.

'My name is pronounced "Law-rens",' she continued, pulling off one glove to shake his hand. 'It's French.'

'But you aren't.'

There was no suggestion of a Continental accent in the woman's evenly modulated voice.

'Half. My father was English, my mother French.'

'Marie Duclos,' Sarah guessed.

'Yes.' A spasm of pain flickered briefly in her eyes.

'I'm sorry,' Sarah was momentarily thrown from her normal composure.

'It's quite all right. We weren't close. They just took letters in for me. It was safer than having them lying in an empty house when I'm away.'

Abruptly she dragged off her hat. It revealed a skull

479

covered in thick black curls on the right side. The left was shaven to an ugly stubble, a thick gouge of angry red scarring stretching from over the ear to the back of her head. 'Straying husband took exception to my enquiries. I've been unconscious in hospital for two weeks. I take it you'd like me to tell your boss what I told you about Donald?'

'She certainly would,' Stamford replied. 'I take it you kept a surveillance on the shop?'

'Out back,' she agreed. 'And only at night. I mean, it was pretty obvious that, without an assistant, Donald would have had to shut the shop if he wanted to nip upstairs for any extra-marital fun in the daytime. And I didn't think he'd want to be that indiscreet. It wasn't a difficult job. The blackout has made that sort of thing a darn sight easier in fact. The only problem usually was the ARP patrols. And the police,' she added with a slight smile. 'Anyway, I soon realised that most of that lot were creatures of habit. Only the ones from the hairdresser's and the cafe seemed to go out after the blackout was up.'

'Not James Donald?' Stamford queried.

'No. He stayed in. The . . . other person . . . came to him. He left the back door unlocked; so they didn't have to wait around in the backyard and be spotted I suppose. Which was lucky for me.' She looked Stamford right in the eye. 'I slipped in and fixed the lock one evening, so that when the other person locked it, it didn't quite catch. I had to be sure you see, before I sent in my report. I mean, the visits might have been entirely innocent.'

'Obviously they weren't.'

'Oh no. When I went in an hour later they were

hard at it in the bedroom. Didn't even know I'd been there.'

'And the name of this "other person"?'

She told him. It took his breath away, although, when he thought about it logically, he realised it fitted all the facts.

'What now?' Sarah asked. 'Are we going round there, sir? Should I call out a car?'

'No. And yes. There's something I want to check out before we question Donald's lover. Could you get me the statements file please.'

While Sarah took a formal statement from Mrs Fox, he made a note of an address in the file and then picked up the phone and asked the operator to get Chief Superintendent Dunn's home number.

When his superior came on the line, Jack spoke rapidly and decisively, outlining his theory and asking Dunn to clear the way for him. 'It's hardly classified information, but you know what they're like these days, sir. Even the colour of the doorman's socks is probably top secret. It might be diplomatic to warn them I'm coming and ask for their cooperation. We'll go round there first,' he said to Sarah, replacing the receiver, 'then straight on to make an arrest with any luck. Leave that for one of the other girls to type up. If we leave now we should . . . Christ!'

He flung himself to the floor a split second after the two women as the window disintegrated with a roar, shredding the blackout shutter that had been fixed over it and sending the loose papers swirling round the room in a mad dance. Throughout the building, he could hear the crash and tinkle of other windows on this side smashing on to the floors. Sarah shuffled backwards and made to stand up again. He caught her wrist. 'What the hell are you doing? Stay down.'

'Light, sir.'

'I'll get it.' He dashed across, flicked the switch to 'off', then cautiously opened the outer door. The corridor had no outside windows but someone had already taken the precaution of turning its row of lights out. In the blackness, figures were coming out of other rooms, moving and calling questions and reassurances.

'Anyone hurt?' Jack shouted.

The station sergeant came towards him, his stooping frame a hazy silhouette behind a shaded torch. 'Just one that we know of so far, sir. Glass fragments. 'Is arm looks like a hedgehog's backside.'

With a sense of inevitability, Stamford saw Sergeant Agnew being led past, the afflicted limb cradled in a makeshift sling. 'I think I shall have to apply for sick leave, sir.'

'Granted,' Jack said promptly. 'Don't come back until you feel completely well.'

'We'll never see him again,' Sarah hissed in his ear.

'Very likely.' Another explosion roared outside. Not so close as the previous one, but near enough for Stamford to order both the women out of the room. 'We'd better take shelter until this lot's over.'

They spent the rest of the night sitting in the narrow corridor between the two rows of cells which, thanks to its thick walls and tiny barred windows, was the safest area in the station, and crawled out wearily at dawn when the siren on the station roof announced it was all clear.

Jack detailed a WPC to escort Laurence Fox to the canteen and get her breakfast; it seemed the least he could do after she'd provided him with the breakthrough in the case.

'Let's get this over.' He rubbed a hand over a prickly chin. 'I must remember to leave a razor at the station.'

'I thought you were going back to the Yard,' Sarah flung over her shoulder, dabbing powder over her nose and trying to pull wisps of fringe across the black and yellow bruise on her forehead.

'I wouldn't know,' Stamford said shortly. 'Are you ready?'

'Are you sure there will be anyone there? It is Sunday.'

'We'll soon find out, won't we?'

As he'd guessed, the building in Gower Street had a skeleton staff working over the weekend. Apparently, Dunn had already managed to contact someone in authority; a reluctant and suspicious clerk produced a ledger for their examination, his yellowing index finger and thumb clamping the ruled pages open so that Stamford could only check the one sheet he'd asked to see.

Having established at least one alibi was no alibi at all, they climbed back into the Wolseley and roared through Mornington Crescent and Camden Town. All around there was evidence of last night's raids; partially demolished buildings, their contents spilling from rooms open to the streets; crater-pitted roads made more hazardous by rubble and glass; a cordoned area with ARP wardens and first aid workers struggling across piles of bricks with a stretcher; open pipes spewing water into the street;

and overall the stench of cordite and gas.

'Most of it seems to have been dropped a bit further south again,' Sarah said, bouncing uncomfortably close to the car ceiling as Stamford drove furiously along Kentish Town Road. 'Wonder if Balaclava received any damage.'

It seemed not. As they progressed eastwards it became obvious that the bombing damage was confined to the west of the High Street. The pale lights of dawn were still too weak to draw any colour from the gardens and houses; they drove into a street still clad in greys and blacks, the misty tinge of autumn dampness rising in a diaphanous haze from the wasteground behind the row of shops.

The upper windows were blind; blackout curtaining drawn tightly over their glass panes. Nonetheless someone was up. Passing the Emmetts' backyard, they heard Lexie calling to someone to make sure that door was fixed properly. A masculine voice answered her from the grocer's shop that they'd have to wedge it until a carpenter could be found.

Ignoring them all, Jack opened the gate to the last shop and went in. His initial knock brought no response.

'Perhaps they went to the shelter,' Sarah suggested.

'I don't think so. They said they never used them.' He pounded harder, a steady, authoritarian knock which said the call was official and the caller wasn't going away until they received an answer.

After a few minutes, the bolt was drawn across and the door swung in a few inches. The moon of her pale face seemed to float in the space between the cap of her hair and the dark clothes. Despite the early hour she was already wearing the maroon dress with the ARP overcoat flung over the top.

'May we come in, please?'

'It's very early. I'm not feeling too well. I haven't had much sleep. Couldn't it wait?'

'I'm afraid not, Miss Fortune. Could you open the door, please?'

Wearily, Helen stood back. The black smudges beneath her eyes testified to her lack of sleep.

Sarah had expected her boss to go straight to the flat. Her surprise when he made for the hairdressing salon was reflected in Helen Fortune's face.

By the time both women had recovered their wits and gone after him, he was already staring at a picture on the salon wall. It looked like a photograph of Primrose Hill from where Sarah stood.

'You've changed it,' he said. 'Where's the other one?'

'It got broken. I threw it out.' Helen drew the overcoat across her breasts, hugging herself with slim white hands.

Jack swung back to look her full in the face. 'It won't do any good, you know. Gwen Donald had hired a private investigator. James had been under surveillance for weeks before his death.'

It didn't seem possible that the pale face could become any whiter, but in the ash-grey light Sarah saw the final traces of colour drain away. Helen's lips formed the word 'No' but no sound came out.

Sarah asked, 'What was in the picture?'

'Miss Fortune as a child. And her father, Joshua Fortune, in his Sunday best. He wouldn't have left his watch and tie-pin to a daughter, would he, Helen? A few personal bits and pieces to Matthew, isn't that what you said? Including, of course, the distinctive pin with the initial "J" in the centre.'

She was too intelligent to believe she could lie her way out of trouble, but she might have tried it if another voice hadn't drawled from the doorway to the stockroom, 'Trust Dad eh, Sis? He managed to damn me even from the grave.'

He was lounging in his usual casual pose, one hand thrust in his jacket pocket as normal. Only it wasn't quite normal, there was something out of place. Sarah wrestled with the problem while Stamford continued to speak.

'All that business about a future sister-in-law was to throw me off the scent, wasn't it? To stop me guessing your brother was a . . .'

'Pansy?' contributed Matthew his eyes too bright. 'Well you just can't tell, can you? I couldn't, about James I mean. Been living next to him for years and hadn't a clue.'

'How did you find out?'

Matthew shrugged. 'He came round one evening. He'd got some metal dust in his eye and wanted Helen to wash it out, but she was at a class, so I had a go. And one thing rather led to another.'

It wasn't hard to imagine. James staring up at the good-looking young man looming over him. The sudden attraction. The revelation that it was reciprocated. The stoop and the first tentative kiss that had rapidly turned into a passionate exploration.

'He'd been in prison for it, you know?' Matthew said in the same chatty tone as if he was discussing James's batting average. 'Convicted at Bedford Assizes; twelve months hard labour. Lucky for him he was a minor. The other, er, participant, got six years.'

It was another piece of the puzzle that fitted into place. 'That's where he was when his parents moved here.'

'Quite right. They scuttled back to London to hide. Even changed the family surname. And guarded their little deviant from then on like he was Jack the Ripper. And when they knew they were dying they made him promise to find a good woman and try to overcome his terrible affliction: their description, you understand, not mine.'

For the first time, Sarah found herself able to feel some sympathy for Gwen Donald.

'Poor Gwen!' Matthew mimicked her. 'The woman's an ignorant lump. I don't think she'd ever read anything in her life except recipes and knitting patterns. But he was going to give me up for *her*.'

Sexual jealousy burned from his dark eyes; bitter and despairing.

'It wasn't just sex, you know. I really loved him. And he said he loved me. He lied.'

'He loved his children,' Sarah said. 'He wasn't prepared to give them up.'

Matthew snorted. 'Boring little brats. They'll grow up into fat, ignorant housewives just like their mother.'

'You don't deny killing him then?' Stamford said baldly. He held his breath. They still had hardly any firm evidence. He needed this confession.

'Not much point, is there?' An expression that was almost triumphant lit up his face. 'He thought it was a farewell party. One final time. He even let me tie him up. I said it was something I'd always wanted to do. I gave him a last chance,' he said seriously. 'But he still preferred that fat frump to me. So I put the pillow over his face and knelt there until he stopped jerking. It wasn't nearly as difficult as I thought it would be.'

Throughout this exchange, Helen had stood like a statue, the strengthening light from the unshuttered shop window creeping across the basins, chairs and driers to reach her wide despairing eyes. Now, as Stamford made to move towards Matthew, she jolted to life and stepped between them. She pleaded: 'Please? Even Gwen doesn't really care any more.'

'And Josepha?'

'He didn't do that. He was at work. You heard him yourself. He had to go back to work after James's funeral.'

'We've checked with the Ministry of Information in Gower Street, Miss Fortune,' Sarah told her. 'He signed out of the building at nine o'clock. Plenty of time to get back to Kentish Town and keep a date with Josepha. When did you make it? At the funeral?'

'Of course I did. It was the first time I realised she'd got that damn tie-pin. I went back to the flat soon as I remembered it. Just before you lot turned up that morning actually. But it had already gone.'

'And what about you, Miss Fortune,' Sarah couldn't resist asking. 'You must have recognised the pin at James Donald's funeral. Didn't you think it was rather strange?'

'I said Josepha must have stolen it,' Matthew snapped. 'Told her not to make a fuss. I'd get it back quietly.'

'Lucky for you she was wearing it. But, of course, you'd have asked her to,' Sarah corrected herself.

'Damn woman had wound it round and round her hair. I had to cut it out. Nearly got caught by some ARP warden. But apart from that it went far more smoothly than I expected. Except for some drunken old biddy trying to wake up the whole damn Row.'

Helen made one last plea. 'He didn't intend to kill her. Just retrieve the pin.'

'And what was he going to do? Ask if she'd mind not mentioning where she found it?' Stamford gripped her forearm gently, pushing her out of his path. He felt her resistance and prayed that she wouldn't start a fight that she couldn't possibly win. He started the caution: 'Matthew Fortune, I'm arresting . . .'

The back door was flung open and Lexie bounded in a cup extended. 'Helen, can yer spare some milk, the delivery ain't come again and I . . . Oh, hello. What's up?'

'Amazing isn't it, how the great moments of our life so often turn into farce,' drawled Matthew. 'I'm afraid your tea will have to wait a minute, Lexie. The Inspector was just about to arrest me for murder.'

'Eh? You murdered someone? Who?'

'Are we so well off for victims now that I can have a choice?' He was enjoying himself. 'James, of course. Oh and Josepha too. Oh look, reinforcements.'

This last remark was directed at Alan who'd come in behind Lexie.

'You killed James and Josepha?' Lexie repeated. 'But *why*?'

'Much as I'd love to stay and discuss motives with

you, Lexie, I think it's time I was leaving. Are you coming, Sis?'

Just too late Sarah knew what had been niggling at her ever since Matthew first appeared in the doorway. He had the wrong hand in his pocket. Before she could move, he drew it out. A lethal silver muzzle gleamed between the fingers.

Helen Fortune's shock appeared to be genuine. 'Matthew! Where did you get that?'

'For heaven's sake, Sis, there's a war on. How difficult do you think it is to get a gun? Get the trap up, we'll lock this lot down there. Don't move, they can only hang me once, remember.' This last order was directed at Alan who'd started to edge forward. 'Get the trap, Sis.'

Helen stood unmoving.

'Sis!' His voice lost its cocky edge. 'Help me, Sis. I *need* you.'

'I don't know. I can't. Oh Matthew.' Tears tumbled down her cheeks.

'You do it.' The barrel was redirected at Alan's chest. 'Go on, open it.'

Alan had no choice but to obey.

'You first.' The gun swung towards Sarah. With both hands gripping the still slimy wood of the staircase she was forced to back down into the dank cellar. Lexie followed her down, the heels of her shoes in Sarah's face as they descended the rungs.

Alan came next, then Stamford. The trap was shut and they heard the bolts being fumbled. Before they could move fully across Stamford seized the edge of the stairs, swung himself up and thrust his shoulder roughly against the door. An explosion reverberated around the enclosed cellar, Stamford spun backwards, seemed to hover in midair, and then fell, blood spurting from his arm. Lexie's scream was echoed by another from the salon above them.

Thrusting her out of the way, Sarah sprung up the slippery steps, closely followed by Alan Milligan. Helen had got no farther than the back door. Leaning against the jamb, sobs shaking her body, she made one final feeble attempt to bar their way. Alan picked her up and moved her bodily to one side.

Matthew had disappeared when they burst on to the back path. For an instant they both scanned the churned field. 'Front,' Alan said succinctly.

Sarah was already sprinting around the side of the shops. He'd had a few seconds' start. She expected him to be well away down the road. Her heart jolted into her throat with shock when she found herself face to face with him outside the front door of the hairdresser's. He thrust her back; colliding with Alan's rush forward she knocked them both off balance. Matt gave a despairing yell, 'Sis, come *on!*'

Someone moved beyond the glass door. But the shape was too tall and too bulky to be Helen. Matthew knew it too.

He spun away. Stamford got the front door open as Sarah and Alan regained their footing and shot forward again.

In the confusion none of them had noticed the delivery lorry.

The train had been delayed again, they'd redirected her all over the place after last night's raid, and just when she'd thought she was on a straight run Ethel had found another barrier flung across the road in front of her. She was nearly opposite the Gardens. And at the bottom, she recalled, there was a gap into the field with another one leading into Leighton Road. It was wide enough to take the lorry. Crashing and banging her gears, Ethel had swung the heavy vehicle right and put her foot down. The Gardens weren't long enough for her to accelerate over the speed limit, but it made no difference. Panic-stricken at the sight of the racing figure which had suddenly materialised in her windscreen, Ethel stood up on the brakes.

The wheels locked. The road surface was still muddy from the recent excavations. The bump as the lorry hit Matthew full in the chest, then rolled over the prone figure, crushing his ribcage into his lungs and rupturing the bowels was no worse than the second jolt as the front wheels rocketed up the kerb. Then the cab slid into the cafe and window and windscreen shattered in an explosion of crashing glass. At the rear of the lorry the tailgate flew open under the force of the impact; metal churns bounced and spun over the uneven surface sending spirals of creamy liquid across the pock-marked road.

For a stunned second nobody moved, then Helen rushed towards her brother. Alan sprang for the lorry runningboard, wrenched open the door, and helped a dazed and bleeding Ethel to safety.

'It wasn't my fault, mister. Tell 'em, mister. It weren't me,' she sobbed.

'Matthew!' Helen knelt in the dust and wet, cradling his head.

'I'll phone for an ambulance,' Sarah said, turning away, knowing that he was beyond any medical help.

She made her way back into the shop as other doors

and windows opened. Maria's head appeared at the upper window, her black hair flying like a banner in the breeze. The military policeman Stamford recognised from the shelter came out of the cobbler's shop together with Rose Goodwin and the kid she seemed to be looking after. A pale, dazed Lexie stood in the doorway of the hairdresser's.

Helen saw none of them. 'Matthew,' she repeated in a gentler tone, stroking his hair.

He tried to speak but his face twisted in pain. Bright red blood filled his mouth and spilt in a thin stream from the side of the lips, staining Helen's skirt a dark black. He made another attempt to talk.

'Stay quiet,' she urged. 'The ambulance will be here soon.'

'Didn't know,' he said with an obvious effort. His eyes sought Stamford's over Helen's shoulder. 'She didn't know. 'Til this morning.' He gritted his teeth and shuddered. When the agony subsided again he gasped out, 'Tried to make me give myself up. Sorry, Sis.'

He tried to smile at her again. Then the light faded and the pain lines melted from his face.

'No, no, Matthew, Matthew.' She was rocking on her heels, the sobs juddering through her body.

Everyone else seemed unable to move.

'Hey, look, miss, look at the cats.' Nafnel pointed at the street.

Afterwards, whenever she thought about the case, it was the picture that always came into Sarah's mind. Cats: ginger, brindled, black, white, tortoiseshell; fat, sleek, moth-eaten, and feral; they'd crept from houses, sheds, ruins and fields and now they crouched under the grey and gold dawn sky; their paws and bellies soaked with milk, their moist tongues lapping at the white lake.

At Nafnel's shout they raised their heads briefly and looked at the drama a few feet away. Ethel was vomiting and telling everyone that it hadn't been her fault. Stamford's bleeding arm was dripping a glowing pool of pinkness into the river of milk and Helen was clutching her brother's limp body as if she could squeeze the life back into it.

The cats regarded it all with glittering quartz eyes. Then their heads dropped and they continued their steady lapping. Death had come again. So what? Death was all around nowadays. What did one more matter?

Epilogue

Three Weeks Later

It wasn't the kind of place he'd normally have met her; but any where with more class might have made it seem like an assignation, rather than what it was: a final settling of the account.

'Thank you,' Helen said as he placed the gin in front of her.

'My pleasure,' he responded automatically.

They sipped in silence for a few moments; each lost in their own thoughts.

It was a working men's place; plain wooden floors covered in sawdust; polished brass pumps for the mild and bitter; a few bottles of well-known spirits behind the bar and a sticky bottle of some fancy stuff a rep had once talked the landlord into buying standing in a film of dust next to the massive cash register.

Jack tipped his pint and scanned the rest of the customers over the rim. The population of the area seemed to be ageing with each week. There were no men under thirty in the bar; and consequently no women either because they couldn't come to a public house by themselves. Several of the blokes were showing an equal curiosity about the occupants of his table. He didn't kid himself that it was him they were interested in.

Helen had noticed it too. 'I seem to be attracting a fair bit of attention. But then I'm getting quite used to that.'

'Have you had much trouble?'

She sipped, the clear liquid leaving a moist film over her red lipstick. Her whole face had been thickly made-up, partly as a defiance and partly as a mask behind which she could hide.

'Not really,' she admitted. 'I was a bit of a nine-day wonder at first. You know, people gaping on the pavement. But they soon got tired of that. Murder isn't the diversion it once was apparently.'

Which was true. He'd given Mary Smith, the trainee reporter, her story as he'd promised, but it had ended up as a few paragraphs on page three. The front pages were reserved for war stories; the more uplifting or morale-bracing the better.

'Are you still working for the ARP?'

'They suggested I might prefer to leave.'

'That seems a bit high-handed.'

She shrugged. 'Perhaps they thought I'd run berserk and start smothering bomb-raid survivors. Perhaps homicidal tendencies are hereditary. Have you noticed that in your work, Inspector?'

'No. Not unless the other members of the family are being subjected to the same pressures that drove the first member to kill. But that's more a question of environment than a hereditary moral defect.'

'Moral defect? That's a polite way of putting it.' She swallowed the gin in one gulp. 'Matt wasn't evil you know? He just . . .' She sought for right words. 'He couldn't bear rejection.'

'Because of your father?'

'Partly. That started it, but it wasn't just Dad. Matt always had to fight to prove he was as good as everyone else. People looked at his arm and were kind, or patronising, or disgusted. But nobody ever treated him as an equal; until James. Do you want another drink?'

'I haven't finished this one yet.'

He'd have fetched her another gin but she seized the glass and marched to the bar before he could do so. Her head held high, she ignored the doubtful looks of the publican and ordered a refill. Jack sensed that if she hadn't been with him, the man would probably have refused to serve her.

'Have you sold the freehold to Bowler?' he asked as she resettled herself.

'Oh yes. He tried to beat me down on price, no doubt he thought I'd be glad to sell and get out.'

'And are you?'

'Yes. But I wasn't going to let that man profit from Matt's death. I made him pay what I was asking.'

'What will you do?'

'Go to America. I've already applied for an exit permit. I daresay there's work for an experienced English hairdresser who can gossip about all the titled heads she used to curl.'

'Did you?'

A slight smile twitched at her lips and for a moment she looked like her old self. 'Well I once worked on an "honourable" when I was an apprentice. But I have a very vivid imagination. And I'll be glad to have someone to talk with again. Everyone in Balaclava Row has gone.'

'I know.' He'd walked past several times and seen the boarded-up shops with the one solitary light burning above the hairdresser's. Once he'd got as far as walking round the back and hesitating by the yard gate before common sense had prevailed.

'Rose went back to her parents, with that funny child she seems to be minding.'

'I've seen her.' She'd come for her tea at the O'Days' house a few times. Less than Pat would have liked, but as much as she was prepared to commit to for now.

'I heard about her father-in-law. Is he going to court?'

'No.'

Rose had been persuaded to drop the charges by her tearful mother-in-law who'd seen the certainty of Jonas getting the sack looming large if he was convicted. In return Mrs Goodwin had promised to make her husband see a doctor. As an added precaution, Eileen had told the Tammies what had been going on, ensuring the Goodwins would get short shrift if they showed their faces again.

'She had a letter from Miss Emmett, from Colchester way somewhere.'

'She wrote to me too. Those military policemen she's friendly with are stationed up there,' Helen explained. 'She and Maria moved as soon as Frank and Josepha's funerals were over. They've got rooms together and jobs in a canteen. I don't think poor Maria knew where else to go.' She drew a folded envelope from her coat pocket. 'Would you like to see?'

> Neither of us can do much, (Lexie had written) but at least we can cook. They're asking for women to join the NAAFI, so I might do that. I don't know really. It depends how *things* turn out. It still seems funny being able to do whatever I like.

Tolly's taken me to the pictures a few times. We're getting on great. I ain't seen so much of Alan, he's had a lot of extra duties for *certain reasons* which I ain't supposed to say on account of Tolly saying his lot don't wash their dirty linen in public.

It's really odd having two blokes chasing after me, after all them years of never having any. Still, mustn't look a gift horse in the mouth.

Maria's still miserable (hope you don't mind me mentioning that but you did say you'd like to know how she's getting on). Several of the soldiers from the camp have asked Tolly to fix up a foursome with her, but she ain't got the heart for it yet. I expect she will soon though. She keeps going on about wanting a family and she's got to get herself a husband if she wants to start one, hasn't she?

Send your address when you move. Perhaps I could come for a visit after the war, I always wanted to travel abroad.

Love

Lexie

'Will you send her your address?' Jack asked, passing the letter back.

'No. I don't think so. I think a clean break would be best, don't you?'

'Perhaps.' Personally he thought that no matter how far Helen went now, the memories would go with her, like an over-heavy rucksack that she couldn't take off however hard she tried.

The silence had fallen between them again.

'I didn't know he was going to kill Josepha, you must believe that.'

'I do.'

'Oh. Good.' She gnawed the lipstick into blood-red globules, her hazel eyes searching for something in his face. It wasn't there.

In a quiet, small voice, she said, 'You know, don't you?'

'Yes.'

'How?'

'I found a white silk thread in Donald's nostril cavity. Mrs Donald said he had no silk clothes, and the bedclothes, including the pillowcase were cotton. What did you use? Your scarf?'

Rather than reply, she looked round the single bar again, seeming to see the remaining customers for the first time.

'They aren't plainclothes policemen,' Jack remarked. 'There's just the two of us. How long had you known about your brother and James Donald?'

'I didn't know. I just . . . something was *wrong*. Matt had been strung up, tense, for days. And then, that day, his mood suddenly changed again. He was, not happy exactly, but buoyant. Caught up on something. And he so obviously wanted me to leave for the post that night.'

'You went back after you'd called into Pratt Street?'

'Yes.' Her sigh could have been resignation or relief. 'I walked the bicycle down the side. I was going to go to the flat and see if Matt was there, but just as I got to the corner I saw him come out of Donald's yard. It was pitch black of course, but I knew, I just knew by the way he was moving, that something had happened.'

'Did he see you?'

'Oh no. I waited by the side until I heard our door shut, then I slipped along to the Donalds'.' Her eyes lost focus as she went back into that flat again. 'He was in the bedroom. I couldn't leave him like that, it was so . . . undignified. So I undid his hands and put the tie back in the wardrobe and then I tucked the bedcovers round him, like he was asleep. I think I thought, oh I don't know, that perhaps people would just think he died of natural causes.'

'When did you realise he wasn't dead?'

'His eyes opened.' She gave a shudder. 'I was tucking the sheet round his chin and then, all of a sudden, he looked at me. Oh God, it was horrible.' Pleading with him, she said, 'I panicked. If he went to the police, if he told them what Matt had done, what he *was*.'

'Is that likely, given that Donald could have been charged with homosexual offences too?'

'I didn't think. I just dragged off my scarf and pushed it over his nose and mouth. He didn't fight or anything. He just went rigid and then relaxed.'

'Did Matt know what you'd done?'

'I don't know. We never spoke about it. When they, you, discovered the body, we both acted as if it was the first we knew about James's death. And after that, well, we just never mentioned the subject. Are you going to arrest me?'

'No.'

'Thank you.' She tried to touch his hand.

Jack moved it out of reach. 'There's no need to

thank me. You're not under arrest because there is no way I can prove you killed Donald, unless you'd care to repeat your confession for the record. I take it you wouldn't like to get it off your conscience?'

'No. I think the state has already had its pound of flesh off me. A life for a life, isn't that the deal? A carrier's lorry might not be quite as formal as a hemp rope, but the effect is just as final.'

'I thought that's what you'd say.'

'Would you have arrested me if you could prove it?'

'Oh yes. It's my job.' He finished his drink. 'Goodbye, Helen.'

He left her sitting in the dingy bar; she didn't bother to turn her head when he parted the blackout curtains and went out.

The night outside was clean and bright with stars twinkling like diamonds against a black velvet sky which, for the fourth night running, was bomber free.

A tall figure slipped across the road to join him.

'I've been feeding carrot tops to that horse of Felonious's. He's quite a softy really. How did it go?'

'As expected, she knows she hasn't got away with it.'

'She has really,' Sarah protested, her breath frosting into clouds in the crisp air, 'if you say we can't arrest her.'

'I didn't say we couldn't arrest her. I said it's so unlikely that we'd get a conviction that I doubted if it would even be taken to court.'

Dunn had agreed with him when he'd read a preliminary report on the case. 'No witnesses, no corroborating evidence apart from one silk thread that a half-decent defence counsel could talk around, and a confession from the brother in front of four witnesses, five if you count the Fortune woman. Take what you've got, Jack, and put it down as experience.'

'She's still got off far more lightly than most murderers, sir.'

Had she? The only person in the world she cared for, both as a brother and a surrogate child, had been taken away from her. And she was faced with the prospect of starting again in a strange country where no one cared whether she succeeded or failed, lived or died. If he had been in that situation, he thought he might find it terrifying.

'I'm getting old,' he murmured. He looked sideways at the tall figure matching his measured tread. 'You're supposed to disagree.'

'Whatever you say, sir,' she said promptly.

'Don't overdo it. You never had any doubts it was her, did you? What was it? Astute observation or feminine intuition?'

Sarah had been asking herself that a lot recently. She'd come to the uneasy conclusion it could have been plain old-fashioned jealousy. But since she could hardly tell Stamford that without explaining the reason; a reason which she had now firmly decided to bury again, she contented herself with, 'Combination of both, sir.'

'Sounds like you're ideal material for CID with those qualities.'

She'd been thinking much the same herself.

More Enchanting Fiction from Headline

PEDLAR'S ROW

HARRY BOWLING

In 1946, Pedlar's Row in Bermondsey is home
to a close-knit community counting its blessings
to have survived the war intact – and full of
curiosity about the new family moving into
number three. And the Priors' move into the
Row is not without incident.

Laura Prior, who's unmarried, having had to
care for her invalid father, enjoys the excitement
of her new home – not least because of her
growing attraction to docker Billy Cassidy. But
her sister Lucy finds life harder; with rationing,
a shortage of homes, having to contend with a
husband who's emotionally scarred from his
internment in a Japanese POW camp, and her
guilt about a war-time affair, it isn't easy to
settle down to normal married life. So the
situation isn't helped when Lucy finds herself
and her family embroiled in local villain Archie
Westlake's shady dealings. And when a body is
discovered on a bombsite behind the Row, no
one is beyond suspicion of murder.

'What makes Harry's novels work is their warmth
and authenticity. Their spirit comes from the author
himself and his abiding memories of family life as it
was once lived in the slums of southeast London'
Today

FICTION / SAGA 0 7472 4520 7

BORN TO SERVE

Josephine Cox

'I can take him away from you any time I want.'

Her mistress's cruel taunt is deeply disturbing to Jenny. But why should Claudia be interested in a servant's sweetheart? All the same, Jenny reckons without Claudia's vicious nature; using a wily trick, she eventually seduces Frank, who, overcome with shame, leaves the household for a new life in Blackburn.

Losing her sweetheart is just the first of many disasters that leave Jenny struggling to cope alone. When Claudia gives birth to a baby girl – Frank's child – she cruelly disowns the helpless infant and relies on Jenny to care for little Katie and love her as her own.

Despite luring a kindly man into a marriage that offers comfort and security to them all, Claudia secretly indulges her corrupt desires.

Always afraid for the beloved child who has come to depend on her, Jenny is constantly called upon to show courage and fortitude to fight for all she holds dear. In her heart she yearns for Frank, believing that one day they must be reunited. When Fate takes a hand, it seems as though Jenny may see her dreams come true.

'Driven and passionate, she stirs a pot spiced with incest, wife beating . . . and murder' *The Sunday Times*

'Pulls at the heartstrings' *Today*

'Not to be missed' *Bolton Evening News*

FICTION / SAGA 0 7472 4415 4